VIGILANTE'S DARE

CERA DANIELS

Copyright © 2016 by Cera Daniels.
Excerpt from *Tiger's Catch* copyright © 2015 by Cera Daniels.
Cover design copyright © Vikki N Charlie.
Edited by Kit Roe.

All rights reserved. This book or any portion thereof may not be reproduced or used in any manner whatsoever without the express written permission of the publisher except for the use of brief passages in a book review.

Man and a Muse Ventures
P.O. Box 24911
Columbia, SC 29224

ISBN: 978-0692688502

Vigilante's Dare
A Relek City Novel, Book 2
Cera Daniels

cera@ceradaniels.com
www.ceradaniels.com
Follow @CeraDaniels on Twitter

Don't want to miss the next tale? Sign up for updates and free reads at http://www.ceradaniels.com!

H.M.:

Thank you for everything you do, every day.

Thank you for daring me to write on.

Thank you for believing.

But most especially, thank you for being.

CHAPTER ONE

FROWNING AT THE BROKEN chain lock dangling from the back of the door, Jay McLelas twisted the deadbolt. He tapped the button on his earbud communicator. "I'm in."

Cinnamon and a hint of apple hit his nose as his silent feet padded through the darkness of apartment 504's tiny kitchen. Out of habit, he checked the leather mask over the top half of his face. *Secure. Time to get this done.* Jay dilated his pupils to amplify his night vision and his gaze swept the room.

Library books about bird care lay scattered across the surface of a battered, round table, and a pair of worn binoculars hung from a nylon strap over the back of the lone wooden chair. A few scattered pairs of shoes—all women's—sat by a couch that looked like it hadn't quite survived an assault by a wild animal. On the counter, a single repeated name glittered on a stack of unopened mail—"Emily Barton. Looks like she lives here alone."

"Civilian. You're clear." His brother's familiar baritone rumbled over the earpiece. "Set all three bugs on Tyrel's place. Nine feet of wire. I want every word nice and crisp. And make it fast. I've got a bad vibe with this one."

Zach's danger-meter was never wrong.

"Care to be a little more specific?" Jay flipped open a sturdy pouch at his waist and snagged a screwdriver.

"Just keep your exits open."

He'd no sooner knelt to loosen the vent on the hallway wall when Zach's voice crackled again at his ear.

"Company's comin'! Murphy's got a contract kidnapping out for Ms. Barton."

Jay's attention caught on the door at the end of the hall, where the target would be sleeping. "How much time?"

The sound of fingers tapping across a keyboard skipped over the line. "They're already in the elevator."

"Shit." He tucked the equipment back into his belt. Murphy expected his masked partner to scope out the La Plaza hotel for the next evening's art heist. If the syndicate boss's thugs caught him somewhere else, Jay would have some explaining to do. "I'm taking the north exit," he whispered, slipping into the small bedroom.

Sprawled across a slim mattress and box spring combo that nearly filled the space lay the apartment's sole occupant. A defenseless target.

Why does that bastard want her? Is he trafficking women now, too?

Fury throbbed behind his temples. This woman lived alone, likely too poor to afford a safer neighborhood—let alone sensible door locks. Did Murphy assume no one would miss her?

"What are you waiting for, bro? Get gone!"

Jay gritted his teeth and crept to the bedroom window. As he brushed the girly curtains aside and eased the lower pane upward, heat poured in to fight the air conditioning. Tainted with a sour hint of uncollected refuse; air humid enough to swim in. Nights like these made him rue the need for a disguise that involved a trench coat and jeans—let alone breathing. Dark feathers swooped to block the exit and an angry barred owl pecked at his gloved hand.

"Torpedo, get out of the way," Jay hissed at his surly spirit guide.

Despite being shooed, the predatory bird bobbed his head and flapped his wings wide, adopting a decidedly perturbed expression on his flat face. He let out a low whistle. Owl-speak that translated as *save her*. Torpedo swiveled to stare at the bed with wide, plaintive eyes and Jay followed the owl's gaze.

A thin cover rose and fell in the slow, deliberate pattern of deep sleep.

Why did she have to be home?

If Murphy was running a new business, Jay could let the thugs take her. He'd follow them into the night and they'd lead him to—*What am I doing? I can't just leave her to them.* The syndicate boss's lackeys could hurt her if he didn't act now. He swore under his breath.

His fingers were close enough to graze the floral print of the heavy comforter crumpled at the foot of the bed. A ruffled blanket had wormed its way down to her calves and ambient light from the apartment complex's parking lot spilled across Emily's shapely body. Cocooned in that nearly sheer fabric, every curve in evidence—sheer. He abruptly jerked his gaze up to her face.

"What do you want me to do? Kidnap her first? I'm not a magician, Tor." It wasn't like he could convince a naked woman to climb out her window in the middle of the night.

Jay glanced between the bird and Murphy's target, puzzled by Torpedo's violent determination. Protecting Relek City was one thing. Focusing on this specific woman... "What's this really about?"

He pushed on his companion-granted ability and took a

closer look at her soft, peaceful features. Colors sharpened in the dark. Rich, clear tones cast away the shadows, and his vision homed in on pale skin above the beige sheet, a tinge of pink highlighting pixie-like cheekbones, parted lips stained almost-red.

Protect.

Hold.

Save.

The thoughts struck without warning, shredded his protests, left him gasping as though he'd been punched with each imperative.

Innocent. Vulnerable.

Sharp possessiveness curved like a raptor's beak at his gut.

Save her, Tor's owlish whistle insisted again, and Jay couldn't refuse. Three years of undercover work in the syndicate—none of it mattered. Murphy wasn't getting his hands on this woman.

Just as suddenly part of his brain was back on the rails, working overtime and frantically searching mental scenarios for one that wouldn't blow his cover. He had to give his partner's underlings a reason: the right excuse to stop an abduction. They'd easily believe his feigned ignorance over the contract. Maybe that he'd finished early at La Plaza. But the woman?

He stepped forward, pulling off a glove, sudden inspiration overriding his brain. He couldn't spirit her away, but what if he didn't have to? Would they buy a relationship? Common sense leapt out the window as his fingers halted a whisper away from her cheek. Diving into an intimate scene with the tenant wasn't quite what he'd had in mind when he'd snuck in for recon.

To keep her from Murphy, he had to risk—

"Why're you still there?" Zach sounded ready to pounce through the earpiece.

Startled from his ill-formed plans, Jay jerked back and

bumped into the floor lamp in the corner. It wobbled dangerously. Grabbing the pole sent the metal clattering against the wall. He cringed as Emily rolled to her right side and faced the door, but the rhythm of her breathing remained unbroken. A mercifully sound sleeper.

He exhaled once.

Jay laid a hand on the shade to rebalance it and took a judicious step away from the fixture.

"They're on your floor—"

"Don't wait up for me." With a quick jerk, he pushed back his hood and shrugged out of his black trench coat. "And tell Ry I'll be late."

The jacket flared on a breeze from the window as he kicked off his boots and stripped the glove from his other hand. Yanking off his t-shirt and tool belt, he used a bare toe to nudge the latter under the bed where it wouldn't be visible from the doorway. He shoved his pistol into his waistband as an afterthought. If the lie worked, he wouldn't need the gun.

Although I might need a therapist.

"Jay—"

Pulling the earpiece out and tossing it with his belt, he caught a muffled string of huffing noises coming from Torpedo's perch on the sill. Laughing. He threw a sideways look at his companion. "This was your idea, feather-head."

Sort of.

The owl took to wing with a hoot that said, *too slow, too slow*. Jay grabbed an edge of the neglected blankets and slipped underneath, pulling them over the pants he still wore. He wrapped his arms around the outside of Emily's sheet, leaving only a meager layer of protection between them when he pinned her back to his chest.

His groin pulsed with an inconvenient rhythm as she woke and squirmed in panic. Her lips were like ribbons of velvet against the palm he clasped over her mouth.

"I'm not gonna hurt you." His voice came out a husky whisper and Jay fought to curb his body's reaction to her movements and the spicy scent of cinnamon that wrapped around his brain. He plunged ahead with the reckless plan. "Men with guns are here to kidnap you—"

She shrieked and bucked in his arms.

"Not me! I'm help—" Teeth grazed his fingers. On what planet had he thought this would go well? "Play along, Emily. Or we both die."

Unable to wiggle off the other side of the bed, she rolled toward him. Two fists shot out, striking his chest. Hazel eyes were wild with fear and fury.

"Stop fighting me," he growled low in his throat, tangling her arms in the thin cotton with one hand. She kicked his calves instead. "I'm here to stop the men with the guns and nasty tempers and I can't do that if you don't—"

Wood splintered in the kitchen.

They were out of time.

"Follow my lead." Jay tugged the sheet back and shrugged underneath. The blood drained out of Emily's face, her dark pupils stark against whitening skin. *Real smooth, jackass.* He pulled his hand from her mouth.

She stiffened, inhaled through full, parted lips.

"Sorry." He dipped his head to hers and swallowed her scream with a kiss.

A soul-scorching, complicated kiss. It jolted up the length of his spine, sent a rush of elation to his soul, his heart soaring through the night air.

What the hell?

He rocketed back to Earth in the next instant to find Emily's luscious body writhing to break his hold, her nails trying to rake his sides. She hadn't felt the bizarre out-of-body connection.

The same sensation that had insisted he join her under the covers rang deep in his core, an internal demand that defied explanation. Somehow enough blood supported his brain functions to remind him he still had a job to do. His fingers buried themselves in her cropped red-brown hair, rumpling her locks as if they'd been rolling around in bed together for hours. If only he'd really had those hours to lose himself in her spicy cinnamon aroma, admire her smooth skin, her flushed cheeks, the lush curves trembling beneath his frame.

Emily's palms settled on his hips and a whimper sounded into the kiss. A sound of surrender. His lips still held her scream at bay, and Jay suspected her apparent capitulation was a ruse to lower his guard. But when her nipples peaked against his chest, his gaze sought hers, night vision colliding with a pair of hazel eyes that flashed with searing heat.

He had half of a second to marvel at that look before the bedroom door caved under the weight of no less than three would-be kidnappers, backlit by the hallway. Shock spread across the goon's faces at the sight of the sexual charade he'd painted.

"What the hell is this?" he shouted. With stronger light, his enhanced sight was unnecessary, and he blinked rapidly as his pupils returned to normal.

Ripping her head away from him, Emily turned a flushed stare on the weapons they carried. One bulb of the four in the overhead light fixture winked on. Black tanks. Rugged cargo pants. Matching crew cuts. Submachine guns. All marks of the more organized street thugs in Murphy's employ. Clearly intimidated, the woman had gone still underneath him, her fingers clenched where they still touched his skin.

"Klepto." The man in the center frowned, dropping his gun to his side. "What are you doing here?"

"Only had one job tonight. Thought of a fun way to spend all that extra time. And I don't recall inviting you." Shifting on the bed, he pulled Emily against his chest, one arm draped lazily over her waist, his palm spread over her skin. She froze at his touch and he heard a strangled gasp catch in her throat. Shoving aside concern and launching into his role, Jay pressed forward with, "Spit it out. What's Murphy want this time?"

"The boss gave orders to bring this woman in."

"The fuck he did," Jay said with a growl.

The goon shifted his weight with apparent unease. "He has need of her unique . . . services."

Her nails tried to impale his arm. Yeah, she wasn't about to be servicing any of the crime boss's "needs". *Sick, twisted bastard.*

"Shame I plan on keeping her for myself," he forced out.

"Nobody's taking me anywhere," Emily's protest came out hoarse, but steady, betraying none of the nerves he felt trembling through their skin to skin contact.

His gaze flicked to where she barely hid under the thin material, her generous breasts pressed taut against the too-transparent fabric. A surge of aggression pounded between his eyes. Posed or not, Murphy's goons didn't warrant a free show.

"You heard the lady, gentlemen." He pressed his lips to Emily's shoulder and hauled the thicker bedding across her chest. He glared at her visitors. "Tell him to find someone else."

They had no right to look at her. *Murphy has no right to take her from me.*

He dropped his gaze to the woman he protected, confounded by the swirl of emotions vandalizing his common sense. Combined with Torpedo's insistence, Emily's sleeping figure had triggered some hidden, primal urge. He hadn't been able to stop himself—couldn't—even if he'd wanted to.

"Get out of the way. Some of us have to actually work for our paycheck." The man to the right took a bold step toward the bed.

"We're taking the woman with us."

"I would advise against it." Jay's voice turned cold, dangerous, and he jerked his head up. He enjoyed the uncertain glances the gunmen sent each other, the tentative shuffle of their feet. Despite his reclined position, his reputation as Klepto had their nerves scattering like field mice.

Emily shivered beside him and he cinched his arm tighter around her waist. A small clicking noise caught his ear, and he tensed. One of them had just cocked a weapon. The act wasn't convincing enough. He had to escalate.

With an exaggerated sigh, he drew up on an elbow and stared down the nearest lackey. These three ranked far lower than his persona in Murphy's organization. Klepto was a partner. They were employees. The gunmen wouldn't dare shoot him, they wanted Emily alive, and Jay refused to cringe at empty threats.

"I'm afraid you're leaving empty-handed, gentlemen," he began. "You see, this woman is my property. She belongs to me. And I'm not partial to sharing or letting anything of mine be borrowed, stolen, or damaged. So you had better pack up those miniature rocket launchers and send Murphy my regards."

Property? He had no idea where the declaration had come from, why his body hardened with each word. Already his cock was determined to rise to the challenge. *Aw, hell.*

"We aren't here to shoot anyone tonight." Disappointment rang on a fourth man's gravelly words. "But Murphy doesn't like folk who come between him and his orders." The thugs lowered their guns and cleared a path for the assassin who strolled in from the hallway with a lit cigarette trapped between his pudgy lips.

Shiv. Like this had to be ten thousand times worse?

Despite the casual, floral-printed attire, Shiv could never pull off "harmless", not with the deadness in his dark eyes and the way he practically oozed slime. And definitely not with the sharp weapons strung about his person like a human porcupine.

The barrel of Jay's gun seemed to sear the small of his back and he was all too aware that Emily lay in front of him like an innocent shield. *Damn.*

"He's got you babysitting now, Shiv?" Jay's mind spun behind his bravado. Ryan and Zach would kill him if he ruined everything, and the appearance of Murphy's second-in-command would not make this a clean maneuver. "You should at least teach them that successful kidnappers sneak. These guys stampeded in like a herd of elephants. Sloppy."

Shiv had once been in the doghouse with his boss, but months had passed and his position had only strengthened. If the assassin whispered "betrayal" in Murphy's ear, if he told him who'd refused to hand her over, the syndicate boss would see a direct challenge. Murphy would step up his kidnapping efforts to show his underlings exactly who gave the orders, both to maintain his credibility and to punish his masked partner's transgression. He'd never walk away from Emily.

The payout for her contract will double overnight.

Shiv barely stiffened at the taunt. Brown eyes, beady as a sewer rat, held steady on the bed. "At least I'm doing my job. Do the words 'La Plaza' ring a bell?"

"As I said: a cakewalk leaves me with extra time on my hands."

The assassin gave a dismissing grunt and pointed at Emily. "Hand her over."

"Who are you people?" Her voice came out the barest thread of a whisper.

Jay's heart stopped, then rebooted with a vengeance, the strong thump threatening to shatter his ribcage. If she gave him away now—His thumb rubbed lightly against her midsection and he nuzzled her cheek, relieved when she took his cue and settled in his arms.

"If my business associate has a problem," Jay kept his gaze on the assassin and his voice low, enunciating each syllable like a calculated threat. "He can discuss it with me personally."

"That can be arranged." Grooves dug into his pocked face as he frowned. "I'm gonna enjoy watching him take you down, Klepto," he said, stalking out of the room.

EMILY SAGGED AGAINST the stranger at her back and inhaled, her breath stuttering in her lungs. Her mind rapped out a frenzied beat of questions. Who was he? Who were they? Why did they want her? Why did he wear a mask? And why on Earth was he *still* in her bed?

I never should have moved here. Muggings, kidnappings, break-ins—Small town girls didn't last in the big city. She'd laughed off her parents' warnings before the move, but nothing about Relek City was safe or sane. Or funny.

Shuddering, she stared at the splintered doorway. Were they gone, or just standing there in the living room, waiting?

She shifted again and tension gripped the stranger's muscles, bunching the blanket against her bare skin. The rock lodged in her stomach overturned and she dragged in another shaky breath. *I don't care how high the electric bill gets with the AC on. I'm never, ever, ever sleeping naked again.*

"You can get off of me now." Emily hated the waver in her whisper, hated her screaming nerves. But the statement sounded a little better than begging for her life.

The muscular arm wrapped around her waist eased its iron-shackle grip, but didn't release. He stayed tucked against her back, his heart thudding against her spine. Steady. Calm. His breath was warm on the nape of her neck. Goosebumps rippled over her skin and her own pulse slammed out of control.

"Let go." Her fingernails raked at his wrists.

"I'm not going to hurt you, Emily."

It wasn't the first time he'd said her name.

The questions in her head crowded into her throat all at once and came out a whimper. She contemplated wrestling out of his imprisoning hold, bounding out of the room, and grabbing a steak knife from the kitchen. But even if the other thugs had left, her body wouldn't cooperate. Her limbs failed to do more than twitch at the mental command to flee.

Why were her mind and body at war?

"Emily." The stranger turned her to face him, his hands gentle as he slipped both arms around her like he belonged.

She shoved her hands between them and pushed at the firm plane of muscle that spanned his chest, the motion as much to keep her breasts from touching his far-too-interesting skin as to get away. He didn't budge, but a wary smile tilted across his lips.

"Are you all right?" Fierce gray eyes gleamed out from a tight black mask, pinched with what couldn't possibly be concern. His shadow-drenched hair pooled on the pillow next to hers.

The possessive words he'd spoken to the gunmen flashed into her head and Emily stilled. "Why did you say that?"

He frowned, cocked his head. "I was just asking if you were okay."

"Not that. The bit about you 'owning' me."

He didn't answer, his index finger tracing a distracting path down her bare back.

"Who are you?" She stared at her uneven fingernails, overwhelmed by an awareness of too much hot, smooth skin. What was wrong with her? "Why did you stop them?"

The feather-light touch threatened to set her ablaze. The same way his kiss had. *That kiss* . . . She bit down hard on her lower lip and closed her eyes. In no way was it normal to be attracted to masked men who broke into women's apartments.

Klepto. They called him Klepto.

"I won't apologize for saving your life, if that's what you're fishing for.""

"That isn't—you—" Her head came up fast, a breath away from his chin. "Why are you here?" She had to see the face behind the thin band of fabric, had to discover why he'd hide his identity from his supposed "associates", had to understand why she couldn't get his kiss out of her head.

Unconcealed interest blossomed in his gaze and his lips rose in a slow grin. "You ask a lot of questions."

"You haven't answered any of them."

The grin widened.

Her nipples peaked against the backs of her hands. *I have another one: What would it be like to kiss you again?* Raw attraction simmered in her veins, answering the call in those intense eyes with a molten rush of desire, convoluting her thoughts.

"I know you're thinking of running. But if you leave before morning, I won't be held responsible for the consequences." He sighed, releasing her, letting her have the space she should have craved.

Running was far from her mind. The sexy stranger lying in bed next to her had her faulty brain dismissing concerns about gunshot wounds and kidnapping. Confusion dominated Emily's mind and her body was reluctant to distance itself from his warmth.

"What consequences?" Her voice wobbled as the word "criminal" flashed through her mind in orange neon.

As if a switch had flicked on for her muscles, her body wrenched backward. The mattress dipped. Only the masked man's fast reflexes kept her from tumbling off the side of the bed. Well, his reflexes and the strong hand he slid across her butt to haul her away from the edge. She flushed at the intimate touch.

"I won't be able to protect you."

"You think they'll come back."

He gave a slow nod. "They'll be watching to see if our little charade is the real deal."

"Why? What do they want with me?" Against his chest her fingers were stiff, like they'd turned to solid icicles. The questions piled into her throat again, clawing, relentless.

"I don't know." His hand tightened on her hip. "Emily, breathe."

"You need to leave," she managed to squeak out.

Her cell phone was on the nightstand. With a start, she dug in with her heels to propel herself within reaching distance. One hand closed around the phone and the other made a fumbling grab for the sheet. She clutched both to her chest with hands that shook.

The stranger stared down at her, his gray eyes smoldering with flecks of silver. "What are you going to do with that?"

"Call the police."

"For a break-in in this neighborhood?" A regret-loaded smile. "They won't help you."

He was right. The short two months she'd lived in the city had been plenty of time to learn the golden rule of the Relek City police force: If you wanted their attention, you either had to have money, or you had to have killed someone who had money.

An avalanche of dread took hold and the phone thumped to the blankets between them.

The room seemed to darken. Shrink. And a horrifying whimper broke loose.

"Hey, look, they won't come back in here tonight. I'll make sure of it." Strong hands wrapped around her quaking body. "Okay? Hey . . . " After a moment one corner of his grim mouth lifted and he fastened his lips to hers once more.

Sensation crashed around her like a gilded cage. His hand caressed its way up her spine and heat feathered into her midsection. She moaned, savoring his kiss for a second time, the taste of need, the heady musk and night sky splashed over his skin.

Then her brain returned.

"Better?"

It wasn't. It wasn't better at all.

Except . . . she could breathe. Her muscles had loosened, her room didn't feel like it was closing in on her anymore. The exact opposite of how his presence should have made her feel.

His lips brushed her ear. "I'm sorry, Emily."

Tenderness. Unexpected care, sending her every assumption into a freefall. Just who was this man? She stared at him as he extricated himself from the blankets and moved to sit on the edge of the bed. His long hair hung like a cape of dark satin down to his shoulder blades.

"Go back to sleep." His hair swept down when he glanced over his shoulder to speak, draping over half of his mask. "I'll keep watch."

Fisting her hands in the blanket helped suppress an insane urge to sweep the wayward strands over his ear. As he reached toward the floor her wandering gaze traveled over tanned skin. A wealth of strength on display, mouth-watering muscles she had no business wanting. Temptation personified. If he hadn't been in her apartment uninvited. With a gun.

Her eyes locked onto the weapon and her next breath burned in her lungs. It worked better than a cold shower to reset her nerves, tempering the bizarre attraction that had held her in its grip.

Shrugging on a dark t-shirt, he hid the weapon underneath. Emily sat up and dragged the comforter with her so she could wrap it tight across her breasts. "And if they come back?"

"I'll tell them they spoiled the mood." He pulled on a belt and a pair of boots, draped a trench coat around himself, and then turned to meet her gaze. "Tonight will be a different story. You should buy some decent locks before then."

Frustration gnawed through her fear. "I need to buy a whole new door." She needed to move with no forwarding address. "Look, if they're going to come after me again, I think I at least deserve to know who these creeps are." Her curious fingertips stretched of their own volition, grazing the ridge of his cheekbone, just under his mask.

"No." Alarm scattered across his face and he sprang from the bed, disturbing two feathers that drifted to the comforter from the window. One final, gruff warning before he set her bedroom door upright and moved into the hall. "Sleep. And be here at dusk tonight."

So his buddies could return and take another shot at kidnapping? Not a chance.

CHAPTER TWO

EMILY HELD THE PERCH over the side of the utility sink in the back room at Partner Paws and scrubbed it under the tap, wishing the water could rinse thoughts of masks and guns down the drain. "The man is a criminal and a creep." She swiped viciously with the sponge and soapy water splashed onto the counter's mint green laminate. "He snuck into your apartment, and he—"

A curious beak pinched her ear. Emily smiled and moved on to the second perch.

"He rescued me, Rain," she murmured to the gray and white cockatiel wobbling on her shoulder. "They were trying to kidnap me and he saved me."

Perched awkwardly with a taped, broken wing, Rain had the toes of one pale foot looped over the collar of her blouse. The little bird made another try for the faux pearl earring on Emily's left lobe, nibbling instead at her skin. A clear dismissal of the villain/hero debate.

She stopped scrubbing and tilted her head to the side to dislodge Rain's focus on her earring. The bird's misbehavior helped ease her mind almost more than the hours-long cleaning spree. "You're right. I've got more important things to worry about."

More important things, like keeping the paid staff employed, roofs over their heads, food on their tables. More important things, like maintaining the vet bills and upkeep for the service animals she'd trained and sent home with her human patients. More important things, like how to make the rent payment for her nonprofit's building so her little furred and feathered friends, like Rain, didn't get dumped on the street.

After her sleepless night, she was more convinced than ever that the streets of Relek City were not a place for any of her non-human patients. A flightless cockatiel, an affectionate cat with three legs—none of her rehabilitating animals would survive.

"Who am I kidding?" She blew out a harsh breath. "The apartments of Relek City are barely livable for humans."

Money and masks. Masks and money.

And she was back to *him* again. Emily frowned, appalled at the stranger's ability to dominate her thoughts. She stared at the sponge under her ragged nails, rinsing clear of soap bubbles. Her palm slapped down on the faucet handle. The taped wing thumped against her neck again, followed by a shrill, warning whistle.

She straightened in a hurry.

"Sorry." She made a much slower grab for a towel and ran it over the length of the perch. Flapping feathers subsided and with another whistle the cockatiel shuffled closer to her face. Rain dipped her head low, an avid fan of cleaning time.

"I'm almost done. Then you can go back to your favorite spot." As Rain rubbed against her cheek she reached up an index finger for the little bird to nuzzle. It worked like magic. The cockatiel nestled in the curve of her shoulder and agitation seeped away, little by little. Every time things got out of control, time with these animals made her calm. Centered. Happy. If only all problems were as easily drained away. "Let's put it all back together, shall we?"

She juggled metal brackets and mesh with Rain wobbling about and trying to enter the half-constructed cage. Nibbling at Emily's shirt for balance like her beak was an extra foot, the bird walked down the sleeve, impatient to be reinstated to a spic-and-span abode. Emily folded a newspaper to slide under the cage floor mesh for a liner. A laugh at Rain's antics lodged halfway up her throat.

The front page.

There, in newsprint quality, was a distorted image from a security camera of the man who'd saved her life the night before. "'Masked Man Robs Foreign Offices'," she read aloud.

His features might have been blurred, but there was no mistaking that powerful stance and the set of those broad shoulders. Mysterious. Sexy.

And a thief.

"Foreign offices, huh? Bet the cops are all over that." Her fingertip traced the grainy picture, residual ink darkening her skin with a bluish tint.

In bold print, the number for the information hotline burned into her brain. "What would I tell them? I've seen your masked man; he was in my bed last night?" She snorted and thrust the paper onto the counter.

Rain nipped at Emily's ear again, adding a perturbed squawk in commentary.

"I'm going, I'm going!" She took a different newspaper off the stack and shoved it under the wire mesh. "You know, you're lucky—at least your front door closes, lady."

A strong, acid-washed odor of flowers and cigarettes alerted her to her coworker's presence a second before Naomi pushed open the door. The heavy cloud of cheap perfume never quite covered the other woman's vice.

"How are you this morning?" Emily hooked the water dish to the wall of the cage and nodded at her entrance.

She didn't answer right away, stopping just inside the doorway.

"Don't let the cats in," Emily warned, adding a sprig of millet to the interior decoration. Rain tugged at her sleeve again, tweaking the fabric out of shape as she tried to get to the food from the outside of her home. "Last thing we need is a riot."

"How long have you been here?" The door snapped closed and neon cheetah print Mary Jane pumps tapped across the linoleum.

The clinic's publicist and on-site family services counselor had a valuable knack for detail. Naomi missed nothing. And when her sharp blue eyes roved over the former storage room Emily knew she'd find Rain's cage was the last to be cleaned to spotless, the floor freshly mopped, every glass surface gleaming, and the dryer already running the previous day's towels. Far too much accomplished before nine in the morning.

"I've been up for a while. Here since a little after dawn."

"Money trouble's got us all losing sleep." The other woman homed in on the cage door and held it open until Rain was safely ensconced behind the thin metal bars.

Emily let the misconception stand. She had a point. Partner Paws' staff was just as concerned about funding. Overworked, overstressed, overwhelmed. A poor time to bring up the break-in on top of everything else.

She shrugged as Rain broke into the usual post-cleaning serenade. "I needed to spend some time with these guys. It helps me focus."

"Well, I'm glad I got in before you decided to 'focus' with the puppies."

Emily raised an eyebrow. "Why's that?"

"You think I'd let you make the rounds for grant applications smelling like wet dog?"

A smile crawled across her face.

Naomi's playful expression drew tight and fuchsia-tinged lips pursed in concern. "Have any others renewed?"

"No." The smile crumbled, her heart cringing in her chest; she was loathe to admit the extent of their dire situation. For the last six months, her little animal-assisted therapy clinic had seen a downward trend of regular donors, some even cancelling renewal commitments early. Even after she'd moved close to cut costs, those grants . . . "We lost two more."

Twin apologetic emails had added to a fierce need to bury herself in work, to ignore the raucous spinning of her thoughts.

"I just don't understand." Her coworker's mountain of red curls shook vigorously, fingers slicing through the air. "Our interviews are consistently positive and we're busier than we've ever been. That's half a dozen places in as many weeks. What am I missing? Where are they going?"

"It's not your fault. You do a great job getting us press time. Things will work out." She'd just try more banks. Credit unions. Private endowments. Someone out there had to be willing to support them for a fourth year.

"Not like it's a hard job, cha? We've got plenty of success stories to share." Naomi rubbed at a smattering of freckles over the bridge of her nose, pinched her fingers there for a moment, and sighed. "You look terrible, Em. With those dark circles the grant folks'll think we're being represented by a zombie, not our illustrious founder."

Her laugh was strained. "You're a good friend."

The outer door cracked open. Julia poked her head inside, her eyebrows furrowed and her long, black braid skimming down the length of the doorframe. "Everything okay in here? Nemo's been pacing and—Hey, stop!"

Like he was on a mission, the orange office tomcat bowled past the office assistant's legs. Captain Nemo darted straight for the canaries, Julia hot on his furry heels.

"Nemo, stop!" Emily shouted, springing forward to intervene.

He stopped mid-sprint, did an about-face and sat, tail swishing, pinning her with an irritated look that bordered on belligerence.

"Don't give me that. You know you're not allowed to go after the birds." She fought to keep surprise at bay. Consistently disobedient, Captain Nemo had never responded to a direct command before. Emily held more sway with the feathered friends at their clinic.

"Impressive," Naomi chuckled as the cat was swept off the floor. "He knows who's boss."

"He's been like this since I got in." Julia lugged the tomcat away from temptation, a frown tugging at high, russet brown cheekbones. "Agitated and ornery."

"He's always ornery. Once, he even tried to follow me home." Naomi scratched under his chin with a set of manicured nails and nuzzled the top of his head with her nose. "No buffet for you this morning, bubba."

Julia nodded as she set the cat down in the kennel room and shut the door behind him. "The only time I ever see him this wound is when Em or Marco are upset. Marco's down the street cleaning up glass at the electronics store. So that leaves you." She directed a serious look at Emily. "What's going on?"

"Another break-in?" Naomi asked before she could respond.

"You got it. They took a couple of plasma TVs. Plasma!" Julia tugged on the dark braid over her shoulder. "Police never came."

Naomi shook her head. "They never do."

A renewed flare of anxiety spiked through Emily's chest,

squeezing her lungs. Captain Nemo's insistent meow came through the door, his claws scraping along the wood.

The police never came, and Partner Paws was in a neighborhood some would consider "respectable" compared to her place in Eddinsborough Commons. They responded to money, power. Not attempted kidnappings or break-ins that involved moderately expensive TVs. In her case, the kidnappers hadn't taken anything of value.

Only because the sexy felon in the Zorro mask told them not to take me.

She shivered as an unsettling memory of mouth-watering kisses took center stage. Rain rubbed against her fingertip through the cage bars but the avian comfort barely made a dent in her mental tangle of doubts this time. Emily filled her lungs with the satisfying scent of dish soap and hard work.

"Ladies, I have to hit the bank for a cashier's check to cover our rent, then more places around town for grants." She snatched for the newspaper and her feet pivoted for the door. When she hit the kennel room, Nemo rubbed against her bare leg, purring. "Don't worry, fella, I'll be back for the afternoon class."

He looked up and Emily bit her lip, enjoying the camaraderie but unable to conjure another smile. Julia was right; the animals were all strangely responsive to her stress level. More than usual. More than they did with the people she assigned them in therapy classes. She made a conscious effort to tone down what had to be a major vibe of distress on her part, taking a series of counted breaths as she walked the main hallway.

Both women followed her out of the back room, but only Julia followed her into her office, making a noise in the back of her throat. Emily turned and found herself wrapped in a tight hug.

Crying was not an option. She returned the squeeze then pulled away to drop the newspaper on her desk.

"You're not just upset about the money," her friend said. She leaned on the back of one of the aging, cushy chairs that faced Emily's desk. "We've been like sisters since high school. I'd think by now you'd know you can tell me anything."

But Julia worked three jobs and took classes at a local university. She was stressed to the limit about the possibility of losing her permanent spot at Partner Paws. Emily didn't dare tell her about the break-in either.

The heaviest part of her money worries, though . . . she could share that truth.

"My savings account hits zero today. Between Partner Paws and my parents' farm, I'm tapped out." She tugged open her desk drawer. Two brown feathers with white stripes brushed her knuckles. Owl feathers. Shoving the physical evidence of her evening drama from her mind, she rifled through a handful of manila folders.

Julia's face was grim. "So this is it."

"We'll get funding."

"Mr. Young called again." The innocuous comment spoke volumes about the unhealthy direction Julia's mind had veered. Options. Unacceptable ones, at that. "Real smooth talker, you know. I ended up giving him an appointment first thing tomorrow, but I think you're in for another pitch to bump his sick kid up the list."

"Partner Paws doesn't take bribes." Emily kept her face carefully blank. Locating the folder of records for the grant appointment rounds, she slid it into her oversized purse as she spoke. "The waiting list is there for a reason, and if someone with money wants on it, they can wait with everybody else. We're running two classes, max capacity on time and space in the facility. Overcapacity, when you add up the bills."

Despite her protest, she knew both of them saw the lure of opportunity. The kind of money Miles Young had offered in the past would be more than enough to cover just one extra patient. Enough to cover another year of rent. A heavy sense of wrongness twisted her stomach.

"We could use the cash."

"Money isn't everything. I don't care what the rest of the city thinks." She slung the purse over her shoulder then stretched out a hand, resting her palm on Julia's forearm. "He wants a miracle cure, and all we can provide is therapy. We'll make it one way or another, but—"

"But we don't take bribes. Got it, boss." Troubled brown eyes crinkling in the corners, she gave a mock salute. Before Emily reached the double glass doors at the front of the building her friend added, "Best grab your umbrella. Looks like the sky's about to fall."

JAY RESCUED HIS morning half-caf, the coffee threatening to slosh onto his keyboard as Ryan slammed his palms on the desk.

"We are not in the maiden-saving business, Jay! What's wrong with you?"

Why on earth *had* he crawled into bed with her? "I stayed long enough to set the bugs on Tyrel after they left." Long enough to make sure Murphy didn't send Shiv in for another try.

His older brother bristled. "But you forgot to turn them on!"

"There is that." Jay rubbed the back of his neck with his free hand. Not only had he made things tense between their alter ego and Murphy Jones, he'd also screwed up a whole day of surveillance on the apartment under Emily's. He'd been so preoccupied . . . "I'll go back tonight and take care of it. It's not like I don't have a reason to be there now that he thinks—"

"You don't even know why he wants her, Jay." Ryan held up

a hand. "Not that it matters. Murphy'll just send someone else to nab her."

"Then I guess we better beat him to it." Jay couldn't allow for anything else. Beyond her broken bedroom door she'd spent the remainder of the early morning hours curled up in a tight ball with a Mag-Lite for protection, and it shredded everything decent inside him that he hadn't gone back in to hold her.

As if he had a right to do that.

"We?" Ryan snorted and cracked his knuckles on the oak surface of the desk, his voice roaring against the walls of the small office. "This is *your* mess. And anyway, how do you propose to find her? Does your cock double as a divining rod? 'Cause she's not going back to that apartment."

Jay held his furious gaze. "You're waiting for me to ask to borrow your lieutenant."

"My wife is not helping you out of this disaster."

"I haven't asked. And I won't, because I can handle it, Ry." He shook his head. "Torpedo's been following this woman all day. I'll—"

"Right. You're going to need something stronger than this crap." Ryan grabbed the weighted mug out of Jay's hands and looked him square in the face. "Your spirit guide's been bothering Zach with that creepy little whistle-snore of his for the past hour. He's roosting in the command center."

Sleeping? "Wait. What? I ask him for one simple favor and he's sleeping?" He let out a frustrated growl through clenched teeth and sank back into his chair. "Romeo never does that to you, does he? Fall asleep on the job?"

Like his brothers, traces of a dying bloodline flowed through Jay's veins. Each of them had come out of the Ohanzee tribe's traditional spirit walk with an animal companion and a shift in physiology; they'd been granted abilities that—no pressure— were supposed to balance the whole good-evil playing field.

Complete with doom-and-gloom prophesies. The shaman had called the changes "gifts": Sight, Sound, and Sense. Torpedo, Romeo, and Drak.

Some gift. After insisting Jay rescue the woman the night before, Tor had apparently decided he wouldn't pull his share of protection duties.

Damn fickle bird.

"Romeo's a dog, not an owl. He doesn't have light requirements."

"It's raining. He does fine when it's overcast."

"Regardless, you kept him out all night and half the morning." Ryan set the mug down and spared a grimace for the swirl of cream rising to the surface. "Even spirit guides need sleep."

Scenarios of a daytime kidnapping chased through Jay's mind. "What am I going to do?"

"Murphy's got her already, bro. If she's not outright dead."

"She's not dead," Jay snapped, palming the rim of his drink. "What if we convince him to drop the contract?"

His brother frowned. "You want me to cut a deal with him?"

"He'll want to meet with our alter ego."

"If Klepto loses Murphy's trust, we lose our in for the drug deal and a lot of big names get away clean. You have to let this go." Ryan opened his mouth to say more, but a soft knock saved Jay from more lecturing.

The door swung open. *Emily?* He bolted to his feet, his heart flaring into overdrive.

Her expression tripped over their grim faces. "I'm so sorry— They told me out front to come right in."

She's safe. And she was right there, in the McLelas Financial office building. Jay fought to keep relief off his face, forcing his shock into a smile.

"No need to apologize, Ma'am. I was just leaving." His

brother's scowl melted and Ryan rapped the pads of his fingers on the desk, tipping his head at her with his public face on, a feigned, almost flirtatious grin that had Jay's fists clenching in dismay.

Her gaze darted between them and the edges of her eyes creased as if she were measuring, calculating. Remembering? His chest gave a pained lurch. Had she somehow uncovered his secret?

Ryan turned a covert, steel glance his way, one eyebrow arched in silent reproach. "See you after lunch."

A flicker of doubt gnawed at Jay's confidence as the door closed behind his brother.

No. She didn't—wouldn't—recognize him in his dark blue suit, his straight brown hair pulled high in a tight ponytail and far lighter under office lights than bedroom shadows. His voice even lacked the gravelly tones he and his brothers affected while behind the mask. He leaned over the desk with an outstretched hand.

"Emily Barton," she said, and her fingers seared his skin.

The same heat danced up his arm, the same inexplicable attraction lunged for his brain. How was that possible?

"Jay McLelas. What can I do for you this morning, Ma'am?" He looked for a hint of recognition. Nothing. Relief rushed through him, but right on its heels came a mental groan at a question rocketing around inside his brain.

What if she remembers my touch?

Her eyes sparked with an intense light and her lips quivered when she let go. Emily tucked a runaway lock of hair over her ear. "I run a small clinic, Partner Paws, over on the East end of the city. Does McLelas Financial have any grants available for non-profits?"

For his part in what went down the night before, he'd just as soon skip the formalities and give Emily money out-of-pocket.

It wasn't like he didn't have the cash lying around from the jobs they'd pulled for Murphy.

Oh, that would go over even better than last night.

"We have a variety." He motioned for her to take a seat and drank in the silver chain around her neck, dipping low over her tight floral blouse, the pink skirt hugging her hips. "Tell me about your organization, Miss Barton, and I'll see what might fit." When she settled into the available plush seat and the skirt rode up, the memory of her fair skin draped in something far more translucent had him claiming his own chair in a hurry.

The gratitude for his broad oak desk was short-lived. His thoughts refused to let go of the reality that had been the press of her body against his. *Get your mind out of the bedroom!* He swallowed uneasily as flames licked at his chest.

She set a manila folder on the surface between them and flipped it open, rotating it in his direction as she spoke. "We match terminally ill or disabled human patients with rehabilitated animals, a relationship which benefits both." At his gesture to continue, she pulled out a sheet of paper with a chart, pointing as she spoke. "Medical studies show that animal companions positively affect human lifespans, illnesses, general well-being; we foster those relationships at Partner Paws through classes and hands-on lessons."

Jay nodded, tabbing his monitor on. The purpose of her group resonated with him more than she could possibly know. Torpedo was more than his spirit guide and constant companion in the night. Despite his inopportune naps, the owl was family. "Nature of the funding?"

"To cover operating expenses and long-term care." Her gaze lowered to her hands, then back to his face, a momentary lapse in her confident façade.

"One of our major grants, then." He longed to capture her fingers between his, to rub his thumb along her slender wrist, ease whatever worry was on her mind. Instead, he had to make do with sitting across a desk, asking more questions just to keep her in the building longer. She was safe here. But once she left... "We can set up an application for the Rhodes grant. It is a big one, but the committee often splits awards out to new applicants, and the award deadline's coming up quick for this quarter."

"That would be wonderful."

He ducked behind the monitor and typed up the beginning of her application. In his peripheral vision, the silky strands of bobbed brown and red hair mesmerized. His heart pounded into his groin. Gulping his coffee to bolster his nerves, he finally pressed a button on the keyboard to print out her information.

"Thank you, Mr. McLelas," she said as he scooped the paper off the printer behind him and pushed it across the desk.

"It's Jay." With a smile, he tapped a fingertip on the bolded words at the top of the page. "Just log in to the website with these. There's an evaluation period. We'll send someone out on a couple of surprise visits—"

His mouth snapped closed and he stared at the paper. Was it that simple? Did he have a legitimate reason for keeping an eye on her during the day? Outside of the office?

"Mr. McLelas?"

"Jay," he corrected again, jerking his head up. "I'm sorry, what did you ask?"

She'd tucked the folder back into her purse and scooted back in her chair. "When is the deadline?"

"Three weeks, with awards shortly after. Tough competition, but I think you've got a great chance." Better than great. Fiscal responsibility demanded the paperwork, but even if her organization didn't actually win the draw, she'd get the money she needed.

Emily thanked him, exchanged another electrifying

handshake. She hesitated, her hazel gaze searching his face like she could find the answer to a question she hadn't asked. Then she was gone, leaving him alone with the dizzying taste of cinnamon and apples on the air.

He stared at the closed door, amazed his voice had remained steady, even professional, during the encounter. He shouldn't visit her again, shouldn't risk her figuring out who he was. But he had to, with or without temptation calling him to her doorstep. They still had to keep tabs on the dealer in the room underneath hers and after last night's declaration, Murphy would have her watched. Jay had to follow up on his end of their farce.

Another night under her covers. If this was how his libido reacted while sitting in the same room with her, how was he going to handle joining her in bed a second time? Animal instinct or protective willpower? He struggled to think beyond the way her lithe form had felt in his hands, wanting her quivering in anticipation instead of fear, yearning for his touch instead of panicking in his arms. Her wide eyes narrowing with passion for him—His next heartbeat skipped.

"Wait. If Tor's sleeping . . . " Jay scrambled for the phone on his desk. "Zach—"

"I'm not tracking down your girlfriend."

Damn it.

ZACH'S VOICE BURNED in his ear. "Okay genius, let's try this again. One in the hallway, one in the bedroom, one in the living area. I best be able to hear something this time."

Jay returned the listening device down the ventilation shaft and tied off the cord on the grate. He tapped the screw on the floor with the magnetized screwdriver and slid the covering back in place. Right under Emily's feet sat a hotbed of frequent, illegal transactions. They hoped to grab the last set of connections for the drug deal with audio evidence. That was why he'd returned. To finish the job he'd been sent to do the night before.

Or so he kept telling himself.

His mind had spent the day wholly overloaded with fantasies of Emily's naked body twisting underneath him in pleasure that only he could supply. Fantasies shattered when he'd arrived to find her missing, her bed made.

"What's taking you so long?" Zach's voice growled into the communicator. "You should be back here listening already."

Jay's eyes glossed over the replacement door to her apartment. A new silver chain gleamed on the wall. "I'm being thorough." Home repair had been his first order of business.

"Told you I should have gone instead," Ryan said.

"We're a team, Ry. Let me work."

He pushed on his night vision and squinted into the kitchen. The digital numbers on the stove clock blazed in his enhanced sight like he stood right in front of it. 12:00. Midnight. She wasn't working late. She just wasn't coming home.

A low growl rumbled in his throat as he stood. *Hell, man, get a grip.* He stalked into the bedroom and shoved open the lone window. Torpedo swooped in and ruffled his gray and brown mottled feathers, tilting his head with a curious look.

"Where is she?" A strange lump formed in Jay's throat. "Find her." A soundless rush of wind caressed his face when the owl whooped a soft agreement and flipped back into the air.

Fear, Jay decided. It was fear that caught at his chest without warning. He hadn't experienced it in so long he barely recognized the sensation. Worry, yes. But not damn near paralyzing fear.

"Find—Aw, Jay," Ryan said. "Tell me Torpedo's hunting."

"Track him. She's not here." He swallowed down the acidic taste on his tongue, gulping in outside air. Long ago he had made the conscious decision to never let anyone make him feel afraid again, had conquered shadow and night. But this fear wasn't for himself or for his brothers. This fear was for the woman, for Emily.

Why? Why now? Why . . . her?

Ryan coughed. "Bossy little—"

"No," Zach cut in. "You want a one-night stand, you track her down on your own." He didn't like his equipment used for anything but the job. "Ry, I got an even hundred that says you can finish up that robbery at two before our baby brother activates all those bugs."

Right, the bugs.

"Know what? For once, I'll take that bet. Pity 'bout all that youth and inexperience."

Jay could hear Ryan's wide grin through the earpiece. His oldest brother had three years on him, a year and a half on Zach. "Sure your trick knee can handle the climb?" He smiled without humor and stopped his feet from pacing in front of the open window.

"Scaling La Plaza? A stroll in the park," Ryan said.

"Park's a dangerous place at night." Jay sighed. "Track Torpedo. I won't go after her until I'm done here."

Ryan's laugh barked out over the connection. "Damn straight, you won't."

"And you'll be done when? Easter?" The distinct rattle of a keyboard being assaulted came over the earpiece, and then paused. "Jay, if you're just gonna stand there . . ."

He ducked around the bed and removed the second vent from its place near the floorboard. That she wasn't in her bedroom shot holes in his bid for ownership. He tapped the plate back into place before heading for the living room. If Emily had gone to a hotel, Murphy would figure it out and call their bluff. Jay just hoped his men didn't find her before Torpedo.

Before he could get to her side.

He lowered the last microphone and tapped on his earpiece again. "Zach?"

"Still moving."

Pulling two more devices from his belt, he kneeled to secure the first under the chipped base of Emily's dresser. Extra security. With bugs in place in her apartment, he'd know if Murphy's men came when he wasn't around. Assuming they both survived the evening. Juggling the other one-handed, he eyed her small kitchen.

Flour jar. It'd be muffled, but otherwise in a prime spot to hear trouble. He buried the device under the white powder then dusted off his gloved hand over the sink. Jay coughed as he asked Zach for the bird's status. Maybe he could follow until Torpedo caught up to her.

"Target's on Hodges and James Streets. Daysleeper Motel. Your girl can sure pick 'em. Murphy's got a warehouse not far from there."

"She's not my girl." *Yet.* The single word launched into his brain like a firework.

Jay peered out of the window, his skin itching to be on the move. Five stories to the parking lot below. One story up to the roof. He swung out onto the ledge and jumped up, just like the night before, leveraging his body weight against the ledge of the window and the decorative architecture on the old building.

"Hey, why are there five bugs on my screen?" Zach cursed. "I swear, if I have to come over there and set these myself—"

He tuned out his brother's words, his heart thumping out a steady rhythm of dread.

Murphy Jones would not have her.

With a careful press of his toe, the window slid shut. He pulled himself up and over the roof, jumping across the narrow alley to the next building. This was his favorite part of the night, leaping shadow to shadow, every limb, every muscle involved in the business of climbing, running, straining to reach the next ledge. Parkour was the next best thing to wings. Quick bursts like flying; stopless feet that knew the city from an angle few others dared tread. This was home now, a comfortable place where no one but Torpedo could best him.

Uneven ledges weren't necessary for long; the grimy buildings became taller and fire escapes were more readily accessible. His feet and hands pounded against metal railings until he made his way back to the ground a block from the street corner Zach had pinpointed.

The flash of a bird on the night wind glimmered on the horizon. Emily was here. When they came for her again, involving the cavalry would only mangle their operation further. Getting mixed up with her was his mistake to fix. He'd start by standing his ground against Murphy's thugs, alone.

"Torpedo's around the Sout—"

"I know where he is." Jay reached up to turn off the communicator, then shoved it into the pouch on his belt. Consequences be damned, he would protect this woman.

CHAPTER THREE

LIGHT FROM THE STREET seeped under the two faux-velvet curtained windows on either side of the double-locked doorway. At the back of the brick building, the clasp on the final motel room window wiggled to the right with a soft *pop*. Emily's fingers tightened around the serrated kitchen knife pillowed under her head.

Damp air rushed through the opening as someone outside inched the window up, sending a new streak of terror down her arms. *Breathe in, 2, 3, 4* . . . Her lungs burned with agony at the slow rhythm, steady despite the shape of her nerves.

She'd registered the room in cash under a false name, prayed no one would find her. The effort had been in vain. A shadowed figure pulling himself over the sill, dropping inside without a sound. She fought valiantly to maintain the illusion of sleep.

The man came closer to her blade; his shadow loomed larger on the wall as he approached the uncomfortable bed. A pause, and then the curtains shuttered again, the shadow obscured.

Twin thudding sounds of a pair of boots hitting the floor made her breath catch in her lungs. Fabric slithered, more heavy things connected with the ground. The held breath turned to ice. She scrambled to restart her counting, but even simple numbers withdrew to the corners of her mind when he lifted the cover, lying down beside her. Exposed to the humid air, her toes curled against the blanket.

Now. Emily gave a shout as she launched herself at him, swinging her right arm over her body, her blade angled at his chest. The intruder's hand caught her wrist, the grip too familiar. He hauled her over his body until she sprawled on top of him, knife dangling harmlessly by his shoulder, cheek pressed to his cheek. A startled gasp ripped from her gut and her next breath dragged him into her lungs.

Juniper enveloped her senses; the scent from the bushes surrounding the motel mingled with a star-touched aroma she couldn't mistake. The masked man. No chance of breathing normally now. *Maybe never again.*

"It's long past dusk, Emily." His whisper at her ear sent streaks of cold fire skittering through her veins. "I thought I told you to stay put."

She pushed up with her elbows and tugged against his grip, staring down into fathomless eyes. "How did you find me?"

"I'm a professional." He nodded at the useless weapon in her hand. "If I'd wanted to hurt you, that thing wouldn't have stopped me."

His index finger tapped along the inside of her wrist. The handle slipped between her clammy, frightened fingers like it had gained forty pounds. He tossed it over the far side of the bed with barely a glance. A clatter against the nightstand drew winces from them both. Two more bounces of the knife toward the motel room door echoed in the sparsely decorated space before silence returned.

"'Let the strange man in the bed and attack him with a butter knife' is not a solid self-defense plan against professionals."

Frowning, she shifted to one hip to escape him. "You didn't honestly expect me to be some midnight booty call, did you?" She met his gaze. "Let me go."

Silver eyes twinkled up at her from the pillow. "So you can assault me with a spoon next?"

Her mouth dropped open. "Are you laughing at me?"

The rumble in his chest gave him away before his lips bent in a rakish smirk. "Not at all."

Emily's knee popped up of its own accord. His eyes widened in surprise, but before her blow hit he'd flipped her onto her back and straddled her waist. Calloused palms trapped her wrists to the mattress, pinning them on either side of her face.

"You should have led with that one." He was openly grinning at her now.

Why does he have to have a sexy smile? Why do I want to smile back? It was much harder to struggle when her body had already crossed him off the threat list. "I'm not good at improv."

"You did just fine last night." The masked man eyed her motel room door.

Emily scrunched her eyes closed against the tightness in her chest. "Why are you here?"

"You're here," he said. "And we still have to perform Act Two."

"Act Two?" She opened one, then both eyes to see his lips hovering above her nose.

"In which the lovers try again to get the kidnappers to leave them alone." The amusement in his gaze shone, lit from a slight glare of the outside security lights.

Terrific. A criminal with a sense of humor. She just wished the punch line didn't involve so many guns. "They can find me too, can't they?"

His jaw tightened and he stared at a spot above her head. "Yes." One word, rasped, harsh.

The masked man cocked his head as if he were listening to something. Over the usual hum of the industrialized city, all she could hear were night noises—the buzz of street lamps, the rarity of a passing car, the grind of air conditioning vents.

When he looked again at the door, she asked, "Why does your boss want me?"

A tic pulsed along her captor's jaw. Like he was gritting his teeth. But he didn't answer.

"He is your boss, right? You work with them?" This time, she caught regret etched in the taut lines of his high cheekbones, the slight slump of his shoulders, the silver-shot glance. She made a guess. "You're an undercover cop. You're really a good guy." Emily really, really hoped he was one of the good guys.

He paused, dragging in a breath. "He's my business partner."

"Not a cop, then," she said, forcing a rigid smile. Stabbing disappointment collected behind her ribcage. He'd said as much the night before—she didn't want to believe it.

"I—" Gray eyes connected with hers, confused and warm on her skin at the same time. Then nothing. He shook his head, refusing to finish whatever he'd been about to say.

She rifled through her mind for another question while he was still inclined to answer. "So does he want me for some freaky woman museum? Does he want to keep my toes in a—?"

"Hell, I hope not. Murphy Jones is sick enough, but I don't know, Emily. I wish I did." His gaze roved over her face, searching. With a sigh, he released her wrists and rocked onto his shins, the taut muscles of his legs cradling her thighs.

Far too pleasant sensations arced from where he pressed against her—straight to her over-eager nipples. She forced her brain off that dangerous path. Her body was out of its ever-loving mind. Her masked avenger agreed that a museum of women's toes was sick. That at least counted for a check in the "good guy" column. Or at least a check in the "better than the other bad guys" column. *Stop it! The guy stalked you to a motel room, crept in through the window . . .*

He rubbed the back of his neck with a frown. Traitorous yearning unfurled in her gut. She wanted to kiss those lips back into the teasing grin he'd spared her earlier. Those lips were too handsome to waste on a frown.

"You've caught Murphy's attention."

She lifted her chin. "And yours?" *Oh, holy crap. What is wrong with you?*

One eyebrow quirked and he leaned in, rubbing a thumb along the inside of her left wrist. "Definitely mine. But that was just a pleasant accident."

"An accident?" Emily took in a sharp breath. "You didn't just fall into my bed, buddy. You *climbed* into bed with me. You're *still* in bed with me!"

"I've never had any complaints before."

Egotistical jerk. "Oh, so you're God's gift to imperiled women, are you?" She leveled a glare at him, yanking free of his grasp. "Out. Get off of me." Her fingertips pushed against the rough denim over his thighs. His incredibly solid thighs. His sexy, incredible . . . Emily jerked her hands away, her pulse racing anew.

He winked, his lips curving back into that full, irresistible smile.

She scowled at him but the attraction simmering her blood was far from fading. *Welcome to Stupidville, brain. Population: You.*

"You're stuck with me now. If Murphy discovers we've lied about our little intimate encounter last night, we're both—" He cut himself off and his head tilted again to listen.

Emily listened too, but she couldn't hear a thing over the incessant hooting of an over-excited owl. "Dead?" She finished his sentence for him, a new realization trickling through her mind. Her life wasn't the only one at stake here. Why was he risking his life to help her?

Humor bleached from his masked eyes as they softened with concern. "They're turning into the parking lot."

Her jaw dropped in mock disbelief. "So what, you can hear them pulling off the freeway? Are they yelling out a window, declaring to the whole of Relek City their intent to snatch me out of my motel room? What do kidnappers drive, anyway? Fake cleaning lady vans?"

He didn't stop her nervous thread of sarcasm. Instead, he swept his t-shirt up and over his chest and head with one hand, tossing it aside.

"Motorcycles? Black Suburbans with brush guards?" Emily's thought process derailed, latching onto the chiseled muscles she'd felt under her palms the night before. "Cute little bicycles with bells and ribbon tassels?" She forced a slow trickle of air into her lungs and then counted mentally on the exhale.

The man had a six-pack meant for a luxurious night of nibbling. "Okay, sure. I can be rescued by *that* again." She looked up at the amused, self-impressed smile on his face and knew from the sudden heat her face flared to molten-lava-red. "I—"

"Take off your top."

"What? No." Reality tugged under her skin, battling with chagrin, diverting the blood flow from her cheeks. "No freakin' way."

"Act 2, Emily," he said. The masked man's hard length slid down her body, charging her nerve endings to the boiling point, his fingers pulling the blankets up around them. "We're on."

"As are my clothes." The bite of fear inched up her throat.

"Not for long." Promise danced in the thin ring of silver around his dark pupils and cemented her to the mattress. He leaned forward, gently tugging the straps of her camisole over her shoulders, his hands cradling her head in the moment before their lips met.

Fear wasn't the emotion arching her body off the bed like an offering. It wasn't what prompted her to twirl her fingers around the tips of that enticing dark hair.

It's all an act, she reminded herself. *For the kidnappers.*

Burning need nibbled first at her toes, zinged through her veins in the next instant.

How long would she be able to tell the difference?

HAMMERING AGAINST THE door made Jay rip his lips away, tugging the blankets around them to cover the fact that Emily still had a shirt on—*Well, half a shirt.*

"Do you mind?" he shouted.

At least they were knocking tonight.

The doorknob rattled and someone's voice trickled through, "They're both here."

"But why are you?" Jay called out.

"Good question, isn't it?" Shiv this time, his voice grating through the closed door. "Least this place looks better than the dive you crashed at last night."

"Hey!" Emily wiggled underneath him.

Focus eluded his hunt for the brilliant excuse lodged somewhere in his brain.

As someone knocked with what sounded like a battering ram, Emily sent a tight smile toward the door. "To be honest, it got a little crowded last night. We thought this would be more . . . private."

Her voice pitched low, arousing, and it slammed the breath

out of him like a blow to the diaphragm. At least one of them didn't need acting lessons. The woman in his arms had the audacity to look up at him and slide her fingers across his masked face, a lover's caress of his cheek and a playful tug at his ear.

"Ignore them," she said, theatrically loud.

Jay jerked his head to stare, relying on the long, dark hair cascading over his shoulder and framing their faces to hide his surprise at her boldness. An inquisitive look gawked up at him, and he knew she'd seen his pupils contract too fast, the silver-and-black whirl of his ability churning like twin turbines. Without voicing the question in her eyes, she closed the distance in a light, uncertain kiss.

Her breath danced against his cheek. "They'll go away."

His already attentive erection strained against the fabric of his jeans and he swore inwardly. How could she do this to him with just a peck on the lips and a stage whisper?

Worse, she was terrified. Jay had no trouble spotting the tiny crease of her eyebrows, identifying the quiver in the posed, sultry angle of her mouth.

"Not up for debate, gentlemen," he said as Emily squirmed against him, arching her back as if she were desperate for his touch. "Get lost."

"This isn't over, Klepto," Shiv said.

Emily's tongue darted out of her mouth to wet her lips and Jay's cock jumped with startling need. Unable to resist her siren's call, he slid a hand under her head and pulled her against him for another kiss.

And another.

He nibbled on her lower lip and she gasped, sweeping her palms up over his shoulders.

"It is for tonight, asshole," he murmured.

There was silence beyond the door, no more knocking. With

Emily's fingers kneading his muscles, her soft breaths panting from his attention, Jay's concern for Murphy's hired guns bent out of focus. A faint car engine cranked in the parking lot, worlds away.

They'd left.

Good.

Jay's eyes filled with Emily. *My Emily.* His hands found her waist, massaging their way up her sides and stomach, tripping over the annoying fabric that remained of her shirt. He angled her head up and dropped a kiss into the dip of her throat.

One knee slipped between her thighs and her eyes shimmered closed. Her hands clutched at his shoulders, restless. Jay felt his control slip away, his mind tumbling into a bottomless well of sensation.

So good.

He kissed her neck again, twice more across her collarbone. His hand cupped her breast of its own volition. When his tongue swept across her nipple she jolted off the mattress. Not an act. Just this, just him and Emily. A nip at the tempting bud rewarded him with a low moan.

Something heavy scuffed across the carpet.

Emily froze underneath him and he shielded her body, staring down at her flushed face and parted lips. Acrid smoke cut through his consciousness. Gravity turned the world into a slow-motion hell as they turned as one to stare at the wall by the door. While they'd been . . . occupied . . . Shiv had picked the lock.

The sound they'd heard was him arranging a chair. Where he now sat, a spectator on the sidelines, taking a long drag on his cigarette.

"Well, don't stop on my account." A cloud of murky smoke puffed from between Shiv's thick lips. Moving a knife over his shoulder, he nudged the light switch with its blade.

Jay blinked hard, the overhead lighting like a slap across the face. A flash like that meant until his spirit guide-amped ability had the chance to cool down, his eyes would look normal but his night vision would run full-bore. He hauled back on his sight, thankful for cheap lightbulbs.

Dim lights meant he could still function. Mostly.

The assassin, monochrome and blurred in Jay's half-blinded state, slid a pack of cigarettes back into the pocket of his highly-contrasted floral shirt.

Ordinary sight ... any time now.

"Get out." Jay eyes settled on the knife the assassin twirled in his fingers. The vulnerable spot between his shoulder blades tingled. Emily's knife.

Had she been as lost as he was? Or had she just been playing along?

"Murphy sent me to make sure you weren't ... acting." Pudgy lips twisted in a perverse smile. "He won't be disappointed."

The assassin's eyes focused only on Emily, warped with base desire. Jay's throat tightened, a growl fighting to break free. Both of them were still covered from the waist down with the cheap orange-and-paisley motel comforter, but now he switched places with her, tucking her against his back to block her from the assassin's too-interested gaze.

"He'd like to make an arrangement. In the morning. Ten." Shiv rose smoothly from the chair and threaded the blade through his fingers, sliding his thumb across the tip. "Sharp."

Jay schooled his face into a look of disinterest and he rolled his shoulders back. "I'll drop by to see him after dark."

"Suit yourself. It's only your woman on the line." Clearly satisfied with the charade, Shiv leaned on the light switch again. Someone had cut the outside lights, pitching the room into complete darkness. "You do know how to pick 'em."

Already halfway on, Jay's night vision jump-started and followed the assassin's blue and orange t-shirt without effort. Shiv grasped the aging door handle and turned as if he could meet Jay's eyes in the night. The arc of his glare angled too high. Using Emily's knife, the assassin saluted in the direction of the bed.

"Do carry on," he said, securing the door behind him.

Not for the first time, Jay wished he had a way to ask his spirit guide questions at a distance, the way Ryan could with Romeo. Was Shiv listening outside the door or had the thugs parked across the lot? As if on cue, Torpedo let out a short string of hoots from the roof.

Watchers watch the Watcher.

There were enemies around, and they weren't going anywhere anytime soon. He tipped his head and frowned. Ryan had a job at two. In a little over an hour. If that robbery took place, and Jay was still here with Emily, their cover would be blown. He'd have to call Ryan on the comm, warn him. That would be tricky. Emily couldn't know about his brothers. But he couldn't leave her unprotected. Not with Shiv involved.

Emily. Irresistible to her very core, lips welcoming as a daydream. *And me too far gone to realize that bastard came in for a front-row seat.*

"I forgot to ask them what they drive." Her thready whisper twisted around the knot of failure lodged in his throat.

Rolling to face her, he tugged at a stray lock of her hair. "Pink tricycles. The lot of them."

He swallowed hard as a tremulous smile travel across her lips, the overcast of fear lifting from her hazel eyes. Fierce urges to protect her, claim her, keep her from harm rose from somewhere in his marrow.

Jay curved his arms around Emily's back. "You did great."

Understatement of the century. She'd pushed him beyond

rational thought. He brushed a thumb over her cheek before moving away.

"Are you leaving?" Her fingers shot out, tentative on his shoulder. Confused emotions clouded her eyes as they hopped back and forth, trying to see his features in the dark.

"I can't leave." He captured her hand in his. "They'll have this place under surveillance all night."

Honor demanded he be honest about their situation. He might not get to truly claim her, but he'd sure as hell keep her close, fake whatever relationship he had to, if it would protect her from a man far worse than himself.

"They'll be waiting for a chance to take you. You're going to have to get used to this—us." Jay took in a deep breath. "I'm afraid I'll be visiting often."

"Why?" She stared up at him with eyes too big for her face.

Because I need to keep you safe. He crushed her against his chest so the words wouldn't make it past his lips.

"Why do they want me?" A tremor rattled through her frame as she inhaled. Her adrenaline high had to be crashing.

"I don't know, but I'm damn well gonna find out." He rested his chin on the top of her head and wished he had Ryan's gift for words. "It'll be okay," he said instead.

"This is *not* okay. Nothing about this is okay." But she didn't pull away.

He held her as the trembling subsided. When her breathing slowed, almost even, more controlled, he pressed a kiss into her hair. "Get some sleep."

In the end he canceled the morning robbery from the bathroom, running sink water providing white noise between Emily and the whispered truth. Dreams had taken her before he scooted back under the covers and wound his arms in a protective circle around her body.

Too soon, the glowing red light of the motel room's digital clock stabbed at his eyes. *Six? Already?* Jay glanced down at the sleeping angel in his arms and rubbed her cheek with his thumb. Their position felt right, his arms still tucked about her like a shield of muscle, her form fitted to his, their legs entwined as if Emily had always been there, a treasure of his own—a treasure he didn't deserve.

He eased himself from the embrace and sat up on the side of the bed. He had to leave before daylight; he couldn't chance her getting a good look at him without the aid of night shadows or sub-par motel lighting. But he'd make sure the thugs had gone, and he'd be watching. Murphy wouldn't take her. Jay pulled on both boots and stood.

"What do I call you?" The drowsy voice sent warmth curling around him, through him.

He cast a look back over his shoulder. She wasn't quite awake, her eyes half-obscured under heavy lids.

Jay reached out a hand to smooth her mussed hair, unable to stop a tender smile from sliding into place. "Anything you want."

CHAPTER FOUR

"SORRY FOR THE SHORT notice."

"Nine thirty's fine, Mr. McLelas," Emily said, her neck cramping as she squeezed the handset against her shoulder. She wanted to believe the sincerity in that mocha-smooth voice. But the phone call was a courtesy. He'd mentioned unscheduled visits when she'd applied. Jay McLelas had a job to do. And Emily's job was to convince him Partner Paws was the best investment for their grant money. "We have a group this morning, but I can be available for the paperwork you need."

"Thank you," he said. "I'll see you soon."

The words resonated like a promise and resulted in a delicious—foolish—shiver across her shoulders as she hung up the phone. Mint-enhanced coffee found her nose and the shiver traced a path down her spine.

"Get a grip." Emily saved the grant application on the computer monitor, rubbing at one temple with her index finger. She'd woken alone in the motel to a plate of fruit pastries and fresh coffee shop brew. Even business couldn't clear her head, tangling images of guns and grants.

Danger, laced with midnight kisses and paperwork.

She dropped her gaze to her hand where it rested on the phone. "Just because a stranger brings you breakfast in bed doesn't mean you can get all hot and bothered by the entire male species."

Quiet laughter made her gaze snap to the doorway. Julia. Relief joined Emily's tumult of thoughts. *Thank God Naomi didn't hear me.*

"This stranger have a name?" Julia asked, the corners of her dark eyes pulled tight in amusement.

"No." Her brain melted just thinking about him, and she still didn't know his real name. Emily shook her head. "It doesn't matter."

Julia stretched her arms out, her teeth flashing in a wide smile. "Have you told—"

"Don't you dare tell her. Don't even hint at it." Emily said. He'd slipped away like a ninja, vanishing with the dark. There was nothing to tell.

"But she'll be so glad something other than money trouble is keeping you up at night." A wink, before Julia's face took on the staid expression that said she had something difficult to say.

A teenaged intern appeared at Julia's elbow before she could speak. "Mr. Young is here."

"Thanks, Britt. I'll see him in," Julia said, nodding at Emily as the girl pelted back down the hall. "Good luck."

Miles Young was tall, thin, and polished in a rich blazer suit of charcoal. As usual, his deceptively easy-going presence was in full force; his confidence was almost palpable in the way he acted as if he'd already gotten everything he wanted—and if he didn't, he soon would. Today, however, his breath reeked of alcohol. Her stomach twisted with unease as the sharply dressed man clasped her hand.

"So, I have the pleasure of meeting with you once more in the flesh, Miss Barton." He clawed his fingers through short brown hair, tipping his head in a gracious smile. "We have some finances to discuss."

A smile slammed onto her face and she reclaimed her side of the desk as fast as she could without appearing rude. The horrible need to put space between them was like a living creature in the room. Julia had it right: He'd returned to attempt another bribe.

Without exception, dealing with these conversations left an empty feeling in her chest. The wealthy tried a multitude of approaches so she'd move their children, spouse, friend, mailman—sick or not—to the top of the list for a pre-trained puppy. But her animals were for therapy, not novelty. If they wanted well-trained pets, this man's echelon of society could shop at breeders instead of hovering like vultures over a little non-profit like Partner Paws. But it seemed the presiding belief was cash and persistence would change her mind.

"As you know, I've been following your charming program for a while now," he began, his shoulders drooping as he sank into one of her armchairs. "Quite a few tales—no pun intended, Miss—have graced the newsstand of such miraculous Partner Paws recoveries."

Brown eyes lit on the newspaper still on her desk. "Actually, there's one in that very issue. May I?"

Her eyebrows lifted. *What's he playing at this time?*

The businessman snatched her paper without waiting for an answer and tilted the front page toward her. "Shame, isn't it? How killers make the front page while the heroes are stuffed way back here?"

"He's not—" Emily snapped her mouth shut. Had she been about to defend her masked visitor? She didn't know if he killed people or not. She didn't know anything about him. Beyond the fact his bold touch could light up her nerve endings like a roman candle doused in gasoline and christened with a flamethrower.

Stop it. Don't think about him. Her throat refused to let in more than a trickle of air as she reached for the paper cup of coffee.

"Ah, there we are," he continued as if she hadn't said anything. "'Partner Paws Pet Cures Kidney Disease'. Lovely picture of their trainer: You, my dear." He threw the paper back on top of her desk, lifting a hand to rub the side of his clean-shaven, chiseled jawline. "I would be most interested to hear how you coach your animals in the art of healing."

If he'd read the whole article, he would know the words under such a sensational headline had nothing to do with miracles. It was a simple tale about improving quality of life and increasing one's will to live. Partner Paws animals couldn't cure a terminal illness.

"I teach them appropriate social behavior and manners, some special commands to keep their companions safe. That's all." She folded her hands over her appointment book and smiled. "They do the rest."

His eyes flashed with skepticism. "You deny you train them to cure your patients?"

"I'm afraid you misunderstand, Mr. Young." Her instincts turned wary as he pulled out a notepad and jotted something down. "This article—Sometimes a dose of companionship is all our patients need to ease their stress, human and animal alike. Stress causes many complications, and a side effect of making our patients feel more equipped to handle the day to day can be that their illness becomes less severe. Not gone, but better."

Bracing herself for the usual sob story, she mentally charged up her bribe-rejection speech. "Sir, if this is about your son's placement on the waiting list . . . "

"Oh, no, Miss Barton. I've run out of options for Stefan's

cancer treatments, and I'm afraid there's only one avenue left for us." Every nerve in her body locked on to the odd flicker of emotion—not grief, but something cold—that passed through his eyes. "See, I'm a widower with too much time on my hands. My son's illness, well." He turned his face away from her and took in a shaky breath. "His time is more precious to me than my wealth. Nothing we try helps."

The tall man slumped further in the chair and Emily's eyebrows knitted together. She came around the desk to perch on into the cushioned chair next to his, offering a tissue from the box on her desk.

"He always wanted a dog." His head dropped and he dabbed at his eyes with his own handkerchief, a bright purple square he pulled from his suit pocket. "I'm sorry, Miss Barton. I didn't come here for pity. And here I am, a hopeless wreck."

He's not here to hand out bribes.

Guilt pierced her lungs and she floundered for something to say, crumpling the tissue into her palm.

"In the past, I've tried to buy him a spot in one of your classes. Stefan gets weaker by the day, and I'm afraid he just doesn't have time to wait on your list." He blinked away the remaining unshed tears.

"I'm sorry, Mr. Young." Tentatively, she rested a reassuring hand on his shoulder.

The purple cloth swiped at his eyes again, its color vivid against his pale skin. His spine turned rigid. "I'd like to make a donation to your organization. No strings attached. To use for other children like him, who might still have time to go through the proper channels for one of the animal companions here. Stefan's legacy, if you will. I've already made arrangements with the bank but it may take a couple of days to clear such a large sum." He pushed the notepad back into his jacket pocket and drew out a checkbook. With shaking hands, he pulled a receipt of deposit from the inside cover.

The slip of paper read "Partner Paws" and there were far too many zeros. More than enough to solve their problems. Disbelief coiled with suspicion in her chest. "Sir," she said, moving to steady herself against her desk, "this is an incredible gesture. Your son—"

"I procured a dog for him. Excellent pedigree, of course." Mr. Young tipped her a charming smile, all hint of shadows gone from his face. "By week's end, I'll have acquired an excellent trainer to ensure a strong companionship."

Emily fought a frown at his misconception. *Friendship doesn't require special breeding or training. It just happens.* "Well—"

Her protest made it no further; he cut her off with a wave of his hand. "The donation is an inadequate payment for your achievements in unconventional medicine. For what your excellent coaching methods—for a single animal and child—will yet achieve. I can go home with a lighter heart. Now, if you'll excuse me—I have another appointment at the top of the hour." He jumped to his feet and turned to leave.

"How can we thank you?" The faint question left her lips as he opened the door. This was the kind of money people renamed hospital wings with, wasn't it? And Partner Paws merely had classrooms, kennels. Maybe she could get a plaque for—

"Your continued work will be gratitude enough." The man turned back around to face her, sorrow in his eyes overshadowed with a flirtatious edge. "And I expect you'll come see the namesake of my donation in person."

At the startled look on her face, he gave a too-hearty laugh. The overwhelming stench of alcohol turned the air between them vile.

"My annual fundraiser? Next Tuesday." He closed the distance between them and grasped her fingers. "I'll send a limo to pick you up. Unless you'd like to thank me sooner."

Drumbeats of disgust hammered at her skull as his kiss lingered on the back of her hand. She'd been thinking of rededicating the dog park outside and he was expecting to see her on his arm. Emily wasn't about to go on a date, no matter how rich or handsome the stranger. *Or how mysterious.* An image of her masked visitor whirled uninvited through her mind. Now, there was a kiss she hadn't wanted to wash off. Of course, her moonlight ninja hadn't been drunk.

"Mr. Young, I think perhaps—"

"Tuesday, *cherie*." He sped out of the room, almost bolting from the building.

What just happened? She stared down at the paper between her fingers and her feet inched backward until her other palm steadied her against the desk. "What did I say?"

Julia barged in. "I don't like that one," she said with a frown. "He's sneaky."

Turning, Emily held up the receipt. "'That one' just took care of our vet bills for the year. And then some."

Her friend snagged the paper and threw it, sending it tumbling in a slow flutter to the top of the desk. "Listen to me, Em. He came in looking completely dejected and when he left he looked far too smug. Something's not right." Distrust furrowed her dark brow. "You think he's really giving us all that money? Money's not free. I don't know what he's doing, but it'll hurt us in the long run."

"I'll call the bank." Emily wanted to believe in Mr. Young's generosity, but Julia kept her hope firmly grounded. Even if the money was in the bank, when the man sobered up he could very well change his mind. "We both need a trip away from the city. It's making us jaded."

"I was jaded long before I moved here."

"He asked me to attend a fundraiser with him." She bit her

lower lip in thought. Her instincts were useless today. *Lack of sleep'll do that.*

Julia snorted and shook her head. "So really what our Mr. Young has done is bought a date with you. For half a million dollars."

"Don't be dramatic."

"Oh, it gets better. By taking the money you've opened yourself up to meet this rich guy's son at the fundraiser, and he knows you're too good of a person to tell a child no to his face." Her waist-length braid bouncing against her back, Julia yanked the door open and headed down the hallway toward the kennel. "I hope I'm wrong."

"You're not on that count. He does expect us to meet." Emily sighed.

"Mm, mm! Would you look at that?" Naomi's soft whistle dragged her attention to the front door. "Was there a sale on sexy this mornin'? It's gonna be a great day, cha, Mrs. Melanie?"

Naomi bumped the automatic door opener to give Mrs. Melanie Bluseau, one of the elderly students in the morning class, more time to maneuver her wheelchair through the doorway. Behind the beaming women another tall, handsome man was walking toward the building. He stopped to stare up at the roof.

As a tug on her arm from one of her younger students pulled her eagerly toward the classroom, Emily felt a smile chase away her worries over Miles Young. "Behave, ladies. That's our grant officer."

JAY SHOVED ONE hand in his pocket. A gust of wind caught on his briefcase as he surveyed the warehouse-turned-office. One lone grocery bag crinkled past the door and blew down the grimy side alley. Partner Paws' façade was well-maintained, at least from this angle, but he didn't see any outside lighting beyond the streetlamp at the end of the block that overlooked a worn bus stop. No security cameras on this building, no alarm system. The parking lot behind him—which held only his car—had been redesigned to be more park than lot, presumably for the organization's animals to be exercised and trained. It would be unlit at night. How had she made it through a whole day and half a morning without being snatched by Murphy's thugs?

He didn't know how long he stood there, staring, but when he finally strode forward his knuckles cracked around the handle of the case.

The door opened with a cheery tingle of bells and a teenaged volunteer gave him a little finger-wave from behind the reception desk. "Miss Barton's just getting the morning class settled in for Naomi." The brunette wound the white cord of her iPod earphones around a finger and flashed him a coy smile. "She said you can go in if you want."

He nodded and continued down the hallway. A series of stepped windows spread across the left wall. Emily stood with her back to the glass, talking to a roomful of people, some sitting in wheelchairs, others standing, still others lounging in a sprawl on the floor. He strained to hear, but the glass stood thick between them.

She took a cat with only three legs from a carrier along the wall and settled it into the arms of an older woman in a wheelchair, patting the cat on the head and the woman on the shoulder. As she spoke to the woman she alternated glances between her and a boy standing just behind the chair. The boy nodded with enthusiasm at whatever Emily was telling them. She kept an arm around the woman in the chair and rubbed her thumb in a gentle motion over the crest of the cat's head until she'd finished speaking. Then she backed away.

Jay's breath caught in his throat when she turned around,

smiling. Emily lit up the room with that smile, inexplicably lifting his heart as well. There was something magical and comforting about the way she flitted about the room to talk to them, the students in the class responding with wide grins and careful motions to mimic her own.

"Well, Mr. Grant Officer? You wanna meet the class?"

He angled to the side and faced another of the Partner Paws staff. The redhead was almost nose to nose with him. She smiled, her lips colored in shock-gold. He blinked in surprise.

"Naomi Triviona," she said by way of introduction, then waved at him to follow. "Come on, we'll find you a seat." Her footsteps clicked against the floor, calling attention to a purple leopard-printed pair of spiked heels.

The flamboyant woman elbowed the door open and Emily's warm greeting beckoned them inside. He fought a reflexive urge to hide his face from her memory. She hadn't recognized him before. She wouldn't today, either.

"Good morning," Emily said, crossing the room to his side. "It's a pleasure to see you again so soon, Mr. McLelas."

"Part of the process is to see you in action. I didn't want to interrupt. We can get into paperwork later." He hoped she'd let him stay to watch her work.

Her cheery demeanor was contagious. "I've just finished with the warm-up part of today's lesson and Naomi will be teaching the rest. Want to see what they're working on?" Without waiting for a reply, she grabbed his free hand and half-dragged him into the center of the room, grinning. Her fingers slipped free from his. "Folks, this is Mr. Jay McLelas, from the McLelas Financial firm downtown. He's here to check us out, see how we do things. Anyone want to share what we're up to?"

"He's one of *the* McLelas brothers? Hot damn." Naomi's not-quite-a-whisper hit his ears. "Sexy *and* rich."

He stifled a smirk and absently rubbed his thumb across his

fingertips where Emily's touch still lingered in his memory. Naomi's sentiment was nice, but only one woman's opinion mattered today.

A sandy-haired man stood uneasy on his feet, gripping a halter on the tall golden retriever beside him. Dark sunglasses covered his eyes. "Mornin' Jay," he began in a cheerful baritone with a slight Southern drawl, "the little lady has been teachin' us all about patience." A chuckle spread across the room.

Emily leaned close to his ear, affecting a stage whisper. "Buster wasn't following directions very well yesterday."

Suddenly empty, his lungs dragged in the musky odor of shampooed pets and her familiar cinnamon before she pulled away.

In a louder voice, she continued, "We've almost got him trained good though, don't we, Hue?" She stooped and gave a conspiratorial wink to the blind man's dog.

Jay laughed too, enjoying the rush of camaraderie she offered. This was Emily's world. Nothing like his grisly nights, three stoic brothers and their spirit guides haunting the streets. He had politeness behind a desk at work, laughter with his family, but there was always an undertone of grim determination. The McLelas name hid danger. Death. In the light of day, she and her room full of strangers offered him life, happiness, sunshine. A side of humanity he'd thought lost to him. He didn't know how she had managed to get under his skin and into his soul so fast, but he didn't regret this moment.

One by one the students revealed anecdotes of lessons past and he soaked up the respect they had for Emily and her team.

She nodded at him. "Okay, guys, I think that'll wrap up my contribution to the excitement for the day; I will leave you in the capable hands of Miss Triviona, as usual." Emily ushered him out of the room, leaving behind the diminishing sound of Naomi's heels clicking across the classroom floor. She reached for the door across the hall and beckoned him inside her office. "Now that you've seen us in action, Mr. McLelas, did you have any questions?"

"It's Jay." He set the briefcase on her desk and slid a handful of papers from the binder. "These are reference forms you'll need to distribute to a few of your participants. We require testimonials. The more you can gather, the better." The word-of-mouth testimonials he'd heard in the room today could secure any panel's decision to set aside the money for her, but they had to have the documentation in the system to make it official.

"Wait right here." She grabbed a few of the pages and darted from the room. When she returned, she said, "I have a few poets in the first group whose stories should be told here, no question about it. The rest of these can head home with the afternoon group." Emily tapped on the remaining forms. "Thank you so much for bringing them by! Is there anything else I can do for you?"

Jay's mind conjured many things she could do with him. None of them involving work. But he was here to keep an eye on her. In his capacity for McLelas Financial. That was it.

He folded his hands on the top of her desk, a perfect captive audience. "I'm impressed by the atmosphere here. The class prepares them for taking care of a pet?"

"And for the pet to take care of them." At his raised eyebrow, she continued. "Partner Paws bridges the distance between ailing people and ailing animals. The common thread of survival against all odds—it brings them together in a camaraderie of sorts. We find matches that suit the owner and pet's needs."

She leaned to the side to dig in one of her desk drawers, giving him an unintentional and enticing view of the lush curves of her breasts underneath her shirt.

Need of his own slammed into his groin and he forced

himself to look away. Jay focused on the coffee he'd left for her. It had to be ice cold by now. Ice cold.

Yes. Think of ice.

"Because both of them have special requirements," she was saying, "I run them through extensive training courses to prepare each one for their roles. On top of that, our animals are observed and guided through behavioral issues, passed through general obedience training, and are extensively handled by the rest of our staff as well."

"And the people who come here for a companion: are they walk-ins? Referrals?"

In response, Emily pushed an application to him and pointed at a series of questions covering multiple ailments, inquiring about mobility, family life, housing, and many other considerations he never had to worry about with Torpedo. Financial concerns were not mentioned.

"Our screening process is quite thorough," she said as he thumbed through the document. "We aren't like a regular adoption agency or shelter. We do have a partnership with Fairview Hospital for referrals but for anyone wanting to go directly through us, we have an application process, a waiting list, and a mandatory training and acquaintance period. We have to see how they mesh together."

He glanced up, found his gaze dipping along her collarbone again as she searched for something amid the papers on her desk, and promptly forced himself to glance around the cozy room. "What if it doesn't work out? Have you ever had any problems matching the animals and people?"

What if she'd caught him staring?

She looked glum for a moment and he wished he could take the question back. "We look at how the person is doing now and where the potential lies for improvement on both parts. We ask ourselves if a woman who is suffering from depression would benefit more from a stoic companion or one with a large amount of energy, a needy pet or one who is self-sufficient. There have only been a couple of disappointing cases."

He wanted to hear more of her lyrical voice but he hated the flash of sorrow that burned in her gaze. His hand lifted, his fingers itching to take her hand, to soothe her distress, but he paused and lowered his palm back to the desk.

A knock sounded on the door and Naomi peeked in. "Sorry to interrupt, Em, but are there any extra cat books?"

Emily stood and grabbed an orange spiral-bound workbook off a short bookshelf. She lingered over the shelf then grabbed a second book, sliding it in front of him.

Jay heard the door close again as he flipped through the pages. The workbook was vivid and engaging, covering daily steps for feeding, watering, cleaning, and caring. Extra pages lined the back for photos and notes.

"Did you write this?" It seemed like the sort of thing an exuberant young woman with a love of animals and people, and experience with both, could create out of air.

Emily laughed, a sparkle of bells. "Oh no, that's Naomi's handiwork there. She's infatuated with cats."

A grin tugged at his mouth. "Guess that explains the shoes."

With another chuckle, she pointed out a few specific pages and pulled a chair close to him so she could show him a few more of the organization's workbooks. She bubbled over the rest of the staff and their individual twists on the teaching process. Jay soaked it all in, reveling in her nearness.

"You've got a diverse group, Emily. Talented," he said, the smile now easy on his face. Her face angled up at him and he continued, "What's your animal of choice?"

Emily's hazel eyes sparkled. "All of them." She grinned. "My specialty is avian, though. Happy chirping is perfect for a pick-me-up in the morning."

"Avian, huh? I've got a bird at home you should meet, then." His expression turned rigid.

What in the hell are you doing, Jay? She can't meet Torpedo!

Never mind the fact that if she saw the owl with him at night she'd figure him out. Torpedo wasn't good with people like her trained Partner Paws companions. He wasn't about to let her get close to the owl's beak, or his talons.

Her face perked with interest. "Really? What kind?"

"Do you have any pets of your own?" He already knew the answer to the question: No. He'd seen every square inch of her apartment and there was not a trace of any kind of creature.

Emily hesitated at his dodged answer, her eyebrows raising a fraction. "I keep all of my 'pets' here." She stepped away to reshelve the books and smiled as she added, "I used to foster one or two at a time, but Marco took that over when I moved into the city."

"Marco?" A cool spurt of jealousy dampened his mood. He shut down the unexpected emotion with a smile locked on his face, but she wasn't looking at him, scooping the workbooks into a neat pile.

"One of our irregular volunteers."

"Unreliable?" His narrowed glance caught on the clock by the bookshelf. Noon. *Damn.* He couldn't justify monopolizing any more of her day any more than he could reschedule all of his daytime responsibilities as well as his nighttime ones.

"Depends on who you ask. I've always been able to count on him for the heavy lifting." She turned to him and shrugged.

Jay stood and thanked her for her time. "I've got to get back to the office. Papers, filing, I'm sure you know the drill."

She wouldn't be left unprotected this time. Torpedo and Romeo, Ryan's German shepherd spirit guide, would both be keeping an eye on her. And following her, if he didn't get back before she left Partner Paws.

Emily took the hand he offered. A frisson of attraction pulsed between them and the corners of her eyes softened.

Jay dropped her hand fast and deflected his gaze, afraid the look might mean she had almost closed in on his identity. "I'll let you get back to work." Before he could turn to go, a newspaper glared at him from the corner of her desk. He reached for it without thinking.

Ryan. I thought he'd killed the camera.

"There's an article about us near the back." Her smile turned white as she pressed her lips together, visible tension ratcheting up her spine.

"Bad press?" He frowned. Her reaction wasn't about Partner Paws at all; her fearful gaze had lingered on the photo splashed across the front page. Klepto.

Criminal. The reminder burned in his throat.

She sighed and took the paper from his fingers, creasing it in quarters. "I was just remembering something Mr. Young said at my morning appointment."

"Mr. Young?" His fingertips flexed against the top of the desk and he leaned forward. It could be a coincidence, but after last night . . . He jumped to the first conclusion and prayed he was wrong. "That wouldn't be a Mr. Miles Young, would it?"

She didn't hide her surprise. "You know him?"

Jay hid the boiling rage behind a tight smile. "We're acquainted."

Miles Young. Alias: Murphy Jones.

CHAPTER FIVE

"NIGHT, HUE. YOU keep the other fellas quiet, okay?" Emily clipped the kennel door closed and skipped backward, her feet unsteady underneath her.

It had been a long day and she was done thinking. She'd sent the volunteers home and taken the dogs out herself to the renovated area of the parking lot for their final run of the day. Exhausting herself out of her woes had felt necessary at the time. Now though, the sensation of being watched crept over the tiny hairs on her arms.

"I have to get some sleep," she muttered, dropping a basket of clean and folded towels on the counter. The back room was eerily silent, absent the squeak of a hamster wheel or the fluff of feathers. She headed for the light switch outside the boarding room door to shut down for the night, hardly relishing the thought of heading home. "Maybe I should just stay here."

Except Murphy's men would know where she worked.

They were probably out there right now. "Terrific. Now I definitely don't want to go out there and wait on the bus."

She ached for a long night of real, uninterrupted sleep. The kind of sleep she'd had just Sunday night. No guns, no masks. Her fingers grazed her lips, but the perfect, delicious memory of her midnight ninja's kiss was stained by the noxious stench of Shiv's cigarettes.

Fur brushed against her legs and her heart tried to vault through her chest. "Just the office cat . . . "

She sagged against the wall. "I can't go out there like this." She flipped off the building lights and her eyes closed as a yawn took her. Exhaustion and dizziness overwhelmed her, her knees colliding with the linoleum. Her consciousness yanked forward, out.

"Should've guessed you wouldn't leave your property unattended," Shiv's acerbic voice cut through the darkness.

Panic made the dream fuzzy. She sucked in a breath, determined not to show him fear. But he wasn't talking to her. The psycho in a riot of blue flowers and her masked man, cloaked in a draped hood and a long trench coat, faced off on the roof of the Partner Paws building. Emily watched the deadly dance play out like a 3-D action movie. They stared each other down, knife against gun.

"How many times do I have to tell your ugly face to back off?"

"Contract's still out, Klepto." The shorter man slashed at him with a long, curved knife.

Her masked man didn't flinch, didn't raise his weapon; he just took a step backward, a bored look on his face. The blade tore through his trench coat. "Tough luck for you," he said. "Murphy canceled it an hour ago. The girl is mine."

"You expect me to believe that? That's just downright insulting."

A strong gust of wind twisted his coat around his legs, buffeted the hood around his face, tried to pull his words away from her ears. She strained to hear the conversation.

"I found him someone else."

As if caught on the air current, Emily's view rushed past the conversation.

Wait, go back!

Her focus zoomed in through the darkness to other bodies creeping up to the rooftop. They thought they were sneaky, but she could see them, recognized some from the nights before, guns aimed at her masked man's back. Adrenaline soared through her veins and she tried to shout a warning, but there was no sound. Like someone had severed her vocal cords.

This is my dream, right? In my dream, he doesn't get shot!

She wrestled with the dream to get him a warning, but she was powerless, a bystander, nothing more. A barrage of gunfire erupted. No!

She twisted, hovering above the scene, then her eyes swiveled, her dream-self following the masked man's easy leap to the roof of the next building.

He was unharmed. "I don't think he'll be pleased to know you tried to off his favorite thief," *he shouted, ducking to the left to avoid one more bullet.*

Shiv snorted, twirling the knife in his fingers. "Murphy's not gonna know. Because one of these nights, his so-called 'partner's' just gonna disappear."

The masked man's teeth flashed white. "One of us will." *He stepped off the roof in a blur, feet connecting with a ladder, hands rapidly grabbing and releasing railings as he controlled a fall toward the ground. She followed his weaving dash down the street then the dream-camera panned to the men chasing him in the night. More gunfire rang out, but nothing touched him.*

He ducked through an open doorway, chest heaving, and he swore under his breath, looking directly into Emily's eyes.

"Get back there and keep her safe! I can handle this."

Was he talking to her?

The vision dipped and weaved back to the front door of Partner Paws.

She woke with a start, blinking in the dim backup lighting and trying to get her bearings. Heat seeped away from her slumped body into the hallway floor. *The hallway?* Purring buzzed like a jackhammer against her thigh and Emily pushed up on her arms to see Captain Nemo curled against her in concern.

The office cat gave a tentative meow, worry in his yellow eyes. He pushed his huge orange head under her trembling palm. She buried her fingers in the fuzzy scruff of the cat's neck, rubbing her thumb over his green patterned collar.

It felt so real.

Lifting one shaking hand, she willed it to be still. Her muscles wouldn't obey. Neither would her pulse slow down. Another rush of comfort came from the tomcat and she let it wash over her without question. She needed sleep. Now. Before her body gave out on her again. Before her brain manufactured any more bizarre nightmares.

She cast a distrustful glance at the front door. "I wonder where Marco stashed the cot."

CHAPTER SIX

"You should be home, Emily. Not sleeping on the couch."

Emily bolted upright and her forehead slammed into something with a sharp *crack*. With a yelp, she backpedaled on the cushions until her spine hit something solid. The slats of the front windows were open and the solitary lamp down the street flickered like a windblown candle. Spots were fading from the edges of her vision but her head throbbed as she struggled to identify the man now crouched beside her makeshift bed.

"Sorry." He rubbed at the bare strip of forehead above his mask and threw her a rueful grimace. "You okay?"

He's alive. She sagged against the arm of the couch, relief striking as cool and fast as the dream had. *And it was a dream, after all. Just a dream.*

His eyes lit up as if encouraged by her expression, and he pushed himself off of his knees. "Shall we?"

"Shall we what?"

"Go back to your apartment." He held out a hand. "Look, the motel last night was pushing it. Shiv won't buy us on a couch."

She frowned and batted his fingers away. "I'm not sleeping on this couch with you."

"It wasn't exactly my plan. But if you insist." The masked man gave an affected sigh and slid onto the blankets she'd laid out, settling against the cushions. Silver eyes focused on her still-pulsing forehead. "I can't let your coworkers think someone beat you. Come here, Emily."

She glared at him, and his cheeks creased in an apologetic grin. That smile . . . Her insides responded with a slow flip. "Tell me your name."

"They call me Klepto." He inclined his head toward her, a small, bemused frown marring the handsome planes of his face.

Not that name. Her nose crinkled, but she eased out of her crouched position and into the seat beside him.

"What's wrong?" His index finger snaked out to trace the bridge of her nose. "Aside from the obvious."

"That's what *they* call you. That's what the psycho with the knife calls you." It wasn't real, and it wasn't . . . him. Late night whimsy took hold. "How about 'Midnight Marauder'?"

The corners of his mouth twitched. "That's a terrible name."

"Well, it's nicer than Klepto. Less . . . " Emily waved her hand in the air, searching for an explanation. "Creepy criminal-like."

"Less creepy criminal-like?" he repeated, staring.

"You don't like it?" A teasing grin crept across her lips as she thought of how she'd considered his appearance earlier in the day. "Let's try: 'Nighttime Ninja'?"

The masked man leaned over her body, his lips brushing her ear. "I'm not a ninja," he whispered. His fingers feathered over her skin, kneading slow circles over the tender spot on her forehead.

"You wear all black, have a mask, sneak around in the dark, and make no noise when you move. Ninja." She ticked off a finger with each point. In her dream, he'd also been agile as one—but he was cocky enough without knowing he'd invaded her subconscious.

"I don't use a sword—"

"Who said all ninjas use swords?"

"You're not calling me a ninja." Ninja's insistent words held an edge of warning even as they took on a low, seductive pitch.

Emily closed her eyes, leaning into his gentle touch. "Thank—" She swallowed the second word because otherwise it would have come out as a groan. The warmth of his lips closed over the injury then took a detour toward her left temple. A jolt of desire spiked down her spine, settling between her thighs with a vengeance. *This cannot be happening. Again.* She shifted against the cushions, losing a silent war against the blast furnace of a blush.

Ninja pulled away. "Better?"

The look of smug, male satisfaction on the visible half of his face made her wonder if he knew exactly how much he affected her.

He stood, extending his hand once more.

"I do need clothes." She already knew his opinion on that front. *Rephrase that before you end up naked in his lap.* Emily held up a finger to counter the sly look in his eyes. "For work tomorrow."

He grinned wider.

How is it possible for that to still *come out wrong?*

"So," Ninja said, dragging out the word, "are you coming with me, or do I get to dig through your underwear drawer unsupervised?"

HALF AN HOUR and one blindfolded car ride later Emily lay curled under a sheet in a tank top and a cute pair of pajama shorts. Trying not to think about the average criminal's salary. With gas over $20 and the roads troublesome for even emergency vehicles, who even bothered to own their own car anymore? She sighed. Maybe that was it. Maybe the thief heading for her bedroom window had stolen one to get her home and hadn't wanted her to see.

It was a cooler night and her AC had been making hideous rattling noises, so off it went. Ninja pushed her bedroom window open and drew her bedroom curtains shut, a trickle of light playing over his dark form. Her eyelids lowered a fraction to watch his approach to the bed. About a foot away he stopped, his masked and cloaked head cocking slightly to the right.

"Are we rolling into act three, or have you just decided to spend the night for fun?" She caught the gleam of his teeth as he unraveled the hood and discarded the fabric and his trench coat on the ground.

He hadn't said a word, hadn't made a sound since they'd left Partner Paws. Even after she'd thanked him for replacing the splintered doors in her apartment. Nothing more than that sexy smile lit by moonlight as they'd entered her bedroom.

Ninja slipped out of his boots with more grace than a man should possess. Then he tugged off his shirt with slow, deliberate ease. Wind played against the curtains and shed flashes of light across one heck of a firm, muscled chest; that set of stunning abs good enough to nibble. Her eyes were suddenly wide, unable to pull away from the utter maleness on display. He unhooked his belt, a loop of small pouches and leather containers, discarding it on the pile of clothing already gracing her floor.

If he continued down this road, she'd have to toss him dollar bills. *My whole wallet.*

The accentuated, slow ripple of muscle as he gripped the corner of her blankets and slid underneath tore her emotions between fear and excitement. They lay there in the silence, his arms wrapped around her, her heart beating so fast and so loud—How could he miss its thumping pressure against his chest? He rubbed the back of her neck, setting her nerve endings on fire, stoking the heat in her body until it matched the intensity in his silver-touched eyes.

She was a realist. She could take care of herself, and had, in the pre-Murphy reality. Her brain kept her out of trouble, her strength rescued animals, her persistence helped others survive. She relied on herself first and friends she'd known for years second. Yet here she was, staring into the eyes of a man right out of the comic books, a man who'd somehow become her own personal protector. Mystery drew her in and surrounded this masked contradiction, a man who exuded danger but shielded her like a precious gift.

She burned for more.

Emily held her breath as he leaned in, pressing his lips to hers. Her body dissolved with the sensation, the energy zinging between them palpable on her skin. His hand slid into her hair, the pads of his bare fingers gentle where they rubbed against the back of her head, drawing her deeper into an embrace where she was safe, protected from the dangers of the night.

Dangers like—Her eyes flew open and she turned toward the new bedroom door with an audible gasp.

"What?" His low voice sent another sharp thrill through her body. "What is it?"

She looked up at him, his body arched protectively over her, arms framing her sides. He studied the door, his jaw rigid, then he dropped his anxious expression back to her face.

"I'm sorry. It's just," she paused, deliberately slowing her breathing to get her body under control. A self-conscious twinge hitched her shoulders. "Every time you kiss me someone with a gun comes through the door. And I wasn't sure if they'd . . . "

Trailing off at his soft chuckle, she wondered if she'd even heard it at all.

A wide grin broke across his face and the tension in his muscles vanished.

"Those gentlemen won't be bothering us tonight."

She stiffened, remembering her dream and Miles Young's label of "killer" from the morning meeting. "Did you kill them?"

"Kill them?" He rolled off of her, one hand still massaging the back of her neck, the other flung wide against the pillows. "I led them on a merry chase around the city until they got a little preoccupied with a police escort, but I certainly didn't kill anybody."

"How am I supposed to believe you?" She drew her arms up, trying to ignore the way the fingers still kneading her skin affected her nipples, spreading stardust through her veins.

Turning his head, he gave her a sad smile. "I've done a lot of bad things, Emily, but I've never taken a life."

Truth. The instinct struck the same way it had in her dream. She wished she could trust it—trust *him*.

"I don't expect you to believe me." He pulled his hand out from under her head and the covers fell away from his parade-worthy torso as he sat up. "But I wish you could."

"I want to."

The masked man's gaze darted back to her face and he lifted a hand to brush her bangs back across her forehead. Then he turned away again to stare at the window. Evidently he didn't know what to say to her admission. Well, neither did she. Why had she said that out loud?

She frowned as one hand lifted toward him, toward the leather hiding his identity. She burrowed her fingers into the blankets and squeezed.

"You're not going to show me who you really are, are you?" Even as she asked, Emily knew he'd never tell her. She'd have to settle for imagined mind-sketches of what she'd find under the mask.

His index finger ran along the side of his mask and he gave a distracted shake of his head. That particular line of inquiry: closed.

She flexed her toes over the mattress. "I guess I'll just have to stick with 'Ninja.'"

He didn't refute it this time. She squeezed the blankets again, her gaze content to lick over his chest as questions crowded into her head and she tried to distract herself from giving them voice. This bizarre connection between them had to have an explanation and she didn't know where to begin searching for one.

It sure wasn't gratitude that set her on fire.

When she snuck another glance at his face, her eyes collided with a look so determined and sizzling there was no question he intended to kiss her senseless. Emily's muscles clenched, tightened. Her nipples itched against the cotton with each caress, demanding indulgence. The time for acting had passed. She wanted him as much as he wanted her.

So what is he waiting for? Permission?

She squirmed as Ninja drew her back into his arms. When he didn't make good on the promise in his eyes, Emily made the first move instead, pressing her lips to his.

It was all the encouragement he seemed to require. He pressed her against the covers, spanning his hands down her sides, exploring the curves of her body, pulling her along on another luxurious, sensual ride.

JAY LET HIS FINGERS drift over her tank top, caressing the soft curve of her waist as he nibbled on her lower lip. Emily joined him in a fiery kiss that made the air around them sizzle with intensity, drugging them both with passion. Her hands wrapped around his hips, sending a cascade of sensation to his already raging hard-on.

With slow, careful movements, he straddled her and pushed her shirt over her head, throwing it over the side of the bed. He kissed her again and again. Driven. Desperate. His gaze flickered over her face, flushed with longing, no hesitation.

His fingers brushed over peaked nipples and gave each a gentle tug. She quivered, her hands cruising over his skin as though she intended to set every nerve ablaze on the way up his chest. He didn't stop to question his good fortune. But he had his own exploring to do.

An unrelenting trail of kisses led down to the valley between her breasts, lower to her belly button. Jay nipped lightly at the soft, silky skin of her abdomen. Emily moaned, inching higher on the bed, questing for more.

His own impatience had him pushing at her waistband, sliding a hand on either side of her pants and easing them over her hips. She lifted her butt and shimmied the rest of the way out of the pajama bottoms, kicking them to the foot of the bed. No underwear. The breath rushed out of his lungs and they refused to refill.

He pushed himself up, surveying the glorious display of her entire naked body for the first time. His greedy gaze drank in smooth, creamy skin, the dusky peaks of her lovely breasts, the inviting tangle of dark curls between her legs. Amazing. "Emily . . . Angel. You're a slice of heaven." He followed the unguarded comment with a slide of his hand up her side, a slow lean to her face.

She pushed herself into his arms, crushing her breasts against the firm plane of his chest. Their lips connected again and Jay pinned her to the bed, his tongue easing between the seams of her lips. He was unprepared for her to suck on it, for her tongue to dance alongside his. His cock jumped against her thigh. Emily was his. All his.

Her hands dropped to the button on his jeans, flipping it open and drawing the zipper down as far as she could reach with him still covering her body. He finished the job, kicking the pants off while he turned his attention to her breasts, suckling one tempting taut bud. Her sharp intake of breath urged him on.

Questing fingers flicked across the junction of her thighs, rewarding him with an arched back and a moan. *She's so wet. Ready. For me.* Her hazel eyes clouded over.

"What do you want, Emily?" He parted her thighs with a knee, lapping and blowing a chilled breath across a nipple. It hardened even more and she shivered, her thighs tightening around his leg.

"You." She was breathless, the word coming out in a gasp as he rubbed his thumb over her clit. "More . . . of you."

He cradled her head with one hand, twining their tongues together again. Jay's other palm rested on the moist heat of her mound, his fingers teasing her entrance. "More of this?"

Her breath stuttered and her hips ground into his touch. "Please, I—"

A soul-shattering scream pierced the night. Emily bolted up from underneath him with a dismayed shout and Jay maneuvered immediately out of knee and elbow range. "Shit!" He twisted toward the window.

The scream came again and this time he recognized the culprit.

He was going to *kill* Torpedo.

"Ninja?"

Oh, she can't keep that nickname.

"It's okay." He shrugged. *Stupid, bird-brained . . . bird!*

"Shouldn't you go to her?" Her voice was laced with concern. "She's in trouble!"

"Who?" He met her wide-eyed stare. Emily's lips were swollen with his kisses and Jay longed to return to that world. His fingers missed her arm, grazing the sheet she'd wrapped around herself instead as it trailed her from the bed. "Emily, what are you doing?"

She threw the curtains aside and squinted into the parking lot lighting. "I think it came from downstairs. What if those men took another woman instead of me? You need to help her!"

Did she think he was the kind of man who rescued damsels in distress on a regular basis? He wasn't the Hollywood superhero she'd painted in her mind. He wasn't any kind of hero. Jay was a criminal, undeserving of an honest woman like Emily. Not that he'd give her up.

Another strike against me.

For a moment he floundered, leaning back against the pillows, trying to figure out how to coax her back to bed.

"Why are you still lying there?" she demanded. "Jump out the window and do something!"

Yeah, 'back to bed' was not happening. Not unless Tor made a more personal appearance. He swung his legs over the side and padded across the floor, reluctantly gathering up a flower-smothered blanket to slip around his waist.

"I don't jump down," he said. "I climb up. It's much safer that way."

"Ninja, this isn't funny."

"Neither is trying to throw me out there without my clothes." He tipped an uncertain grin at her. An appealing wave of red colored her face and he crowded her, one arm around her waist and his other hand rising to stroke her cheek. "That wasn't a woman screaming. It was just Torpedo."

As if on cue, the owl swooped onto the windowsill. She jumped reflexively back from the sudden rush of air and the large bird blocking part of the streetlight. Jay moved with her and felt her heart pound where their chests connected. He swore under his breath.

"Do you have to be so dramatic, Tor? Stop scaring her and apologize."

Emily stilled in his arms, comprehension crawling into her hazel eyes as she glanced between them.

"This wasn't quite how I envisioned the two of you meeting, but here goes. Emily," he dropped his hand and gestured toward the owl, who smoothed down his feathers obligingly, "this is Torpedo. Torpedo, Emily."

"The scream," she said. "He was hunting."

"Yeah." He felt her relieved sigh against his shoulder, the moment she relaxed and accepted his embrace. "Probably spotted a rat."

"Or a snake."

Jay remembered she was a bird enthusiast as she turned out of his arms, closer to Tor's ferocious beak and talons.

"Don't make the mistake of thinking he's not dangerous," he warned, tugging her lightly away. Torpedo was fine with him, but he could be testy, and at any moment he could make a lunge for the hand she extended in slow motion.

"He's just like you." Her voice sounded distant, as if she were entranced by the owl's presence. "Fierce but gentle."

Jay blinked at her calm assessment, confounded when the powerful owl craned his neck toward her with a light rub against her fingertips.

Emily ruffled his head feathers, a contented smile aimed at Torpedo. "A handsome fellow," she whispered. "Where did he find you?"

Jay caught the sideways look from both the bird and Emily and knew he was in some kind of trouble. Torpedo had never let anyone touch him before, other than himself. Not even his brothers could get close. How had she gotten him to acquiesce so readily? And as for how they had found each other . . . That was a story that touched a little too close to his family's gifts.

She cocked her head to the side, a bemused look on her face. "Ninja, what would possess you to name an owl—that flies through the air—after an underwater missile?"

His face burned. Another long story. "About this 'Ninja' thing." If his brothers ever caught wind of that name . . .

"Complaining about your nickname," she scoffed, petting his spirit guide again. "Think of 'Ninja' as karma, tough guy. You may as well have called him 'U-boat' or 'Submarine'."

As she continued to fuss over the names, Jay felt a grin win over his attempted scowl. He strode back to the bed and lifted the covers, digging through his mind for a way to lure her away from the window.

"Or, hey, how about 'Sonar', Ninja?"

The nightstand rattled as Emily's phone did a jig across the wood.

"Julia Meadows," he read on the display, already plucking it off the surface to deposit it into her outstretched hand.

"You just get off work?" she asked by way of hello. "That call center has to give you better hours . . . worse, right . . . suppose you could be walking home in the dark."

Things would not be returning to sex. Not tonight. Jay sighed and reached for his pants.

After several moments, she covered the receiver. Her gaze caught on the clothes he'd donned and she bit her lip. "She's got a test tomorrow and needs a pop quiz. Is it okay if—"

"It's one in the morning."

She frowned. "You know, before this week, this is the kind of thing that counted as an emergency."

He gave a startled laugh. "You need a ride to her place, then?"

Her hand clenched around the phone. "No. I've got a cheat

sheet in the living room. I'm not going anywhere."

He'd never have made the offer if Shiv wasn't thoroughly occupied, but from the way tension stole over her limbs and made her movements jerky, she didn't believe they were in the clear. He nodded and waved toward the door. "I'll keep watch."

As Emily left the bedroom, Torpedo's stare drilled into him. Out came the most complicated series of sounds he'd ever heard emerge from his companion's beak. With none of the usual translation, the owl's words bypassed Jay's ears and collided directly with his mind:

If you screw this up, I'm keeping her. Not you.

CHAPTER SEVEN

JAY TIPPED HIS HEAD to the perch hidden in a curtained-off corner of his personal office. "I know you're not sleeping, Tor."

Fluffing of wings came first. Then the low strain of the owl's whistled response. *I'm tired.*

I know just how you feel, friend. It wasn't a thought shared man to bird, despite his bizarre experience the night before. He didn't have the same connection Ryan had with Romeo. And if Ryan's hope that telepathy came as an extension of their bonds with their spirit guides, Zach would be next in line anyway. Jay hid a yawn in the next sip from his coffee mug as Torpedo bunched his legs underneath him and swooped out the open window.

"You look a few carafes short of a brain," Zach commented, his shoulders and the pristine white suit he wore blocking the doorway. He didn't pause to grab some coffee of his own as usual today, instead throwing himself into one of the chairs on the other side of Jay's desk. His fingers tapped the arms of the chair in uneven rhythms.

"And you've had a bit extra," Jay said. At least he'd caught some winks with Emily on his shoulder but Zach . . . did he even sleep at all anymore? "I could've come downstairs."

"Commander in chief's orders."

As if prompted, Ryan appeared in blue pinstripes, shutting and locking the door behind him. "I know I said he pulled the contract," he began. A few swift, economic steps later and he was standing next to them, his palms braced on the back of the other empty chair. "The terms are a little dicier than I wanted."

Jay frowned. "I thought you said you'd redirected him." Otherwise he'd never have taunted Shiv with a lie.

A harsh exhale. "Delayed. And believe me, he is *not* okay with it." Ryan's knuckles blanched against the leather of the chair. "Murphy is edgy on our whole partnership now. The only reason that bastard hasn't put a hit out on our persona yet is because we've bringing in some nice bags of coin and fresh bottles of rum. He's livid about that stupid claim you made on her. Livid, Jay." His expression drew tight, a cross between anger and disgust. "I've never seen him like this before. Not even when I confronted him about Old Town."

At this, there was utter silence between them. Their mother had lived in Old Town—had burned there years before, when someone razed the district to the ground—and up until a month ago, all three brothers had kept up this farce of a partnership under the belief their current syndicate target was responsible. Unfortunately, Murphy had known nothing, which meant their only link between past and present remained a psycho who liked to play with sharp objects.

Gut churning, Jay leaned forward and braced his forearms on the desk. "What exactly does 'delayed' mean, Ry?"

"Tuesday." He held up a hand. "I convinced him it'd be better for her to come to him of her own free will—"

"Never gonna happen!" Jay growled.

"—and he agreed. Amicably, if you can believe it." None of them did. "Jay, I didn't say we'd play fair. But the contract's down. Shiv's on the back burner. I bought us time to figure this thing out."

"'This thing' is an innocent woman's life." Jay rose to his feet, fury blasting through his veins at his brother's casual suggestion. "Forget it, Ryan. No way in *hell* am I giving her to Murphy."

"You're not listening."

Zach chipped in. "You've only known the girl for what, three days? I knew you had a touch of hero complex but geez, Jay, you're completely obsessed with her." He had the audacity to smirk.

"I'm not obsessed with her!" The volume of his protest made Zach's eyebrows snap into a furrow and brought him from his own chair. Jay glared at him. "I'm *not*."

"Right. You just want to know where she is twenty-four hours a day, skip out on comm duty, and go offline for entire evenings without a trace. Did you know that little cat and mouse game of yours last night almost got Ryan tagged? We've got a schedule for a reason. A system, so no more than one of us at a time is pinpointed on the street. So they still think there's only one of us. Since you decided we didn't need a second heads-up, last night he had to shift his time again so Shiv didn't catch on. The alarm went off and he had to rough up four beefy guys in uniform. You *know* how much he hates that." Zach stalked away, but he wasn't gone long. He slammed his chair against the desk, sending dark liquid sloshing out of Jay's coffee mug. "While you were sexin' up your woman!"

The truth in his older brother's words struck like a knock-out punch. His drive to protect Emily was dangerous. If Ryan had been caught by the police, he'd have been unmasked. They'd all pay the price. Worse, he'd have had no way to know if those cops had been in the syndicate's pockets or not; the possibility Ryan could have harmed people determined to do the right thing cut at them all. Jay had taken too many risks and his brothers had every right to be pissed.

"No one knew I was with her last night." He hoped.

"What about the night before? Cancelling a job so you could be with her? Jay, it's a bad idea to challenge our 'partner' right now. We need him to keep us in the loop until the final bid."

Ryan tapped his fingers on the desk. "Boys . . . "

"What?" Jay and Zach both spat the word at the same time.

"Sit down. Now. Z's not going to give her to Murphy, and neither am I." After they complied, Ryan rested a hand on Zach's shoulder and his lips thinned. He brought his other hand up in a pinching motion. "We're this close to having these bastards right where we want them. I can't push him any further than I did last night, and *obviously* we're not giving him your girl."

Jay's jaw clenched at his oldest brother's pointed look.

"Which means we have less than a week to lock this in. Find out why he wants her, nail down the time and place for the drug deal, and get Emily under lock and key until it's over."

His eyes widened. "You want to end it."

"We have to start working around Murphy. Not with him." Before he could explain further, Torpedo came barreling through the window in the far corner of the office. Screaming. He did a full soar-over through the office, feathers shedding over the carpet.

Watchers watch the Watcher's Consort.

Jay went momentarily immobile with shock. There was no mistaking it. The scream had been noise, unintelligible. But the words? Clear, crisp, and inside his head. He shook his head at the bird's designation of Emily. Consort? They would have been more than that, if Torpedo hadn't decided on a dinner of rat du jour.

"What was all that about?" Ryan cocked his head to follow the owl's flight pattern back out the window.

Like Jay's eyesight, Ryan's hearing had been amplified by his spirit guide. Yet the eldest McLelas had only winced for a moment, which meant he'd tuned his super hearing way down to avoid the blast. Zach—and Jay himself—had been less fortunate; his other brother rubbed his ears with a grimace on his face.

Spreading his fingers over the surface of the desk, Jay confessed. "I think things are changing."

Ryan was hyper-focused now, a sharp gaze drilling into his skull. "How?"

He tapped the side of his head with a finger. "It's not just me translating. It's . . . in here." He swiveled a look at Zach. "But that's not right, is it? It's your turn."

"Leave it to my superpower to fuck something else up," Zach quipped about his spotty luck with making his own ability—his danger sense—work for them. He hummed in the back of his throat. "Did you kiss her?"

"Huh?"

"Emily. The woman you're obsessed with. Because that's how it started with our besotted brother, too. Things changing. Spirit-mate shit."

Jay's insides buzzed like an earthquake had rolled in under his feet. She couldn't be. Could she? A Spirit-mate. That was a family word—a destiny thing. Cosmic manipulation. Ryan had found the filter for his ability—in truth, his other half—in his lieutenant. Were they right? Had Jay found his in Emily, or was it wishful thinking?

Ryan smiled. "It'd explain a few things, but the shift to telepathy with Romeo . . . that happened before I met Amanda. It could be natural progression." He glanced at the time bouncing around Jay's monitor and shook his head. "I've got to check in before Lilah hunts me down. Wire taps are now priority. You'll need to visit this woman to keep up appearances, Jay, but we need intel more than appearances, and we don't have time to waste."

Both Jay and Zach nodded. No more entire nights spent watching over Emily—but if Ryan was right, he wouldn't have to. Tor would be enough to report if someone was creeping around too close. Unless Emily was truly Jay's, bound by a prophecy to fight by his side. To balance his power—and how would she manage that? Ryan's Spirit-mate was a cop. A vetted warrior with a stake already in the fight. Emily was an innocent.

Ryan hung back as Zach took his leave. "If she *is* your Spirit-mate, we may have even less time. I'll put a call in for research but Jay—if anything else changes, you tell me. Immediately."

Jay nodded. As much as it'd be nice to have an explanation for the possessive way he felt about the woman Murphy had targeted, he couldn't make it settle inside his head. An innocent. How could it be her?

CHAPTER EIGHT

CAPPUCCINO SCALDED EMILY'S FEET through her peep-toed heels. Her courtesy-of-Ninja cup of caffeine slipped through her fingers and rolled, halting against her trash can with a final slosh of liquid. The hot beverage soaked into papers strewn across the tile and seeped into the fibers of worn rug under the furniture.

A steak knife stood, impaled, in the center of her desk. *Her* steak knife.

The room before her which had once been her office—her locked office—finally came into focus and she jolted from her spot with a furious rattle of the doorknob as the fingers of her other hand relinquished the metal. Crumpled workbooks spilled from one overturned bookshelf, the corner caught on her slashed desk chair its final attempt to avoid face-planting on the floor. The contents of her two upended file cabinets were missing.

No, not missing. Those were the papers she stepped over to get to her desk.

Her attention centered on the knife. And the big, red "See

You Soon!" note cheerfully pinned over the teeth on the blade. Signed with a single "S".

Shiv had dropped in for a visit.

Emily strode around the desk and grabbed a tissue. She wrapped it around the handle of the steak knife, then worked the blade free of the particleboard slab. Throwing both note and knife into an already opened and empty drawer, she slammed it shut with all the frustration she could push through her muscles.

She hadn't seen would-be kidnappers in several days and Ninja hadn't been determined to resume their "acting". Obviously she'd let it ease her worries more than she ought; she'd taken the vision to mean she was no longer hunted, closer to fact than dream.

She'd become complacent.

Behind her, the bookshelf rocked free of its anchor and finished its fall to the ground. She jumped at the crash and shot a glare at the debris, then swiveled her chair and sat down. The easy chairs on the other side of the desk were slashed too. Stuffing popped out of numerous knife-plundered gashes in the cushions. Emily turned a stare on the desk drawer as if the blade could somehow come out and attack. *It's cold in here.* With shaking hands, she massaged the sleeves of her pink blouse.

Ninja. Where was her masked repeat-visitor now? He cared, right? He cared whether or not Murphy got his hands on her. But Emily didn't exactly have him on speed dial and he wasn't here now, had only been dropping in to check on her for a few hours each time instead of spending whole evenings with her like he had at first. And no matter how late he stayed—or didn't—he always vanished at daybreak. She'd have to wait to tell him about the knife until evening. If she stayed un-kidnapped that long.

"Oh my God." Julia stood in the doorway with the Tuesday paper, her usually olive complexion paling in shock. "Emily, what happened? Are you okay?"

"I don't think so, Julia." Her limbs moved of their own accord, numb, folding her hands on the desk like they'd decided she should at least appear calm. Raising her now-blurry vision she watched her friend tiptoe over the spilled cappuccino river. Had anyone checked on the animals yet? She usually did after she set her coffee down . . . and it was definitely down. Emily pushed herself up. "Need to see the kennel."

"Britt was just doing that. I'm going to grab some paper towels. Why don't you come out and watch the phone for me?" Julia reached for Emily's arm and helped her out of the office, settling her into a rolling chair behind the reception desk. "Britt, can you bring over a glass of water? Em. I'll be right back."

Britt tried to reassure her that the animals were doing just fine, but once Emily's blood flow returned to normal, she had to see for herself. They were untouched. Safe. All the same, she stopped by each area to check on her friends, letting their early morning playfulness soothe her nerves. She squared her shoulders and prepared to tackle the scene in her office again.

"Sorry, Julia," she said, catching a glimpse of her friend with a handful of wet paper towels for the trash.

Julia wiped her hands on her jeans and leaned over the reception counter. "Someone ripped apart your office and *you're* sorry? I'm gonna nail the little punks who did this!"

The ferocity shining in her pacifistic friend's eyes made Emily's lips remember how to smile. "You, personally?"

"Well, the cops sure won't do anything about it." Julia bobbed her head with a frown. "I doubt she's up, but I left a message for Naomi."

"Morning, ladies," a cheerful male voice burst through the front door. "Surprise donut fix, incoming!" Marco's swarthy face peered over the counter at the pair of them. "Julia, *cariña*, they were out of lemon cream." He balanced the box on his forearm and frowned. "I know that look. What'd I do?"

Emily led him to her office, absorbing a second shock from the damage to the room. This time, she exchanged her fear for fury, an emotion echoed by a long string of Spanish curses from Marco's direction. As he calmed, his questions turned more practical.

"Are the animals okay?" He scooped up paper by the armload. "Is anything missing?" The red tint to his features burned with aggression.

Glad I'm not on the receiving end of that. "Both rooms are fine, though the animals know something's up. As for this mess . . . I won't know until I go through it all."

Marco shook his head and the harsh color faded from his face in splotches when Julia stepped into the room, as if he were trying to haul back fury for her sake. Emily's gaze darted between them, catching the strange, shy look her friend gave their donut-bearing volunteer and the affectionate crinkle of his eyes that softened the rest of his anger.

Marco? Marco is Julia's 'hot Latino number'? Julia had taken a night off the previous week with that excuse and Emily hadn't thought anything of it at the time. She opened her mouth to ask how long they'd been seeing each other—anything to distract her from this insanity—when Marco threw the jumbled mess of papers onto a chair cushion and marched across the room.

"We should keep an office Doberman." He inched his fingers under the facedown bookshelf and grinned back over his shoulder. "Then again, Nemo might have some blood on his claws we can analyze for DNA."

By the time the mismatched piles of paper became organized stacks and the furniture was right-side up, it was late afternoon and they were long out of donuts.

"The only thing that sticks out is my appointment book. I'm

not going to know if my own head is attached." With a weary smile, she slumped against one of the torn chair arms. It all had to be alphabetized and re-filed, but at least her schedule was the only thing—She sat up sharply. "Where's the stack of papers for the grant?"

Marco gave her a blank look, but Julia patted the top of a short pile of folders. "It's not here. And I don't think I saw it on the floor, either."

Emily rifled through paper after paper, slapping each stack down. "The testimonials are gone. Why would . . . they . . . take that?"

"AFTERNOON, MISS BARTON. What brings you to our office today? Turning in paperwork?" His smile warm, Jay closed the door behind her and slid into his desk chair.

"I'm afraid quite the opposite," Emily sighed, meeting his curious gaze. "Thank you for seeing me on such short notice, Jay." She probably looked like hell. Lack of coffee and sugar, along with an overload of stress, had surely forged a permanent wrinkle between her eyebrows, worn dark circles under her eyes. "My office suffered some casualties in a break-in last night and I'm afraid someone stole the forms."

Jay's eyes widened with surprise. "What? It wasn't—Have you called the police?" He looked like he was about to leap over the desk to her side. Like some big, handsome knight in a business suit.

Her chest warmed at the chivalrous thought. "We can't. Well, we could," she corrected quickly when he raised an eyebrow. "But while you might not have any difficulty around here, they're not exactly helpful on our side of town. It'd just be a paper chase anyway, and there wasn't anything important on them yet." *Why would Shiv steal a stack of personal stories?*

The threat was to her, not Partner Paws. Right? She shook her head, threading her fingers into a ball on his desk. "Can I trouble you for those testimonial sheets again?"

"I'll take care of it." He touched her clasped hands as if to reassure her, feeding her a burst of attraction that sent her veins tumbling into a confused, slow sizzle.

If he felt it too, she couldn't see it through his half-angry expression.

He turned to his computer, but glanced back once, his gorgeous blue-gray eyes refilled with concern.

Her libido was completely out of whack; it had been since the aborted, spontaneous tumble under the sheets with Ninja. Every time she looked at Jay McLelas, she could feel Ninja's fingers against her scalp, the cradle of his shoulder that seemed to be the only place she could easily to drop off to sleep for the past few nights. And every time Jay looked at her, now or during his surprise visits at the clinic, she felt like there was more to his concern than just his being a genuinely nice guy. *This is why you shouldn't have almost-sex with strangers. Every dark-haired guy you meet will set off a freaky mask-fantasy.*

He typed something into the computer. "Were any of the forms filled out?"

"Only two," she shrugged, avoiding his gaze. "Handed in after class yesterday. I was going to gather the rest of them this weekend but I guess I'll have to redistribute them now, right?"

"Addresses, phone numbers?"

"Those were on the forms, yes." Her veins turned ice cold. She clenched her fingers around the handles of her purse. "What if he tracks our students down?"

"He?"

She startled and her gaze jumped to his face. "The thief who took our papers." That sounded like a reasonable assumption, right?

He studied her for a moment and his forehead creased like he was about to ask a difficult question. "Emily, I don't want to sound—but your hands are shaking and you look..." He rubbed his palm over the back of his neck and threw her an impulsive grin. "Do you want to go grab some coffee?"

The unexpected invitation threw her completely off-balance.

"I appreciate your offer..." She stopped at the disappointed look he tried to hide from her. *Oh, what the heck. He's only trying to be nice because I look like I haven't slept in an age. My other option is to go home and get that sleep . . . and I'd probably wake up in the basket of Mr. Knife-Man's tricycle.*

Her heart skipped a beat as Ninja's face jumped to the forefront of her mind. Emily tucked a few stray strands of hair behind her ear and focused on generating a smile. Maybe it would steady her nerves. "That's sweet of you, thank you. Mine spilled this morning, so I'm running on fumes. But I'll need to make some calls first."

Piper Stevens and Melanie Bluseau, the two students who had turned in their paperwork early, weren't at home. After leaving twin messages on their answering machines, she closed her cell phone and followed Jay to the break room instead of the coffee shop down the street.

"Coffee" turned out to be code for "come to my cushy office." Jay's fifteenth-floor personal, keypad-secured "break room" was more befitting of his rank as a full partner in the McLelas Financial company name than the standard office on the ground floor. The black swivel chairs and luxury couch in the second office must be nice for unwinding at the end of a long day.

It wasn't all a ruse, though. There was indeed coffee. The kitchenette counter displayed the prominent coffee bar of a wealthy caffeine addict. Four large carafes sat steaming on what looked like a long hotplate.

"How much of this do you actually drink?" Her fingers traced the green marble countertop.

"On a typical day? All of it." Jay gave her a sheepish look. "They're set to brew at different times."

"*All* of it?" She thought her days needed a kickstart. How did one consume gallons of coffee in a single day?

"I do share," he added absently, grabbing a pair of mugs from an upper cabinet.

With a flourish, Jay flipped the lever on a thermos and black liquid trickled out. "This is my strongest blend, and you look like you need it today." He topped off both mugs and slid one across the counter toward her.

She took a reflexive step back, but the mug remained upright and didn't fling scalding liquid all over her. "Your blood must be made of this stuff."

Jay laced his drink with some kind of creamer. "That's what my brother Ryan tells me." His face cracked in a grin as he stirred, an infectious smile that warmed her to her toes.

When he moved to sit behind his desk, she aimed for the sugar.

"You want to drink that straight." He raised his mug at her. "Trust me."

Hia eyes shimmered with amusement but the corners still held concern, the same look that'd had her agreeing to stay for coffee. Emily blew cautiously on the liquid, dark as a gap of starless night sky, then flicked a covert glance at him through the steam. He didn't have the same kind of "I'm rich" smugness she associated with money. There was a comfortable, sincere draw to Jay McLelas.

"Is a second office a perk of owning the company?" she asked.

He took a sip from his mug and settled both hands around it when it touched back down on his desk. "Technically, this is my only office. I'm better with the morale boosting than the loan and grant officer thing, but I'm covering the desk downstairs while one of our employees is out on paternity leave."

Jay tipped his head and held up a hand. "Not because we're short on staff or anything. I rotate time with each of the departments; gives me a ground floor view of how our employees conduct the day to day business. And it makes it easier to understand where they're coming from if you have to bring them up for coffee to discuss a problem."

"You double as a psychologist?" She smiled over her mug, blowing cool air over it a second time.

He shrugged. "An accountant might need an attitude adjustment, or a middle manager might need a pep talk. One can vastly improve relationships with a steaming cup of joe and honest conversation."

"Counselor, then."

Jay ran an index finger around the rim of his mug as if considering her suggestion, but when he spoke, he changed the subject. "Tell me about the break-in, Emily. Was it just the grant papers, or is there more to it than that?"

She couldn't begin to explain the sharp push in her gut telling her to trust him with the truth about Ninja. And the kidnappers. And Shiv. And Murphy. With the concern dominating his face over a little thing like a stack of paper, well . . . if he knew how her nights had been going, she'd bet he would drag the police to her apartment himself.

A frown tugged at her lips but she found herself speaking anyway. "My office was trashed. We managed to get things ready for re-filing but—whoever—did it only took the testimonials and my planner. I think they were just trying to scare me."

"Why would someone want to do that?" Jay released his mug and leaned forward, his eyes glittering with dark, intense emotion.

"I don't know," she lied. *Because Shiv wanted me to know he knew where I worked? Because he's done not taking action?* "They didn't have to go through the effort. I'm already half-terr—uhm." She stopped, dropping a stare to her mug. She shouldn't have said anything, but her mind still shrieked at her to tell everything. A quake went through her hands, rattled the liquid in her mug. Emily glanced up at his patient face as he waited without a word for her to continue. "The thief stabbed a knife in the middle of my desk."

He rocked back into his chair in a visible effort to appear relaxed, but she'd already caught the way his hand rewrapped around his mug tight enough she was afraid it would shatter.

Rubbing at the back of his neck, he flashed her a sad smile. "I'm sorry."

"Why? It's not your fault some psycho roughed the place up." She took her first sip of the coffee unconsciously, a reflex to cover her nerves. Warm, satisfying liquid hit her throat and she sighed with pleasure. Already the caffeine shook her blood awake. "This is fantastic." Emily blinked at the mug, surprised by the lack of bitterness despite missing sweetener.

"Fresh roasted yesterday and ground just this morning."

She arched an eyebrow at him, but before she could ask anything further, two men burst into the room. Or rather, one burst in, the second sauntered in, the epitome of casual in a blindingly white suit. Jay looked ready to slide under his desk.

"Jay, we've got—You have company," the first man's excited voice waned in its enthusiasm as he looked her over, sending a questioning look toward her host.

She'd seen him before.

"Emily Barton, these are my business partners, Ryan and Zachariah," Jay introduced formally, rising. Emily followed suit, extending her hand first to the man with the glasses. "Zachariah is head of security and Ryan is—"

"In charge," Ryan broke in, catching her fingers in a firm grip and bowing his head.

"It's just Zach, Ma'am. And don't let him mislead you with that whole 'partner' nonsense," the second man said, thumping his chest with a fist, "we're related."

Oh, there was no mistaking the family resemblance. All three men had the same tall stature, bronzed skin and broad shoulders, long, dark hair, the same classic jaw. The same radiant confidence and self-assurance. All three of the illustrious McLelas brothers, dominating the same room.

Naomi would swoon.

Ryan made a face at the steaming mugs. "Some vamp's gonna bite you and fry on the sidewalk come morning when he can't fall asleep." He said it with the practiced ease of a joke that had been repeated far too many times.

Jay's now-murderous expression was far from effective. Emily bit her lip but a laugh bubbled in her chest.

"Ryan's more of a 'tea' kind of guy." Zach poured himself a mug and shrugged as Ryan raised an eyebrow in his direction. Jerking a thumb at Jay, he added, "Hey, I don't drink as much as *he* does."

Jay sighed and threw her a suffering look. "These miscreants fulfill the other two-thirds of the McLelas requirement."

"So, what brings you up here? My brother behaving himself?" Ryan raised his eyebrows at Emily.

The smile she'd been about to send to Jay froze, numb on her lips. All three of them were overwhelming in their sensuality whether playful or standing still. Lock that in with the break-in and her present dark-haired protector? Her brain was quickly heading toward meltdown. Jay steadied a flat palm against her spine and her breathing stalled.

"Miss Barton is a client who's been through quite a lot

today." *So shut up and leave her alone* were the unspoken words pouring off of his rigid frame.

She could have kissed him. As it was, her lungs remembered to work, pumping in coffee-loaded air.

"Then I hate to interrupt business, but we do actually have something pressing to discuss." Ryan spread his hands in apology. "It won't take long."

Relieved, she took that as her cue. "I should run some errands anyway." Emily stole a quick, final gulp of her drink and slid the mug to the surface of the desk behind her. "Thank you for the coffee."

For a moment, Jay looked like he was going to insist she stay. But then he turned that look on his brothers, and she could have sworn Ryan's head shook just the slightest fraction.

"I'll drop the new papers off at your office." His hand dropped away. "Wait, Emily, before you go . . . " Jay grabbed a business card and flipped it over, scribbling something on the back. "My direct line. Cell phone."

He didn't have to say anything else as her feet headed out the door. *If you need anything, call me.*

"So, that's Emily." Zach's teasing smile forced Jay's focus away from the closed door. "Glad to see you're chasing after her while the sun's up, like a normal guy."

He ignored the jab and any news his brothers had was secondary to the fact that their time was up. "We can't let her leave. Shiv trashed her office; Murphy's got him back out there."

Ryan sent him a chiding look. "How do you propose her grant officer keeps her here?"

They ganged up on him then, moving in close and blocking his view of the rest of the room. Zach jerked his thumb over his shoulder. "Deal's got a date and time. They're moving the new product at the end of the month."

"Do we know where? How?" Jay asked, his need to keep Emily safe overriding his usual filters. "Do we know what they're moving? Do we know anything of actual value that can shut down Murphy for good?"

Ryan snorted. "I get that you're impatient. I get that you're worried and frustrated and pissed off. But this impacts an entire city, Jay, not just one woman."

My woman.

Splitting his time between intel-gathering and exploring things with her had been beyond unsatisfying. Not just because he hadn't figured out a way to come to terms with the wild pull between them or the changes in how Torpedo spoke, but because he still knew next to nothing about the crime boss's motives. Zach at least had uncovered where Shiv was meant to take her: a warehouse where Murphy notoriously kept women to reward his syndicate lackeys. But those women were paid for their services—and he'd been planning to take Emily against her will.

Why? What was different about her?

"I know what's at stake, Ry," he said into the tense silence between them.

A flood of new, highly addictive drugs shifting between syndicates would give Murphy a stranglehold on the city. It couldn't happen.

"We have to stop it, and it'll be harder with Klepto on the outs. Bloodier, probably." Ryan and Zach shared a sober glance and Jay held up a hand to stop them from cutting him off. "We've been out before. We have other informants. And we still have the taps."

Ryan shook his head. "We agreed to dissolve the partnership, but we're not going to waste our last night with it, either. Relek PD loses traction too; the undercover cops

Amanda's got working with her. Klepto vetted her, she vetted them."

Jay stared at him but it was Zach who continued, "He won't go after them. They aren't high profile enough. Klepto's the one who'll have a target on his back. But we still have a night. We have to make their commitments count. So, the deal's not happening tonight; we have time to branch back out, but—"

"Exactly," Jay interrupted. "We have time. Emily does not."

"She has a little. And it's not like we don't know where she'll be if he does." At Jay's growl, the middle McLelas brother backed away a few steps and angled toward the door. "As I was saying: The deal isn't going down, but a few high profile meets in range of our ears are.

"Early evening, so it's before Shiv'll be due and you know it'll be shit we can move on, that the ladies and gents with Amanda's taskforce can wrap up with a bow. Bigwigs'll have counter-tech, so I'll be too busy trying to keep the lines clean to really listen. Which means I need you and Ryan to monitor."

"Monitor—" He had to be joking. Jay's fist clenched around his mug and he took a quick sip that did nothing to cool the burst of helpless fury. "I'm not sitting in the HQ listening to wires while that psycho is on his way to kidnap Emily! Is that why you're both here? To stop me? Are you planning to tie me to those taps? Is that it?"

"Grow up, Jay," Ryan snapped back. "What happened to, 'I know what's at stake'? You'll have hours to spare and this isn't about you. It's not about Emily."

It was bigger. A city already well under the thumb of criminals about to plunge itself deeper into the abyss.

"Our spirit guides will all have eyes on her, okay? We'll have enough warning, and you'll have enough time to get there." Zach's placating tone only made Jay want to punch him in the face.

An hour later he'd dulled his aggression on a bag of sand and now sat staring at dots on a screen. Listening to a whole lot of nothing.

Ryan's head tilted to the side as he sifted through the sounds in the headset.

Jay snuck a peek at his oldest brother's board. Ryan had pulled up two locations, tuned separately for each earpiece of his noise-reduction headphones.

The HQ room was deftly hidden behind a panel that extended off of Zach's security office in a subbasement of McLelas Financial. Half-built electronics, extra costumes, gear necessary for their nighttime endeavors, and reams of research materials filled tables against another wall. The air conditioner cranked to blasting to keep the overabundance of computers, and Zach's own temper, from overheating.

"So, you in love with her?" Zach ventured quietly, but it still caught Jay off-guard.

He sighed. "No. I'm not in love with her."

"Please. You were holed up in your office sharing coffee. The good stuff. That's like a geeky marriage proposal. You've been visiting her night and day—"

"She doesn't know that."

"—and I've never heard you yell like that, man."

Ryan threw a distracted glare in their direction.

Jay mashed a button in frustration, cranking the volume on the parking garage he was supposed to be waiting for a bunch of suits to start gabbing in. Still nothing, still burning daylight. A covert glance showed Zach's attention was occupied by the text on a monitor. *Just five minutes,* Jay promised himself, *then I'll check the parking garage again.* His finger deliberately tabbed to the bugs in Emily's apartment.

It was already seven, full dark barely draped over the city, but she was home. Jay tuned in to her evening, the easy to interpret sound of opening cabinets. *Dinner?* He picked up sounds of bags opening and heard the clang of a pan, multiple trips to the fridge. Sudden static met his ears and he murmured absently to Zach, "Sounds like one of your babies is having a glitch."

"My bugs don't 'glitch', Jay," came the retort.

"Let me take a listen." Ryan was already switching over to his frequency before Jay could change the channel.

Brilliant, Jay. Just brilliant.

Ryan frowned. "There's a pretty annoying crackle on the feed, Zach."

"Told ya they'd have jammers." Zach switched to the same channel. "Let me see what I can do."

Jay hung his head. "Guys—"

"Maybe I can pick through it." Ryan's eyes closed. "Hey, Jay, where is this? I think I hear someone singing."

Zach took in the coordinates on the panel and yanked the headset off his ears with a growl. "What the fuck is wrong with you, Jay? A couple of hours! That's all!"

"Emily?" Ryan lifted one earphone off his face.

Jay's voice cracked. "Well . . . "

A sudden squeal of piercing feedback had him and Ryan clutching their ears over the comm desk. Jay peeled off his headphones with stunned effort, his head spinning, only two thoughts coming out clear in his mind: *Emily.* Then: *Ryan.* He froze. It was as if reality had slapped him across the face with a tire iron. His brothers were right. He'd lost perspective with Emily completely if he could be thinking of her before his own family.

Zach darted around him, kicking at Ryan's chair as he looped his wrists under their brother's armpits and lowered him to the floor. "Ry! Ry, say something."

His urgent whisper barely registered over the ringing in

Jay's ears. Their older brother didn't respond with more than a mumble of unrecognizable expletives. Then Ryan's eyes rolled closed and his body began to shake. Jay threw himself to the floor, pinning Ryan's forearms to the ground.

"Get some ice." Jay's order came out slurred and muffled to his ears, but Zach seemed to understand him.

Murphy has Emily.

Two bags of ice wedged on either side of Ryan's neck, just under his earlobes. Zach took Ryan's head between his palms and held him steady as his limbs tried to convulse under Jay.

"Don't do this, Ryan. Reach for Amanda." Jay gritted his teeth together, watching the slow ooze of blood escape from his brother's left ear. "No, no, no . . . "

Ryan's eardrum had ruptured. Both Jay and Zach had seen it happen before from over-exposure to sound. Before Amanda. They'd thought him safe, through the unique bond he shared with his wife. Ryan was lucky he hadn't had both ears to the speaker.

"Shouldn't she have been able to protect him?" Jay asked. He and Zach exchanged a bleak look.

If Ryan could still fall prey to his ability . . . what hope did that leave them?

"What did you hear?" Zach looked over at him, brushing a damp cloth over Ryan's forehead.

"Feedback exploded over the line." Jay frowned. His own ears fast approached normalcy, but Ryan had been straining to hear through the static. To hear Emily. *Emily's gone.* "He was wide open."

"Exploded?" Zach's whisper turned incredulous. "What'd they do, blow her up?" He looked up at Jay's face and blanched at whatever he saw there, held up his hands. "Whoa, whoa. Easy."

Jay's face pinched tighter with worry, both for Ryan and for

Emily. *Murphy's either got her or she's dead, and I've deafened my brother.* Add to that he'd screwed their chances on getting the intel Zach wanted, and guilt joined the worry in eating him alive.

"He just meant it was loud." Ryan coughed and his eyes snapped open. He stared, his eyes unfocused. "I reached past it; didn't hear anything go down, Jay. Your girl's okay. Was the bug, that's all."

Jay's hand had frozen in a partial sign language motion, set to ask if he was okay. "Ry, I'm sorry."

"Don't croon over me like a woman." Ryan tried to shake his head, but Zach's fingers held firm across his head. "I'll be fine."

They didn't let him sit up, but Jay released the death grip on his arms. "You're staying put until—"

Ryan's gaze swept over his face and he ground his teeth. "Get your ass dressed and go after her." He made an angry swipe at the blood trickling down the side of his face. "If it were Amanda I'd do the same. Just . . . " He coughed, then grimaced. "Go."

Jay rose to his feet as the worry he'd been trying to hold at bay rocketed through his bloodstream. *Not Emily.* His shoulders numbly shrugged out of his blue suit jacket and one hand yanked at the band holding his hair. He reached for a set of clothes, his mask, his hood, functioning on autopilot.

Zach watched Ryan for another minute and when he angled his head up, he gave a small nod. The deep frown released from Zach's features. "I've got him." He angled a distracted look at his equipment. "I'll track things from here."

Jay didn't hesitate any longer. He dashed for their private elevator with one arm in his trench coat and an earbud still in his palm. His floor was abandoned after dark and Zach controlled the flow of security cameras, so there was nothing to do but run. He leapt out the window he kept open for Tor, digging his fingers into handholds concealed on the side of the building.

Clicking on the comm as he ran, he sprinted through the night air. His feet hit pavement and he weaved through early evening shadows in the alleyway. Up. Across. Over.

"Our guides are still at her apartment building."

He climbed up, hand over hand, feet inching over the brickwork on the outside of her complex. His forehead furrowed in concentration. *I'm not too late. She's still here.*

"Jay, watch it," Zach's voice warned over the line. "Go in armed and stay off mute."

He flipped a switch on the earbud mic to set the line to conference from his end. As her empty bedroom came into view his heart lodged in his throat. Bringing the heavy magnet up to the glass, he dragged it across with more haste than usual to raise the metal latch on her window. Torpedo flew in behind him, landing with a soundless bounce on the bed's comforter.

Jay drew his gun with his right hand and his left hand turned the knob on the door, easing it open. The only light came from down the hall, the kitchen.

He tamped down on his suspicion and crept forward until he could see her moving around the kitchen, her head bobbing and hips swaying to an inaudible beat.

Dancing.

Dancing? His mouth dropped open. Emily showed no signs of tension, in fact, this was the most relaxed he'd seen her . . . outside of his arms. He remained in the safety of the hallway, needing to bring her into those very arms once more, to capture that wisp of a smile with his lips. Wild with the urge to be near her and ensure her safety, Jay let it override good sense. He had to be certain there was no threat and so he pushed his eyes to their limits, harder than he usually dared. Anyone could be hiding in a corner, a shadow . . . a gun could be trained on her because of him and with her music on, she might not even be aware.

Something sizzled on the stove as she plundered through a cabinet and juggled a few different bottles of seasoning down to the counter. She was definitely dancing, her lips moving with silent lyrics. Screwing a cap off one of the bottles, Emily lifted it over the pan on the burner and then her chin came up with a gasp. Whatever spice had been in the container splashed over her in-progress meal.

"Ninja?" Emily's voice shook. She yanked her earbuds out. "You're early."

"Did she say 'Ninja'?" Zach asked. Jay's hand hovered over the earpiece for a moment. Paused. He'd agreed this time. No cutting his brothers out of this until he was 100% sure.

"Is there someone here with you?" Jay barely recognized the words, the rasp in his voice was so harsh. His eyes continued to rove the room.

She tilted her head, her lips parting. And heaven help him, but the sudden flash of alarm that obliterated the former happiness in her eyes nearly brought him to his knees. "No one's here but me. And now you."

A thin smile, but her hand shook as she moved her phone, where the earbuds had been plugged in, from a pocket concealed in her skirt to the counter.

Jay holstered his firearm and went to her, running his hands over her arms and taking in the room from the new angle. "Are you okay?"

"As okay as can be expected, right?" Watery hazel eyes focused solely on him, impossibly huge. "Are *you*?"

The concern in her question—for him, when he deserved none—had Jay tugging her against him and resting his chin on the top of her head. What wrong with him? It was one thing to go ga-ga over a woman. But he'd been desperate to hold her, careless on the mad dash to her windowsill. Unsettled and restless until he took in a deep breath of her, cinnamon and apples and simmering onions and maybe chicken with far too much pepper from the stove.

The slight imprint of her body seeped into him, her hand rubbing his shoulder as if to soothe. Stranger still, it was working. But before he could acknowledge his fear for her, before he could think of an answer at all, the kitchen behind her popped with a miniature explosion.

Fire flared and he reeled backward with her even as his vision crumpled from the assault. Smoke he couldn't see burned his nose in the next instant. Emily turned in his grasp, pulling at the hands that had locked around her. The fire alarm in her living room wailed and his earpiece was filled with shouts from his brothers. Words he couldn't process any more than her efforts to get away from him and over to the stove, because the flame that rose from the pan felt as though it had set his eyes ablaze.

CHAPTER NINE

"Let go!" Emily twisted, wrenching at his gloves. Over her shoulder she caught a glimpse of wide eyes, the tension that she could feel in his arms lining the parts of his face that she could see. Was her big, muscled protector fire-phobic? It was a small grease fire, but if she didn't get to the extinguishing spray under the sink fast, it would quickly grow, the cabinets would catch, and the room . . . "Ninja! Now!"

Sluggishly, his chin tipped toward her.

His fingers loosened, but not before she caught a glimpse of pupils that had gone from a natural black to stark, unearthly white ringed with pale, shimmering silver.

Certainly a trick of adrenaline and flame. The moment his fingers loosened on her hips, she dove for the sink, snagged the bottle of Fire Out, and yanked on the ring. The spray covered her stove. In moments, all they were left with was a bit of dark smoke and gray foam. And the blasted fire alarm.

She cut off the stove, cut on the vent, then ran through her tiny apartment to open the windows. The one in her bedroom was already open, but she pushed it further, propped the tiny one in the bathroom open and nudged a box fan into the rickety frame of the living room window—the one she couldn't even use for birdwatching thanks to its view of only bricks—hoping it would draw the smoke outside. That done, Emily climbed onto the chair at her kitchen table, then onto the table, to knock down the detector. It stopped wailing when it hit the floor.

Silence descended.

So did a fine layer of ash. She had a sinking feeling it would be everywhere, sneaking its way into every crack and crevice and even into closed drawers. And her security deposit? Toast.

"You know," she said into the quiet. "Compared to a madman and his lackeys, that was a cakewalk."

"Emily?" Her masked visitor was still standing against the fridge. Hadn't moved an inch.

Unease crowded out the thin wave of victory in the hungry pit of Emily's stomach. "I'm right here," she said, pouring all the reassurance she could into the words as though she were calming a wounded animal. His head jerked toward her and she brought her palms up. "The fire's out. It's okay."

"No. It is not."

"The fire's out, Ninja. I promise. And you don't have to worry about someone coming in and finding you. A fire alarm means more than a break-in, but most folks around here don't roll in until much later. Like you."

"It's not the fire. I—" He cut himself off and turned slightly, swallowing with visible effort. His hand slid inside his hood before dropping to his side. Fingers curling against denim, an uncertain motion where he was usually so arrogantly confident. Emily's heart squeezed even before he spoke his next words. "I can't see, angel."

"You . . . can't see? Did some grease hit you?" She blinked at him, at eyes still washed with white. Not rheumy or dazed but pure white. She'd thought it a trick of her own eyes before but now... Was it possible to have a panic attack that left one blind? They couldn't have been close enough to the stove for him to have burned his eyes—or anything else—and the fire hadn't lasted long. Sliding up beside him, she fit herself under his shoulder and her arm inside the trench coat. Around his waist, where muscle clenched under her fingers and made her feel even warmer. "Let's get you to a chair."

"You're shaking." His grip was almost brutal on her shoulder. Locking her to his side. "This is my fault, for distracting you from your cooking. I'm sorry."

"Easy, big guy. I'm a little rattled, sure, but I handled it. Far easier than the other nonsense in my life lately." She smiled up at him. Half the day, she'd warred between wanting to rail at him and wanting to lean on him when he arrived—both because of Shiv—and instead here she was, holding him up and steering him around her counter so he didn't ram straight into the cheap particle board corners. How could she help him? What did her protector need? Her lips turned downward. "You really can't see. Has this happened before?"

His fingers twitched over her sleeve. "Pretty sure your chairs were closer than this."

"I'm taking you to the bedroom. Smoke doesn't smell as strong in there." She glanced up at the serious set of his lips. "Did you avoid my question because you're trying not to fall over?"

"I'm fine. Just disoriented." The grumbled words almost made her smile. Emily's free hand crept up to her shoulder and instantly he entwined gloved fingers with her own. "It's never been this bad."

A yes, then. "What's it usually like?"

He leaned into her, resting his chin awkwardly on top of her head as they shuffled across her worn carpet.

"Okay," she said. Emily didn't understand what was happening to him, but this man lived in a world of secrets. She wouldn't have his true face, his true name. Here was one more truth he refused to divulge. "Talk about something, though, so I know you're still with me."

He hugged her against his side. It was barely there, almost imperceptible, but she felt the slight pressure, the way his tension eased the longer she stood by him.

"Words, Ninja."

"Your voice does this sort of breathless thing when you're irritated with me," he said. "I like it."

Emily let out a huff of air.

"That too."

"You're impossible." She drew back the coverlet and settled him on the bed. Not to be deterred, he gripped her forearms and pulled her down against him, bumping her nose with his.

"It's surreal," Ninja whispered, his lips a blaze of electric current as they brushed hers. "I want to tell you everything."

That fast, he released her to lay back on the pillows. The loss of the glow of white—and bizarre as she knew it was, she also knew it had definitely been a glow, not mere reflection from outside lighting—told her he'd closed his eyes. Disappointment cut at her, like he'd lied. When she knew he'd only voiced the exact same thing she'd had on her mind.

She shook her head, strands of hair sliding over her cheeks. It didn't make any sense, this draw they had to one another. It wasn't in the caring; Emily was always driven to help, human or not. That wasn't the problem. The problem lay in the near-strangling frustration that she didn't know how to fix whatever was happening to him.

"At least tell me what you need." Maybe he could concede to that, ease a little of each of their burdens at the same time.

"Time," he said with a slow drawl that was somewhere

between amused and concerned, but it still wasn't an undiluted truth, "I just need some time."

"How much time?"

"And maybe a cold washcloth."

She squeezed the fabric of his shirt between her fingers, barely restraining a childish impulse to pinch him. "Ninja."

"I wish I could give you more, angel."

It wasn't the first time he'd used the moniker but the husky edge to his voice made her hormones stand at attention. Reluctant, she released him to grab a cold pack from her freezer. It took her away from his side and her skin felt itchy, like she had to be closer to him, not with the entire length of the apartment between them.

"Which means I need space," she said to the dusty emptiness of her kitchen. "I'm losing my mind. Maybe I've already lost it."

She surrounded the chilled wrap in a soft cloth and returned to the bedroom to see he'd wiggled to the left. Emily took the seat by his side and slid the compress into his hands. Immediately, he set it over his eyes with one hand, reaching for her fingers with the other. After a tense moment where his breath hissed out of his lungs, his thumb began to roll over her palm, the rhythm constant and, she suspected, soothing them both.

Instead of a thank you, he said, "It's a genetic thing. Bright light sometimes throws in flashes of white. Patches. Like you'd see spots from a camera flash. Except it washes out everything completely. After a while it'll come back to normal."

She didn't say anything, not one single question though her mind roiled with them, her ears straining to hear more of whatever he felt safe enough to tell her. Minutes passed.

"Shiv was at your office today," he said next. Once again unexpected.

Ice prickled in her veins and her breath caught. Ninja's thumb stopped for a moment, squeezing the center of her palm. Grounding her, reminding her she wasn't alone to face this. "You know? You knew?"

"And I was unable to help you," he admitted, the growl of his voice strained with frustration she felt to the bone. "I am limited in what I can do during the day. People tend to notice a masked man skulking about their place of business."

She smiled. "I think they'd notice you no matter what you were wearing."

His lips curved and before she'd realized it, the fingers of her free hand were tracing them of their own accord. She shivered, and he moved the arm he'd flopped over the compress to press those fingers firmly against his lips. Branding her. A lingering kiss that made her ache.

Trying not to squirm, Emily strove for a different topic. "Were you expecting trouble? Is that why you came in all guns blazing?"

"I thought I heard trouble." He shifted, letting her reclaim her hand. "I had to be certain you were safe."

Her eyebrows furrowed. "You heard it through what, the actual bad guy grapevine?"

A sound that might have been a laugh. Strained. Tired.

"Are you in pain?"

"It's not bad."

She pursed her lips. "Let me get you something for—"

"Stay." He gripped the hand that his thumb continued to stroke. "Emily, I keep telling you not to expect something you shouldn't. I'm not the man you're building up inside your head. I'm one of those *actual bad guy* types."

"Right, because Shiv would totally come to make sure I'm safe and sound."

He grimaced. "I was listening to a wire tap. It went out; I

don't know why. And—"

"Wait." She clamped her fingers around his this time. "You *bugged* my apartment?"

"Case in point." He shifted on the bed as though restless.

She shook her head. "You're not a bad guy. You're an idiot."

The laugh rumbled in his chest.

Meanwhile I'm the one keeping a strange man in my bed. Who's been playing with surveillance equipment.

Oddly, she wasn't upset that he'd had the gall to bug her place. His need to ensure her safety, a measure of what had been his concern for her . . . It was as if she could feel the physical impact of these thoughts through their connected hands. Imagined or not, she'd heard as much through his words too. No. What hurt was how he continued to see himself in that light: in doing something to let him better protect her, he believed he was exactly like the would-be kidnappers.

She opened her mouth, but Ninja spoke first. "I'm sorry. And I will ask next time."

Her words dried in her throat even as emotion plucked inside her chest. What kind of bad guy apologized? What kind offered concessions? Why couldn't he see it?

There was an empty window in one moment, a fluffed-up owl in the next. Torpedo hadn't made a sound on those impressive wings of his when he'd come in for the landing. "Hello, handsome," Emily greeted, and smiled as he shook out his feathers with a little trill of welcome.

"Keep an eye on her for me, Tor," Ninja said. "Two, if you can spare them."

She grinned. An owl would certainly be up to that task, every inch the perfect night predator and watchman. And Torpedo, it seemed, took his protection duties seriously. He swooped in to perch on the top of the open door. Emily sighed as she glanced down the hallway. The smoke had definitely lessened, but there would be so much to clean. Her stomach grumbled at the same time as if to remind her the cooking utensils and her countertops weren't the only things that had suffered from a lack of successful meal preparation.

"I'm going to let you rest," she said, "but I'll just be in the kitchen."

Ninja gave a slow nod. "Go. Eat. Just don't go far." She heard his teeth click together, felt the untamed, impossible compulsion to protect her rush between them once more before her hand separated from his and it was lost. "Please."

"I won't," she promised.

Surely she hadn't imagined it? The emotion? The way it had severed the instant she'd stopped touching him?

She stopped herself from touching him again, from seeing if it would come back with renewed contact. *Distance.* With effort, she wrenched herself from her curiosity and the bed. *That's all I need. Perspective.* After closing the door behind her she followed Torpedo to the ashen battlefield that had become of the rest of her apartment.

She leaned on the counter, her palms smudging the soot. *I was just relieved to see him, after the little present Shiv left for me.* "After seeing things creeping in the shadows all day," she added aloud as she wet a cloth and began to scrub. Eating could wait. Right now, cleaning would settle her thoughts.

It wasn't until she'd worked her way to the stove that she spotted it. A charred piece of debris among the hunks of inedible meat on the stove. Plastic of some kind, and if she wasn't mistaken, the metallic flake coming out of it was a bit of wire. Since when did floured chicken come with electronic devices? The battery might have heated just enough to spark the grease, or maybe the extra spice she'd dumped when he had startled her with his broody, silent act had started it. Either way, she was looking at Ninja's bug.

"Oh, you idiot."

Torpedo puffed up into a ball of feathers on top of her little TV and Emily smiled wryly over at him. "Where was it hiding, you think? Inside the meat drawer? My flour? He didn't think I might use these things? I realize nearly burning my kitchen down isn't a great first impression on my cooking skills, but come on."

The owl came closer, his claws tapping on the counter. He bobbed his head several times, hooting away at her as if they were having a real conversation, just like he had with her masked man.

Humor smothered a fraction of tension she hadn't realized still weighed down her muscles. "I have no idea what you just said, but it sounds like we're on the same page." Reaching out a hand to ruffle the feathers at the side of his head, she sighed. "I wonder if he's hungry—"

A knock sounded at the door and she jumped. Torpedo bristled, his stance changing from preening at her attention to alert guard owl.

I'm so not answering that.

The brisk rap of knuckles on her door burned her ears a second time.

I'm not even going to look. But her feet took to pacing the linoleum in front of the door. Her eyes flickered to the remaining mess of her kitchen. It was probably a neighbor about the smoke. Not Shiv. He wouldn't have knocked.

"Miss Barton?" The voice was muffled but familiar. Mr. Young.

She paused her pacing and lifted herself to the peephole. Standing in front of her apartment with a single perfect rose and at ease in an expensive tux was the man who had donated a fortune to Partner Paws. Miles Young. *Why is he here?*

"Oh no," she whispered. "The fundraiser."

She'd completely forgotten. Emily chewed on her bottom lip. She strained to the limits of the peephole's sight range. She didn't see anyone else, but they could have been standing further down the hall. Miles Young's face settled into a downcast expression as he gave up on knocking. Emily felt a pang of guilt. She'd already done him an injustice by thinking the worst of him during their previous meeting; she couldn't just ignore him. He stooped as if to leave the flower on her doorstep.

Emily twisted the doorknob and pulled, the chain going taut and leaving a gap for her eyes to peek through. She hoped her body blocked the view of the kitchen. "Mr. Young?" Her gaze met his face then skittered to the left and right of him. There was no one else in the hallway.

"Miss Barton. I was afraid you weren't home. I had thought to pick you up for the event this evening." Extending the rose, he smiled. Alcohol didn't seem to linger around him tonight. "If you aren't ready to go I can wait here for you to get changed."

"I'm afraid tonight is not the best night." Apprehension saturated her thoughts. Wait in the hallway? When Murphy's goons could show up at any minute? Not happening. She didn't know Shiv's standards for kidnapping, but she bet he wouldn't be able to resist the money smiling at her through the crack in the doorway. There had to be other options, another way to repay his generosity. "Is there a different function I could attend instead?"

He bowled right over the question. As if she hadn't spoken, he dipped into a short bow, his brown eyes warm. "Why don't we dispense with the formalities? I'm Miles, and I would be honored if you'd be my date for the evening, Emily."

Ninja was safely ensconced in her bedroom; it wasn't like she could—or would—let Miles Young traipse through her personal space. She had to make him leave.

"Miles," she said with deliberate emphasis, "I can't. I'm

sorry. I had a bit of a cooking incident tonight and I really should—"

The man's hand came up to the crack of the door and Torpedo suddenly swooped in behind her, sounding off with a horrifying screech, beating his wings past her head as his talons forward as if trying to get to the man's head. Emily gawked at him in horror, threw her hands up to wave him away. The bird had been so friendly to her, she hadn't considered how he would react to anyone else.

"Torpedo, no!" She flung the silver chain from the door, shooing the bird back so she could slip into the hallway after Miles's retreating form. Snapping the door shut behind her, Emily sagged against it with a sigh. Her eyes narrowed with a start, taking another glimpse up and down the hallway. *I've got to get a grip.* "I'm so sorry, Mr. Young. I had no idea he would lose it like that."

"Oh, it's quite all right." He regained his composure faster than she did. "I guess you haven't gotten that one trained yet for your organization."

Her hands had started shaking again. Emily pressed her palms against her thighs. "This really isn't a good night. I'm sorry I can't go with you." Scraping came from the inside of her apartment. Torpedo screeched again.

"Why don't you go back inside and change. I'm a very patient man." The warmth didn't touch his eyes this time.

She could tell he was far more shaken than he attempted to appear, a hint of irritation lacing the tight curve of his lips. *I would be ticked too, if my would-be date cancelled last minute and then sicced an attack owl on me.* She considered herself lucky Torpedo hadn't gotten hold of his skin or his expensive tux.

She glanced down and caught her breath. A dotted red line appeared on the back of his hand. "Oh no, he did get you. I'm so sorry! I've got Band-Aids," she murmured, turning to open the door again. Sharp, stabbing pain hit the side of her neck. Her palm flattened against the door, trying to hold her up as her legs suddenly turned to jelly.

"A very patient man," he might have said again.

A new voice came from down the hall and clipped footsteps approached, but her head wouldn't turn to look. Emily slid to the floor, unable to see beyond the crack of her closed door, her head nudging the wood. *What's wrong with me? Why can't I move?* Panic flared everywhere at once and the owl inside the apartment beat again at the barrier between them. Emily couldn't feel her fingers, her toes.

"Emily? Emily, are you okay?" Miles held her around the waist, his voice ringing strangely in her ears.

"What happened to her?" a vaguely familiar female voice asked.

"I'm not sure. She just collapsed. Maybe from the smoke—do you smell that? I'll have to take her to the hospital." Miles shifted his arms to her knees and the center of her back. "Could you help me?"

The hospital? Wait... Dark fear bit at her mind, remembering the sharp sting of pain at her neck and the brush of his hand. Had Miles Young drugged her?

"Oh, yes, of course!" Two delicate hands plucked at her feet and pushed her head against Miles's chest. "I'm her neighbor. Henn Collins, over in 506. Let me give you my cell. I'd like to know she's all right."

No! Don't let him take me! Her eyes, sluggish, tugged away from the silk threads of his tux jacket, her heart rattling in her chest in an attempt to break free from her ribcage. The woman had already stepped away, and she wasn't looking at Emily.

Miles's heart thumped steadily against her ear. Icy calm. "I will send someone by to let you know personally."

So smooth, even as he abducted her from her home.

Ninja!

A crash sounded behind the door. Either Torpedo, knocking things around, or her masked man, having heard the commotion, trying to get up from the bed. Blind. Her heart tumbled. He'd been so worried . . .

She squeezed her eyes closed as her vision swirled.

Miles Young carried her to a vehicle—*his limo?*—and passed her off to someone who smelled like a cigarette factory. Emily was lowered back into his arms inside the car, cradled in his lap while the vehicle rumbled into action. Her head rocked uselessly against his chest.

"See? She wasn't difficult to retrieve in the least." Long, thin fingers cupped her chin and tilted her head up, his other hand creeping around the back of her neck. Miles stared down at her with a fanatical gleam in his brown eyes. "Don't worry, Emily. I'll take good care of you."

CHEST LEVEL, EMILY'S wrists were bound with loops of satin cording to a metal ring off the right side of the mattress. The white sheeting underneath her body tucked into a wooden frame surrounding the bed. She couldn't lift her head but she could turn it, a shackle of metal holding her in place. From the feel of her legs, she guessed her ankles were in similar bonds. The walls of the room held a collection of newspaper clippings and glossy photos, some torn, some slashed through with big, red X's.

Where am I? She tugged against the wrist restraints.

"Oh, you shouldn't do that. You might hurt yourself. How do you feel?"

A bit like psycho-bait. Emily swiveled her gaze up to Miles Young's face. He towered over her, a wicked grin twisting his thin lips. She opened her mouth to speak but nothing came out.

What did he give me?

Glancing at the pictures on the near wall, she bit her lip. An article with her picture sat among them. Her inked self kneeled with a smile, arms draped around a tri-colored collie. The hair on her arms lifted. *Get a grip, Em. You're not going to stand a chance if you lie here shaking in your shoes.* Her eyes narrowed, the pound of fear in her heart tripping over the gap into anger.

His eyes followed the angle of her gaze to the line of tattered decor on the wall. "Failures, all of them," he said. "I know you'll fare better."

He perched on a folding chair by her bedside and crossed his arms over his chest as he leaned back. "Miss Barton, when I saw your face in the paper I knew you were the one. I tried things the conventional way. Money works in most circles. But not with you. I suppose that's because your talents far surpass the other professionals I've worked with." He reached out and fingered a lock of her red-brown hair, then dropped it and flipped a knife open by her ear. The flat of the switchblade traced the curve of her cheek.

This isn't real. It's a nightmare. A hellish, freaky, stupid nightmare. She pushed air through her vocal cords, willing them to create words. *Ninja will find me.* Hope spiderwebbed through her dread.

The whimper of a frightened dog met her ears. "Murphy, where do you want this thing?" One of the men who'd first attempted her kidnapping blocked a now open doorway.

Murphy. Her brain flared into overdrive. *Miles Young is Murphy.*

"The bedroom." A knife severed her bonds and Murphy grabbed her free wrists in one large palm. "Come along, darling."

Unable to struggle with her drowsy limbs, she lay still as he unlocked the fixture around her neck and cut her ankles free.

The crime boss yanked her up by her forearms. "You have work to do."

Her eyes tripped over the dark stains embedded in the gray carpet under her flat pumps. Emily's brain dimly cataloged the marks, old splashes of blood. With Murphy's hand clamped around her arm, her stumbling footsteps followed him into a large room hazy with drugs and sex. Lavender fabric spun out across the ceilings and walls, and glassy-eyed women undulated on circular stages. The audience featured thugs like the ones who had tried to kidnap her before Murphy had apparently decided to take matters into his own hands. Her heart sputtered. Had he brought her here for his personal harem?

But no, he tugged her past the coarse display of flesh and down a side hallway, winding into corridor to the right. The last room in the hallway held a white-draped bed with a small human-shaped lump under the coverlet. Toys were scattered around the room, and a desk with crayons and markers in a neat tray dominated the far wall. The crime boss's hand thumped between her shoulder blades and she pitched forward, a yelp escaping her lungs. She sprawled face-first on a carpet of plush green, her limbs too useless to break her fall.

Murphy stepped around her to the side of the bed. "Everything will be all right now," he said.

She strained to push herself onto her side and caught a glimpse of Murphy's hand cradling a much smaller one. A nasty expression tugged his lips down as he watched her struggle. Finally, he tugged her upright by her bicep. "You will recover from the anesthetic soon. And then you will heal my boy."

CHAPTER TEN

"You will train this beast to cure his cancer. I know you only work with injured animals, but my son insists I can't have the mutt's leg broken." Murphy sighed and shifted a quivering mass of English mastiff—maybe a year old, already bulking up on sleek muscle and grown out of his pudgy baby phase—toward Emily first with an ugly shove of his toe, then the side of his foot. "I will therefore give you two chances. If you fail the first time because the animal is intact, know there is a remedy for the situation."

"And the second time?" Emily croaked, dropping to her knees to awkwardly cradle the terrified dog in her arms. A dark muzzle pressed against her leg and she ran a hand over his beautiful, fawn-colored flank. She didn't waste her breath correcting Murphy's assumptions. The man was insane. At least the boy didn't follow in his father's footsteps, if he wouldn't let Murphy hurt it. She hoped. Willing the puppy to calm, she pitched her gaze toward the bed, genuinely wishing she possessed the ability to help both of her charges. But how could she, when she couldn't even help herself?

"You have an hour." He stalked toward the door out of the

room without answering her question and slammed the door behind him, sealing her in with the click of a key in the lock.

An hour? Yeah, right. Animals reacted to her moods more than they did with other people. The puppy was no exception, still shaking against her, his speckled tongue lolling out of his mouth as he panted. She closed her eyes and sought to calm her heart rate while she stroked her hands across the short bristles of fur. "It's okay, it's okay."

"Can I see you?" A youthful voice emerged from the pillows.

Suspicion tainted the breath she took in around the lump in her throat, but she pushed herself off the floor to meet the boy she was supposed to save. The dog butted its head against her knee and she let her fingers trail over the ruff of his neck for reassurance. As far as companions went, Murphy had indeed picked well, and with the crime boss's money, it would be pure-bred. Mastiffs could be well-suited as service animals. She'd have loved to have one join the ranks at her clinic. This one would need something, too, with whatever trauma the dog had obviously suffered, the near-constant trembling . . .

"Stefan, right? I'm Emily." She forced a wary smile at the bald child in the oversized bed.

He nodded slowly, his pale skin glowing under the fluorescents. "You're pretty. I thought you might be. Your voice sounded pretty." Stefan gave her a wan, lopsided smile in return. "You should go. Before he comes back."

Her eyebrows lifted. "Go?" The door was locked from the outside. It wasn't like she had an escape route.

His lips tugged into a frown. "I know I'm gonna die." He tugged the blanket up with pale fingers, his eyebrows furrowed in concern. "But my father's convinced there's a cure. He's tried everything. All the experts."

Her stomach gave a sudden lurch, recalling the room where she'd woken. The blood on the floor, the X's over faces on the wall, the shredded articles—a roll call for others he'd tried to use to cure his son's cancer. Just how many 'experts' had Murphy brought in? And where were they now?

"Father thinks I don't know what he's doing, but there's nothing wrong with my ears." Stefan plucked at the blanket and the mastiff rose onto his hind legs, thumping his front paws on the mattress. "You should escape before he kills you too." The boy draped a languid hand over the large dog's stubby snout.

What kind of monster kills people in front of his own son?

Emily's hands covered her mouth to stop a cry from escaping as she sank to the bed near his legs. Here was a boy no older than ten who, if she could believe his father's bribery attempts, had undergone chemo and radiation, had been diagnosed terminal half a year before. Instead of coming to terms with his son's condition, Murphy had sought out alternative methods. Which in normal circumstances, she encouraged. But Murphy? He clearly cared for his son Stefan, but this wasn't about quality of life. He'd become obsessed with a cure that didn't exist.

Ninja's masked face jumped to her thoughts. He'd tried and failed to protect her from his boss. Now she had to face the same fate others had, alone.

A red X would denote her death.

Because if there was one thing she couldn't do, it was heal the boy who looked up at her under the canopy of white.

"I can't cure you."

"I know. No one can. Not the Catholic priests, not the voodoo masters, not the medical doctors. I'm not possessed and I don't have a cold. I'm dying." Stefan sighed and scratched at the mastiff's ear. Tipping his head to the side, the child's gaze drilled into hers with more maturity than he should have had to have. "Leave while you still can, Miss Emily."

Her lungs churned with stale air. She rose, bowed her head,

and finally exhaled. Leave this boy with a monster who killed people, ran a crime syndicate, drugged and kidnapped innocents? Her eyes shot toward the door and her throat spasmed.

"What about you?" She couldn't do it. She couldn't turn away from someone who needed her help.

"I won't go with you. He's my father. I love him. I can't leave him. I'll do that soon without running away."

Emily closed her eyes, hoping to strengthen her resolve. Involving Stefan in the training like she did at Partner Paws with her regular students might make him active enough to bring some color to the child's face. At least then she'd feel like she'd been able to help him in the little time she had left. Her mind jolted, calculating. Would that be enough for Murphy to think her so-called techniques worked?

"What's your dog's name?"

"Titan." Sad eyes roved over her face. "Why won't you go?"

Because there was nowhere to go. Determination seeped into her muscles. "Because I'm here to teach you how to care for your companion."

STEPHAN WAS IN high spirits and giggling within the allotted hour while Emily ran Titan through some basic hand commands. Stefan pointed toward the floor and the mastiff puppy squatted, then sprawled, on the floor at the side of the bed. Titan rolled over, his tongue almost touching the floor, begging for a tummy rub.

"I don't think he's catching on." Stefan hid a smile behind one pale hand.

He would. Emily had a miracle worker's knack for getting animals to do exactly what she asked. She would have pinpointed it on the relationship gained through her rehabilitation work, but the result came out the same on the healthy too. The task was to get them to understand and connect with the person she wanted them to respond to in addition to herself. If she could just have a few more days. And with luck, the shift in the boy's behavior had bought her that time.

"Thank you." The boy grinned down at her.

The key turned in the lock and the dog flipped over in a rush, slamming his quivering body against the side of the bed, wide eyes focused on the door.

Hour's up.

"Is it working?" Murphy took in her position on the floor, hand on Titan, and stepped forward.

Just how long did he think it took to train a dog? "Mr. Jones, I think—"

"I didn't pay you to think. I paid you to heal my son."

Emily froze. "Pay?"

"You didn't really think I'd drop half a million on well wishes, did you?" A scowl rippled across his face and his eyes narrowed at the dog. "Come with me, Miss Barton. And bring the mutt."

The check for Partner Paws. So much for no strings. Her face drained of blood as she stood. Stefan's hand snaked off the bed to wrap around her index and middle fingers and he angled his head toward the door, though he couldn't see Murphy from the bed. "Father, don't hurt her. Don't hurt Titan. I feel good. Better." His eyes scrunched in a silent plea. "Don't let him hurt Titan," he mouthed at Emily.

"Well, I'm glad to hear that, son." Murphy's hand rubbed slowly over the door handle. "Very glad." He jerked the door open. "I'm just going to have a nice little talk with Emily while you get some rest."

Emily forced a smile and followed Stefan's father, trepidation simmering in her veins.

They didn't go far. He relocked his son's room and led her, with Titan pacing obediently by her side, to an office off the small hallway. Closing the door behind them, he whirled to seize her forearms and shoved her against the wall. She bit her tongue, tasted metal.

"Is it working? And don't lie to me." His eyes bored into hers, mad with hope.

No man, monster or not, deserved the false hope that his child could be cured when there was no chance of recovery.

She couldn't do it. "He's learning the hand signals—"

"Hand signals?" He shook her until her teeth rattled. "Hand signals don't cure cancer!" Then he pulled her further into the room and let her go. "My kid's laughing. I like that. He's feeling great. I like that, too. But I think you can do better." He paced in a circle, Emily at the center. "I've spoken with your coworkers, and I think your progress will be faster if you deal with something more familiar."

"What do you mean, you've spoken with my coworkers?" A cold chill stabbed at her toes and spread throughout her body. If he'd hurt them . . .

"I made a few phone calls. Shuffled a few papers." He waved his hand to dismiss her question. "If your work with rehabilitated animals is as effective as they say, I can expect results within the evening, yes?"

"I need more time than that." Her fists balled at her sides as she stepped in front of Titan. "You promised your son you wouldn't harm this dog."

"He doesn't realize that sometimes I have to do things for his own good."

"Like kill people?" Anger fueled a second step.

"Yes." The sadistic curve of his lips sent twin strings of goosebumps up her arms. He flipped open the switchblade knife in his palm and started forward. "Move aside."

"No. I won't let you do this." She held her ground, her eyes narrowed with determination. "You can't go around pointing sharp objects at people and animals and expect them to listen."

He laughed and grabbed the front of her blouse, huffing out a breath once again rank with liquor. "I said 'move'." He shoved her aside and slashed at Titan.

When the blade gleamed under the florescent lighting, she darted in without thinking, her hands aiming for a solid push at the crime boss's chest. Metal bit into her palm but she couldn't scream. Murphy's hand had wrapped around her throat.

Titan barreled forward with a growl. With his weight, he could've thrown the crime boss off-balance, but he did no more than snag his teeth on the fabric of the man's pant leg. The crime boss kicked the dog away and the mastiff puppy backed up with a fainter growl, huddling in the corner. Gasping, Emily dug her nails into the back of his hand, struggling against Murphy's stranglehold until he slammed her to the ground.

"That was foolish." He kneeled beside her and she saw the shredded leg of his tux pants through spots in her vision. Titan hadn't even broken skin. Turning his knife over in his hand as if to admire the blood on its slick blade, Murphy clicked his teeth in disapproval.

He shook her by the neck and her teeth rattled. Emily had thought she'd known what rage looked like. She'd been wrong. The expression on his face was something so full of hatred and murder and anger it had to hit at least ten levels above her previous definitions.

I'm going to die. Emily cried out in her head and Titan let out a pained howl.

"You need time? If you have time to train the dog to attack me, you have time to cure my son." He bunched her hair in his fist and dragged her up beside him, out into the hallway where he could separate her from Titan. "I'm going to give you a second chance to work with that beast properly, after you have an opportunity to think about what you've done wrong."

"I was trying to help—" Emily managed to croak before he tightened his grip and made her cry out.

"And you will."

Murphy snapped his fingers. Smoke puffed through an open door halfway down the hall and a shirtless, heavily-tattooed man emerged.

"Gag her and put her on the wall. I want Miss Barton to understand her place here."

"No!" Emily squirmed against the firm grip on her scalp and thrashed in vain to escape the velvet cloth descending across her mouth. Yanked tight at the back of her head, the knot of fabric pushed a dull ache to her temples. She was hauled into a great room and around a raised platform that ringed the area, then fastened to the wall with chains.

Hot liquid coated her fingertips and made her bonds slick where the shackles gripped her wrists. Her mouth went dry under the gag.

Blood. My blood.

"Murphy, when you get a free moment, I believe Ares is on the line." Out of the smoke cloud by the door emerged Shiv.

Emily ground her teeth as he let a hungry glance fall over the length of her body.

"I'll take the call now, assassin." Murphy rubbed his hands together and patted Emily on the cheek once before striding back across the room. "Never too busy for business."

When his boss had left, Shiv took her chin in his fingers and sneered as he leaned close. "If that were true, I wouldn't be required to eliminate his distractions."

She watched, helpless, and the man withdrew a hypodermic needle from his pocket. She bucked against the wall, straining against the bonds until his hand moved to span her throat.

"Hold still." Shiv angled the needle straight into her carotid. "This will hurt."

Pain vaulted over her neck and shoulder, overloading her mind. Her thoughts jumbled out of control, pulling up a sharp image of her masked man. *Ninja, please* . . .

Muffled behind the gag, the scream dragged out of her lungs only made the Hawaiian-shirted criminal's twisted smile broader. Something snapped in her head under the onslaught and a shudder wracked her body. In her mind, she saw a web of threads launching from her consciousness, spreading out as if searching.

What's happening to me? Her eyes flared with agony.

Shiv turned to walk away, puckering his lips as if to whistle. Then he froze, turning to stare at her face. "Now, that's interesting."

Her eyes snapped shut and her helpless mind followed the threads. The lines connected to animals around and inside the building. Torpedo shrieked and Stefan's dog sent a low growl into her thoughts. As if the drug called out through her pores, she felt more creatures enter her mind, their rage and terror reciprocating her own.

"It appears you are . . . special." Bony fingers clamped around her jaw and yanked her head to the left, to the right. "If you survive, my employer will want to meet you."

CHAPTER ELEVEN

BLOOD DRIPPING FROM HER *bound hands set Jay's mind on fire. Emily's murmur of pain echoed in his head. He had to get to her, had to break the skylight and save her. Emily! He tried to hit the glass, but his limbs wouldn't cooperate.*

The warehouse-turned-harem spread out underneath him. His vision streaked over velvet, satin cushions, little stages where women danced half-naked; past the glistening palms of sweating and grubby hired thugs; and zoomed through the dirty glass, pushing everything out but Shiv's hands on the woman chained to the wall.

She's drugged. Son of a bitch drugged her and he's going to add her to this freak show. *Jay railed against his mental prison, unable to feel his physical body at all now.* Arms, legs, do something!

But how? This wasn't his normal night vision. This wasn't normal at all, his body not his own.

"May I have everyone's attention?" *Murphy clapped his hands and gestured to the woman hanging from the wall as he joined Shiv at her side. "This is Emily. She is a perfect example of what happens to bad girls." His fingers wrenched her chin up from where it drooped to her chest. "Bad girls don't get to have fun, do they?"*

I have to get in there before he kills her!

Jay's vision swiveled to take in the rapt attention of the other women in the room. Some of them shook their heads but others just looked dazed, their faces pulled into the gaunt draw of drug addicts.

He's keeping them all high?

Murphy was on the move, reaching for one of the women who seemed clear-headed. She perked up under his attention, arching into his palm when he held out a hand. "But I don't have to worry about that with you ladies, do I? Because you're all my good girls." He threw a glance back at Emily. "Do let me know when you've had enough."

Jay blinked, then all he could see was a close-up of Emily's face, her attempt to lift her head on her own, the glimmer of despair lurking in her eyes.

"Ninja," she mouthed.

Spirit-mate.

The owl-word danced across his soul like a tuft of cotton on the wind.

I cannot fail her. I will not fail her.

His gaze fell back as if he'd turned his enhanced vision off and relied only on weak, normal eyes. The scene spun below him, whirling out into the night. He shoved against the images, fear and the feel of something pummeling the crap out of his physical body tinting the corners of his eyesight red.

"Snap out of it!" Zach slammed his back against a brick alley wall, shaking his shoulders. A look of relief jumped over Zach's features. "You're back. Jay, Jesus."

"What happened?" He pushed his brother's hands away and

rubbed the back of his head. "Where are we?"

"Close by. We were almost at the warehouse when you fell off that fire escape." Zach pointed to a ladder a few feet away. "Your eyes went orange. We thought you'd gone into a coma or some shit."

"I was there." Snippets of the vision replayed in his head. It was real. *And Emily* . . . "The warehouse. The room in the middle. She's chained to the wall."

Zach cocked his head. "What do you mean you were there?"

"I saw her. I don't know how. I just did." He started down the street, Zach keeping a fast pace at his side.

"Tor," both of his brothers murmured, Zach by his side and Ryan into his ear.

"So it's true then," Ryan continued in a low tone. "She really is yours."

Spirit-mate.

The word ran over his heart like a Ford F-150 this time.

Blood dripping from her fingers flashed in his mind and he gritted his teeth. He let the pavement punish the soles of his feet, jarring his knees on the run. This was his fault. He should've been able to protect her. Torpedo's furious tearing about her apartment had urged him into action, but he hadn't even been able to figure out how to open the damned door. If he'd just practiced pushing his ability to the brink more often. Worked through his weakness instead of copping out and only using what he had to.

For so long his priorities had been simple. Hold down the fort. Keep the peace. Help his brothers stay alive and together in the fight for their city. But even for family he'd never ignored the safe limits, never pushed his power so desperately to ensure their welfare. Only for Emily.

His Spirit-mate.

His mind reeled; his steps wobbled. If Zach hadn't caught

his elbow, he would've simply sat down in the middle of the alley. Stunned. And there wasn't time to waste on figuring out if his brain had flown the coop or not.

"Whoa," his brother said, "you good?"

Jay waved him off, sucking in short, shallow breaths. "Ry, what's the score?"

"I've got line of sight. She's not—Place is crawling with goons," Ryan confirmed. "It's gonna be near impossible to get her out."

"No, it won't. Murphy took something that belonged to me. To Klepto. He'll know I'm coming."

"You're pushing yourself too hard, Jay."

Zach swiped at his sleeve and tugged him to a halt. "We need a plan. You go in there like this . . . If you have any feelings at all for this woman, you won't put her in any more danger."

Feelings. The Spirit-mate legend manipulated their introduction, not their relationship. Oh yes, he definitely had feelings.

He swiped at his mask, swearing. "We agreed. We have to cut our ties. Our persona just lays low until we knock out the drug deal and then being on a dead-or-alive list won't matter. Murphy'll be done."

"And Emily?" Zach hissed at him.

"Safe house."

His brother couldn't argue that. Zach had designed the new condo's security system himself; Murphy's thugs couldn't break her out of a fortress. Neither brother responded and when Jay saw Zach wasn't doubled over in pain—his ability's way of saying bad things were about to happen to one of his brothers—he took the green light.

Sprinting now, he rounded the corner of the alley. "Take cover. I'm going in."

When his brothers spoke again, it was pitched too low for

him to comprehend with the pavement flying under his feet.

"I can't believe he's been drinking the Kool-Aid too."

"Believe it." Ryan said. "I called Brennan. No word yet."

Zach scoffed. "Maybe she finally took the money and ran."

"Murphy!"

The male voice penetrating Emily's fogged mind burrowed into her memories. He sounded angry, furious, but she wasn't afraid of him. *Familiar. Safe. But why?* Her vision streaked as a hand tilted her head.

"Ah. Your owner's arrived. I do hope he brought his own leash." The blurred man in black and white dropped her face again and she watched his feet step away, followed by a second figure in bright, garish colors.

They were gone. She tried to force her limbs to test the chains, but the drug held her tight. Despite her need for freedom, Emily's eyes fell closed.

She could see.

The room was empty except for the single royal throne near the back. A tumbler with an umbrella and amber liquid rested on the arm of the chair. At the front of the room, two double doors stood wide open, and wind billowed through the door, blowing in plastic bags and other loose garbage from the street.

Another dream?

Ninja stood in the middle of the concrete floor, a demon in dark cloth. The wind tugged at his hood.

He'd come for her.

"Murphy!"

Behind him, the doors rumbled closed with the help of two thugs.

Murphy stepped through an entrance behind the throne

and approached with an outstretched hand, a greeting.

The masked man didn't step forward to take it. "I know you took her. I know she's here. Bring her to me."

"I can see why you wanted to keep her," Murphy said as he crossed the floor to the red velvet chair and slid into the seat. "She's a regular little firecracker in bed." He crossed his arms over his chest with a dark smile.

Disgust at his lie rippled and spread down the threads in her mind. There was a way out through the faint, glowing web, but she was too lethargic to find it and couldn't fight the vision.

"How much did you have to drug her for that?" Ninja barked out a humorless laugh.

Murphy stilled, then he plucked the umbrella from the drink on the arm of the chair, flicking it at Ninja's feet. "She is most undisciplined. But do not worry. Your pet is learning her lesson as we speak." He pulled the glass to his lips and licked at the salt decorating the rim.

"Perhaps I should teach you a lesson of your own." Ninja stalked forward, drawing a gun from the holster at his waist.

You said you weren't a killer. Hope tilted sideways at the sight of the weapon. She knew her kidnapper was a murderer, but the healer in her rebelled. *Isn't there another way?*

Murphy laughed, a hollow, bitter sound. "For this false accusation of theft? Since when has honor been a quality engendered by thieves? I gave you time to have her come to me of her own accord. She failed. You failed. You have more tasks to complete, partner. I'm sure by the time you've completed them, I'll have tamed her, and you can have her back. If she performs to my satisfaction." His smile curved higher, arching his cheekbones. "You really should be thanking me."

"I am not bartering for what was stolen from me." Ninja strode up to the throne. "Our arrangement is over."

"If that's what you would prefer. Since you started having

kinky masquerade sex with your pet you've chosen to cancel arrangements on a whim, made headlines, set off alarms—She is a distraction. Now, I'm afraid my offers of recompense for her ownership have expired." Murphy snapped his fingers. "But I'm a fair man. Our arrangement entitles you to thirty-five percent of my take."

One of Murphy's men entered the front room with two women on leashes. The queasy sensation in Emily's stomach increased as the women did a sensual crawl across the floor. They each wore little more than a bikini and a thong, with a gossamer skirt that draped over their legs, open in the front so it wouldn't impede their movement.

"These two should be sufficient."

Distaste twisted Ninja's jaw. "We're through, Murphy." He hefted his firearm and shot twice, severing the length of the leashes which tethered the girls to their handler.

Don't kill them! They're drugged; they haven't done anything wrong! Even her mental voice sounded hoarse.

The guard screamed and his legs buckled underneath him; he rolled, clutching his calves. One of the girls laughed and stumbled back through the doors that led into the middle of the building. The other simply shifted to a seated position, her eyes glazed over. Horror washed over Emily as the woman didn't even seem to notice the guard had been shot. Her fingers quested into his hair and massaged his head while blood dripped down his legs.

Murphy turned a dry smile on Ninja. "Perhaps you'd prefer to pick your own."

"Bring her out, or the next bullet lands between your eyes."

Murphy sighed and set his drink down, flicking at invisible dirt under his nails.

Ninja swung the gun in his direction. "Now!"

"Very well. Follow me." Murphy headed for the back of the

room and Emily's dream pulled away.

She soared through the night air, coming to rest on the roof above the more populated room. She saw herself hanging from the wall, her body limp as if life were fading from her. Blood dripped from her shackles. The lurch of dancing bodies had stopped, and Murphy's men were tense, ready, aiming guns at the door on the far side of the room. Her gaze rotated to the doorway. As soon as he stepped through, Murphy swung to one side and gunfire rang out from the center of the room.

Ninja!

The shriek of an owl reverberated in her head. In a spark of orange, the vision merged with reality and Emily returned to her own body, her mind crumbling into a nonsensical tangle of images instead of thoughts. Through the drug-induced blur of her natural eyesight, she saw an eternity of battle, bodies, struggle engulfing the room. Blaring fire alarms struck her consciousness, peppered by gunshots. The dark blob of the warzone thinned out and her peripheral vision caught streaks of movement fleeing the scene.

The chains holding her shattered, metal cascading over her shoulders. Arms, strong, masculine. His. He scooped her up against a solid chest. Her lungs claimed the musky, star-touched scent of the man who held her, who rescued her. And she remembered who he was. His name was Ninja.

Blue and red lights detonated in the haze of her eyesight, flickering strobes across a background of white. Ungodly loud sirens continued blasting into her skull.

"Hang on, Emily."

A rush of air slid over her skin like a satin blanket. Her stomach fell away and she was weightless. Flying.

CHAPTER TWELVE

JAY'S ELBOWS PROPPED UP on the comforter, his thumb tracing idly over the bandage wrapped around Emily's hand. She slept in his bed, dressed in one of his longer short-sleeved button-up shirts since her blouse and skirt had both been torn and bloody. "I should grab her a change of clothes for tomorrow."

"It's already tomorrow. Past midnight, Jay. Why don't you get some rest? Let me take a turn." Zach settled a hand on his shoulder. "The drug wore off the other girls already. Probably has for Emily too. But if she was as rundown as you are, it's good she's sleeping."

He shrugged the hand off, twisting his head to look at his brother. "You can't be here when she wakes up. She'll know the difference."

Zach rolled his eyes. "How? No one else can tell us apart in this getup."

"It has nothing to do with how we look. Just trust me."

"Oh, I get it. You think if I'm in here she'll try to have sex with me and I'll do a better—"

"Zach!" Jay hissed under his breath. "Give it a rest."

A low murmur came from the pillows and his gaze fixated on Emily, her rest uneasy, the fingers of her free hand clutching at the blankets. His arms longed to hold her, to remind her she was safe, even in her dreams.

His Spirit-mate. He'd had time to process the possibility, knew what it meant to the men in his family. What it meant to his control. It morphed an already complicated attraction into a necessity, and Jay wasn't sure he had it in him to be honorable if she found out . . . and then left.

Zach's hand clamped on his shoulder again and Jay met a gaze that crackled with something between sympathy and ferocity. No matter what happened, his brothers would have his back. "Ryan said you can trust what you feel. That the Spirit-tastic mojo doesn't—"

"I know what he said. But I can't just—it's not fair to her. It was different for Ry. Amanda's a fighter. She was made for this. Emily . . . "

"Survived. She is a fighter Jay, just a different kind."

"Not helping. I'm grasping for sanity here, Zach."

"Sleep. You'll find it."

"That work for you?" Jay gripped his brother's forearm but released him the moment he felt a tremor race through his own muscles. Even caffeine wouldn't take the edge off this exhaustion. "I'm not the man she needs."

"Yeah, okay. Sure." Zach strolled to the side table and plucked a McLelas Financial company pen from its surface. He waved the pen at Jay. "Missed one."

"Thanks." Jay rubbed his eyes with his free hand. "I'll be fine."

"Bullshit." Zach shoved a hand through his hair and gave a frustrated sigh. "Look, Jay, waking up in a strange place is going to have the same effect whether you're hovering over her face or spooning." His brother paused, his gaze searching Jay's face. "Get your tired ass up in that bed so you don't embarrass yourself by falling out of the chair."

"No, you can't," Emily protested in a low, drowsy voice. "Don't kill them."

Nightmares chased across her features.

Jay's gut tightened. He couldn't let her go through that alone. Pushing out of the chair, he cast a look at his brother, whose hand was on the doorknob.

"I'll be in to rewrap her hand around four." Zach flicked him a thumbs-up across the room and slipped into the hallway.

In a matter of seconds, Jay joined her under the covers. He cradled her against him and his agitation faded. Comfort threaded into his heart. Jay had needed to do this since he'd brought her home, had needed to hold her in his arms. To admit—if nothing else—he cared for her more than he ought.

If nothing else? Ha. She'd seen him at his lowest—his power shattered—and he'd rescued her from hell. He was far more invested than simply being concerned for her well-being.

Emily went from sound sleep to wide awake in a flurry of limbs, kicking at his shins and twisting to get away. She rolled to her back, whimpering. He trapped her forearms lightly under his palms, hooked an ankle around her right leg.

"Easy, easy, angel. It's just me." He pressed a gentle kiss to her forehead. Her eyes focused past the nightmare, homed in on his gaze. Relaxed. "It's just me." Jay eased his grip as her struggle subsided.

Her arms flew around his neck. "Ninja?" His nickname came out of her mouth in a croak.

"Well, yes . . . But I'm not a—"

"Murphy?" One word. So much fear in the questioning lilt of her voice. Her head shifted from side to side as if trying to scan the darkness for danger. "Shiv?"

"You're safe, Emily." He tugged at her arms to loosen them and stared down into her eyes, little wells of hope. They were clear now, free of the haze of unrecognition he'd seen when he'd pulled her from the wall. Zach was right. The drugs had run their course.

"Thank you." Her unbandaged hand traveled down the side of his face and caressed his cheek. "For rescuing me."

Jay leaned into her touch. "Emily," he said, tracing her eyebrow with a finger.

She lifted her head and her lips brushed against his. One light, perilous kiss.

"Shouldn't," he murmured, though she seemed to take down all his walls.

"Have to." Emily pressed her lips to his again.

The second time, Jay couldn't pull away, couldn't stop himself from plunging his fingers into her hair, couldn't let her go. The sweet taste of cinnamon filled his mouth. Their kiss deepened and one of his arms slid around her waist, melting them together. Lust-fueled adrenaline bolstered his energy reserves as it raked through his veins like talons of lava.

Both of her hands tunneled through his hair and rested at the nape of his neck. At the touch of the bandage against his skin, enough brain cells returned to warn him.

Stop, Jay. Stop.

Bracing himself against the mattress, Jay tried to convince his limbs to let go of her body. His teeth scraped across her bottom lip and she smiled as the kiss came to an end.

She sucked her lower lip into her mouth and her eyes lit with drowsy wanting. His cock jumped with awareness.

"Angel," he managed to get out as her fingers tugged his hair, pulling him back down, "you've just been through hell and I—"

Their lips met for a third time and a new wave of heat

assailed his insides.

He couldn't convince himself to stop now. Not when she groaned into his mouth. Not when her skin felt so smooth under his fingertips. Not when she seemed to want him with the same fierce wash of fire that threatened to consume him whole.

She was here. She was safe. She was his.

One of his hands slid around the back of her head. The other grappled with the buttons of the short-sleeved dress shirt covering her breasts.

"Emily," he murmured again, shoving the fabric to the side.

"Yes. Please." She whimpered the words, bucking against him when his thumb located a nipple through a bra of satin.

Her hands pushed at his chest and he pulled her into a sitting position with him, her tongue tangling with his. Jay's loaned shirt fell from her shoulders. His hands covered her fingers even as she reached back for the clasps of her bra. With two quick tugs, he unfastened and pulled it down her arms.

Then he crushed her to his chest again, his fear for her safety, his hunger for her warmth, and the emotions he couldn't yet voice searing through the embrace. Emily's hands slid down his back to the waistband of his jeans and traced along the edge over his t-shirt. She tugged the shirt out of his pants and danced her fingers over his abs. His muscles tightened, jumping under the playful caress. Jay let her strip the shirt over his head and grinned inwardly when she lay a set of tentative fingertips on his mask.

He dipped her back against the mattress, a smirk traveling to his lips. "The mask stays. But everything else . . . " He stared pointedly at the purple lace panties still hiding her entrance from his hungry view. "Everything else goes."

"You first." Emily crossed her arms behind her head and wiggled into the pillows.

The teasing movement sent pleasure of a more innocent sort

dancing through him. Everything about her pose was languid, happy, content with this moment between them and he wanted to bask in it too, had to breathe her in . . . and taste.

"Hmm." Jay was certain his lips curved with an edge of the wickedness he felt at that thought. Hazel eyes were locked to his, the smile on her face never wavering as he moved down her body. He dipped his head to indulge his senses. A faint hint of sweetness already greeted his tongue, stronger as he teased through the fabric. When his attentions passed over her clit, Emily's hips shot off the bed and she moaned, her fingertips tapping the back of his head as though helpless to do anything else.

He forced himself to leave temptation behind, traveling back up the length of her body and chuckling low against her cheek. "Sure about that whole 'you first' thing?"

"Not anymore." And yet she didn't move to remove the barrier, fast little puffs of her breath hitting his chest as her fingers hooked into the belt loops at his waist.

His heart had a rhythm of demands for his body to take hers in all the ways he could think of before morning. He needed this. They needed this. But the windows were closed for this round, they were safe in his house, and he wasn't about to push her faster than she wanted to go.

Jay yanked his jeans and his boxer briefs off and rolled her on top of him. Letting her take the lead, take almost anything she wanted. "Your turn, beautiful."

"If you insist." Emily let a hungry gaze drift down his body before she dipped her fingers under the lace edge of her panties. She slid them over her hips in a slow-motion reveal. With a dainty kick she nudged the satin over her toes and then settled the vee of her body against his jutting erection.

It was Jay's turn to squirm. She leaned over him and her tongue laved one of his nipples, short ends of red-brown hair barely dusting his flesh. Damn. He'd kissed her before, knew they burned hot together, but their interrupted tryst was nothing so decadent as this. Over and over she licked patterns on his skin, lower and lower while his hands bunched in her locks and he murmured her name. Slim fingertips kneaded their way down his body, tracing over the two old scars that decorated his side.

"What happened here?" she asked, then her lips followed the length of each one she'd encountered, as if memorizing by touch and then by taste. "Here?"

"Bullets. Grazed," he answered, unintentionally vague as all the blood had rushed southward.

"Rescuing people?" Her nipples jutted against him, sliding down his abs until she'd gone lower still, until she nibbled lightly at the top of one thigh.

"Not that guy, angel, remember?"

"Are to me." She shocked him with the words and then with her tongue, swiping a heavenly path up the length of his cock.

Jay groaned and pulled her back up to his lips. He kissed a path across her cheek then sucked the lobe of her ear into his mouth. Slow? Forget it. He couldn't wait. His lack of restraint alone should be enough to prove to her how useless he was in the role of hero. In one smooth motion he had her under him again and her ankles hooked around his legs.

"I want to show you how much I've needed you." How torturous the past week had been. How much he'd wanted to return to soft sheets and moonlight. Her underneath him. Just like this. Jay teased her opening with his cock, feasting on her expression, desire echoing his own.

She gave a slow, sultry nod of her head, her eyes dazed with lust. "Then show me already."

He rocked into her again and she bucked against the gentle stroke to her clit. Driven now, Jay didn't wait any longer, thrusting deep, gasping when the ready heat of her body clamped around him.

"More..." she whispered when he held himself still inside her, reveling in the connection overlong.

Carnal invitation in that softly spoken demand. He reared back, driving into her with one hard, sure stroke. The rhythm his heart required soon caught them, each thrust sending sensation flaring to his chest. Again and again he surged forward, her hips pumping to match his demand.

His hands slid to the backs of her thighs and he pinned her wide. Colors flared behind his eyes, warping his night vision with an entirely new spectrum of rays. His lover glowed like a beacon in the darkness. Her head fell back to the pillow even as her breasts arched against his chest.

Spirit-mate.

"Faster." Her voice was husky with sin now and her head tilted back up at him, her hazel eyes like tiny suns to his enhanced sight. Emily's teeth tugged on his lower lip.

"With pleasure." He obeyed with a smirk.

"Ye—yes," Emily stuttered out, moaning as his fingers explored the contour of her backside, gripping her hip to hold her still as he drove them higher.

She let out a whimper when her upward spiral began. He tried to hold on, to carry her further. Riding through the storm with her as pressure built low. Washed in a fresh wave of passion and colors. Her soft keening shattered them both. Jay went over the edge with a final press of his body against hers, tumbling into a chasm of sensation.

Eventually he realized Emily's fingers were running up and over his muscles. Jay wasn't sure if it was her who shook, him, or both.

"I'm glad you found me," she said.

He smiled down at her and caught a quick glimpse of the

nameless, peaceful emotions that swam in her eyes before she squeezed them closed. Jay pressed his lips to the hollow of her throat and rolled to his side next to her curvy form, circling her waist with his arms. *Me too, love.* Exhaustion slammed into him on the heels of pleasure, an inconvenient reminder of how little sleep he'd been claiming for himself lately.

"Ninja," Emily murmured, wrapping her arms around his neck and kissing his jawline.

Too drained to protest the name, Jay curved around her, nuzzling his nose against her shoulder. She succumbed to her fatigue before his own eyes fell shut.

JAY BOLTED AWAKE at four, a soft knock at the bedroom door reminding him of Zach's promise. He glanced down at Emily's naked, sleeping body and pulled a down-filled blanket over them, brushing a lock of her hair over the curve of her ear. With a sigh, he shifted, dropped a kiss to her forehead, and slid out from under the cover.

"Be right there," he called into the darkness, reaching for his pants. He answered the door half-dressed. Ryan rested on his forearm against the doorframe and Zach slouched against the wall with his arms crossed, a first aid kit dangling from one hand. Both had changed out of their masks for the visit. *Fine by me.* His brothers weren't getting anywhere near Emily in her present state.

"How is she?" Ryan asked, his forehead creased with concern.

Jay nodded. "Sleeping soundly now."

"You got sleep, too." Zach pushed his shoulders off the wall. "Now you only look half-dead. Ready for me to work some more of my magic?"

Jay held out his hand for the first aid kit. "I'll do it. It's just a rewrap. What?" he added when Ryan narrowed his eyes and threw him a full-body onceover.

"Best let him look to see if she ripped her palm back open while you two were 'sleeping'."

Zach grinned, a wicked gleam in his eyes. "Also: I'm gonna need to move some listening devices a little further from your bedroom. . . . Maybe outside."

"Not cool, bro," Jay grumbled, snagging the plastic box out of Zach's fingers as both of his brothers chuckled. "And if either one of you goes for the 'our baby's all grown up' crap, I'm throwing punches."

"Better you than me, Jay," Zach said solemnly. "I'll be damned if I ever let a woman get that far under my skin."

Jay grimaced. "Like a woman would ever try. You're about as charming as a bucket of ice."

"With or without the champagne?" Ryan shoved off the doorframe, humor playing on his lips. Then his smile faded, something dangerous swirling in his eyes. "Zach, did you bring in her clothes?"

Zach looked between them, then nodded. "Bag's by the front door. Gimme a sec." He trotted down the hallway as Ryan turned back to Jay.

"His vibes have been getting worse."

Jay flicked a worried glance at their brother's retreating back. "He doesn't usually hide that from me." He frowned at Ryan. "No seizures, though?"

Ryan shook his head. "Romeo said he was puking his brains out about an hour ago. It's probably something to do with the little hit Murphy put out on us. You."

"Kill orders? We expected that." Jay rubbed the back of his neck. "We didn't exactly part on amiable terms." Throwing up wasn't good, but at least it wasn't a seizure. Any time Zach was sick was a cause for concern. His brother's immune system was iron-clad. However, Zach's ability more than made up for that, letting him know danger was coming for one of the three of them by throwing him curveballs of pain. The worse the pain, the worse the trouble.

"And on Emily."

Jay's eyes widened.

"We've got her things moved into the condo. I want you to move her to that safe house as soon as she's up. Put her on lockdown until we see Murphy's ass in a jail cell."

"Done gossiping?"

Ryan sent a grin over his shoulder. "It's not always about you, Z."

Zach snorted as he returned around the corner with a shopping bag but an unusually weary look passed through his eyes. "It's not like I can pinpoint where it's coming from or who it's for. I'm blind and deaf as usual, eh?" He forced the bag into Jay's hand. "We already know Murphy's after us—no big mystery. Just have to be alert. Now go reset her bandages before I take that kit back and do it myself."

Jay nodded. "Thanks, guys."

"And Jay," Ryan paused a beat, then frowned. "When you've got her safe, pop over to the office. Brennan's still not picking up, but there's nothing saying we can't go through her notes ourselves."

Jay sighed. They'd contracted Brennan to dig through all of their father's documents, every piece of Ohanzee history that had survived the Old Town fire. She would have contacted them if she'd uncovered anything in it regarding his or Zach's powers. Or their Spirit-mates. If Brennan hadn't found anything, neither would they. It was an exercise in futility waiting to happen. They all knew it. "Fine. You can count me in."

He ducked back into the room.

Still intact, a clear line of medical adhesive sealed the cut across the center of her palm. He tossed the used gauze in the trash can in the bathroom and cut a fresh length to wrap the wound.

Emily stirred before he'd finished, her half-bandaged hand stretching up to her mouth to stifle a yawn. "What are you doing?"

"Finishing up." He wound the gauze around her hand two more times and taped the end.

"Thank you." Her eyelashes dipped low over her face, guarding her expression.

Sweeping her underneath him again wasn't an option. Instead, Jay sat on the mattress and slipped his arms around her. Her head rested on his chest, her hand sliding over his heart as it had every night that week. Now, though, the embrace felt . . . heavier somehow.

"How did you find me, Ninja?"

"Shiv's plan was to take you to that warehouse; figured that was still the place. I came as soon as I could. And . . . " *And then I saw you in a vision.* He tried to think of a way to bring that up that didn't involve adding "psycho" to his criminal title. But then she tilted her chin and those heart-stopping hazel eyes called the rest forward.

Jay found himself explaining how he'd seen Murphy speaking to her, chaining her to a wall, and being powerless to help her. That a vision showed him exactly where she'd be in that building. The tumble of words ended and he felt her breath, steady and warm, on his chest. Silence draped the room. He refused to look down to see the horrified expression on her face, to see her rejection. If he'd blurted out instead that she was his Spirit-mate, or worse, that he wanted to explore the less supernatural pull between them . . . *Idiot. This can't work. She can't be with you like this. Not without knowing who you are. And she definitely can't have a future with a criminal.*

A bitter laugh scraped his throat and he let her go, stepping to his bedroom window and flinging the panes open. Torpedo flew to the sill then hopped onto his ungloved hand, the owl's cautious talons walking across his skin with light pinches. He ruffled the silent bird's headfeathers. What had he been thinking? He wished she would just say something. Anything. Even if it was to condemn him for the criminal he was, for ever coming into her life, for adding to the danger.

Torpedo's owlish gaze met his eyes and Jay felt a rush of sympathy course through his mind, as if the bird had somehow connected with him to send him reassurance. Soft feet hit the floor behind him and he waited for her to come to his side.

"Whatever Shiv drugged me with must have given me some kind of out-of-body experience. I could see you, talking with him. You canceled your deal with him—for me. You threatened to kill him if he didn't let me go. But I couldn't reach you. I couldn't say anything to stop you from shooting the guard." With a thin sheet draped around her, she propped her forearms on the windowsill.

She'd seen him? She'd shared a vision? Already his ability had reached for her, changed her, and he had no way to stop it. No way to reassure her it wouldn't get worse. He settled his free hand over her wrist. She didn't pull away. He had to tell her. She had to know what she was to him. It couldn't be any more difficult than telling her he'd had a vision in the first place, right?

"But it really can't be the drug if we each had a vision, can it?" she asked, shaking her head in disbelief.

His Spirit-mate, connecting the dots on her own. Jay's throat was too dry to do more than make a mere sound of agreement.

"Ninja, this isn't the first time. I saw you the night you came to my office. On the roof..." Emily stopped and angled a tremulous smile at him. Her fingers traced over his side, over the places she'd learned there were scars. "They shot at you. Just like tonight. And it's not the first time for that, either. You need to stay away from people who shoot at you."

Torpedo's claws tightened on his arm and Jay lowered the owl to the sill. The bird stepped to the wood and rubbed against Emily's bicep like a cat.

"He knew about Miles, about Murphy," Emily thought aloud, her eyes following Torpedo's launch back out the window, the wheeling and dipping of feathers on the breeze. "He attacked him at the apartment, and I didn't listen. I walked right into Murphy's hands."

A safer topic. Sort of. He curved an arm around her, holding her for a moment while his tongue remembered how to work. "That was not your fault, Emily. I should have been able to protect you."

She shook her head. "No. Although I do blame you for putting the bug in my flour. That little explosion's what did your eyes in in the first place."

A chuckle forced its way up his throat. "Not my smartest decision."

"You meant well."

He felt those words like a punch. Would she feel the same when he locked her in a tower to keep her safe?

"Murphy thinks I can cure cancer. He brought me there for his son, Stefan." She tipped her head toward the night sky. "Miles kept after me for months at Partner Paws and I never realized . . . " Her words trailed off and she leaned back against his chest as if seeking comfort.

Jay wrapped both arms over the thin blanket and rested his chin on the top of her head. "He gave me an entirely different impression." In a way, her admission helped him breathe easier. From the scene he'd arrived on, their intel and the vision, Murphy'd certainly worked the sadistic sex club angle. He rubbed his thumbs in a soothing motion over her crossed arms.

Her hair shifted under his jaw. "I stopped him from assaulting his son's dog and he blamed me when the puppy attacked." Emily's shoulders hitched. "I don't think Murphy planned on hurting me until I'd proven I couldn't heal Stefan. He needed me alive and conscious."

"He made Shiv drug you."

"He did it himself." When he stiffened at her back, she slid her fingers over his arms. "At first. To get me to his car. But on the wall . . . Shiv did that when Murphy wasn't looking."

Jay lowered his head to press a kiss to her temple in an attempt to mask a fresh blaze of anger. "*Shiv.*" He couldn't stop an even harsher growl from edging into his voice when he asked, "Why?" The woman in his arms shifted, rolling her head so her ear pressed to his chest and she looked up at him, her eyebrows creased with worry.

"I don't think he's loyal to Murphy. He has his own agenda. Someone gave him different orders."

He frowned. "Are you certain?" That could change a few things. They would have to be more careful than ever to avoid mistakes if another player had joined the field.

She nodded, then shivered in the night air, and Jay gave her a light squeeze. "Come back to bed with me. We're safe enough for now, but we both should get more sleep." He pushed on his night vision to claim a sharper view of his spirit guide's aerial maneuvers. *Keep a lookout, friend.* Imagining Torpedo on the heights and patrolling for danger, Jay sent the errant thought into the brightened world of his enhanced sight.

He never expected a response.

Torpedo dropped to a nearby tree and sent a flurry of hoots into the night that saturated Jay's mind. *Your Spirit-mate is safe. Keep it that way, Watcher.*

Watcher. Jay blanched, following Tor's winding pattern

through the darkness. Torpedo. Sudden comprehension slammed the breath out of his chest. Of course; he'd just been too wound to notice before. The vision of Emily had been through eyes similar to his own. An out-of-body experience like she'd said, but just different enough to be . . . an owl.

CHAPTER THIRTEEN

EMILY BLINKED INTO SUNBEAMS streaming from the windows in Ninja's bedroom. Disappointment drummed its fingertips across her thoughts. He never stuck around for daylight.

She tugged on the gauze around her hand. Did he have to run away in his own house? Or maybe it wasn't his. Pushing back from the sill, she surveyed the room with interest. Blues in a number of shades surrounded her like clouds. His furniture was all thick beams and lush fabric. The dresser, bed, and low, sprawling bookshelves which crept around two of the walls were all carved from the same rough, dark wood. Books ranging from animals to gardening, electronics to business overflowed the shelving.

One of them had to have his name under the cover, but when she pulled a volume from the shelf, she couldn't bring herself to open it. She didn't want to find out this way. With a sigh, she returned the book to its spot and wandered toward the open door of the bathroom.

Emily wanted him to trust her with the truth.

Even after last night, he'd never tell her.

The bathroom was the size of her apartment's kitchen. Maybe bigger. On the decadently long counter sat a towel and a bag with a change of clothes. "Good plan."

After wrestling the learning curve of far more shower controls than was natural, she stepped under the water and memories flooded her mind. Leaning on the cold tile, tears sprung to her eyes, mixing with the heat of the shower on her face. Murphy could have killed her. Shiv tried to. Either man could have killed Ninja. Instead, they'd survived.

Ninja had saved her.

He'd seen her in a vision—the same kind of vision she kept having—and he'd come to take her from Murphy. And then he'd brought her here to protect her. For a bout of incredible sex under cover of his favored darkness. To hold her while she fell asleep. She'd been safe, cherished. But in the end, he'd gone, and she was still alone.

Her head insisted she couldn't fall for the man in the mask until she knew the man behind it. Her heart already knew she was a goner.

She closed her eyes and tilted her head into the stream. Sex with Ninja had been the one shimmering spark in her evening. An amazing, transcendent spark. She'd felt like soaring through the skies, on the wind. He cared for her. The emotion had shone clearly in his eyes, poured from him in every touch, made her heart yearn for him to say the words out loud, despite being unsure if she was ready to hear them.

It wasn't until she grabbed the liquid soap from a shelf inside the tub and began to wash that she realized they hadn't used a condom.

"Oh. No. He probably thought . . . " No, there hadn't been much thinking. She'd wanted him with a desperation that had thrilled her, and he'd tried to stop them. Failed, because he'd wanted it as much as she had, but he'd at least given voice to a token protest. Emily hadn't even considered risks.

Sinking to the floor of the tub, she wrapped her arms around her knees. The warmth in her chest turned frigid as a ski slope. Things had been hot between them since they'd met, but she hadn't exactly had time to hit the drug store for condoms or to get a prescription for birth control pills. Before this mess started, she'd had no need for either. She sat there until the water ran around her in cold rivulets.

"What will he say?" she wondered aloud to her foggy reflection, toweling her body and then wrapping the overly fluffy cotton around her hand. Ninja was too hard on himself. What if he used this mistake as another one of his self-professed 'bad guy' excuses? "What on Earth do I do?"

Telling him this truth could go wrong in a million ways, but Emily didn't make a habit of deception. Something else that had begun to sneak into her life since Ninja and Tor and Shiv and Murphy appeared. She needed to talk it through.

She needed Julia.

Re-wrapping herself in the towel, she crept back into the bedroom. Still no sign of her masked man, but there was indeed a cordless phone on the bedside table. A landline, when folks so rarely had the money to spare to keep one at home these days. She grabbed the device and hurried back into the bathroom, locking the door and sinking onto the lip of the tub.

"Partner Paws—Hey, Em!" Julia's greeting chipped at the ice in her chest like it sought to thaw her out. "You running late this morning?"

"Yeah," Emily said, then closed her eyes. She'd been concerned with how to have a conversation with Ninja but hadn't considered how many lies she'd have to tell her best friend in order to ask for advice. "Actually, I might not be in at all today."

"Want me to cover for you at Bluseau's?"

"Is that today?" She passed a hand over her face. "Yes. Please, and give her my regards?"

"Can do!" The sound of a pencil scribbling a note came over the line, then Julia sighed. "Okay, spill. You sound awful. Lack of sleep finally catch you, or . . . ?"

"Or. Definitely or." Emily smiled wanly at the receiver. "I . . . can't tell you everything."

Anything.

Could she even ask for advice?

"This was a mis—"

Julia cut her off with a chiding sound. "You can always tell me everything."

"Not this. It's too. Messy. Messed up. Just," Emily sighed as all the frustration from Shiv's hunt, Miles'/Murphy's deception, her abduction, everything, poured out of her in waves. "A big, giant disaster. And I don't want you mixed up in it. Any of it."

"Em." Julia's usually steady voice wavered. "You're scaring me, girl. Is this about the break-in? Our money?"

"I'm sorry."

"Don't apologize. Just tell me what's happened!"

"Still can't," she reiterated. *Wouldn't.* She had to give Julia something, though. "But I . . . there is something I do want to talk about. Need help with. I . . . you remember how I mentioned a guy?"

Silence. Then, "Sugar, are you pregnant?"

"I don't know."

Silence again.

"We didn't use a condom," she blurted out. "Things were so . . . last night was . . . and I don't want him to feel . . . anyway, I—I don't think he knows."

"Well." Julia's sigh filled her ear. "You can't read his mind, can you? Or decide what he feels? 'Cause as far as I know, the only other way to know those things for sure is to ask him."

"I intend to. Once I figure out how to start that sentence."

A short laugh. "Accidents happen. Though take it from me, it's not something the kid would ever want herself to be called, yeah? You'll know what to say. You always do."

"I guess."

"You haven't known him long, right? Are you afraid he'll feel obligated?"

"Maybe." Would he feel like he had to tell her who he was? The cold pit in her chest made a return.

"Afraid he'll walk away?"

Emily chewed on her lower lip. "I gotta admit, Julia. I like him where he is." No, that wasn't true. "Actually, I'd like him closer."

Julia chuckled longer this time. "You have to talk to Naomi about him, you know that? Soon as you figure this out, you know she'll want deets. He treating you right otherwise?"

"Yes." No hesitation there. *He's been a lifesaver. Literally.* "But what if—"

"No." Julia's sudden change in tone made her flinch. "This is not a 'what if' scenario. He puts his big boy pants on and talks with you about this like an adult, or he's not for you, Em."

The tough talk settled over her like battle armor, smacking around the doubts she still had burrowing into the corners of her mind.

"Hey listen, we love you," Julia said. "Get some rest, sort this thing out with your man, and come back to us, okay?"

People in her corner. That was one thing Murphy couldn't take away from her. "Thanks, Julia. I'll see you soon."

She took the phone back out, then took her time dressing, drying her hair, and letting the measure of calm that came with getting even a fraction of the weight off her shoulders bolster her confidence. Composed once more in a dark blue blouse and floor-length skirt, Emily shook her head as she reached the bottom of the bag and realized he'd forgotten shoes.

Oh well. She could face him without them. Brushing at her skirt with her injured hand, she pressed the fingertips of the other on one of the other door's handles.

If this door goes to a closet, I bet it's loaded with black t-shirts and trench coats.

Her curiosity won out and her hand slid around the brass doorknob, then twisted. The door swung silently inward and she took a long, steadying breath, willing herself to step over the threshold. Why was she so nervous? *Because I'm afraid of what I might find.*

And her heart was on the line.

Never mind that she needed to find him and have the dreaded conversation: Was she about to wander into some secret armory or lair? Discover his true identity? Emily left the door open behind her and she crept forward, the light from the bedroom window barely penetrating the darkness.

She felt for a light switch but nothing stood out along the wall. *Maybe it's further down.* After a brief hesitation, she took a few more tentative footsteps down the corridor.

"Where do you think you're going?"

Emily whirled to face him, then froze, her toes digging into the plush hallway carpet. "Are you guarding the doorway?"

"Of course." Ninja lounged comfortably in an overstuffed sofa chair to the left of the doorway. "I really can't have you wandering around in my personal space."

He didn't have a problem with personal space last night. Heat rose to her cheeks at the wanton thought and she shoved it aside for safer ground. "You've gone through my things. You went so far as to bug my home, if I recall."

"I did that when you weren't looking," he said, swinging his legs down from the arm of the chair and stretching like a cat.

"It's not remotely the same. I have to know about you so I can protect you; you don't need to know anything about me."

Ouch. She squared her shoulders against the unexpected sting in his words. No, he couldn't shut her out so thoroughly. More, she couldn't let him. Especially not now. "You're not sitting there to protect me; you're sitting there to protect you."

"Quite observant this morning. And I haven't even gone for coffee." Amused steel eyes roved over her skin.

Emily crossed her arms over her chest. "We need to have a conversation before you confine me to your bedroom."

"No." Ninja leaned forward, his elbows on his knees. "Where you'll be staying is not up for discussion."

Obstinate, high-handed—"I'm going to come back to that, because it absolutely is," she promised, then said, "but I'm not talking about that kind of conversation."

His expression turned wary, as if he'd expected a battle and was thrown by her momentary retreat. "What, then? Is your hand bothering you?"

Emily rubbed the palm in question and shook her head. "It's about last night."

He didn't assume she meant her abduction. His lips—those addictive, memorable lips—curved. "Regrets, angel?"

"It was incredible." She met his gaze directly. "But we forgot to use protection."

The silver in his gaze flashed wide and his jaw flexed, but he was motionless everywhere else. When he spoke, the words lacked his usual composure and came out husky, pitched softer than his usual grumble. "So you want . . . to go home for your birth control . . . ?"

She simply watched him for a moment. Truly, she didn't know what to say any more than he did on the subject.

"You're not on the pill."

She shook her head.

"Emily. I'm sorry. I didn't—God, I didn't think." A long blink of those glowing rings of silver. "This is just one more reason—"

Her throat constricted like her own emotions were intent on strangling her. "Don't you dare. Don't make this something you think means you're a bad guy. It takes two to make a mistake like this—"

He was on his feet in the next breath. "Last night was not a *mistake*."

She tilted her chin upward. "You 'forget' condoms often?"

His nostrils flared. "No. Obviously. I wasn't saying—"

"Not 'obviously,' Ninja. I barely know you." She smoothed her hands on her skirt even as the unplanned words dragged her heart over splinterings of glass. "I *don't* know you. And I don't mean just your name; we haven't known each other long enough for me to get anything 'obvious' at all. I have no idea how you do things on a normal date night. I assume you don't have to deal with fires and rescuing women from their kidnappers on the regular. If you even know what a normal date night is. I had no idea how you'd even react when I told you. Did you know I thought you might just walk away? Just leave?"

"Leave you? To Shiv? To Murphy?" His voice was back to gravel again. He strode forward, backing her against the far hallway wall and clasping her shaking fingers in his steady ones. "How could you think I'd consider that for even a second?"

"*Because I don't know you*." She hauled in a breath that scoured her lungs. Wild frustration battered at her mind with him this close. "At the start, it was just acting, to protect me. How am I supposed to expect you'd stick around?"

"It hasn't been acting for some time, Emily." He growled, and the frustration shoving against her own emotions grew heavier. "You wanted this as much as I did. And you do know me. You might not have my name, but I swore to you I'd keep you safe. If you can't trust my—"

"I wasn't finished!" She yanked a hand from his and thumped him on the chest. "I want to trust you, I do. I want to count on you. But I don't know how to handle what's between us. With you, and the mask, the secrets. There's the visions we're getting, the way your eyes what, shorted out? I don't understand what's happening and I think it's pretty darn safe to say, where you and I are concerned, there's no such thing as 'obviously'."

"I get it; I screwed up when I let him take you. Don't think I don't feel every ounce of that failure." A noise clawed up the back of her throat but he bulldozed over it. "I charged into that warehouse last night for one reason. You. And one misplaced condom, you think is going to make me forget the rest of my honor, too? I'm not going anywhere. And neither are you."

Something was wrong. Really, really, wrong. She didn't feel this desperate. She didn't feel this utterly out of control. The floor didn't feel solid, and Emily's mind felt battered by a sense of urgency to keep herself in his arms.

"Ninja," she whimpered. "Let go."

"Let me figure this out." He lightly squeezed her good hand and instantly the emotions swamping her doubled like a kick to the solar plexus.

As it had the night before, orange threads draped her mind like webbing, spreading through her, from her, thicker and thicker and grasping for something she couldn't understand. Emily coughed, her vision swimming with tears from the emotional overwhelm. "Let go!"

"Okay. Okay." Ninja said. He raised both hands in surrender but he was anything but calm. Aggression was bound tight to his movements, as though he was afraid of accidentally unleashing it. A hand went to the back of his neck. "Emily, there's such a long list of things we need to talk about. How about we take a breath, then continue this at your new place?"

"New place? So you're not keeping me here, then?" She

stared at him, her arms dropping to her sides like twin lead weights.

He shook his head. "Don't worry though. Everything is like you left it, just . . . in a safer neighborhood."

"Wait. Everything? You . . . You moved my things to another apartment?" Emily's fists clenched at her sides. Without touching him, some of the foreign emotions had eased, the webbing in her head dimming to shimmery strands instead of cording. It left room for her own emotions. Chief among them: fury. "Were you planning to ask me for permission? For a budget? I can barely afford the one I'm in now!"

"It's a condo, and rent's not a problem." He waved his hand to stall further argument. "I have to keep an eye on you. We can't have another repeat of last night, and I can't protect you when you're across town. So you'll be staying at this new place instead."

He said it like he couldn't fathom he'd done something wrong. Like moving her whole life from one apartment to another, removing her option to go home, going through every single thing she owned without even asking, wasn't in itself the problem. Pain seared through her palm and she winced, forcing herself to unclench her fists. No, in this case, arguing got her nowhere.

"I'm getting some air." She ducked under his arms to stalk down the dark hallway. "If you don't want me to know who you are, I suggest you show me the way out before I go somewhere personal."

A sliver of light peeked around a corner and she angled toward a door that appeared to lead outside. He dove to intercept her, blocking her escape.

"Your house does have windows I can climb out of," Emily warned, spinning to look for another way out. Her skirt brushed light against her ankles, swirling as if it echoed her agitation.

"Emily."

Her cheek turned into his solid chest, rocketing her heart rate past safe levels. Ninja leaned down and brushed a kiss across her temple, sending a traitorous thrill down her spine and a whirlwind of dangerous emotions circling in her brain. His. His emotions. How was this happening? Shiv's drug?

"I can't allow you to go out there alone, either."

"Well, it's a good thing I don't require your permission." Emily bristled and squashed her reaction to his nearness, fighting the extra senses, backing up a step. Rebellion surged through her limbs. He couldn't *allow* her to go outside? How could he act like this after last night? Protecting her was one thing, but this? She caught a glimpse of light from an archway to her left and edged toward it. "You're being ridiculous."

He growled.

Her footsteps faltered to a stop. "Why are you doing this?"

"Murphy wants us both dead."

His blunt words hammered like an ice pick into her chest. "I can't just hide under a rock and wait for him to find me. I have the day off, but people count on me, Ninja. Animals, too." She shoved her hands to her hips and turned to glare at him, but her confidence flagged as a new realization stabbed home. "You were planning on stopping me from working."

"I just need a few days." He lifted a palm to her shoulder and she shrugged away from him. "That's all. I thought you could stay at the new place until I get this straightened out."

"Out of the question. Graduation is coming up soon at Partner Paws. I'm not going to just *abandon* all of my—Ah!" Her insides contorted in agony and she pitched forward into his arms.

"Emily!" Ninja's arms tightened around her corporeal body, smoothed back her hair, lowered her to the floor. His worry swamped her senses. "Angel, look at me."

She tried. But it was like being drugged and chained all over again. If she moved, she might splinter out along the sudden wealth of thick, orange threads. Lost for good. He shook her shoulders, but reality fell away.

"What do you want from us?" a terrified voice asked.

Melanie Bluseau. A patient at Partner Paws.

Emily's vision expanded and a panoramic view warped her perception.

The older woman's forehead bled and her wheelchair was backed against the wall. Red, thick blood seeped across the floor through the archway on the other side of the room. Emily wrenched her head around, trying to see what Mrs. Melanie's horrified eyes stared at, to see whose blood spilled into the room, but her vision body felt covered by heavy fabric.

"Can't have you telling anyone what you saw, can we?" The gruff male voice didn't belong to any of the psychopaths she'd run into lately. "Loose ends aren't pretty."

"You, though. You can tell them Miss Barton sent her regards." A bulky form surged into the room and Mrs. Melanie screamed as the man yanked her chair to one side, throwing her to the floor.

No! No!

Emily heard another scream, this one rage, and stared in horror when Julia staggered into the room and leapt onto the man's back, scraping at his face with bloody fingers. He flung her off, smashing her against the wall. Julia's chest didn't rise again.

"No!" It came out more a screech than a word, pouring through Emily's veins, clawing its way through to reality. "Julia!"

The man turned toward her and growled. "Get away from there!"

Emily's thoughts fragmented. She sped towards him,

flailing with inhuman limbs at his face, leaving gouges in his skin, swooping and whirling away from his hands.

He scooped a baseball bat off the floor and swung. Connected.

The vision floundered into a monochromatic and soundless moving picture. She flew on unsteady wings through the front door, arcing toward the sky.

JAY KEPT EMILY'S forearms pinned to the ground as she lashed on the floor. Her eyes were neon orange, unseeing, and she was screaming. A vision, like he'd had in the alley. One he couldn't pull her out of.

Ryan plunged into the entry hall wearing his trench coat, his hands over his ears. "What the hell did you do?"

"Call Zach. Find Tor. Supposed to be watching Shiv." If the whole iMax movie screen-o-vision effect truly had come through the eyes of his spirit guide, whatever the owl was seeing must have been terrifying.

Or maybe it's just the fact it's a vision at all. What do I know?

"On it." Ryan backpedaled toward the kitchen.

Emily's scream cut off and she went limp in his arms, her eyes still glowing in that eerie shade.

"Emily?" Jay scooped her into his lap and shook her shoulders. "Emily!"

Ryan popped back into the room and squatted behind her head, a spare earpiece in his palm. "He's tracking. Fill me in."

She had a pulse. She was breathing. But helplessness and McLelas genes didn't see eye to eye. Jay spared his brother a nod. "The vision I had last night, the ones she's had—"

"This isn't her first one?"

"Third." He rested the back of his hand on her forehead.

"We're seeing through Torpedo's eyes, the same way you and Amanda had your ears tuned into Romeo. Zach finds my owl, we find out what she's watching."

Frowning, Ryan clipped the mic and speaker combo over the shell of Jay's ear. "Your spirit guide needs to learn control. It could take time."

"You think Tor's doing it on purpose?" He swore under his breath. "When I went under last night, did I have a fever?"

Ryan shook his head, his expression grim. "You weren't screaming either."

"You didn't tell me it'd be like this." He couldn't keep the accusation from his tone. The panic that plunged into his heart like one of Shiv's blades.

"The bond wasn't like this for me. Jay, if I had answers, you'd have answers." His oldest brother draped his arms over his knees. "Bren's notes. There's got to be something. Has to be."

Jay leveled a look at him. "This is not something I need my big brother to fix."

Ryan shrugged. "I honestly don't think I could if I tried. This is between you and Emily. Tor, too, if he's providing a bridge. But you're going to need all the help you can get to figure it out. The two of you going down for the count like this . . . it's stronger than what we went through. Ours was disorienting. Not painful. Not violent."

Silent, Jay rocked the woman in his arms. Willed her to wake.

"You said she studies birds, right?" Ryan ventured after a long moment.

"It's her specialty, yeah. You think there's a connection?"

Another unhelpful shrug. "I was thinking maybe you could both work with your spirit guide a little easier, is all. He gives you a hard time; maybe he'll open up to her. But now that you've mentioned it, I'll check the notes for anything sounding bird-like, too. You know, aside from eyes and visions."

"Why'd it have to be visions? Why couldn't I have gotten something cool, like wings?"

"Fuckers would be tough to hide in a trench coat, Birdman." Zach's voice cut into the conversation, streaming into Jay's ear over the comm unit.

An uneasy roll of laughter shared between brothers was exactly what he needed to ease some of the tension in his body. There were few avenues of recourse. Their Ohanzee tribe no longer existed. The gifts their individual spirit walks had granted them hadn't exactly helped when Jay, Ryan, and Zach returned to Old Town to find destruction, death, ashes.

Little was recovered from the aftermath of the mysterious fire that claimed a city block's worth of lives, including their mother. Journals hand-scrawled in a symbolic language none of them could translate. Bags of camping equipment for an excursion that left too late to escape the fated attack. Unless they cracked Shiv's secrets, they'd never know what really happened, and even knowing didn't help them explain Zach's seizures and Ryan's unstable ability, let alone visions, orange eyes, or how to protect the woman in his arms.

His hands slid to Emily's sleeves, and it felt as though the rigid lines of her muscles eased slightly. A good sign.

"Got Tor," Zach said. "Bird's taking a turn around Kingsford Park. His tag's erratic."

"Get over there and see if you can spot trouble," Ryan ordered, pulling on his own mask. "I'll join you shortly."

"Erratic?" Jay frowned. "Is he injured?"

"On my way; you'll know as soon as I do," Zach said.

Emily was so very still. Too still. Jay brushed a damp strand of hair back from her face. Instantly, her muscles locked, and Jay pulled his fingers from her skin.

She relaxed. Though her eyes were unchanged, her body

slumped in his lap.

Ryan gave him another worried glance. "Do that again."

His fingers were already in motion, a lingering touch against her cheek.

She whimpered.

"It's you." Ryan motioned for him to let her go.

The absolute last thing he wanted to do.

He stared at his hands. "I'm the one who did this to her? Not Tor?"

Recalling her distress during their earlier argument made him frown. At the time he'd assumed she'd wanted space. Being skin to skin certainly hadn't been a problem the night before, so what was different now? Or was it only during the visions?

The questions would have to wait. Emily gasped and bolted out of his arms, the orange in her eyes dimming to hazel. Disbelief held him in place, and he wasn't fast enough to block her view as his brother double-timed it backward to the living room archway.

She blinked rapidly, shaking her head even as Ryan concealed himself along the wall. Looking at Jay, then the shadow that Ryan had tried to vanish into, she scrubbed her face. "Ninja? Two . . . "

"Emily. Emily, what happened?" Jay asked, drawing her half-focused gaze. His brother dodged around the corner. "What did you see?"

"I was flying," she murmured. "But I was hurt. Then the colors came back." A lunge, her fingers gripping at the edges of his trench coat, her knuckles bone-white. "Julia! Ninja, there was so much blood. So much." She turned into his chest and rattled violently. "I should have been there. It should have been me. He said it was me!"

He stroked her cheek out of an automatic need to reassure, to comfort. A slip that made her wince and had him jerking his hand back. Was he an idiot? He couldn't touch her. He wouldn't hurt Emily. "Tell me what happened."

"Mrs. Melanie—she's one of my students—and Julia—she's like family, Ninja, and I asked her to be there!—and then there was some guy with a baseball bat. So—So much blood." Her eyebrows knitted together as she remembered the vision. "Julia wasn't breathing . . . I have to get over there."

"Over where?"

"Mrs. Melanie's house. I give her a private lesson some mornings because her son can't always bring her—"

"Give me an address, Emily."

She recited it from memory and he threw a look to the living room shadows. Ryan flicked him a thumbs-up in the darkness and fled through the back of the house.

Murphy's hit had some takers.

And it sounded like Julia's stand-in for Emily may have cost her life.

CHAPTER FOURTEEN

"When I get back, we'll talk." Ninja pulled the blindfold from Emily's eyes and gestured broadly around the condo.

A curt nod was all she could manage. She was done trying to reason with her masked man. Still-bare toes took her away from him, stepping onto the cold stone tile of the kitchen floor. Low, but unmistakable, a curse had her sending a look over her shoulder.

"Wait." He seemed to hold himself still for a moment, then brushed his hand against her fingers, his jaw taut.

Regret, relief, an underlying thrum of fear.

She held herself still, focusing on her own emotions over his. Anger, hurt, confusion. Refusing to grab onto him to see if there was a way to sort through this bizarre connection, not when he wouldn't listen. His touch moved up her sleeve, where the sensations eased almost immediately. Was it her lack of prompting for elaboration that had his breath whooshing out of him so heavily? If so, he had another thing coming.

Instead of 'allowing' her to help her friends, Ninja expected her to sit here. No amount of protesting on the drive over to her new prison had convinced him to let her wait at the hospital when he'd already made up his mind to go solo. No. He wasn't solo at all. She pulled away.

"There are two of you," she said. "Two Ninjas."

He grimaced. "There's only supposed to be one. It's . . . easier to cover ground this way."

Not a denial or a "not right now". She frowned.

"I sent him ahead to check on your friends while I got you to safety." Ninja took a step toward the door. "And I need to meet up with him now."

She turned to hide the way her eyes turned watery, worry surfacing for Julia and Mrs. Bluseau.

"Emily," he said with a sigh at her back, "I know you're angry with me, but we'll sort it out when I return. When your friends are safe too." A light *click* sounded behind her and she whirled. Gone, the front door locked with some sort of electronic device.

"You can't lock me in a tower!" she screamed at the control panel on the living room wall. It had to be the main circuit board for the security system that kept her trapped here instead of running to Partner Paws to get help. Emily assaulted the baseboard with a series of infuriated, useless kicks and threw herself to the floor, slamming her back against the wall.

They have to be alive.

Her fault. She'd asked Julia to cover for her. Murphy wanted her dead.

Murphy wanted Ninja dead.

Her good hand glided over her abdomen as she worried and when she finally noticed, she flushed. Concern for him hadn't been because of their mutual What If. "I'm not pregnant. I can't be pregnant *and* going insane *and* hunted by a crime boss." A pained laugh—hysteria, maybe—left her huddled inward. "Oh, God. What have I done?"

Shaking, she got back to her feet.

An hour passed before Emily gave up on looking for a phone and trying to wedge the locks off the door and windows in the condo. She curled up on a couch much nicer than her old one—so much for everything being the same just in a new place—and closed her eyes, wishing one of the clinic cats were with her so she could bury her fingers in the scruff of his fur.

One shimmering orange thread sprouted in her mind. Spiraling outward, reaching.

Reaching?

She tested the strange sensation, the measure of reassurance she sought meeting her halfway. A soft purr. Equally orange fur. Squares on a green collar.

Captain Nemo?

Purring amplified down the thread, rumbling in her mind. Her eyes snapped open. Impossible. Yet the visions had been real. Why not this? The threads she'd sensed weren't drug-induced. They weren't imagination. Contact with the office tomcat had felt as though he was cuddled up against her thigh, and the reassurance had definitely come from him. Not her own mind. Not her own emotions.

Just like with Ninja.

Or else she should start looking up insane asylums.

"*You are not crazy.*" A series of faint owlish whistles—understandable—in her mind.

"No." She kept her voice stern in the empty condo. "You visions, whatever you are? You need to stop. I have enough insanity in my life right now."

Rummaging through cabinets to make a pot of coffee to stabilize her nerves and maybe forestall the hallucinations, Emily heard buzzing. She followed the sound to her familiar bedside table—in her new master bedroom. After a sideways wiggle and tug of the wobbly drawer pull, it popped open.

My cell! Without looking at the caller ID, she mashed a button. "Hello?"

"Where have you been?" Naomi was practically shouting.

"I—"

"Never mind. Em, there was an accident at Mrs. Melanie's. She's fine but Julia's in the ICU and our staff's heading over there now. Get over to Fairview soon as you can."

The line clicked off and Emily pulled the phone away from her ear, staring down at the display. *Easier said than done, friend.* Frustration renewed in her gut and she snapped the device closed. Why was she hearing it from Naomi? Why hadn't it been Ninja? Better yet, why wasn't he here? He'd promised to come back once he'd gotten them out of danger. Had something gone wrong? Absently tightening her grip on the phone, the center of her injured palm protested. She crossed into the main room and dropped it on the kitchen counter next to the useless keys he'd left behind.

Pacing to the security system panel, she rapped her knuckles on the obnoxious series of lights. She could worry about Ninja later. Right now, she had to get to Julia. Which meant getting out of the condo.

"Okay, think. All this stuff has to run on electricity, right?" The logic sounded good, anyway. *The breaker.* "I'll just shut the stupid thing off. Short it out somehow."

She tore through every room in the condo for the second time that morning. Tucked behind a water heater in an extra bedroom closet, she found it. Emily pulled the lever on the breaker door open and stared at a double row of switches. "OCD much?" Every single one was tagged like a kindergartener had gotten hold of a label maker. *Kitchen, Master Bathroom, Laundry, Security* . . . She snorted. "It can't be that simple." Her finger snaked over the switch and flipped it to the right anyway.

Clicking caught at her ears, resounding through the condo.

Her fingers looped into a pair of low pumps and after slipping them onto her feet she returned to the security panel. Smiling at her exhausted expression in the darkened array, she grabbed her phone, keys, and purse from the kitchen counter. The front door to the condo and the downstairs atrium of the building swung easily open on her way to the nearest bus stop.

JAY PACED ON the plush living room carpet, no longer dressed in his nighttime disguise.

"And it's *my* fault he didn't put a tracking device on his girlfriend?" Zach yelled over their comms.

"It is *your* security system, Z." Ryan shoved his hands into his pockets. "You didn't get an alarm on your end?"

"The system's still live here. She's probably just hiding in a bathroom or a closet. The place is pretty big. You sure you looked everywhere?" Shuffling papers sounded from Zach's end. "Maybe she's hiding in a cabinet."

"We were quite thorough before we called you. She's gone, the keys to the exterior lock are gone, and all the exits are unlocked." Ryan leaned against the wall next to the security panel.

"That's impossible. Check under the bed."

"The breaker's tripped." Jay shoved a frustrated index finger toward the secondary bedroom door. "Why is the breaker even accessible?"

"I designed the system to bypass the breaker. It shouldn't matter." Zach swore and they heard more papers flying on the other end of the line. "No one's ever gotten out of there before!"

Which was true. They'd either underestimated Emily or overestimated the system's ability to protect her with such a tempting contract on the line for a host of cash-hungry mercs.

I will not let him kill Emily.

"Didn't you have an emergency backup?" Ryan closed his eyes and shook his head.

Zach went silent for a moment. "Technically, there's still power going to the box."

Sighing, Ryan pulled his hands out of his pockets and shoved them across his chest. "You accounted for overload but not a straight cutoff of the circuit. No warning of any kind? That's a serious flaw, bro."

"I didn't install it; I just built the damn thing. It's not my fault the maintenance team hooked it up to the wrong circuit. There's nothing wrong with my system. It's not my fault!"

"I don't care whose fault it is!" Jay slammed his fist into the wall and growled.

Once more, Emily was gone and he hadn't been able to protect her. Torpedo had been pummeled with a baseball bat and—though the bird couldn't die unless Jay did, though Tor would heal at an unnatural pace—his wing would take far too long to heal for him to help Jay track her down now.

Ryan's eyes slid to his face. "Romeo's out searching and Zach's going over the security tapes. We'll find her. We will." He rested a hand on Jay's forearm, weighing it down so it fell to his side. Zach's comm line went silent, probably muted as he hustled through footage.

The phone at Jay's waist trilled. He blinked at the display, staring at the number. Partner Paws? *Emily!*

He picked up in a rush. "Emily?"

"Jay McLelas?" It wasn't Emily, but the girl's voice was familiar. One of the volunteers, returning his call.

He wracked his brain for her name. "It's Britt, right?"

She confirmed it, and then said, "You were looking for Emily? I overheard Miss Triviona say they were heading to the hospital. But Mr. McLelas, you should know—"

He thanked her and hung up before she finished. Emily

would be at the hospital, and that was all he needed to know. Everything else, he'd figure out on the way.

"He doesn't have her yet," Ryan said, even as Jay broke into motion.

His feet hit every other step on the way down to the first floor, putting on speed at the thought of Emily alone, dying, murdered in some hospital supply closet.

His older brother barked out a laugh. "How about we get to her before that comes up?"

"That was the idea," he snapped, ignoring the fact he'd been thinking out loud again. The thoughts wouldn't stop coming, no matter how much he tried to distract himself.

Ryan punched a string of numbers into his phone and brought it to his ear. "The longer we guess at what Murphy's going to do, the further away he gets. We can still take him down. He's good, but we're better." His free hand chucked Jay on the shoulder as they hit the landing.

"I won't even be able to touch her." A weak smile tried to find his lips and vanished almost as quickly. His hands fisted by his sides.

Ryan shook his head as they pushed through the double doors. "Skin to skin, right? You'll just have to be careful. And I'll back you up at the office."

Assuming Jay got to her in time.

Before they headed opposite directions, Zach broke radio silence. "Hey, guys? We have another problem . . . remember when you said Murphy paid her a visit as Miles Young?"

"He was showing off. That he knew where she worked." Jay already didn't like where the new problem was headed. "Wait. Emily knows who he is now. What possible—"

"Apparently some money changed hands. Money that's now 'missing'."

"I'M LOOKING FOR Julia Meadows. They said she was in the ICU?" Emily's eyes roved over the large waiting room, alert for anyone too attentive to her presence. The bus trip had taken too long, but at least there she hadn't felt alone, hiding in a crowd of commuters. Here, she felt as though every unoccupied corner she turned was going to be hiding a man with a baseball bat.

The pink-clad woman behind the desk slid her finger down a paper listing patients. "They just settled a Meadows in room 271. But visiting hours are restricted to—"

"I'm her sister." She quietly gave her name and shuffled through her purse for her ID, mental explanations already forming. *I'm recently divorced. My maiden name is Meadows.* Almost believable. Except for the part where she and Julia looked nothing alike.

The volunteer raised a skeptical eyebrow, studying what had to be a frantic look on Emily's face, then she ushered her through instead of bothering with questions. Too easy, but slipping through the doorway to see her best friend on the stark white hospital bed had her dismissing caution for overwhelming concern.

"Em," Julia's voice sounded thin and reedy.

Emily yanked a chair to her bedside and grabbed her hand. "I'm so sorry, Julia."

"Mrs. Melanie did good this morning. So did Nutmeg." She lifted her other hand to point at the sparkling ring on a tray next to her bed. "Marco asked me to marry him last night."

Tears jumped to Emily's eyes. *I'm sorry* looped through her head on endless playback. Guilt tromped through her chest, a riot of her own failings.

Julia shifted, her eyes falling closed. "I know what you did, Em. I just wish I knew why."

Huh? Does she know about the vision?

But she didn't get a chance to ask as Julia's hand slipped

from hers and her body went limp on the blanket. Hideous beeping met her ears. A host of nurses filled the room to stabilize Julia, propelling Emily out to the small intensive care's lounge. It felt like she waded through hip-deep water. Tears blurred her line of sight.

"Are you here to finish the job?" a male voice spat.

Her spine straightened like a metal rod and she turned to face Marco's reddened, furious expression.

"How dare you? You have the nerve to put on the sympathy act? You have no right!" He shook a folder stuffed full of papers at her. His fist crunched the manila as he took a single menacing step forward, and small slips of paper fluttered to the waxed floor between them.

"I'm sorry, Marco—" Emily held her ground. This was familiar trouble. This, she could handle. Marco's infamous temper only worsened when he felt like he had the advantage.

"No! You don't get to say sorry. We were your friends, Emily! Julia found you out, you tried to keep her quiet. It's all here!"

Her jaw dropped, her stomach rolling over. More paper fell, scattering around the toes of her pumps. She caught glimpses of dollar signs but didn't dare take a closer look, not when it was clear he expected her to know what it was already, not when he was accusing her of something so despicable.

"I would *never* hurt Julia. Never."

"We have the statements! You're not getting away with it!"

"Statements?" She choked back a sob and held her hands up, surprised when they didn't shake in front of her chest. "What are you talking about, Marco?"

"Like you don't know." His lips twisted into a snarl. "Money, Emily. The half-mil you stole from Partner Paws."

Murphy. Of course he'd take his money back. She hadn't kept her end of the one-sided deal that absolutely had strings;

there would be no payment if she didn't cure his son.

"Marco, stop!" Naomi bolted in to the lounge. "You'll only make it worse."

I'm being framed. Murphy . . . She'd entered a new kind of hell. "I didn't take anything. I swear to you."

"What about my fiancé?" Marco growled and covered the ground to Emily in four fast steps, shoving his index finger in her face. "You gonna fake innocence on that too?"

The phone call, Julia's question about money, the brutal attack in her vision, her name on the thug's lips. *No. Nonono.* Her lungs felt an eighth of their size, squeezing until she was dizzy, a mere sip of air able to pass between suddenly cold lips. "How could you think I'd ever hurt a woman I count close as a sister?"

"We didn't want to believe it, Em. I still don't. But Julia found the papers this morning while she was putting your office back in order. And now she's in there." Tiger-printed heels thudded dully on the thin carpet and Naomi stepped between them, tipping a sad look toward the milling nurses. "The police are on their way . . . if it's a mistake, we'll figure it out, okay?"

She'd been called to the hospital, sure. But not so she could see Julia. So she could be arrested.

Trying to convince them now would never work.

"Naomi, you know me. You know how much I put into Partner Paws, and you know how much I care about all of you. I would never . . . "

Behind them, she caught a glimpse of a man she definitely didn't expect to see, his smile grim. Jay McLelas's eyes gleamed with a sharp ferocity.

"Miss Barton," he greeted, broad shoulders brushing Naomi and Marco easily aside. "I'm glad I caught you. It seems there's been an issue with your accounts. If you'll accompany me to McLelas Financial, we can sort out this misunderstanding."

She stared at him. The grant they were trying to get was through McLelas Financial, but she didn't have any accounts there. A movement down the hallway caught her eye. Two police officers, heading straight for them.

"It's a matter of some urgency." He shifted slightly, blocking her view of the hallway. Blocking their view of her. And then he winked.

Mute, she clenched her fingers around his suit jacket sleeve as he extended his arm. He drew her toward the elevators, Naomi protesting at their heels.

"You can't leave. The cops—"

"Can come see us at my office," he shot over his shoulder, and then they were behind steel, hurtling toward the lower level parking garage. Jay met her stricken look in the elevator door's reflection. "We need to have a chat about your donors."

CHAPTER FIFTEEN

EMILY FOUND HER VOICE by the time they'd reached the parking garage. "Jay," she started. "What just happened?"

"Still happening. Car first. Questions later." He opened the passenger side door to a shiny black BMW parked curbside in the fire zone.

A fortune in metal and precious fuel. Emily's mouth snapped shut. Talk about a completely different stratosphere. People on her planet took public transit. Not cheap, but smarter than maintaining and fueling a personal vehicle. No one she knew even had a car on their radar, though one or two would've loved to take a motorcycle for a spin. She took buses, or her bike if she needed to think. Gas was a commodity for the elite, the politicians, and the city-funded. Or the well-off criminal element.

Ninja had a car too.

Her eyes widened but she obediently ducked inside. Shutting the door behind her, Jay bounded around the front of the vehicle. Emily sank back against the leather seat. It didn't

have the same feel of Ninja's car, but she'd been blindfolded—
She shook her head sharply. What was she doing? Comparing her daytime rescuer with her nighttime one was far from sane.

Then again, running from the cops wasn't either.

Once sealed in the relative privacy of the car, he tipped her a worried look. "You okay?"

She was pretty certain she was shaking. "Are you..." Pausing, she licked lips that felt parched. "Are you helping me run from the police?"

"Were we running? Surely not." His smile didn't reach the usually expressive blue of his eyes as he turned the key in the ignition. "Buckle up."

"Why?"

"Safety. Plus I'll be driving over the speed limit."

She buckled herself in, but he'd answered the wrong question. "No, I mean, this is well beyond the bounds of being our grant officer. And isn't it... illegal?"

"Ah." He eased the car onto the mostly-empty city streets. "You haven't lived in-city long enough to know what happens when someone goes in for police questioning at the behest of a man who wants to keep them there."

Emily's heart thudded dully against her ribcage. She could guess. She'd already learned what happened when a crime boss wanted to keep her, after all. But how did Jay know? How could he *possibly* know? "You mentioned Partner Paws' donors."

"You're being accused of a major theft from a banking institution, of clearing out the Partner Paws' accounts. Specifically, the money that came from a donor. We've talked about him before, remember? Miles Young?"

"Yes..." She twisted the seatbelt between her palms, barely breathing.

"The bank is on his side, those police officers..." He shot her a quick, sympathetic look. "...your friends. All on his side.

Which would be bad enough, if he were just another man with money, like myself or my brothers."

"You can't..." He had to have meant just in terms of money, but she couldn't shake the impression she got from his tone. Like he honestly placed himself in the same class of human being as a man who could frame her for assault and theft. He'd been nothing but helpful since she'd met him. Sweet. Concerned. And now he was rescuing her before she was trapped by Murphy in a different way. She stared at the side of his face, grim determination etched in the tightness of his jaw. "You can't think that. You're nothing alike."

He shrugged. "Money solves—and causes—a lot of problems here."

"Jay. You're not like him."

"I believe you're being framed," he continued. When her breath rushed into the space between them, Jay's hand came up as if he intended to take hers. He dropped it to the gear shift instead. "McLelas Financial, as it happens, is in prime position to address the issue of missing money. Our firm has an excellent team, and they've been called on for things like this before—our forensic accountants. We're going to help."

"Thank you," she managed to stammer. Hope was in a low fizzle in her gut, not able to go far when she knew exactly who Jay would be up against. "But I really don't think that's a good idea."

"It's the only one we've got."

But Emily still had Ninja. She couldn't let Jay and a bunch of accountants go after Murphy. Not when the crime boss had just put her best friend in the hospital, not when he would no doubt have zero issues with taking out a nice guy with money and a coffee obsession.

How did she stop him from taking this on? How did she stop him from getting hurt too?

The car took a tight corner, the tower Jay owned with the rest of his family looming up ahead. He nudged a folder in the center console with his elbow. "Look there."

Inside the folder was a stack of printouts with a lot of numbers, none of which made much sense. "What—"

"The last page," he urged.

She flipped through, the world around them darkening as he pulled the car to a stop beneath a concrete overhang. In the glossy photo she uncovered, the crime boss waved to the camera, an expensive watch on his wrist. At the very bottom of the print was a sticker where someone had handwritten "Murphy Jones".

Emily gasped. Jay knew. And if he knew who Murphy was . . . how much else did he know?

"Like I said, if he were just another wealthy player here in Relek, it'd be one thing. But he's not. Turns out, Mr. Young has another name on the streets. And the police—the ones he hasn't paid off—have been after him for some time. Theft, forgery, drugs, prostitution—they've just never been able to peg him before." In the shadows, his eyes caught like silver. A trick of the light. Still, she was breathless again as Jay leaned over to press the button on her seatbelt. "It might not be a good idea for us to try, but doesn't he sound like someone who should be behind bars instead of you?"

TAKING A WALK around Jay's office while he made a phone call, Emily paused to run her fingers over a pink wooden chew toy on a glass end table. Deep scratches scored the wood and the rope had frayed. She peeked around a curtained corner and caught a glimpse of similar toys, a series of miniature wooden swings suspended from the ceiling, and a tall, wooden perch stand on the floor.

He'd mentioned a bird, but though she surveyed the floor around the perches she didn't see a trace of feathers to betray the species. From the variety of toys, she guessed parrot. Maybe even a macaw. But where was it? She eyed the grooves in the largest perch. *I wonder if it talks.*

"Emily?" Jay beckoned her with a wave, the phone still pressed to his ear. When she drew closer, he held out a steaming mug. "Sorry. This won't take much longer."

"No, it's fine," she whispered, warming her hands on the ceramic. "I don't have anywhere else to go." She caught the flicker of a conflicted set of emotions darting across his face when he angled his head away from her to return to his hushed phone call. *What was that about?* Before she could analyze it further, his office door swung open.

"Okay, we hit paydirt with—aaand he's on the phone." Ryan kicked the door closed behind him and cast his eyes around the room, looking for a place to set down the stack of folders in his arms. "Let's get back to it, Em. He'll catch up."

She pushed the chew toy aside so he could set down the pile. "These are all Partner Paws records?"

"Nope. This," and he shoved a folder into her hands, "is your innocence." Cocking a half-smile at her, he gestured to the couch and flopped down into the seat himself. "The rest are leads. Sit. I'll show you."

After she settled on the couch next to him, Ryan opened the folder to a glossy printout. "You know this woman?"

Blond, straight, shoulder-length locks, a pair of dark sunglasses with rhinestones on the side. The slender woman in the photo stood in front of a bank teller, handing her a card.

She frowned. "I've never seen her before."

"Ann-Marie Bonds. She's the one who ripped off the Partner Paws account this morning. Under your name. McLelas Financial's security—well, you met Zach—he phoned in a tip so some folks would pick her up for fraud."

She nodded slowly. "So that's it, then? She cleaned out the accounts? But what about Julia? Mrs. Bluseau?"

He held up a hand to stall her questions. "One thing at a time. Miss Bonds claims money was wired to her account in exchange for her part in this. Which is where our team comes in." He picked up another folder and flipped it open.

"The..." What had Jay called them? "Forensic accounting?"

"That's right. Our team is working with the police." He held up a hand again at her skeptical expression. "We'll track the funds that were pulled in for Miss Bonds to see where they came from. And we're auditing your personal accounts, as well as the Partner Paws account, to see where all that money went."

"I thought they said it was gone."

"Well, sure. There's 'gone', like cashed out in unmarked bills 'gone', and there's 'gone'—" he pointed at the ledger paper in her hand, "—like redistributed to other accounts 'gone'."

"But this doesn't equal the amount that was taken." Her shoulders sagged. "And they're different companies."

"Companies all owned by the man who donated money to your organization in the first place," he said, a guarded look in his eyes. "Murphy targeted you pretty hard, from the looks of things."

Her spine should have made a cracking sound, she sat up so fast. "So now they can stop him? With this deposit list?"

"Not quite." Ryan rubbed his hands on his knees. "Like you said, the amounts don't match. It took some work just to prove these were the real ledgers, instead of the ones they found planted in your office, your computer, that bank's files. But we're betting men, and they didn't get to our systems. If we keep digging, we'll find the rest of it. The guy keeps his hands clean," he continued, "We can suspect him all we want, but he's got money. The police can't hold him—and keep him there—unless we get the puzzle pieces in a nice little frame for them."

"And as for the attack, your friend will be okay."

She could have kissed Jay for those reassuring words. "Thank you."

He smiled as he slung himself down into a chair across from them. "The police have a composite on the attacker from their descriptions. They're running a search to see if they get any matches on the guy's face. But even he turns up, there's no evidence—real, physical evidence—to then tie Murphy to an assault and attempted murder charge."

Ryan nodded, taking the folder out of Emily's hands and sliding it to the top of the stack.

"What do I do?" Technically, she'd seen the man too; maybe she could identify—*Yeah, because that won't look suspicious at all.*

"Nothing. Let us handle it." Ryan's forehead creased.

Emily stared at the folders. "I need to do something to repay you for your help. I'm no good at sitting still."

A strangled sound came from Jay's throat, dissolving into a fit of coughing. She cocked her head at him in concern.

"Coffee down the wrong pipe, bro?" Ryan grinned at him, waiting until Jay waved for him to continue. Then he turned a more serious look on Emily. "I wouldn't mind help going through records. The tech team can do it, but extra eyes never hurt and Zach's busy unraveling the extra complication of witness testimony."

Jay cleared his throat a final time and rubbed the back of his neck. "Miss Meadows and Mrs. Bluseau both heard their assailant name you. Julia also saw someone taking the false records out of your office, as if you were trying to cover it up. She'd already made phone calls to look into it before he moved in for the attack."

"Murphy's really got it in for me." She forced in a slow count of air. He'd staged everything. The timing made everything look worse. She pitched a look between the two brothers. How could they believe in her innocence when even her closest friends accepted Murphy's setup?

"The biggest thing he's got going for his scheme is how desperate your organization—and you—were for funding." Jay said. "I didn't realize how bad it was."

Emily dropped her gaze to her hands. "I kept it from them. That's why they're not trusting me, it has to be. Naomi, Marco, the others, they knew it was bad but not exactly how little we were working with. Murphy's money had only just cleared. Julia knew. I just . . . I didn't want to let everyone down." Despair felt like a weight on her shoulders as she shook her head. "We had plenty of funding in previous years, public and private grants. We'd been getting more press.

"But a few months ago I stopped boarding out of town, moved into the city. It seemed like just after we doubled our kennel space and took on more staff, our donors dried up. Funds were coming out of my pocket. We were trying other sources—I came here to try to win that grant. I certainly didn't want to take his money." She looked up into blue eyes that crinkled in the corners, eyes filled with concern. "We'd tried everything. He didn't give me a chance to refuse and we were out of—" Her breath caught and Jay's eyes narrowed.

"Options," he finished darkly. "That's what he was doing. Then and now. Cutting off your options."

CHAPTER SIXTEEN

THE REVELATION THAT MURPHY was responsible for her nonprofit's lack of funds in the first place seemed to deflate Emily instantly; her shoulders stooped and she rubbed the back of her bandaged hand over her forehead, wincing as though her skull ached.

"He doesn't want me dead," she said so softly Jay had to strain to hear. "He wants me back."

For a moment, neither he nor Ryan responded to her worried words. They weren't supposed to know how she'd spent her night.

Finally, Ryan cleared his throat. "Back?"

She bit her lip and hunched further into herself. Jay didn't know how to make her feel better, how to say it would work out when, as Klepto, he and his brothers were so tangled in syndicate dealings that stopping Murphy was no longer simple.

He wanted to hold her.

Doing so would make everything infinitely worse.

Every breath he took in his office was filled with his Spirit-mate. The cinnamon and apple warring with coffee was too much, especially when he couldn't haul her close. Not when a mere brush against her skin brought searing pain.

"I best bring Zach some coffee too," he said, standing to leave. Ryan sent him a thunderous look, but he ignored his oldest brother's disapproval.

He wasn't running from her.

He only needed to breathe some air that wasn't laced with everything he couldn't let himself have.

"You and your girl have a fight?" Zach answered his office door with a raised eyebrow. Despite the greeting, he practically inhaled the fresh mug.

Jay moved to sit in a rolling chair. "How are you feeling?"

"I'm fine. And nothing happened to any of us, so it must have been a false alarm." Zach dropped into his own chair and flung himself toward his computer.

"Tor was hurt."

"Which sucks, don't get me wrong." Despite the fact his fingers were still moving across the keyboard, he glanced over. "I just don't get sick over one of our guides taking a hit."

Jay nodded. "You don't get false alarms, either."

"Why are you here, Jay? Really?"

"Any progress with who Shiv might be working for?"

"Not yet, and you're full of shit. Try again. I know it's about her."

"I just needed a minute." He frowned. "I don't know how to do this."

"Be in the same room with a girl? What are you, 15?" Zach's lips twitched. When the jibe met with silence, his brother swung his chair completely around. "Ohh hell, you want to talk again. Go get Ryan. I'm busy."

"Ryan's with Emily." Jay sighed, bracing his arms on his

legs. "I can't hold her like I did last night. She needs to hear everything's going to be fine."

A snort. "Does she now?"

He thumped his knees with his fists. "You haven't seen her, Zach—"

Zach thrust his thumb over one shoulder. One monitor was focused on Jay's office couches. "Next. Come on. I've got places to go, people to see."

Straightening, Jay asked, "Witness testimonies?"

"Yep. Murphy did a number on her, but I want to hear how bad it really is." He gulped at his coffee. "Maybe you should tell her."

"Tell her what?"

"Klepto. You."

Jay gaped at him. He'd expected some taunt about his emotional state but no. Zach, keeper of all secrets until his dying breath, was actually suggesting he tell Emily about their identity? "Just how do you think that's going to go down? Admitting I'm a criminal isn't going to be reassuring."

"Hey, you're the 'criminal' who got her away from Murphy. If you count your Shiv interventions . . . " He shrugged. "It'd show her we know who we're dealing with."

And maybe boost her confidence that they could truly help. From her protests, he knew she thought Klepto the better man for the fight. She should know they were one and the same; Jay fought the pull in his chest wanting that very thing, the part of his thoughts that clamored he'd have to let her know sooner than later, especially with his powers affecting her so strongly.

"She looks at me differently in the daylight." His non-masked identity hadn't broken more than the speed limit in her eyes. She'd never called Klepto "sweet". "I'm not ready to give that up."

"Hey, you're the one in my room looking for some kind of

epic fucking wisdom. You don't want to listen, fine. Just keep pussyfooting around it and get her home before dark." Zach leaned back to mash one more button on his keyboard and the displays changed over to surveillance footage. "I'm out."

NUMBERS SPUN IN her head from all the computer scenarios on Ryan's printouts. By the time the third McLelas brother joined them, the afternoon had worn into evening and Emily felt like they were no closer to Murphy. Zach scooted around a black German shepherd that darted in after him but the animal beat him to their huddle.

"Not tired of them yet?" was the first thing out of the tall security officer's mouth.

Wagging his tail at Ryan, the large dog slid down beside him where he reclined on the floor, surrounded by paper. Ryan rubbed the dog's head even as he directed the animal's gaze to Emily. "This is Romeo. Romeo, give the nice lady a kiss."

She grinned when Romeo obeyed, licking the back of her hand while a happy tail wag wiggled his whole body. "Nice to meet you," she said, scratching behind one prominent ear. He tilted his head and his tongue lolled happily out of his mouth.

Zach wheeled over in Jay's desk chair and rocked back in the seat. He spared a smile for the exchange before all humor seeped from his face. "I spoke with your friend, Naomi. Seems Miles Young—Murphy Jones—had some nasty things to say about you. She seems like a smart woman," he shook his head, "beats me why she'd believe half the crap he fed her."

Emily watched Romeo slide to the floor with a light thud and lay his head on his paws with a dejected sigh. Ryan flicked a strange glance between them, but she was too wrapped up in trying to understand her friend's betrayal to ponder imaginary orange threads. She nodded at Zach. "Such as?"

"My favorite of the bunch? You deal drugs," he began, baring his teeth at her when she sputtered. "Got into trouble with someone with muscle and had to use the cash. You asked Murphy for more money after he donated the lot of it to Partner Paws; he refused. He's also the one who put it in their heads that you'd had Julia whacked for finding out. They found her before . . . " Zach took in a quick breath. "Before the cops got there."

Cigarette-fouled memories ripped through the edges of her mind and her vision flickered, blocking out the rest of his words. Chains. Syringes. Blood. Exhaustion pummeled her body without warning.

Zach snapped forward in the chair and Jay's hand landed on her knee. Concern lit both faces. "Emily?"

"Hmm?" She pressed her bandaged hand to her forehead and willed the daze to leave her head. "Sorry. It's been a long day." *Was the kidnapping just last night?*

"You don't look like you've slept well in a few days, not just this one. Having crazy people set you up for a bank heist can do that to a person," Ryan said, throwing her a grin. "Maybe we should talk about this tomorrow. After you get a nice long nap."

"That's not it." Zach frowned, narrowing his eyes at her. "Headache?"

"Yeah." Today had been too much. Too much of everything. "It's probably food, though."

He still looked doubtful, turning to Jay like he had a different suggestion, but Jay was already on his feet, making a beeline for the kitchenette. She would have laughed if a sound of dismay hadn't come out first. She'd only meant it was probably time to go home and cook a decent meal.

"I didn't mean—There were granola bars," she protested.

"Plus she had coffee," Ryan offered too, raising his voice over the rustling noise Jay made tunneling through the cabinets.

Zach rolled his eyes. "Just because that's all Jay consumes doesn't mean coffee qualifies as food."

She lifted the papers off her lap to scoot out of the chair but Jay appeared in front of her before she could stand. He traded another granola bar for the stack, heading for his desk to drop them off. Her fingers fumbled with the wrapper until Ryan plucked it from her hand and tore the foil for her.

"Thanks." She chomped down on the bar and her stomach rumbled in discontent.

"Don't mention it," Ryan said. "Just doing my brother's girl a favor."

"I hate to break it to you, Ry, but she's not my girl."

Zach chuckled. "Naomi seemed to think so."

Emily rolled her eyes at the ceiling. When she lowered her head to look at them, Zach and Ryan were shaking with silent laughter. "What?"

"I didn't realize they made face paint in that particular shade of pink," Ryan choked out, waving his hand in Jay's direction.

Jay's face had taken on a darker, charming red.

Ryan made a show of stepping forward and taking Emily's free hand in his own. "I should be delighted to escort you to dinner this evening, once he passes out from lack of oxygen." Clearly up to nothing but trouble, Jay's oldest brother brought his lips to the back of her hand even as a sly twinkle sparked in his eyes.

Jay's gaze locked onto her hand, and Emily noted the stiffness in his shoulders with interest. When she pulled her hand away from Ryan, the look met hers for what could have been an accidental moment before landing safely on his desk.

"Please. Ryan'd eat all the food and forget to let you order." Zach stood and offered a hand to take the empty wrapper.

"That was one time!" His protest brought the laugh higher

in her chest but it still didn't break free, only a smile making its way to her lips.

"Meredith," Jay said into the intercom on his desk phone. "Can you put in a call to House of Wok's?" His voice sounded relaxed, but the aggravated ripple of muscle under his suit jacket told a different story.

"The usual?"

"Plus one."

CHAPTER SEVENTEEN

"No, you hold it like this," Jay said, holding up his own chopsticks. "Then you just pinch them together and . . . voila!"

Emily tried to mimic the motion but lost one of her pair and the wooden stick rolled, disappearing over the edge of the coffee table on Ryan's side. Yet another piece of steak bounced off the glass, leaving a soy sauce smudge on the table and a delighted German shepherd at her feet. Romeo stared up for thirds.

Ryan snorted back a laugh. His hand hung in the air, his own sticks loaded with a tangle of noodles. "Haven't we starved her enough today?"

Jay waved him off, grinning. "She'll get it."

"It smells fantastic." Emily stared down at her white and red takeout containers, exaggerating an expression of longing. "Are you *sure* you don't own any forks?"

They all chuckled and Jay pushed himself away from the aromatic Chinese food. "I know how to fix this." he said, snagging a fresh packet of sticks from the table. Heading for his desk, he added, "Be right back."

She heard the rip of paper but couldn't see what Jay was up to. Ryan's hand scratched absently at the dog muzzle that pushed up under his hand to peer over the surface of the table. A heavy paw snaked up toward his egg fried rice.

"Manners," he said, giving the dog a light push.

When he returned, Jay extended a fresh pair of chopsticks to Emily with a sweeping bow. Instead of pulling them apart, he'd wedged a rolled piece of paper between them until they formed a slight "V", then rubberbanded them together so the sticks kept the shape.

Laughing easily now, she accepted the improvised utensil with a flourish and scooped at her dinner to collect a new piece of steak. Balancing it on the prongs, she finally managed a full bite of food. She gave a happy sigh as the salt hit her tongue, and, grabbing up the takeout container, commenced shoveling at her rice.

"See, that wasn't so hard, was it?" Jay grinned and pushed her an eggroll.

Emily smiled around her box, reveling in the camaraderie of family. The bond she shared with Julia had been the closest thing to what the brothers shared, and lately there'd been too much work to spend time letting off steam. If Julia made it through this—and she couldn't believe anything else, nor that their friendship wouldn't survive—she'd have to set up regular girls' nights.

"House of Wok is a regular thing for you guys, huh?" She nodded at the three chopstick pros surrounding the low table.

"Best Chinese in the city," Zach said.

She chuckled.

"What?"

"I never would have imagined three wealthy businessmen sitting down for takeout. The place must make a killing."

"We do tip well. Wouldn't want them going out of business."

Ryan winked. He pushed a piece of chicken off the table with the back of his hand. "Oh, Romeo, I didn't see you there." The dog chomped happily at his free snack then grinned up at his owner with his tongue hanging out of his mouth.

Jay snorted at him. "Smooth." Turning to Emily, he added, "You see what I put up with?"

Quiet chewing commenced but after a few minutes Ryan frowned. He took a final bite. Setting his sticks down, he folded his hands in front of him and leaned forward, forearms on his knees. "So tell me, Emily. How did you cut your hand?"

Time froze like someone had hit pause on the movie of her life. Silence engulfed the low table. Emily could have sworn Jay and Zach glared at their brother. She sighed and poked at a piece of steak in her takeout container. *Should I tell them about the rest of this madness?*

"Something at work?" Jay suggested in a soft tone at the same time Zach cut in with, "Maybe she doesn't want to talk about it."

She had to tell them. Maybe it wouldn't help them pin down Murphy's transgressions, but it'd make her feel less like a deceiver. At the very least it'd help them see exactly who they were up against. The McLelas's—for some reason she was certain now, down to her bones—they were men she could trust. Just like Ninja.

Stop it. Just stop it, Em. They're not superheroes any more than your masked visitor is. All they're doing is helping stop someone from framing you. Yes. That was *all*.

Emily cast a look out the window where dusk had coated the sky beyond McLelas Financial. Was Ninja already waiting for her at the condo; was he finally ready to talk? Frantic that she wasn't there? No. He would have already tracked her down. In fact, he was likely watching from a miniature camera stuffed into her Chinese food. The last weary thought crossed her mind and she made a sound between a giggle and a hiccup.

Emily set the rest of her takeout on the table and forced a new smile at the concerned expressions crossing the brothers' faces. "Murphy," she said. None of them looked surprised.

"What about him?" Ryan prompted again.

This time Emily couldn't mistake the dark look Jay shot him. "It's fine. You're all helping me; I can't just sit here and keep pretending that this isn't my fault. I've got to say something."

"No, you don't." Sliding lightly over her knee, Jay's hand reassured her. Steadied her nerves.

"Murphy has been after me since before he dropped that deposit in my organization's lap. He sent men to my home, my workplace. His thugs left me notes . . . "

The hand on her knee squeezed.

"Last night he kidnapped me. Drugged me. And when I couldn't do what he asked, he strung me up on a wall in a warehouse. Some kind of sick strip club. A few of the women looked pretty happy about being there. Others were high. But—" She shook her head to clear the images. "I cut my hand when I tried to stop him from hurting his son's dog, that's all. I got in the way."

Zach actually looked a little green.

"But you're here now. Safe." Jay's hand stilled.

"Yeah." She flashed him a wry grimace. "But he's so mad I got away that now he's turning my friends against me, making it look like I'm a thief, sending thugs to kill them instead of just coming after me, and paying off police officers to put me in prison. I don't suppose meeting with him would make it better?"

"No, it wouldn't." Jay gave her leg another squeeze and his hand slid away to roll into a fist at his side. "You'd only be putting yourself back into his hands."

"After all our hard work, you're not going through that

again. With Murphy or his dirty cops," Ryan said, a somber pitch to his expression even with the upturned curve of his lips. "Thank you for trusting us, Emily."

She'd never seen any of them look so grim. "I have to trust someone, right?" Confronting the memories of her kidnapping should have rubbed her emotions raw. Instead of feeling exposed, however, she found voicing the events fueled a new well of confidence. Pinched nerves in the center of her forehead relaxed amid the brothers' genuine concern.

"You just have to remind those trusty someones to feed you more substantial meals," Zach said.

And just like that, the middle McLelas brother rolled the topic back to a light, frivolous conversation about favorite—and most disgusting—takeout dishes from a variety of the restaurants Relek City had to offer. A companionable hour passed, Emily's headache faded, and the sky outside Jay's office window turned dark.

Rocking back from the table, Emily set down her chopsticks and smiled. "I really should get home, gentlemen."

"It's been a pleasure, Emily." Zach said. He'd finished eating well before the other two and now looked up from a folder of papers. "I wish it were under better circumstances."

"Back to work already?" She nodded at the stack in his hands.

"I don't think crime sleeps. But on the off-chance it dozes off, I want to be there." His eyes lit with good humor but his gaze followed Ryan and Jay to the kitchenette trashcan where they cleaned up the evening's meal. "Don't worry. We're going to do everything we can to catch this guy."

Jay returned, a ring of keys in hand. "I'll give you a lift home."

In the car, Jay didn't say much. Emily inhaled the strong, masculine aroma of interior leather, directed him to the building where she'd spent the morning, and was stunned to realize just how close it was to his place of business. He escorted her to the door on the second floor of the complex.

She turned back to him, gripping the door before it could shut in his face. Her temples throbbed with a fresh wave of headache. Emily hoped Ninja had left her Tylenol accessible. "Thanks for letting me stay, for letting me help with the numbers this afternoon. I don't know what I would have done holed up in this place all day. Just waiting around for him to come grab me again."

Rooted in place in the hallway, Jay's eyes gave the condo a haphazard onceover. "At least the place looks pretty safe. I don't think he's going to bother you here." His fingers closed around the brass doorknob. "Since you're taking the week off, why don't I pick you up in the morning? You can help us go over more data."

She cocked her head at him and the pain in her temples sloshed like a million grains of sand, abrading her nerves with ribbons of orange. She pressed a hand to her forehead. "More busywork? You sure you won't get more done without me? Maybe you should just loan me a coloring book."

His eyebrows furrowed and the fingers on his left hand twitched. "I'll find something for you to wrestle with. How's eight sound?"

"After the week I've had? Too early. I think I'll sleep for a few days at this rate." A yawn hit her and she managed to throw him a sheepish half-smile. "Case in point."

"Nine, then. I'll be back. And I'll bring coffee."

Coffee. Her heart bounced with the thought as their eyes met, rippling between flaring interest and a sick feeling of helplessness in the face of the dangers that plagued her evenings. Maybe she should have asked to sleep in Jay's office. Ninja's face punched into the foreground of her thoughts and she rested her temple against the doorframe. Jay McLelas. Ninja. Two men. Both cared for her, helping her in vastly different ways.

It wasn't fair.

Jay's voice interrupted her turmoil, bidding her a good night. His hand lifted as if to brush her hair over her ear but he dropped it again to the doorknob. "And, Emily?" He snuck another look into the room.

"I'll be okay." Emily stared at the curve of his fingers, then she met his gaze. The wealth of concern hidden there drew her hand to his forearm. She wished he hadn't backed off, wished he'd have followed through with the apparent impulse to touch her.

How had she gone from office cats and wine to falling for two sexy men—who understood the importance of coffee, no less—in the space of a week?

"You know we're not far away. Two blocks. If you need anything, call me. I don't care if it's just that you're out of eggs."

She nodded and her hand slid from his jacket. Jay gave her a final gut-wrenching smile and tugged the door closed.

MENTALLY, THE ENCOUNTER continued with him pulling her into his arms and kissing her headache away, cradling her against his chest, safe, where she belonged. Heated cinnamon on his lips. He pressed his palm against the door and pushed away. Touching her wasn't an option, no matter who he was at the time. A foot further along the wall, his fingers tripped over a panel, slid it aside, and punched in a code. Jay nodded as the security system kicked in with a hum. She'd be safe now. So long as she didn't figure out some other way to leave. Rolling his shoulders as if that'd shed the anxiety, he headed down to the condo on the ground floor of the building and vowed to return sooner than nine in the morning. But under the darkened armor of night, not the auspicious business suits and offices of the day.

Torpedo was sprawled on the dining room table, Jay's sister-in-law hovering over the bird's wing.

"Hey, stranger," Amanda murmured as she moved to the counter, shoving aside a container of hot cocoa to get to a sadly neglected 4-serving coffeepot. "Is your guest okay?"

"Don't worry about the coffee." At the raised eyebrow he waved her away from the counter. Not only would it be instant—a thought that made his insides rebel—but for once, just once, he actually wanted to experience a longer bout of what he had the night before in the arms of the woman overhead. "I need sleep tonight."

Sleep, nothing more—not even the talk he knew they were due.

Thin blond eyebrow climbing higher, she asked, "Are *you* okay?"

He didn't answer but took her post next to his spirit guide and grasped the edge of his wing with a cautious slide of fingers. Though Tor—like all of the McLelas companions—could heal quickly, Jay still wondered if it'd be necessary to bind it like one would put a sprained arm in a sling.

Emily would know.

The clink of a mug hitting a polished counter sounded behind him. "Ryan said Emily was *with* Tor when he was hurt." The emphasis ruined Amanda's neutral tone.

Jay couldn't blame her for the curiosity, not when his Spirit-mate's existence meant someone with whom she might be able to compare notes. "She saw Murphy's thug hit him with a baseball bat."

"*Yes. Your Spirit-mate was Watching.*" The translation of his owl's softly hooted reply shimmered into Jay's head. Torpedo ruffled his wings and added, "*Do not fret, Watcher.*

Just a bruise."

"What did he say?" she asked, coming up beside him now and dipping a spoon into her mug to stir.

"A lot more than usual." He gave Torpedo a pensive look. They'd been together for years and in the past few days his spirit guide's words had gained clarity, expanding beyond simple danger warnings. Jay sent Amanda a sideways look. "Ever since I met Emily."

A pleased smile. "Visions, a chatty owl . . . anything else changing since you found her?"

He frowned. "Not for me. But Emily . . . she's in pain. I can't touch her. It hurts her."

Amanda's spoon froze in place. "That doesn't sound right. Our gift is hearing. Yours should be sight. The visions make sense, but touch?"

"It's not like Tor's been forthcoming with answers on the subject, either."

"*Don't have any to give.*"

He got a definite mental image of an avian wing-shrug and stared at his spirit guide.

"*You Saw?*" The words translated, and then pictures appeared—one of himself, and one of an owl's eye.

Jay blanched.

"*I'll take that as a yes. Excellent. We'll talk more now.*" Once more with flashes of images thrusting into his head.

"Do you need a chair?"

"I'm fine," Jay said, and then added to Torpedo, "Just not sure I need the visual repartee."

"'Fine.' Uh-huh. You're as bad as your brother," she said dryly.

"*Just need practice. Your Spirit-mate does too.*"

"We're not practicing anything, Tor." He growled and tugged out the metal clip and elastic band holding up his ponytail. "Not until I figure out why she's hurting."

"*She is sensitive*." Instead of imagery that flowed with the sentence this time, they came a beat afterward: people crying, laughing, yelling, cowering in fear.

He passed a hand over his eyes as a headache threatened. "Too much, featherhead. And I don't know what any of it means."

Amanda gave a soft laugh. "Believe me, practicing is the only way you're going to figure the bond out. Whatever Torpedo's up to, things will keep changing. Practice will make things better. Frankly, I wish we'd worked on ours sooner."

He swiped his hand through the air. "It made things better for you and Ry. Pretty obvious things are different for us. And there's literally nothing that says Emily and I improve. Not a damn thing."

"Hmm." She paused, sipping her cocoa with a calculating look in her eyes. "I wouldn't have pegged you as the stubborn one."

"*She is sensitive,*" Torpedo repeated, then vaulted into the air. "*I will Watch until you return.*"

The lock at the front door clicked and Ryan came strolling through the entrance, ducking as Tor skirted the top of his head on the way out. Amanda sidled up to the doorway and Jay made a face, turning to give the couple some privacy.

After a nearly intolerable array of kissy-face noises and a snort from Amanda that said the pair of them were pulling his leg, Ryan cleared his throat. "I'm sorry, Jay."

"For the makeout session?" Jay turned and found a trench coat hurled through the air at his face. He caught it, then the rest of his gear, in quick succession. "Hey, thanks."

"Figured the least I could do was keep you from having to hit the office." His oldest brother rolled his shoulders back and Amanda took his glasses and suit jacket, nodded, then disappeared into a back room. "Dinner . . . Look, I thought she'd throw us some excuse about her hand. None of us had brought it up and it seemed like something someone should have asked about, you know, before she managed to piece something together. Like her realizing we already knew." He paused. "Never in a million years thought she'd tell us the truth. About Murphy, anyway."

Jay growled as he rushed to change. "Give her some credit."

She'd never been anything but transparent. Trusting. He was the one who hadn't yet told Emily what she needed to understand his ability, their connection—much less the real reasons he'd been working with Murphy.

"Oh, I do. She puts up with you, doesn't she?"

"I'm tired of lying to her." Only, with so much between them, where did he even start? Jay tugged on his shirt, jeans, and jacket. With the last button, as if on cue, Ryan's wife returned to scoop up her mug. "You know . . . Zach said I should tell her about us. Klepto."

"He what?" Both Amanda and Ryan stared at him, the latter shaking his head. "You sure he wasn't teasing?"

"He meant it." The mask was on the countertop, and he bunched it under his fingers. Jay hated that he had to hide from Emily. Truth . . . identity . . . heart . . . "I wish it was that easy, that I could just lay everything out for her, but it's not."

"I'll talk to him." Ryan's thunderous expression was soothed only by the way Amanda was tapping her fingers on his arm. "He knows better. You tell Emily everything now and Murphy gets his hands on her despite our efforts, he'll make her talk. You know that."

Jay bit off another growl. "And if I don't tell her, if we screw this up and Murphy gets his hands on her again anyway? Then what?"

"Then he can't torture her for information."

"No, Ry. Then he kills my Spirit-mate and she'll never know."

Silence filled the room. When Ryan spoke again, his voice was low, serious. "We're not just talking about masks right now, are we?"

He was still trying to work out how to answer when a violent clash of images pounded into his skull, too many to isolate. "*Nownownow*!"

"Ow! What the—" Clutching at his ears and swallowing to keep down the earlier eggrolls, he barely registered Ryan and Amanda staring at him with alarm, knew in the back of his mind they hadn't heard or seen any of the horror-laden scenes Tor had thrust into his mind. Jay bolted for the atrium, dashing up the stairs. "Emily!"

Disabling the tighter security took precious seconds, and when her door swung open he spotted her prone, sprawled half on faux stone, half on plush carpet. No blood, no attacker, no flare of orange from her closed eyes, but her muscles clenched so tight he thought she might be locked in a seizure. His owl had draped a wing over one of her feet. Wide, avian eyes swiveled toward him, frantic as the trills coming from his beak.

"Is that what it was like before?" Amanda gasped.

"Emily?" Jay dropped to his knees, scooping her into his lap, careful not to touch her skin even as Ryan checked her pulse. Torpedo followed, and a moment later Romeo was nudging at her other ankle. "No, no, come on."

"Fast, strong, and she's breathing."

"Barely." He shooed both animals from her legs. They gave about an inch apiece. "Knock it off!"

"Call the doc." The order wasn't for him, so Jay continued to helplessly hold his Spirit-mate until Ryan's hand gripped his knee. "Is this Tor? It looks different."

"*Not me*," came an irritated retort. "*Pay attention.*"

"It *is* different. It can't be my touch either. I was careful, Ry. So careful." The infernal noise from his owl's beak stopped and Jay breathed a sigh for the reprieve.

Until there was a muted crash downstairs. Emily began to move in his arms, restless twitches of muscle, pained expressions forcing their way across her face. Like she was trapped in a nightmare.

"Stay with her," Ryan ordered.

As if Jay could do anything else. He pulled his gaze up to see Amanda hanging up her cellphone, crouching in the entryway with a gun drawn. Ryan jogged past her and disappeared, mumbling to Zach about surveillance. Their spirit guides, however . . . dog and owl simply tucked themselves around Emily's feet. Before he could shoo them away again, a mangy-looking, maybe once orange cat careened into his peripheral vision, and he stared as the stray shoved against Emily's thigh. Purring roared from the thin creature and a moment later, his Spirit-mate's eyes opened.

"Jay?" Emily's voice was breathy, weak, but it was her gaze that sent a shock through his veins.

Her eyes weren't glowing orange. They were shot through with it, bizarre neon lines crackling through the hazel like lightning. Thin, shaking fingers reached for his cheek.

Jay reared back before she made the mistake of touching his skin. "Emily, you can't."

She made a tortured sound, her fractured gaze traveling over his chest then bouncing back to his face, and that was when he registered she'd called his name—not Ninja's.

In his rush to get to her, he'd left the mask behind.

"Touch." The single word was hoarse with strain.

"It hurts you," he whispered back.

Another whimper, another attempt to press herself closer. "Help," she pleaded.

"How?" His heart rioted at her pained attempts to speak, thundering in his chest. "Emily, hang on. Just hang on."

Amanda holstered her weapon, dropping into a crouch beside them. "Ask Torpedo what's happening. There's got to be some way the two of you can pull her through this."

He spared a glance at his owl, who'd made a feathery blanket with his wounded wing. "Tell me what we need to do."

"*This.*"

"This what? What do I do?"

"*Nothing she's not.*"

"Nothing?" Incredulous, he glared at Torpedo. "What, are you fucking guessing? Come on, Tor!"

Affronted, his owl snapped his beak with a sharp click and fluffed himself up as if preparing to stalk toward Jay's fingers for a bite. The orange in Emily's eyes pulsed brightly and she struggled for breath, her muscles locking once more.

"No, angel, stay with me." Jay cradled her tighter.

"*Touch,*" Torpedo said, his tone harsh in Jay's head.

Jay shook his head but Emily finally stopped stretching for his face. Instead, she sank her fingers back into the fur by her side. It was almost instant, the way her tension eased at the contact. Not gone but receding, and Jay felt his eyes widen. Touch, yes . . . but not his.

"Okay, that was just bizarre," Ryan was saying as he came through the doorway, and Jay caught sight of a fuzzy tail winding around his ankles. "Some stray knocked over the trash and there's a bunch of them swarming it, but for a minute I could've sworn—"

"That they wanted in?" Jay asked. Quiet certainty filled him as he waited for the second cat to join the huddle. "It's Emily."

"Huh?" Ryan asked, then cursed as he almost tripped over the striped beast who'd snuck in with him.

"The animals, the way my touch hurts—it's Emily."

Scarred over one eye and at least twice the size of the first, the cat parked itself between Jay's knee and Emily's bicep. He held his breath as more purring roared between them. Emily's muscles went lax, her cheek rubbing against his trench coat. Romeo was fur to skin with her too, and when Tor settled in Emily's muscles further.

"She's . . . they're here because of her. For her." Jay blinked down at the collection of creatures, the tormented woman in his arms. "I don't understand how, but whatever's happening to her, they're helping."

Their personal doctor came and went, both stray cats underfoot and vanishing into the streets when he left with bloodwork. Perhaps the animals felt their work was done, though another endless hour passed before Emily roused enough to murmur Jay's name again. Orange eased to paler and paler lines of peach, until the streaks shimmering in her eyes were now an electric white. He hoped that too would disappear, given time.

"I tried to call," she said, pointing into the living room.

He followed the direction her fingers spread. Embedded in the carpet were his business card and her cell phone; they must have fallen when she had. "I'm sorry I wasn't here."

"But you weren't far, were you?" Her palms scrubbed her cheeks and then her head tilted back until she was glaring at him upside-down. "Tell me—" Her whisper caught and she shook her head before trying again. "Tell me you didn't leave just to go around the building and pop in through a window."

Amanda laughed and Emily bolted upright in surprise. Pulling her back to his chest, Jay wrapped his arms around her waist. "It's okay. You're okay."

He let himself breathe with those words, the reassurance he'd offered her seeping into his own pores. *Emily. Emily is okay.* And like this, he could hold her enough that his own nerves were soothed. Not too close. The instinct to kiss the top of her head had to be curbed. He squeezed lightly when her fingers gripped the sleeves of his coat. An interminable night, but she still lived.

Ryan gave a belated introduction as his lieutenant's palms came up. Amanda sent Emily a conspiratorial grin. "Sorry, it's just nice when someone else calls these goons on their antics once in a while." She nodded to her husband. "There's nothing more we can do until those blood tests come back. Why don't we give these two some space for the night?"

"Might be nice to catch up on sleep," Jay agreed, though sleep was now one of the last things on his mind. Emily knew who he was. He knew her well enough to know she would be brimming with questions. Hell, she had a bizarre ability of her own; she wouldn't be alone with those questions.

The others slipped out, leaving only Torpedo behind. The owl burrowed into a set of brown, coordinated pillows on one of the low couches. Settled for the night. Just like he and Emily should be, finally alone, finally out of danger.

"Sleep?" Though her body sank against his, exhaustion lining the cheek she rolled toward his shoulder, Emily gave a soft laugh. "You think I'll let you get away with that, Ninja?"

"Not a chance," he said, chuckling. "But we can talk just as well under a comforter."

CHAPTER EIGHTEEN

WHEN JAY SLID UNDER the covers to join her, his night vision was active, Emily's gaze wide as she took in the more normal, silver glow that signaled his ability. "Not just a reflection."

He shook his head. "No."

She raised a thin eyebrow, her gaze roving over the trench coat he still wore. "That can't be comfortable."

Smiling, he slid his arm beneath her pillow. His grin widened as she snuggled into the crook of his shoulder. "Less skin for you to accidentally brush against in your sleep."

She nibbled on her bottom lip for a moment, then froze mid-bite, glancing up as if she felt him staring at her mouth in the darkness. Longing for it under his own. "So it's not just me, then? When we touch?"

"Whatever's happening when I touch you, it's not happening to me. The only pain I feel is knowing that our being skin to skin hurts you."

"It wasn't a problem last night," she whispered.

"I know. Something changed." Attempting to soothe them

both, he moved his hand in a slow circle, the thin cotton sheet between his fingers and the silk of her arm. No tension rode her face, not yet. Good. Sheets were safe, too. "Maybe it's a mystery best left for morning."

"After coffee?" She leaned up on her elbow with a tired grin. "Be honest, were you bringing me the goods from your personal coffee bar in a coffee shop cup?"

"Like I would've left to fetch the only decent brew in town while Shiv was watching you." He slid a look down her form as she shuddered. "You're taking this well."

"Kind of like the lot of you took my kidnapping story in stride during dinner?" Patting his chest when he stirred, she continued, "It made me feel better to talk about it . . . but you all already knew about Murphy. Not one of you was surprised; no one took it as a joke. I would have. Chained to a wall by a crime boss who thinks I can work magic?" She scoffed. "I should've kept going and brought up the visions too."

Only, now that she brought it up, he had to wonder. Emily might not be able to heal the man's son, but she was clearly capable of something beyond normal human capability.

She wasn't done. "There was more than one Ninja—I saw him this morning. Was that Zach? Ryan?"

"Ryan."

"And why else would a grant officer jump to the rescue of a woman he barely knows?" Her eyes twinkled for a moment. "You had me literally running from the cops, Jay. My legs aren't as long as yours."

He shrugged. "Prison was an immediate concern."

"Right. Because Murphy had paid them off. Are you starting to see yet why this isn't that shocking, in the grand scheme of the past few weeks of my life?" Her chin tipped up, his eyes tracing the contours of a face he'd rather memorize with his fingertips, his lips. "I wanted you to kiss me tonight. You, Jay.

What does that tell you?"

"Emily." The voice that emerged was gravelly enough to have been behind the mask. God, what he wanted with her... "We can't."

Emily sighed, the sound so frustrated he smiled. "Because you're worried about touching me?"

"That, and because this," he gestured between them, "is terrifying." Lifting a hand to smooth away the frown that dug grooves in her skin, he held it there, immobile, unable to touch, unwilling to cause her pain.

A muffled sound of protest came from his Spirit-mate, and she grabbed the wrist of his trench coat. "Me knowing?"

"Everything we *don't* know." How his ability would yet shape her. The way she'd connected to the animals a mere hour before. A madman even now seeking her doorstep.

And yes, what would happen when she overcame the shocks of the evening and finally put together the part where the removal of his mask meant her daytime and nighttime rescuers were one and the same brand of criminal. He didn't want to lose her. With the mystery of their intertwined abilities there was still time to keep her close, but what happened after? What happened when he ran out of excuses? When she walked away?

Emily quieted and let him hold her for such a long, silent stretch of time he wondered if she'd fallen asleep.

"Tell me about your eyes. How you met Torpedo. Something like that."

He shifted so he could meet her drowsy gaze, the hazel of her eyes now half-hooded. "You want me to give you stories?"

"I want you to give me truth. Something you *do* know."

"Even if it sounds like fiction?"

She went up on one elbow, short edges of red-brown hair draping along her jaw. "I feel your emotions in my head, and I'm having visions. I'm already part of your truth, whether you like it or not, Jay. And I think at this point, I can handle a little stranger-than-fiction. So. Your eyes, or Torpedo? What's it going to be?"

Wonder was a strange creature that prowled through Jay's veins, cautious, too cautious to be hopeful. Of all the things they needed to talk about, this was probably the easiest. "Both. Okay. I get my eyesight from Torpedo. He's bound to me through a ritual I went through when I was a kid. A spirit search. And I can see in the dark because . . . well. He can see in the dark."

"And the visions?"

"Those are new." He paused. "We're . . . seeing through Tor's eyes, Emily."

She nodded slowly. "I thought it might be something like that."

He blew out a harsh breath. "In your apartment, when I couldn't see, I said it was genetic. It comes from my heritage. The spirit search bound us together and over time, Torpedo has been able to share that particular ability with me."

"Has he shared it with anyone else?"

Jay frowned, suspecting her line of questioning was going to a more complicated place than storytime. "We're the lucky ones. But it's getting late, and you asked me how I met Tor."

Her lips pursed, but she nodded.

"The week before my thirteenth birthday, my mother took me to the Weaver. The shaman for her people. He drove me out to the countryside." Jay shrugged a shoulder. "Gas was cheaper back then."

Emily cocked her head. "I remember; we'd gotten permits to switch our farm equipment to solar."

She'd grown up on a farm? The juicy mention of her past almost had him stopping to ask for more, but she must've assumed his pause was because of the interruption because she apologized and motioned for him to continue.

"He drove me right up to this cornfield. A corn maze. I don't know if you've ever seen one, but it was this massive, towering green thing . . . " He heard a noise suspiciously like a giggle from her side of the bed. "Hey, I was short then. Scrawny. Everything was taller than me and those stalks were like something out of a Grimm's Fairy Tale."

She'd pressed her lips together, but the laugh escaped anyway. "Sorry. I can see the field, maybe a city boy terrified of corn stalks, but you, short and gangly? No way."

He flashed a grin, then focused on the past. "The spirit search had one rule: don't come home until you're done. I'd known some people who had gone through it before me—"

"Your brothers?"

He raised an eyebrow at her, though he wasn't certain she'd see.

"I'm sorry. It's just . . . You have a lot of secrets, Jay."

"You have no idea, angel." Even so, she curled into his side when he continued his story. "Some came out with animals, some came out with . . . other things. And going in, I knew I wasn't going to come out without an animal of my own. A wolf, for sure, because that would've been badass."

They both chuckled.

"The Weaver looked at me, pointed at the field and went: Go. See." The last part he said in an even deeper voice than he normally used for Klepto, and couldn't help the feeling of satisfaction when Emily's smile grew.

"So I walked through the corn. It grew dark, and the field opened up into a forest. And then it got darker. I'd never known things could get that dark until then." He stared at the ceiling, seeing the woods from that night clearly in his mind.

"Always lights in the city. But there, through the tops of the trees, I could actually see stars. A cloud had gone over the moon, so . . . " He shook his head. "Anyway. I got tired after a while. Sat down next to a tree, thinking—oh, they wouldn't send me anywhere dangerous. I fell asleep, and when I woke up, it was to the sound of a baby crying. At least. I thought it was a baby."

The horrible wailing of the wind was easy to remember, how it continued into louder, closer howling. "I started walking toward it; I wanted to do something to help. And then I heard growling, too. This awful, awful scream."

Glancing down at her, Jay watched her hands flex and wished he dared hold one of them in his own. "I didn't know what to think. Cougars, maybe. Or a woman had been attacked, and her baby was in danger too. I ran forward—because I was an idiot."

She laughed again but he slid upward on the bed, staring at his palms instead of the woman by his side. "The cloud must have moved out from in front of the moon or something, because suddenly the light hit the woods in front of me just so . . . and there was a massive wolf and an owl, tearing at each other." The wolf had had the bird between its jaws, the owl's beak ripping at the canine's eyes and shredding his neck with frantic claws. "The sight was horrifying. The sound was even worse. But I kept hearing that crying . . . and I turned . . . "

There'd been a pile of feathers. He'd gotten close enough to discover the body of a large barred owl broken and prone at the base of a tree. Bad enough, but then, there'd been movement under the large wing.

"I saw him, a bundle of nothing but down. And past him . . . eyes. In the darkness. A dozen of them. I didn't stop to think—I just grabbed him up. He fit in my palm back then, just this little ball of fuzz. He stopped crying when I picked him up, looked me right in the eyes. When I looked up, the rest of the pack was coming closer. So I backed up, tripped over a tree root, landed on my ass."

A soft sound of dismay.

"Wolf bait, right?" He smiled wryly, still staring at his palms, still seeing the past repeat itself in his mind. "I tucked him into my coat and as soon as I did, the screaming stopped. This massive cloud started going over the moon and wolves were closing in on us . . . and then all of a sudden, they turned, and walked away. I knew then my spirit animal wasn't a wolf, but that tiny dust-mite in my right jacket pocket. We sat there until daybreak, and then I walked right out of that maze and got another silent ride back home."

"You should've seen my mother's face when she saw him. She was so—so . . . " His voice caught. She'd been . . . proud. Owls were wise, protective of their families and had good sense, she'd told him, and then she'd told him his brothers would need that.

If she'd only known then the path he'd take for flesh and blood.

Emily tugged at his arm. "You don't have to keep going if you don't want to."

He shook his head, trying to shake the tears from his throat. "It's one of the last memories I have of her. I'm . . . glad it's a happy one."

She tugged at his arm and he let her slip underneath it, his arm draping over her neck. Emily hugged one of her hands around his knee, the other around his back. "I'm sorry."

"There was a fire. Arson. Not long after." He hung his head. "It took the whole block, the whole community."

He gave her a sideways glance after they'd sat in silence for a moment. Her mouth had dropped open. He felt her give a little shake. "What about your father? Was he . . . was he home?"

"He lived in the city . . . " He would have left it at that, but she was staring at him with eyes as round as Torpedo's and twice as piercing. "Heart attack."

"Oh, Jay," she said.

"It didn't happen all that long ago, but he was distant when Mom passed. Ryan did a lot to keep us together. Sane. Safe." He squeezed his arm around her. "Emily?"

"Yes?"

"We should probably consider sleep."

Long lashes folded over her eyes and swept upward again, something haunting in her gaze that he couldn't read. "You'll stay this time?"

"Yeah." *As long as you'll keep me.*

They slid further under the covers and he cradled her tighter, over-cautious where her bare skin was concerned. He was nearly down for the count, had thought Emily there too, when he heard her drowsy voice say, "Next time you can tell me how he got his name . . . "

EMILY ADMIRED THE picture he made after breakfast, a blessed thermos in hand, blue suit and . . . "Sneakers?"

He followed her look and his grin was positively boyish. "Don't tell my brothers. Ryan's all about appearances, and Zach's ensemble? Phew. Talk about prissy."

She laughed. "They were both a lot to take in at first."

"Better after dinner yesterday?"

"Less imposing, more . . . trouble. It was nice; I didn't have siblings to joke with like you do. Julia's the closest thing I have." Her voice almost failed her, but he pressed a hand to the sleeve of her blouse.

"She'll be okay." He sent those reassuring blues over her and something inside her settled. "The sneakers help some people let their guard down a bit around me. Good for running around, too. I've got a couple of HR appointments today and I'm taking a shift downstairs."

Her hands tightened around her still-steaming mug. "Is

there anything I can do? More numbers?"

Even if the files they'd worked on yesterday made an appearance in her new ivory tower, Emily wasn't sure she wanted to work on them. But there were notebooks among the things he'd packed up; she could always dig them out and get to work on a new guide for Partner Paws.

He shook his head. "You might be trapped in a fortress while folks work on proving your innocence, but it doesn't mean you have to stop helping the people and animals you so obviously care for."

"I don't think any of them will want to talk to me right now." The memory of Marco's accusations, the anger on boil under his skin, Naomi's betrayal—she wasn't ready to face them, even by phone.

"Not all do. But Zach's visit helped." He held out a hand and she moved into his embrace so smoothly it was as if they'd done it all along. "I know it won't be the same, from here. But the video conference should give you a bit of the outside."

The monitors, as well as a mounted camera, stood in place of one of the couches, a projector balanced on the middle cushion of the other, a laptop perched on a tiny glass table. How had she slept through this? "You know when I asked you to stay until morning I meant with me. In bed."

His chest bounced under her ear as he laughed and Emily had no other words to counter the thoughtfulness behind what he'd done to the living room. Despite wanting her tucked away safe and sound and being loath to have her out of his sight, here Jay was, trying to find a way to prevent her from feeling locked in. She'd have familiar faces—if he was right and they wanted to see her—and she'd be able to keep working toward her patient's graduation goals, without stewing over her whole blasted situation.

Her fingertips twitched slightly where they'd burrowed into

Jay's jacket. "Every morning, work or not, I'd go in and see everyone, clean cages, check on how each animal was doing."

"And you will do so again. Soon." He spun the equipment up.

Maybe it was a good thing for now. She didn't know what the orange threads were capable of, and now that it seemed to take a more active role in her head, she didn't want to wind up having an episode and suffocating to death in a literal dogpile at the clinic.

Soon Britt appeared larger than life on the center screen. Bubbly as always and looking unfazed by the drama engulfing the situation, she grinned a toothy grin and popped two thumbs up at the youngest McLelas, then at Emily. "Hey, boss."

It didn't take long to bury the questions in her head under business as usual. Working with them over the conference line wasn't the same as working in person, but she'd known this round of students for some time and the animals even longer. She had to be a little more creative with commands, and with the software, as she had to make sure her hand signals and facial expressions could be seen at all times.

It wasn't an experience she wanted in any degree of permanence. Face to face it might have been, but it wasn't up close and personal. The energy was different. She'd have made more progress if she wasn't cooped up and hiding from a maniac.

Still, she was proud of her students and happy that there was indeed progress. They'd be that much more prepared when graduation day came around and they were sent off on their own with the animals they'd trained. Partner Paws would be quieter for a time, until she was able to take on more service animals—and more furry, fuzzy, and feathered things for rehab.

If they could afford it.

Her stomach churned over the fact they were now more

than unfunded for the fourth year of service. It remained that way until Jay came to get her for lunch. Then it simply revolted.

ZACH CAME PLOWING through Jay's office doorway, a tablet in hand.

"Morgue reports," he announced, and for once the only one with Jay was Ryan so the abrupt intrusion wasn't unwelcome, "from some of the women Murphy was keeping."

"Morgue?" Ryan asked, sliding a stack of financial statements to one side of Jay's desk and claiming the screen full of hacked data for himself. "I thought they all recovered from the warehouse—at least the drugs."

Zach blew out a rough breath. "Withdrawal with this stuff had an extended window."

All airflow to Jay's lungs stopped. Those women had been dosed with the same thing Emily had. They'd died from it.

"So it's not your standard street drug," Ryan was saying. "Something new killed them."

Killed them.

"Designer," Zach confirmed. "Autopsy says trace amounts of it were found in their systems—along with other things that should have been long gone from their bloodstream. It'll take a little while longer for them to get around to an ID on the full composition but I think we're dealing with free samples from the shipment we've been waiting on. I'm having the doc run Em's blood samples against these, but I'm pretty sure—"

"Zach." Jay cut in, feeling dazed.

"Hmm?" His brothers both glanced over at him, and Ryan immediately gave his wrist a quick squeeze. "Easy. She's okay. He was about to say she's out of the woods. Look at the report."

Zach smacked the tablet down in front of him with an emphasis that made them all wince. "Those girls died from seizures yesterday afternoon. What Emily went down with last night . . . same M.O."

Except Emily was alive. A thrum of joy struck him, but it was too quickly tainted by the fact that others hadn't been so lucky. There was more, too, a bigger problem his brothers weren't seeing, clinging to his insides like tar.

Ryan snorted. "In that she collapsed. I'm gonna go out on a limb and say what happened wasn't standard. Or did their police escorts note an uptick in the stray population too?"

"Worsening headaches, then an attack to their nervous system," Zach explained with a roll of his eyes. "Jay. Are you listening? She's fine. I mean, we'll keep an eye on her but I'm telling you, she's going to continue to be fine."

He tried to smile.

Ryan reached for his arm again but Jay shook him off.

"She called those animals to her," he finally said, "intentionally or not. They kept her with us. Her ability—whatever she's doing—it's the only reason she's still breathing from this drug. The new drug. The one we're no longer on the inside to stop."

Because he'd wrecked everything, taking her from Murphy. He couldn't let himself regret that. But they all had to deal with the consequences. Both of his brothers turned grim as he met their gazes, following his thoughts to their conclusion before he voiced them.

"What happens if we fail to keep it off the streets?" Jay asked. "What happens if this drug, that kills people when they stop taking it—after one dose—gets out there?"

CHAPTER NINETEEN

IF SHIV DISCOVERED SHE'D survived the withdrawal, would he come for her? Emily wasn't sure if she'd be able to keep down spaghetti, not with the news Jay had brought over during the day sitting so heavily in her gut. Still, by the time the sun had begun to work its way out of the sky, she'd wrapped up a session with the volunteers regarding the upcoming graduation plans and the sauce he was concocting in the kitchen filled the air with a heavenly tomato and basil aroma.

He sent her a glimmer of a smile as she came out of the bedroom, changed into a more comfortable tank-top and jeans. But like that afternoon, she had the impression that the whole planet sat on his shoulders. She hopped into a stool that slid under the bar side of the kitchen counter.

Fancy. Everything about the condo was fancy and spacious and absolutely made sense, now that she had the key to Ninja's identity. "How much of this city do you own?"

"Not enough to save it." He stirred the sauce hard enough to make it splash over the side, a streak of red across the stovetop that gave a violent sizzle.

She reached through the light steam and grabbed the handle of the spoon. Just under his hand. Close enough to touch but still too far away. Blue-gray eyes that went silver by moonlight locked with hers. "Set it to simmer."

A minute later she had her arms around his waist and her cheek to his chest, his embrace suffusing her with now-familiar warmth.

"What's wrong, Jay?" This couldn't still be about the morgue files. "Did something happen with the accounting trace?"

He let out a sigh and one hand slid to the center of her back. "No. We're in over our heads in other ways, though." His fingers continued up until he lifted his hand to lightly tap the ends of her hair.

It didn't hurt, and she grinned. Her heart did a strange hop at the way a smile battled for control over his lips. "I'm a good listener."

The smile gave up and disappointment quashed the tender emotion that had been building in her chest.

"I know," he said, and his gaze darted over her face. "I want to solve something else tonight."

She leaned into him, and this time the smile came back. Weak, but it stayed. A victory. She'd take it, however slim.

"Close your eyes, Emily." A commanding whisper.

Ah. Good. He wanted to solve the same thing. Her eyes slid closed. The array of threads in her mind brightened as if they'd been waiting for her call.

He set his hands on her waist, even now not daring to brush her bare skin. It chafed. Until they solved this mystery, Jay would never touch her where she needed him to. "What is it you see, angel?"

"I see . . . lines. They're orange . . . like a massive bicycle wheel with me in the center of all the spokes."

"You said you could feel me. Can you feel Tor, too?"

"Yes. And there's more . . . " Dozens of threads shimmered in her mind's eye. "I can't tell who—"

"Focus on just us for now."

It was easy enough to isolate the two strongest lines in her head. They blazed, Jay's a tether that seemed to pulse with life and spin as though a whirlwind of emotions would be found within, Torpedo's steady and seemingly enduring as the other strands in her head—just stronger. In her mind, she reached for the safer of the two, touching it carefully, imagining she were stroking a feather.

The owl, who'd been perching on a stand Amanda left earlier that day, let out a hoot that cackled in her ears like laughter. "*Good. You learn fast.*" Along with the translation, which was shocking enough, Emily caught images. A gold star coalesced in her head, then rapid and forceful as punches images of her, a stack of library books, a dizzying swoop through a pocket of clouds. Both she and Jay gasped.

His hands tightened on her shoulders. "Tor, what the hell?"

"You saw that too? Did you hear . . . " She turned too quickly, on the verge of opening her eyes to stare at Torpedo when Jay's pinkie caught on her sleeve. He cursed and pulled away but it was too late. The thread in her mind spasmed. A jolt of confused energy pushed its way toward the center of the web—her. Knees buckling, Emily felt a strong arm wrap around her midsection.

"Okay. That's enough for today."

"No," she murmured, letting him take her weight. She'd seen the reaction in her head, identified the timing, and they already knew the cause. "I saw it move. There's something to work with now. Let me figure this out."

"It hurt you."

"And it will continue to do so, if you don't give me a chance to practice. I touched your owl's thread, and he felt it. I bet I can do the same to yours."

He sighed, but shifted so his arms cradled her, one smoothing over the hair on the back of her head. As she studied the threads in her mind from different angles, she nuzzled into his chest, her nose against the soft cotton of his t-shirt and the star-washed scent of him that made her whole body smile. The communication through imagery was something new to contemplate, but it came with her connection to Torpedo and though shocking, it wasn't painful. Nor did it threaten her ability to stay on her feet. She tried to focus on the man with her instead, the puzzle of how to stop his emotions from breaking through.

Lost in thought, she plucked at Ninja's thread like the string of a harp.

His next breath went in with a hiss.

Her eyelids popped open. "I'm so sorry!"

"I'm fine, Emily."

"I should've been more careful. Let me try something else."

She reached up to caress his cheek, his jaw tight from the jarring lance of her ability. This time, he didn't pull away. A flare of acceptance coursed between them. She watched it smooth over the thread, back and forth as if the emotion were shared. A tender stroke against her mind.

Nice as it was, she shook her head. "There has to be a way to shield—"

An idea struck like she'd downed a sludgy mug of convenience store coffee, a jolt that made her heart riot. Maybe she could build one. A shield. Something that would prevent her from absorbing his emotions. Let them roll off, like . . . rainwater. He was saying something but she didn't hear, building her mental umbrella over the center point of the threads.

"Kiss me," she blurted out when she'd finished her mental exercise, and met eyes that whirled between silver, gray, and blue, as if he'd been using his night vision.

"Emily."

"Do it. Please."

Lips pressed to hers and she shut her eyes. Monitoring inwardly, she watched the center of the threads sparkle with desire—hers. His surge of emotions coursed down the strange tie between them. Jay's emotions, however, were not the stuff of a light drizzle. The umbrella snapped inward, her mind drenched in moments with a flood of want that matched her own and threatened to overtake it.

Emily shoved away. "Oh."

"It happened again." He stepped back from her, yanking at the decadently long ends of his hair.

"Trust me, that didn't hurt. At all." Her skin still tingled from the torrent of need. "It just . . . wasn't me."

"I don't know how to keep from—"

"This isn't on you," she protested. Emily caught a finger in one of his belt loops, refusing to let him retreat further as she explained what she'd tried to do, how it had felt. "I just have to come up with something stronger."

Maybe not an umbrella. Something she could build, and safely forget about over time—because she had no intention of kissing this man and being stuck in her head, successfully blocking his emotions yet unable to enjoy the moon and coffee taste of him.

There had to be a way.

"Bricks," he suggested, and the expectant look in his eyes told her he had begun to believe there might be a chance.

Emily bricked up the path between them and then pulled his head down for another kiss before he could think to reject her. It was dizzying this time, easy to fall into his embrace, heady euphoria seeping into her body until the room went fuzzy. She hummed into the kiss and felt him smile against her lips. His tongue dipped achingly slow into the corner of her mouth and she parted for him.

More.

She wanted more, and when she closed her eyes to see the strands, she could tell he did as well. Except that unruly burst of energy wasn't reaching her mind. The only thing she'd need to rely on in this kiss, this kiss that continued until every inch of her skin tingled, was what any other woman would—a healthy dose of her own lust and body language. And right now, her body wanted all of his.

"We can't." He drew back when she wrapped her arms around his neck.

The rejection was disappointing and happened too soon for her to let go. Whatever concentration she'd held onto to keep the bricks in place shattered; she was once more awash in the full force of emotions: Fear, guilt, frustration, sadness. Not desire, not anymore. Desire hadn't hurt, but these emotions were like a sledgehammer. She couldn't catch her breath, and he hurried to put fabric between them as he sank to the floor with her. The emotional intrusion eased, but it wasn't instant, and she guessed it had something to do with his internal war literally sliding into her head.

"Better that time," she said.

"No more kissing, Emily. Not until we solve this."

"I was able to block it for a little while. And figure some of it out." She smiled up at the concern on his face. Her finger traced the soft collar of his t-shirt. "When you're worried, when you're upset—that's when it hurts."

He closed his eyes and after a long moment, carried her to the table. Over a dinner they both barely touched, they talked about work. Things that mattered but didn't seep into the harsher places in their reality. But come bedtime, he held her so tightly she was worried about the things rolling around in his head.

"Hey," Emily said, her arms tangled in sheets and curving around him. "Whatever's eating you . . . I know you won't tell me, but would it help to go talk things over with your brothers?"

He made a sound of irritation and nudged the top of her head with his chin. "There's so much we need to figure out. I feel like we're running out of time."

"For what? Us? Jay, I'm not going anywhere."

"And anyway, even if I wanted to bother them, I can't." Eyes that were blindingly bright, a core of steel. "It's Ryan's turn to skulk about in a mask. Contract's eased up but it's still live so he can't have any distractions."

"What about Zach?"

"If I come back to the office tonight he'll rig every piece of tech I own to play showtunes every twenty minutes."

"He wouldn't."

"He keeps his promises."

"That's horrible," she said, giggling. "So going to them is out." Coiling a strand of his hair around one of her fingers, she tugged. "Be here then, with me."

His muscles relaxed, her body able to sink into his; he'd been more keyed up than she'd realized. Not a peep of protest when she moved to knead his shoulders. It took time, but eventually the man beside her nuzzled the top of her head again, his rigid embrace going slack, his pulse slow and steady under her ear.

JAY'S DAYS AND nights with Emily coincided for another increasingly comfortable week; him digging into Murphy's accounts and dredging through every tiny sliver of intel they could scoop up to nail the drug deal, her teaching students remotely, working out of the makeshift conference room. Both working on control between themselves and Torpedo—emotions and visions alike.

It seemed her pain was lessening in leaps and bounds so though they hadn't yet had sex again, there'd been plenty of time for other exploration. Dragging her into his arms, dipping between the sultry cinnamon of her lips, her hands cruising over his sides and tiny fingernails biting just-so. It was no longer a question of if, but when.

This one run, and then he'd go home to a warm bed and a willing woman. Who'd hopefully still be willing, after he told her the truth behind their bond.

"What's got your big boy panties in a twist? She's safe." Zach spun in his chair, watching Jay don his trench coat. "Not security again?"

"Not that I doubt your repair skills or anything." Jay frowned and buckled the heavy belt around his waist.

His brother reclined, folding his hands at the nape of his neck. "Oh, come on. It was one time! And it's not my fault she got creative."

"Creative? She used common sense. And your OCD tendencies against you."

Zach's smile turned rueful. "She can't do it again. Promise. But if that's not it, then—"

"She goes back to work soon. In person. Graduation." He sighed, hating that he couldn't keep her in the two places he knew best. Neither could he clip his Spirit-mate's wings. "I'm telling her tonight."

His brother straightened. "How much?"

Jay tugged at his mask. "She has to know everything, Zach, not just the bits of my ability that suit me."

"Oh. The Spirit-mate thing. Right. So not the whole 'love' issue, then?"

"Don't go there." He was certain he was long gone over Emily, but there were too many things standing in the way for a declaration like that to ever mean what he'd want it to mean. Forever wasn't in their cards. Only right now, and getting her through this insanity with Murphy. Dropping into the chair next to his brother, Jay toyed with a tiny gadget Zach had left half-assembled. "Emily and I need to sort out this thing between us. I have no idea how she feels—"

"No idea—What the hell have you been sorting out the past few weeks?" Zach flipped a switch on the console and grabbed a set of headphones. "Get out of here, idiot. Get the data, get home to your girl. Promise I won't listen in on any touchy-feely shit."

Jay shoved the chair back and headed for the window.

"Ah. Jay?"

"Yeah?" He looked back over his shoulder.

"Keep your exits clear."

A tinge of green bled into the skin of Zach's face, and Jay hesitated.

"Go." His brother waved him out, then pointed to a bottle of pills on the desk. "I've got it handled."

Jay frowned, but he left, making his way upstairs to his office window and jumping to the neighboring roof. The condo was two blocks over—a short rooftop jog away—but he had other places to go first tonight. There hadn't been activity in days, not from Murphy's contracts, not from the usual dealers. What could possibly happen in the next twenty-four hours that Zach's sense of trouble had him back to popping pain meds?

"I better not see you 'til sunrise," a voice pitched low in his ear as Jay landed on the last fire escape before the downtrodden office building he needed to case.

"What happened to radio silence?"

"I had something else to say." Zach coughed. "Okay, okay, I'm gone."

The line went dead.

Jay's eyesight glazed.

Hovering outside a curtained window, his wings beat against the glass. His vision self shone back in the glass, orange eyes beaming in the reflection.

Torpedo? What's wrong?

The alley experience had been completely different. This time, Jay maintained some semblance of control over his new limbs.

"Watcher, you must hurry." *The owl-words resounded in his mind instead of his ears.*

What are you showing me?

Torpedo-Jay reeled back and a wide-screen view of their condo claimed the vision.

"Jay! Breach!" Zach. Reality returned with a flame of anxiety. "We're suiting up, Amanda's on her way back. Watch yourself."

Metal railing cut through his gloves where he had gripped the fire escape. Thank God the vision hadn't hit while he'd been airborne and unable to see his landing.

He didn't bother razzing his brother about security on the way; a litany of curses over the open line told him Zach was doing just fine in that department all on his own. It took an eternity to reach her. He leapt down and sprinted for the atrium doors, Torpedo darting around his shoulders. His lungs seemed to shrink as he spotted the wide-open entrance to her condo. Pulling out his pistol, he dodged inside.

Please be here. Please be alive.

A warning bubbled at the edges of his fear. Her touch, somehow, an unknown distance between them.

Emily.

Torpedo aimed for the bedroom and Jay nodded. Faint light glowed under and around the sides of the door. He pushed it open with his foot and swung the gun toward the bed.

"Do you know how many knives I can buy with fifty million dollars?" Shiv tightened the silver blade he held to Emily's throat. She looked paler than the stark white comforter and her clothes were torn. "I'd never again have to sharpen a blade."

A thin red line slid into Jay's enhanced sight, beading along the weapon's edge. Protective rage erupted in his chest, screaming and ripping at him to tear her away from the murderous bastard who draped around her like a lover.

CHAPTER TWENTY

Torpedo clung to Jay's shoulder, throwing a shadow on the wall that reminded Emily of an avenging angel.

How was he here? She'd failed to reach Torpedo, failed to sound an alarm. All their practice, and forming the threads wound up impossible under the crushing influence of terror.

Maybe he and his brothers had bugged the new place too.

"Release her. Now," he said, growling behind the mask. "Or I will kill you."

"We both know you'll try that anyway." The man at her back laughed, a high-pitched, hysterical sound as he tightened his grip. Nodding, he added, "That hunting creature of yours so much as flaps in my direction and she's dead before you pull the trigger. She's a special commodity, Klepto. I'd hate to waste her. But there are always other jobs, and I do so enjoy inflicting death."

Emily froze under the blade. The stench of tobacco smothered her, dipping her thoughts toward chaos. She'd missed her only opportunity to scream a quarter of an hour before. She'd been in the condo alone all day. There was no warning that he'd gotten in, and he'd waited to strike until after she'd slipped into her pajamas. Even now, trapped in his slimy grip, her insides lurched at the thought of him watching her change.

And he'd been so fast. Crushed underneath her, where Jay couldn't see, her right arm bled into the blankets, a neat line carved into skin. Already numb. Emily bit her lip and blinked back panicked tears. Throbbing pulses of fear battered her skull without mercy.

Hers alone.

Her ability didn't work on Shiv; there was no thread to pull, no way to send her emotions catapulting back onto him.

"How many of you are there, Klepto?" Shiv asked. "Two? More?"

Jay's gun didn't waver. "Get your hands off of her."

"You must think I'm a fool. All those jobs for Murphy, with you two going at it all night long? Who are you working with?" Shiv's voice grated against her temple as he scraped a stubbled cheek against the side of her face.

A horrifying whimper leaked from her throat.

"Ah-ah, we had a deal, Miss Barton. No sound, remember?" He pressed the flat of the blade against her throat, tipped her head back against his chest, and smiled at Jay. "She's quite obedient. I just don't understand why Murphy had so much trouble."

No sound, or death. Some deal. Orange threads wended through her mind on command, but now they weren't merely snapping. They frayed. Her thoughts couldn't hold them solid enough to even attempt to try something new, like warning Torpedo that Shiv had changed his game pieces. He had a gun.

"What do you want?" The question came out strangled with anger.

"I'm awed you think you're in a position to ask questions. But I'll bite." Shiv chuckled, the eerie sound causing ice to spread in her veins like clawing fingers. "Your employer wants her for her skills. My employer wants her for her body. My employer pays better, and both of them want you dead."

A low growl came from the far side of the room and Emily shut her eyes tight, wishing it all away.

"Pitiful, really. All this effort wasted for a boy who'll be dead by morning. Ares has had enough of Murphy's distractions and false messiahs."

Her eyes flashed open. *Stefan?* What had this demented creep done to the boy? Craning her neck away from the knife brought her tighter against his body. She shuddered, and Shiv idly traced a path down her arm with one ragged fingernail. Jay's gaze homed in on her face.

Gun, she thought to him, picturing it hard in her head, as if the images his spirit guide could send them worked the other way around. He didn't look like it got through at all. Ruffling feathers came from his side though. Torpedo shifted; the tufted down around his legs quivered. His wide gaze rested on her.

He intended to fly.

Shiv would only be able to shoot one of them, and it wouldn't be the bird.

Not Jay. Please . . .

"I'm actually a little disappointed," Shiv purred in her ear, deliberately baiting his opponent. "I'd heard she liked to sleep naked."

Something snapped in Jay's expression.

No . . .

"He's got a—" Her warning cut off with a yelp. The knife pinched into her neck as Shiv rose up over her body. Warmth trickled down her throat and Emily saw Torpedo launch into the air, the slash of steel in Jay's eyes, the flare of his gun.

Emily screamed, the sound otherworldly and tangled with the second explosion—the one that fired beside her ear. Ringing engulfed her senses.

Slow motion. The bullets moved in slow motion. She hovered above the scene and watched each man jerk back with the force of the other's attack. Hit.

Jay dropped his weapon.

Shiv's gun bounced to the bed in front of her body.

Emily felt Shiv's grip slacken around her physical form and she fought against the pull of the vision. Jay took a step forward, backward. Wavered on his feet.

His back hit the wall.

"Tor, let go! I've got to help him!" The half-thought, half-yell earned her a screech in return, but the vision shimmered away.

The owl clawed at the would-be assassin's limp arm and Emily slipped out from under the dead weight, off the bed, and straight to Jay's side. She wrapped her arms around him even as he slid to the floor.

"Emily," he whispered against her hair.

The trench coat gaped open to reveal a shiny dark spot on the upper right side of his t-shirt. Her lungs compressed. Then refused to take in more air. He couldn't shrug out of the jacket on his own, so she pushed it back off his shoulder. His fingers clamped around hers.

"I'm calling 911." She pressed her left hand to his chest, a new flicker of fear arcing up her spine to join the high-pitched ringing in her head as she touched liquid.

"Help already in . . . coming," he said slowly, panning her neck with his bare hand, just under the cut.

"You need a doctor!" Emily waited in a disconnected haze, unable to call the threads in her mind at all now, expecting his emotions to come through the touch unchecked.

But nothing happened when he touched her. No extra

emotions. No new pain flaring around the injury. Numbness had instead gripped more of her body, starting with her useless right arm.

"Tor'll rush them." On cue—but not hers—the bird made a gurgling sound from the bed and took to the air, out the door. "Not the first time I've been shot."

Alone with him in the dimmed room, Emily stroked a quaking hand over his face. Her fingers left a streak of blood. A cold sweat had broken out on his forehead and his eyes closed.

"Bandages," she said. Exhaustion yanked at her eyelids. "Need those."

His left arm slipped around her waist and tugged her to the floor beside him. Her head drooped to his good shoulder.

"I have to get a towel . . . keep pressure on the wound . . . " *So tired.*

"I'm fine, Emily."

No, you're not. Her hand slipped over the wound in his chest and time fizzled out.

SOMETHING PUSHED HER arm down and another shadowed figure filled her sight.

"Need to get help." She managed the words, tried to push herself into a sitting position next to Jay, lolling her head sideways to look at the intruder when that failed. One of his brothers, unless there were more ninjas than he'd let on, a mask slipped across his face too.

"Stay still, Em. He'll be just fine."

"Which one are you?"

"From the looks of things, I'm the doctor." Ryan? Zach? gave her a tight smile, his eyes narrowed. Gloved fingers snaked out to grip her chin and pulled slowly up until he could study the cut on her throat. His other hand dabbed at the wound with a damp piece of cloth. Without looking away, he added, "When you're done in there, I could sure use an extra hand."

"Doctor Ninja?" Emily blinked against the muffled sound of his voice. Why was her head so foggy?

"Ninja," he said under his breath. With a click of his tongue against his teeth, he added, "You got a little scratch and he took a nick to the shoulder from the dead guy on the bed. I've seen worse, and I can patch this mess up in a jiff." A pair of tweezers materialized between his fingers. "Except for the dead guy."

If he'd meant to be reassuring, he missed the mark, the quip forced rather than flippant. Her vision blurred behind tears.

Torpedo flew in above their heads and landed on the nightstand. She watched him crane his neck forward as though supervising.

"Don't cry, little sister." The doctor spared an anxious look at her then seemed to plaster on a smile as he jerked his chin at Torpedo. "Why don't you tell me what happened? We obviously missed the party and the bird was a little flighty on the details."

She stared at him. *I don't . . . understand him.* Emily heard the words, they were spoken in English, but they didn't make sense. *Why doesn't he make sense?*

The doctor whistled low. "What the hell is this?" Some kind of capsule was trapped between the prongs of the tweezers.

"So, I was right," a voice rasped from behind her. "More than one of you."

Emily tumbled backward, helpless to stop the lift of Shiv's gun once more, aimed at the doorway. *He's still alive?* She followed his line of sight to yet another masked man at the door. The figure blurred into two or three men in her faltering vision. *More of them?* No, that couldn't be right. A jolt of movement tugged at the corner of her eye and her gaze slid back toward Jay. The doctor fired a shot, waited, then set his own gun on the floor and returned to the tweezers.

"He's dead. Bugs?"

Shiv? Dead? The thought sent a rapid-fire pattern of relief through her system. She practically shook with it. And then she couldn't stop herself from shaking.

"Place is clean. Amanda's doing a perimeter sweep but we think he was alone."

The doctor ripped off his mask and rubbed his sleeve over his forehead. "Then get over here and hold her."

Muscled arms wrapped around her waist and pulled her away from the wounded man on the floor. Her fingers scrabbled to keep a grip on Jay. The only Ninja here who was hers. *Hers.*

An affirmative noise rumbled in the chest against her back. "How is he?"

The man hovering over Jay looked up, and despite his bare face she couldn't recognize him through the fog. Holding the tweezers high, his eyebrows knitted together. "If this is a regular bullet, I'm a professional doctor."

"Was that in his chest? Why isn't he wearing a vest? Son of a—"

"You're not really a real ninja doctor, are you?" *Were those words? What's wrong with me?* Emily's eyelids shuddered closed; the man holding her gave her a gentle shake.

"Emily?" A concerned, maskless face filled her sight and dark eyes roved over her neck. The look traveled across her shoulder, down to the floor, widening as it went. Even in the dim light of the room, his skin paled. "Z, we have a problem."

"I know she's in shock. Just keep her warm until I can . . . " The tweezers caught the light again and he dropped his arm to look over at her. His nostrils flared, the barest betrayal of concern as his eyes followed the angle of his brother's head to her side, ending in a stare at what she imagined would be a giant sticky puddle by now. "Oh. Shit. Well, that's not good."

She saw the worried look they exchanged, the new tension

that inched across their jawlines until they looked like a twin pair of moody grim reapers. The McLelas holding her rolled her against his chest and she let out a muffled groan.

"Too much . . . hospital . . . " was the last thing she could make out over the ringing in her ears.

CHAPTER TWENTY-ONE

JAY JOLTED AWAKE, STILL in the master bedroom of the condo but squinting into the morning light. His eyesight flared at the unexpected brightness.

"He's up, Z."

He directed his view toward Ryan and frowned as his brother's skin gave off a psychedelic series of colors. Zach dashed into the room with more energy than the tired face dazzling in Jay's enhanced vision would have given him credit for. A comet trail of light lingered behind him. Afraid the lightshow meant he was about to spend the day blind, Jay snapped his eyes closed.

"Still playing nuclear power plant?" Zach asked. "Maybe we should blindfold him for a little while. Just until that shit wears off."

"I'll be fine." Why was his ability on full-blast? He gave it a ruthless mental tug, but it was as if the reins he normally kept in place had disintegrated, leaving his vision untamable. A hint of cinnamon caught at his nose and he noticed the extra weight of a body propped against his right side. "Emily?"

"She's fine too. But she'll be out for some time. The hospital—"

"Hospital?" Jay bolted upright against the headboard, fighting the instinct to open his eyes again to see her for himself. She let out a soft moan and he spread his palm over soft fabric. From the way she leaned, probably her back. "Are you insane? You took us to the hospital? Which one? Not Fairview."

They never went to the emergency room, preferring a clinic downtown for serious wounds. Too many questions arose at the major hospital and bribes were too easily mislaid, both prices one paid for state-of-the-art technology, silence on the subject of bullet wounds, and convenience. But more importantly, Julia was still at Fairview. Any one of Emily's coworkers could have seen them bring her in.

The woman in his arms must have been near death for them to even consider the risk.

"Just her. And Fairview was the closest ER." Ryan's feet shuffled closer. "Keep your eyes closed and just listen for a minute, okay?"

Jay nodded, struggling for air.

He'd almost lost her. Again. Good God. Once his eyes got back to normal, he was never letting her out of his sight again, mask or no. When she woke, he'd tell her everything this time. Before something else went wrong.

"Your Spirit-mate lives." Feathery reassurance from his spirit guide.

The tightness in his chest didn't ease, but he nuzzled the top of Emily's head and dropped a kiss there, grateful he had this much. He could still hold her in his arms. Her heart still beat alongside his own.

"The hospital gave her a good sedative," Zach continued with a sigh.

"We didn't have a whole lot of options," Ryan added. "Zach's great with field dressing, but your girl needed a transfusion. So yeah, we took her to the emergency room."

"He must've diced her up before you got here. Her arm—"

"No." Sickened, Jay pried open his eyelids. Jagged rays of orange and red snaked into his peripheral, but not before he saw the cascade of white beams highlight the bandage on Emily's arm. He leaned forward to rub his chin over the red-brown crest of Emily's head. "He had a knife to her throat, not her arm! I didn't know—"

"Easy, bro." Jay's vision swirled as Zach held up his hands, and he closed his eyes once more. "She's safe now, and Shiv's out of the picture."

A slow burn of anger kindled in his stomach. He rubbed at his chest with his left hand. A bandage wrapped around his shoulder, extra layers of gauze over the hole Shiv had blasted into him. *Shiv. Guess that makes me a killer now.* Who was he kidding? Tell her everything? *She saw me take that shot.* How could they take any step beyond practicing abilities and sharing meals now that she knew what he really was? What he was truly capable of? She wouldn't stay with a murderer.

At least now she had proof of what he'd told her from the beginning: he wasn't one of the good guys.

"Jay?"

He nodded. "What time is it?"

"Mid-afternoon, Friday."

That explains the daylight. "I'll need to call her work. They'll be expecting her."

"Already done. Naomi thinks she's laying low." Ryan sounded as rueful as Jay felt. "I don't like the reason any more than you do. But for now, she's safe." He paused. "Did Shiv say anything to you about Murphy?"

"Just some threats. Mentioned the payoff." Jay shook his

head. "Emily was right though—He didn't have loyalty to Murphy; he was working for someone else. Someone named Ares."

Ryan mulled that over, the tap of his fingers against his leg an irritated ruffle of coarse fabric. "All right. When you've worked all the poison out of your system and can open your eyes without going spaceman on us, we'll talk more."

Jay's jaw went slack. Poison? Was that what had his vision running on overexposure? "Now, not later. I need straight answers." Never mind his brain ached as if it couldn't decide if it should start spinning in circles or wear itself out by pounding around his skull.

"Shiv hit you with some kind of capsule. A laced bullet—I guess we can call it that—it hit your bloodstream and went nuts. The thing was designed to dissolve, but I got to it before it could dump the whole dose." A bump sounded against the wall, where Zach had probably leaned heavier than intended. "You went in and out for a while. Every time you woke up your eyes did that weird glowy thing. Like when you or Emily have visions. I figure the drug somehow snagged onto your spirit guide bond and sent it into overdrive. Torpedo was here the whole time."

Ryan jumped in. "It's the same drug he used on Emily. Higher concentration. We were hoping you knew why Shiv used it on you. On one of us, specifically. See, I was under the impression that Shiv—"

"—doesn't ... didn't ... use guns. You're right." Jay ran through his memory of the encounter from the beginning. Something important was missing, but he couldn't shake it loose. "You don't think they've caught on to those side effects and are trying to weaponize it instead of selling it street-side, do you?"

"Doc's testing everything and then some. I have my suspicions," Zach said. "Shiv couldn't have known about our abilities. Most likely he was just trying to get fancy, killing you with the side effects."

Jay swallowed hard. "Withdrawal."

"If it hits, I've got stuff here to counter it. But to be on the safe side beyond that, you're not leaving this condo and Klepto stays underground. Just in case this is more than a chink in our shadowy trench coat armor." He cleared his throat over what Jay was certain was a low growl from Ryan.

"All that for me, and you still bypassed the clinic." To keep Emily alive. His tongue thick in his mouth, Jay cracked open his eyelids, nodding at each of them in silent gratitude.

"Let it go, already. Shiv was on the bed; the two of you were on the floor bleeding to death." Zach threw himself into a kitchen chair someone had dragged into the master bedroom. Red and orange lights streaked after him, leaving a Zach-imprint still standing in the room.

Jay blinked at his brothers, back down at Emily, then up again. "Thank you—"

"What, you think I'd let you both die?" Zach swiped at the air with his hand, a small, but trippy movement. "It was a busy night. No one noticed her in with all the other bodies."

"What other bodies?" Jay's eyes widened.

Ryan added, as though calm reassurance solved insanity itself, "Don't worry. We made a few friends last night and I think we'll be able to call in some favors in a pinch."

Yeah, no, that wasn't going to keep his head from exploding. Jay rolled his eyes.

The room spun like a macabre carousel.

Ugh.

"How do you end up with people owing us favors by taking her to the hospital and getting the staff to keep it off the books?" He paused. "You did make sure the records . . . "

"I'm a wizard."

His wizard of a brother had used his super-ears to dig up dirt, maybe even listened through a wall. Blackmail was handy when calling in favors. Jay let out a relieved huff of air, but it was short-lived. What did it say about him that he could feel good about blackmail? He rolled the palm of his hand over Emily's shoulder.

Winking, Ryan spread his hands wide and wiggled a light-smudged glob of fingers. "How many fingers am I holding up?"

Jay held up a middle one in response.

A snort came from the chair against the wall, and Zach rubbed the back of his head on the wall. "Wizards and Ninjas. That's us. Look, Jay, there's something else. She's—" His hands lifted in exaggerated defeat as he stood, returning the sharp look on their older brother's face. "I know, I know. I promised."

Ryan tugged on the off-white lampshade on the dresser lamp. "Thanks for restraining yourself, jackass."

"What did you do?" Jay asked. He stopped short of stroking Emily's hair and held up his right hand. "Wait. Did both of you go?"

"Does it matter? We did what we had to do. For you and for her. Let. It. Go."

"But there's only supposed to be one of us. One masked man visible at a time to make it look like we're one and the same. Ry? Guys. Spill. What happened to the cover?"

Zach turned to leave and his shoulders lifted in a shrug. "It's intact."

Ryan spun the shade and Jay had to close his eyes as it morphed into a miniature sun. His next words were barely audible. "She's pregnant."

The blood drained from Jay's face and he swore his fingers and toes went numb. "She is? You're sure?"

"You're not even surprised." A snort. "I know you said you kids were holing up to work on the touch thing . . . but damn."

"There's a chance the trauma . . . " Zach started, the warning just as soft as Ryan's initial announcement. "Well. You know."

"She could've lost it." Jay barely recognized his own voice, raked over a bed of coals. No more wondering. Now they'd know for certain what that one night of bliss had brought—and the true cost of Shiv's attack. His hands shook, and he tried to still them by hugging the woman in his arms even tighter. "How am I going to tell her Shiv killed our baby?"

"Give it time, test again," Ryan suggested. "Maybe you won't have to. We shouldn't have brought it up." The last had to be directed at Zach.

Jay shook his head. "This is not something that gets to be a secret."

"Unlike the rest of our delightful lives." Zach's footsteps tromped from the room.

What the—Jay tipped his head up to listen, their trip to the hospital fading from importance when the bathroom fan down the hall kicked on. "Emily almost dies, I get shot and poisoned, our nemesis is dead, and he's *still* sick?"

"Yup." Ryan said slowly.

Not for the first time, Jay wished Brennan's research had been more fruitful. She'd focused on Zach's invisible premonitions, the middle McLelas rather than the last in line; it made sense. That the connection between him and Torpedo had come first instead felt . . . wrong.

"Jay, look at me. We need to talk."

"About Zach? Or parenting?"

"About you. And guns."

Jay's eyebrows shot up as he opened his eyes to a more normal light spectrum. He didn't have much time to linger on why; Ryan's tone had gone from supportive to grumpy and he had a thunderstorm of an expression to match. The mire in his gut grew heavier. *Is he upset I killed Shiv? We lose Old Town but surely he knows I didn't have a choice.*

"I had no less than three Kevlar vests sewn up. One for each of us. So we don't—I don't know—die. How many nights have you gone out without it on? How many weeks? When were you going to tell us you no longer needed yours?" Ryan's voice pitched to a near-roar. "When were you going to tell us about your new, so-obviously-bulletproof superpower? When, Jay? And you have the *nerve* to wonder why Zach's sick?"

Jay shrank against the pillows. Okay. So it wasn't about the assassin. This was about the chink in his own personal armor.

He didn't have a defense. "Ryan, it won't—"

"You know what the worst part is?" Ryan asked, still set to deafen. "You knew you might be a father. A father, Jay! And you *still* didn't wear one! You want your kid to grow up like us? Missing a fucking parent?"

God, no. Jay raised his voice to match. "I'm sorry!"

"What if he gets some shit superpower and you're not there to answer questions? What then, Jay? Answer me!"

"I said I was sorry!"

"Yelling is-is not helping."

If the shreds of Jay's heart had started to reconnect with Emily safe in his arms—pregnant or no—they were torn like tissue paper by the taut, pale face emerging from the hallway.

Zach's hand quaked where he touched it to the wall, his face drawn. He closed his eyes, and when he opened them, a blaze of willpower seemed to spark from some well of reserved energy. "We need a plan, not an argument. Ryan . . . I'm sorry. Murphy knows Shiv's dead by now and we're short on options. We need all of us on this one. He can rest some other time."

A curt nod cut across the room.

Zach shoved a tired hand through his hair and pulled the chair to Jay's side. "While we were at the hospital, there was an influx of cases involving the goons who were at the warehouse

VIGILANTE'S DARE

the night you went for Emily. Different accidents. Some shot, some drowned, some burned to a crisp. Murphy's taking people out. They're all dead, Jay. They didn't make it. Even some of the prostitutes, three of the other women he was paying to hold down his personal strip club—who hadn't been dosed." Zach's tone rang with disgust. "It's like the man came completely unhinged."

Horror blossomed in Jay's chest. He was killing everyone? Why? And why now? "How did he arrange that many kills in a single evening? I thought Shiv was the only one on Murphy's payroll that competent." Jay's eyebrows crinkled inward. "But he wasn't really working for Murphy. Someone's wiping the floor, guys."

Ryan flicked a glance to Zach. "Ares?"

Zach sighed. "If Shiv's mysterious patron is behind this, I can't see his handiwork yet. I've been burning starlight for weeks going through the financial records. As soon as they hit the accounts, they get pulled. And this newest batch? No. Looks to me like Murphy's giving out payoffs to take out his own crew."

Jay's right hand clenched in the fabric of Emily's shirt. "Why would he do that?" His left hand balled into a fist. At least that explained why Shiv had used a gun. Someone wanted everyone who was there that night dead. "Is there anyone left who can talk?"

Ryan spread out his palms. "He's down to a loyal few, though after this I doubt they'll stay quite so loyal. Pretty soon it'll just be Murphy."

And his son. Jay's memory finally clicked. "Shiv threatened to kill Murphy's boy. Said he'd be dead by morning."

"Shiv's dead, so the kid's probably fine. Murphy keeps him under lock and key."

"Paychecks can be transferred."

"Zach can check if there's a contract out. But that's all. We're not touching him. I'm not setting off a bigger bloodbath by triggering someone's over-protective parenting mojo."

Jay closed his eyes at the dig. "Fair enough." He raised an eyelid to peer at his brother. "But if anything happens to him, things can only get uglier."

"I don't know how." Ryan sank onto the foot of the bed and rubbed his hand on his knee.

"We give it a couple days and then—" A coughing fit made Zach crumple into himself. When it was over, he gave a weak shrug. "Maybe Klepto doesn't have to be in hiding. Say we get in on the takeover or screw up Murphy's plans. Wouldn't that garner attention from Ares? Draw him out? We play it rough, amp up some filters Murphy's been using to skim off some other business prospects so it looks like he's getting greedy on top of this whole mess, then run in and snatch whatever's left of his operation before it's all gone."

"Whoa. Wait. What?" Jay's mind whirled with his suggestion. "You want us to take over Murphy's operation?" What happened to getting out? "Dig us in deeper on the boss level? Hand ourselves over to Ares? I don't know that that's your best plan. Kind of drops us onto the scene without, oh, I dunno. Adequate research."

"It's dangerous, but it might be worth seeing where it goes," Ryan said, his voice suddenly quiet.

"Don't gang up on me because you think I should be bedridden and blindfolded. Think about it." Under Murphy's thumb, the brothers had leeway to work the covert angle. They'd made sure only the criminals paid in injuries and prison terms. They'd managed to avoid the innocents and control the situation, arranging arrests from the sidelines. "If we take over for Murphy, there'll be that much more blood on our hands. Innocents will die."

"Innocents are already dying."

"Shiv was sent to kill me. Emily and I were both on the guest list from the warehouse, right? But if you were at the hospital last night, and someone knows we're still alive, well, we're still on the hit list."

"I've got it covered, Jay."

"No, I don't think you do. We can't take over Murphy's organization, because whoever's cleaning up after him wants us dead."

A slow smile spread across Ryan's face. "Ah, but Klepto doesn't need to cower from a madman. I know where Murphy keeps his hedge funds. Zach can play with the numbers. He's scrambling. We take those and the accounts you were betting with, wipe him out, he's got nothing. Turnabout's fair play."

"Look at it this way, Jay." Zach shoved himself out of the chair and dragged it toward the bedroom door. "When we're in charge, Murphy's men won't be after your girl every day. The dark side's not pretty, but this thing's too big to let loose. I want them all, not just him. And to do that, we gotta stay on the inside track. Find out who's pulling the strings on this."

Jay coughed. "Look, I killed a man tonight. Sure, he attacked Emily. Sure, he was a monster. That doesn't mean it's something I want to do every day. And if we go into this without looking, that's exactly what we're going to have to do."

Zach and Ryan exchanged a look.

"What?" Jay growled, slamming his back against the headboard. "Ah." He winced.

"Your soul can rest easy, little brother." Zach said, tossing a clean shirt and coat on top of the comforter. "He's dead, sure, but you didn't make the killing blow."

Jay turned a sharp look to Zach. "You—He was still alive?" What if Shiv had managed to kill Emily while he was unconscious? Finish the two of them off? *But that means I'm not a killer.* The tension in his chest twisted instead of lifting as he looked down at the woman slumbering against his chest. *She still saw me shoot him.*

"Zach handled it. While you were sleeping." Ryan's face pinched in anger. "In the future, if you shoot someone, shoot him again."

Zach barked out a laugh. "Or, you know, disarm him. At the very least."

Jay closed his eyes. "Shoot him again. Great. In my defense, the bastard did poison me."

"I'm not mad at you, Jay. Except for the vest. That, I'm pissed about." Ryan took up pacing at the foot of the bed. "We'll all need to be more careful. Nothing left to chance. And when you can join us—"

"You're not going after Murphy without me."

"Fine. We'll just leave Romeo, Drak, and Torpedo to stick around and watch after your maybe-pregnant girlfriend."

A low note of discontent rumbled in his chest.

"Don't growl at me, Jay. You're the one who went and got yourself shot."

CHAPTER TWENTY-TWO

MOIST, WILD AIR TUGGED at the copper strands of Emily's hair where she stood on the edge of a vast lake. Fog clung to the shore, dotted the air over the water, draped around her like a cloak.

"It is time," a gruff voice said from the murk.

When she spun around, a campfire warmed her face. She stood on a vast plain now, no water in sight. Her throat clenched. A figure stood on the other side of the blaze, shrouded in ash and flecks of rising embers.

"Who are you? Where am I?"

"I am called Weaver. We have met before." He stepped around the campfire, his russet face creased like worn leather, hair black as the starless night above their heads. "You are in Dream."

She raised an eyebrow at the apparition. "So I'm asleep?"

"Yes." Weaver took another step toward her. "And no."

Her chest tightened and she backed away from the fire, away from the unearthly man. "Am I dead?"

"You Feel, always Feel, but you must also See. Like the Spiritwalker. The Watcher." He lifted his hand and Emily found herself in another world.

Her heart sank as she took in her new surroundings. The tent held shelves of herbs, glass bottles, animal bones.

Weaver appeared on the far side of the tent. "His Spirit-mate must See."

"Spirit-mate?"

Two faceless men—no, one a man grown, one much younger with an over-long, tousled mop of dark hair—in the tent spoke in a different language, but her dream-self's mind translated it easily.

"Okay. I can conquer the dark. What does that mean, exactly?" Frustration rode the teenager's words, more demand than question.

Weaver's mouth moved as the second man spoke. "The mysteries of the soul are not classroom journeys, Watcher."

The dream changed and now she knew who they were. A younger version of Jay sat at the foot of the second Weaver, his mouth set in a stubborn scowl.

"None of our abilities work right."

"You are not . . . whole. You must find the one who can ease your soul, your spirit. Be as one. Watch together. Only then can you truly See, and only then will your heart and your fear be content." Weaver threw a rug onto the floor.

The teenager's frown deepened. "This ability has nothing to do with my heart."

"Then you are blind. And you can never use the power as it is meant to be wielded."

"Tell me what to do, Meadows!"

Meadows. Now Emily knew where she'd seen him before. The tall, swarthy man going by Weaver was Julia Meadows' grandfather. She'd seen pictures.

He'd passed away half a decade ago.

"Return in two moons' time. All will be revealed." Weaver vanished into the ether of dreams. The tent fell away to a star-flecked night sky.

"But you weren't there! It was all gone!" Jay, suddenly as old as she knew him, ripped himself to his feet and screamed into the darkness. Then he turned, saw her standing there. "My Emily." He held out his hands.

The dream figure vanished before she could fall into his embrace.

Letters, symbols, words flashed across her vision, flooding her with information, the bulk of which she couldn't begin to comprehend. A single symbol caught at her mind, weaving itself into her conscious thought: Spirit-mate.

THE ROOM WAS dark when Emily emerged from her dream. "How long was I out?" she asked before she was fully awake.

She drew in a long breath. Musky, night-kissed. Jay. Her face burrowed against the soft cotton of his t-shirt, the fingers of both hands kneading the fabric. His chest rose and she remembered Shiv.

We're alive.

Her headache had vanished and she lay on a bed, not the floor, on her opposite side now. Against his right shoulder. His injured shoulder.

Emily bolted upright. Pain flared through the right side of her body and regret danced about in her head. She sucked in a breath and held it. As if sensing her pain, one of his hands twined with hers in his sleep. Squeezing his palm steadied her balance, her focus, and the onslaught lessened. When she checked the thread between them, it pulsed, a steady strand of emotions, neither his nor hers overtaking the bond.

"Meadows," Jay murmured. His free hand clenched in the comforter.

Was he dreaming about Julia's grandfather too? The connection they had... did it extend past visions and into sleep? She frowned. It had to have been her subconscious working overtime to make sense of everything he'd told her the past few weeks, an amalgamation of his truths and her role beside him.

So why, then, did her heart thunder as she stared down at his restless form in the dark? Why did that symbol, that word—Spirit-mate—singe her to the bone?

Twisting to the side of the bed, she felt for a nightstand. As she'd hoped. A lamp. Her lamp. She tugged on the pull string and the room became engulfed in soft pink light, tempered by the silky lampshade. They were in the bed at the condo. Emily looked down at the fresh, dark blue sheets, then dropped a glance at the floor where Ninja had fallen. If there had been blood in the room, every trace of it was gone now.

His brothers must have cleaned it up. Because that part had been real, not a dream. She certainly hadn't imagined the terror of having Shiv's blade tearing at her throat.

As she shuddered, Jay took in a sharp breath and coughed, rubbing the side of his face into the pillow. She pressed the back of her hand to his forehead, burned by the heat of his skin. His face twisted in discomfort, and a wealth of compassion torqued through her abdomen, a sensation she tried to share through their bond. This man and his sexy silver eyes had come for her, had saved her life.

Again.

"Will it always be like this?" Emily's hand found the side of his face and stroked across his cheek.

"No!" He screamed without warning, twisting beside her and wrenching the covers.

She jerked away from him, then realized his answer wasn't aimed at her. He still slept, fitfully tossing against the pull of a nightmare.

"Jay?" She threw an arm out to shake his shoulder. The skin under the white bandages decorating her injured limb pulled taut. Emily bit back a moan of pain.

"You can't go! Why?" His eyes squeezed tight and his head fell to one side, then the other. "Tell me what to do!"

"Wake up, Jay," she said louder, framing his face with her hands to keep his head still. "Wake up! It's me, Emily!"

He twisted, fighting her grip on him as if he were wrestling his dream foe. "They're all dead." Gasping, he flew up off the mattress. As her hand gripped his good shoulder he struggled, and she tried to keep him from sailing across the room. "No!"

She flinched at the additional pressure. Something along the length of her arm tugged. *I'm not strong enough*. The flicker of realization broke through her own weariness and she released his shoulders with a start.

Silver slits appeared as he opened his eyes, a look dashing across her face and then widening. His rigid stance crumbled and his arms immediately wrapped around her to crush her to his chest.

"You're alive." His nose nuzzled the top of her head. "You're awake."

"You were having a nightmare," she said into his chest.

"I know." He pulled back and a frown tugged at his lips. "I thought Shiv was going to kill you."

"I thought he did." She shook her head. "But you were dreaming about—"

His palm cupped the side of her face and that was her only warning.

The kiss said he was calling off all former parlay on physical contact. Switching to the all-Jay, all-the-time channel in her brain, Emily folded into him, letting his tongue trace her lower lip. Days and nights of careful practice and keeping tabs on her ability, of careful playing, cautious testing, were forgotten. If it was her passion alone or his bleeding through the skin contact, she didn't care. She only knew she wanted more of his hands roaming under her camisole, her fingers tracing the warm skin of his abs, his breath tickling her cheek, his solid body beside hers. Skin. Lips. More.

"Jay. Jay," she murmured between breaths, between desperate kisses.

It was an embrace that said "Mine", and she wanted him to feel it as much as she did. Her fingers slid under his t-shirt and he deepened the kiss, sending a host of wicked fantasies coursing through her core. His hand burrowed into her hair, tugging on the short strands like he'd keep her captive. Tension ebbed from her muscles as she went boneless. Everything in the world fell away. The arm on his injured side wrapped around her waist and he made a pained sound in his throat.

She broke the embrace, seeking the wound. "Oh, Jay." Under his t-shirt, there would be a bandage where he'd been hurt trying to protect her.

"I'm fine. But we've got to do something about this danger-prone streak of yours."

"Zero days since the last incident?" She turned into the light touch he set again at her cheek and rubbed against his palm. The thread was stable, strong but not laced with too-strong emotions. A smile tugged at her lips. "Tired of rescuing me?"

"Nah. Keeps me on my toes." The silver glow of his eyes turned almost orange under the lamplight. "I am tired of putting you in danger." His eyes closed and he leaned back against the headboard.

"Now, hold on," she said. "Murphy was after me before you arrived on the scene. So if anyone's to blame, it's me, for catching his attention in the first place."

"Yes, it's a pity you're so attractive." He chuckled and pulled her into the curve of his shoulder. "How about we just blame Murphy and leave off with the guilt, then."

"You know he wanted me for Stefan." Emily stilled. "Shiv said—"

"Zach's on it." He angled a drowsy, concerned look at her. "If there's anything he can do, he will."

She frowned, cupping her palm over the lump on his chest. "Will Murphy ever stop?"

His face darkened but he rubbed a comforting thumb across her cheek. "I'm staying right here to protect you until this is done."

"Because you don't have a life or anywhere else to spend your days?"

"Exactly." The gloom lifted from his face.

She laughed. Emily hadn't noticed the weight of her worries until the tension in her chest loosened. Burrowing against his chest, she inhaled his shadow-kissed scent. His fingers dug into her hip a moment later.

"Do you remember anything from last night? The hospital?" When she shook her head, he said, "There's something you need to know."

She pulled back to watch his face. "What's wrong?"

He frowned. "Are you feeling—"

"No, I'm not sensing anything from you, but that body language isn't exactly a mystery."

A slow nod. "Good."

"And?" she prompted.

"You were pregnant."

"*Were*?" The word stabbed at her like another of Shiv's blades. Left of center, twisting between ribs. "I'm . . . you mean I was, but now—" She choked on the rest of the question and he squeezed her tight.

"Okay, wait. I botched that. Big time." His palm caressed her cheek, his thumb wiped away a fat tear on the descent. "Angel, angel, don't cry. Please."

"All that wait and see, for this? For a murderer to—"

"Stop, love. Listen." Jay shifted, holding her face between both palms. "We might not have lost the baby, okay? It's early. So early. I only meant at the hospital the test came back positive. Your body went through hell, though. So it is possible Shiv messed things up. I wanted—needed—you to know. Needed . . . " He trailed off as she shook her head.

No amount of facts could make her feel any better about Shiv possibly causing her to no longer be pregnant, and it didn't matter how far along she'd been. Trying to grapple with a shred of rational thought, Emily's head reeled. He'd called her 'love' instead of 'angel'. And despite his reassurances, Jay wasn't any more okay with a possible loss than she was.

She refused to read into it, to think he'd been hopeful. Even now, she wasn't sure how she felt about a baby with a man caught in two worlds.

"I get it," he said softly, and tugged her against him. "My head went to the same place."

Stopping the shake of her head, she met the bleak look in his eyes. "Knowing makes it worse."

"I'm sorry." He shook his head. "No, I'm not sorry. I wasn't going to keep it from you."

Squeezing him lightly around the waist, she nodded. Her heart ached for him, tumbling end over end.

"When this is over, and God willing that'll be soon, we'll test like we planned and see where we stand." He pulled her close. "This, we figure out together."

She rubbed her forehead against his t-shirt. "Deal."

They rested against each other for a long time. Emily

relaxed, her mind finally settling into a mode that could let her focus on one worry at a time. The biggest concern was still in the form of a crime boss, and Murphy was on the front of her mind as she began to doze. Jay suddenly stiffened. His palm splayed across her shoulder, traced down to her elbow.

She glanced up to see shock jerk across his expression. "Your arm."

"Hmm?" Her eyebrows furrowed as she followed his look. Red dots were growing rapidly through the gauze.

"I've got to redo your stitches." He slipped out from under the covers but before his feet hit the floor he groaned, his palm flying to his forehead.

"Jay!" She grabbed him backward and saw the whites of his eyes smoldering orange. "What's wrong with your eyes?"

"I'm fine. Just a little too much light. Can you turn off the lamp?"

She leaned off the opposite side of the bed and pulled the metal cord. The room pitched into darkness.

"Ah." He let out a sigh of relief.

"Are you going blind again?"

"I don't think so. I'll be right back." When he returned, he handed her a glass of water and two small pills. "Painkiller."

Oh, they were painkillers alright, and effectively smothered additional questions about his eyes, babies, or the dream she began to remember as sleep again hauled at her eyelids. Down the length of her arm stitches wove like lace, tainted by smears of blood from where they'd torn loose. By the time he finished unwrapping the gauze and threaded the needle, darkness reigned.

EMILY WOKE IN the morning with her face still nuzzled into a muscled chest. The same muscled chest of the man she'd fallen for in less than a month. He was still here. He was still breathing. So was she.

Time passed with the rise and fall of his chest its only marker. She smiled, watching him sleep, listening to the steady beat of his heart under her ear. How many times now had he done the same thing for her, held her while she slept, watched the emotions flit across her face in dreams? He wasn't having a nightmare this time. She brushed the back of her fingers across his cheek and he clasped his hand around hers, wound their fingers together. Her heart ricocheted around in her chest like one of the office cat's bouncy balls.

"Morning, angel." Sleep-rough words. "You okay?"

"Better. Still not dead." She smiled against his t-shirt. "You?"

"Still worried."

"You're going to spoil me with all this honesty."

A chuckle rumbled in his chest. "Look at you, all chipper and full of painkillers."

"I've been up for an hour." She stretched, winced at the stiffness in her arm. The new wrapping was tan instead of white. How long had it taken him to do that? Emily took extra care not to strain the wound as she rolled to stare at the stuccoed ceiling.

"Fifteen minutes," he corrected.

She pursed her lips. "How would you know?"

"I mastered pretend-sleeping years ago."

"You were awake?" Emily didn't hide her smile as he feathered his fingers through her hair. "How's your shoulder?"

"Stiff." He rolled both shoulders back, muscles rippling under the tight cotton fabric. "Like some other parts of me." Grinning, he tipped his face in her direction.

Her eyes bulged. "We almost died, Jay." Their baby might have. And Shiv? Definitely. "This is hardly an appropriate time for seduction." The look in his eyes sent a flood of want diving between her legs anyway.

"You didn't complain about seduction when I saved you from almost-dying at Murphy's." He waggled his eyebrows suggestively.

Laughing, she tugged on a length of his dark hair. It seemed lighter than usual with the extra light trickling in from the window, but her post-painkiller brain wouldn't hold on to the detail. She'd had it with worrying. She needed a break, she needed to let everything out somehow—and sex would be a perfect way to take care of the stress. Her thoughts spun violently with want. Sex with him the first time had been fantastic. The earlier kiss lifted the moratorium on touching. She squirmed.

Weeks of nights together, the bonds between them only stronger through the careful, teasing and experimental touches, intimate despite holding desire at bay. Had that desire reached its peak? She certainly wanted him with the same intensity that shone in his eyes.

Emily flexed her arm again. If she wasn't afraid of pulling the stitches out again, she'd already be straddling him. "I think we should avoid rolling around on the mattress. Unless you plan on taking up sewing as your new favorite hobby."

His lower lip jutted forward in a pout, the pose ridiculous on the handsome planes of his face. "I was good all day yesterday. A perfect gentleman."

"Not much of a feat, considering you weren't conscious for much of it either," she said.

"Point." He sagged against the headboard and closed his eyes. "I came nowhere close to death, you know. It was just a little bullet wound."

The weary droop of his shoulders helped temper her hunger, dulling it to a steady thrum. Neither of them was in any shape for sex. No matter how much they wanted more. His eyes connected with hers, daylight catching on little flecks of blue mixed in with silver.

"Mm-hmm." Emily pursed her lips and walked her fingers up his chest. "I told you to stay away from people who shoot at you. So what did you do? You got yourself shot."

His hand slid to the back of his neck. "Trust me, you're not the only one who's voiced that complaint."

She bit her lower lip. "Ryan and Zach. They were here, after."

"Yes. Zach was starring in the role of 'Doctor Ninja'."

The wicked gleam in his eyes did him in, and she gave him a light shove. "I was pretty out of it."

"He thought it was cute." He dropped a kiss to the tip of her nose.

Her nose wrinkled under his lips. "I need a shower."

"I think we can do something about that."

"Oh?" She sat up as he shifted under her and tossed his legs over the side of the bed.

He came around the foot of the bed to her side and scooped her up, careful not to jar her arm. "The bathroom's just down the hall."

"Oh no, you don't." She squealed, wriggling in his grasp. "Put me down!" Then she stilled. What if he tore the wound on his shoulder open?

He carried her to the near wall, his grip solid as he hooked his ankle in the crack between the partially opened door and the wall.

"Put her down," a deep, frustrated voice came from the kitchen as they passed. Zach. He looked more tired than she and Jay put together.

Laughter rumbled at her ear. Jay's stride paused at the doorway to the bathroom.

"If you pull either of your stitches out again I'll keep you sedated 'til next year." She couldn't see the other man now through the muscled chest against her nose, but Zach's irritation was clear.

"Just heading for a shower."

"Bath," the other man corrected, his voice drawing closer.

Emily tipped her head up and smiled at the humor dancing across Jay's features. When he looked down at her, he flashed her a rueful expression.

"Keep her arm out of the water or we'll have to rewrap it again." A hand slipped over Jay's shoulder and he flinched. "And no funny business. I'm not carrying you back to bed. You're heavy."

Jay's grip tightened. "Fair enough." He shrugged away from his brother and kicked the bathroom door closed with his foot. Settling her on the fuzzy purple and green toilet seat cover, another holdover from her old apartment, he nudged the switch for the fan.

"Why would he have to carry you back to bed?" She asked, watching him turn the knobs on the Jacuzzi tub. "And if you tell me you're fine again, we're going to have words."

As the steam lifted from the basin, he turned to her and scrubbed at his cheeks with his palms. A flare of orange burned around his eyes again.

"Shiv drugged me," he finally admitted, sinking to a seated position on the side of the tub. "It's wearing off, but Zach's afraid I'll overdo it and pass out."

"Drugged? You'll pass out? What did he give you?" A pang of guilt worked its way through her middle. "You shouldn't have carried me. There's nothing wrong with my legs."

"No, but it was fun." He dipped his fingers into the tub water and adjusted another dial above the spigot. "I wanted to. Hell, Emily." His liquid gaze sought hers, and her mouth went dry. "There's a lot of things I want to do right now."

She didn't say anything. She couldn't speak around the lump in her throat.

"Come here." He held out his arms.

She slipped off the toilet seat to the side of the tub where he could wrap her in warmth, care, security. His chin rubbed on the top of her head, comfort for them both.

"Know what's crazy?" he asked softly. "As much danger as you've been in, I can't say I regret it. Not all of it."

She lifted her head, pressed a kiss to his throat.

"If Murphy hadn't come after you, we never would have . . . " He shook his head.

It was definitely crazy. Her heart had bulldozed her brain. A different kind of fear tumbled through her head with the realization that she might just skydive off a cliff to be in the arms of this man. She'd already let her heart claim him, she'd slept with him, beside him, and now she was about to join him in the bathtub.

But not if he was evading questions.

She pushed out of his embrace and settled a hand over the side of the tub. "What did Shiv give you?"

"Same thing he gave you at the warehouse. Stronger."

"Jay!" she cried.

"You know how your ability helped you push through it? We think mine might do something similar. That's why Zach's here. To make sure." His fingers slid under the hem of her shirt and he slid a pair of warm palms across her skin. "I'm trying not to worry unless it gets worse. Is this hurting you?"

Emily shook her head, worrying anyway. "Neither did the kiss. Although that could have been because I didn't really care if your good emotions spilled over."

He chuckled. "That's good, because I think it might be time to test with more skin."

"Not arguing."

Jay lifted her shirt, coaxing her good arm through the sleeve and pulling the fabric over her neck. Gently, as if he thought she would shatter, he drew the top over her wrapped arm. He dipped a kiss to her bared shoulder and waited for her to nod, then tucked her head into his chest for another eternity.

Well, it would have been eternity. Emily could have stayed there forever if the water hadn't started sloshing against her fingertips. She jerked her hand back and he bolted off the side of the tub. How long had they been sitting like that?

"Whoops." Lunging for the faucet, he cut off the gush of liquid from the spout. "Water's ready." The grin he gave her as he yanked off his t-shirt was sheepish. "Come on in before it gets cold."

Her gaze settled south of the bandage that decorated his chest and happily kept going.

"You can't get in the tub with all those clothes on, Emily."

Divesting themselves of pants and undergarments, and after draining the tub of a few inches of water, they finally stepped into the warm bath with a duet of contented sighs. Jay settled against the bottom of the massive tub and pulled her down on top of him, propping her injured arm up on the side, out of the water.

Still no extra emotions. She smiled. Maybe practice really had paid off.

She just wished the other part of her ability—her reaching out the way she'd automatically done with the animals—would work with Jay. It would be nice to have an early warning system in place.

His lips found the curve of her neck and a shiver rippled down her spine.

"I think your brother mentioned something about funny business." Although for the life of her, she couldn't remember exactly what Zach had said. Or why it mattered. At least, not now that she and Jay were naked in a Jacuzzi tub. Emily's head fell back against him and she smiled.

Unfortunately, Jay did remember. His kiss ended and he moved to sit across from her. He reached an arm out and his fingers dribbled a trail of water down the side of her face. He looked disappointed. A twinge of matching regret squeezed her lungs. Her own, not his.

Reaching to the back of the basin, Ninja's hand wrapped around a bottle of soap and he squeezed it onto a washcloth. Her eyes followed him as he dipped it under the surface of the water, brought it up dripping. He came up onto his knees with a genuine smile and dabbed the cloth around the nick at her throat. Emily's breath seized at the tender motion.

His lips brushed against her ear. "We'll have to save the funny business for another time."

She brought a wet hand out of the water to span the section of muscle under his gauze wrapping. "When he shot you," Emily said, "I thought I'd lost you, Jay."

His chest rose sharply. "We're safe now. Shiv can't hurt you again."

"Tell me about the mask," she said as his washcloth rolled over her good arm. "Why the pretending? The persona? The disguised voice? Why are you all supposed to be the same person?"

"We're trying to shut Murphy down, along with all of his big, powerful crime boss buddies. It's a massive—"

"Ha! I knew you were really a good guy." She smiled as his washcloth curved around the underside of her breast.

That ended his ministration of soap. Jay's hand pulled away and he rocked back on his calves with a serious look in his eyes. "I'm not a good guy. I'm not a hero. I'm just a guy who had to do *something* to stop a psychotic, drunken bastard from getting away with turning our city upside-down."

He rubbed a hand over his forehead and water dribbled down his nose, cheek, chin, all places she wanted to kiss. "Emily, I've done a lot of things I have no reason to be proud of. It took a lot of work for Murphy to trust us. For the streets to accept a masked man. They couldn't exactly verify our identity. We went through a lot of trouble to make it work. To get on the inside so we could find a way to shut him down and get the cops to take him in. Him and all the people working with him on the higher end. In some ways, we've made everything worse. In a lot of ways."

He dropped down into a seated position on the other side of the tub and Emily waded through the water, wrapping her arms around the back of his head, curling into his lap. He closed his eyes and rested his cheek on her shoulder.

"Now you're no longer partners. So that's worse?" she asked.

"We needed the connection for a deal that could have been the endgame for Murphy, yeah. But before that, before all this." He pulled his head up and stared at her as if willing her to see him for who he thought he was. "I helped him steal. I gave him money to increase his operations. I made it possible for him to pay off more of the cops in our city, to turn the law enforcement crooked. I've helped as many criminals as I've hurt. But I'm no better than they are. Not really."

"You haven't murdered anyone. You didn't kidnap a bunch of women and drug them up in a rundown warehouse. You didn't cut anybody up with a knife."

He blinked down at her, a lost look in his eyes. "My bullet didn't kill Shiv."

"I know." Yet he'd had every intention of killing. Emily's heart throbbed painfully in her chest. "I know you're capable of it. But being able to, shooting to defend someone else, and running around doing it because you can, or because you *like* it . . . they're different things. Just because you can kill doesn't make you a murderer." Her hand traced the side of his face and he clasped it in his own. "You're not a bad guy. You're not. You're not one of them."

She ached for him, longed to take the worry from his face and welcome him in with a—dare she think it, love—that could merge their very different worlds into something suspiciously like a real relationship. Emily bit her lip against hope and the confusion of her feelings. Could he reconcile his guilt enough to give them an honest chance? And could she really, truly, with every fiber of her being, accept how close he walked the graying shadow realm between right and wrong?

CHAPTER TWENTY-THREE

GRADUATION DAY MEANT EMILY had to leave the relative safety of the condo. Jay knew what the event meant to her, a chance for her to return to something normal—the job she loved—and to finally tell her students the truth behind the attack. He'd even agreed she could take a side trip to Fairview to check in on Julia. But with Emily's name still on a psycho wishlist, he didn't want her to go alone. The concern in his blue- and silver-slashed eyes had nearly made her acquiesce to staying indoors. In the end, he provided transport in his more official capacity as grant officer. It felt good having him so steady by her side. She no longer had to wonder if a masked man was keeping an invisible lookout for trouble from the rooftops, and that was good too.

Her pocket vibrated, a phone call from Naomi. The woman's greeting blistered with panic.

"What is it?" Emily asked. "What's wrong? Did someone else get hurt?"

"What? Oh no, Em, nothin' like that." Naomi's voice shifted into a higher pitch. "Setup's behind and I'm short on hands and trophies and I don't know what I'm doing."

"Naomi? What—" She was about a register and a half from wailing. Naomi didn't wail. "Take a deep breath. I'm sorry I haven't been there to sort things out, but it'll be okay." Was the uncharacteristic bout of nerves an attempt to warn her someone else wanted her out of hiding? Emily shifted the phone on her ear, forcing her stomach to steady. They could do this. No one was lurking inside Partner Paws. "Okay? We'll make it through the day just fine."

Naomi let out a shaky breath on the other end of the line. "I don't know what's wrong with me, Em. My head's gone completely wacky and every silly little thing is hitting me like a bomb. Maybe if you just talked to me for a bit, tell me we can order more trophies, tell me where the dog bows are so I can fluff them all pretty after their baths, I'll be better. I hope."

"Naomi," Emily paused, dreading the answer. "Is someone there with you?"

"Britt's manning the desk. We've got a few more volunteers coming in, but Marco's jumped ship. We're due to kick off after lunchtime and it won't be ready in time! I still have to bathe Hue and Brina and Lacey and Captain Nemo's hiding from me—"

"No, I mean . . . never mind. Look, the ribbons are in the far right cabinet, the," and she closed her eyes to get a mental image of the back room, "second from the top shelf. Get Britt to throw some treats around; I'm sure the office kitties will come running. Nemo will turn up." Emily chewed on the inside of her cheek. "I'm about five minutes away now, and we'll see if we can't track down an extra case of trophies in storage."

"You're on your way over here?" Naomi sounded relieved.

"I promised I would."

"Yeah, but, hun." Her coworker's voice dropped to a whisper. "I thought that guy was still after you."

"I've got a friend looking out for me." She smiled against the receiver, flicking a glance at the driver's seat.

She heard Naomi click her tongue against the back of her teeth. "Oh! That's why Mr. McLelas is coming over. Is he bringing you, then?"

Emily almost dropped the phone.

When she hung up, Jay said, "I should have hired a car for you."

"Hmm?" She studied the frown on his lips. "Why? What's wrong?"

"You've been in hiding, things have quieted down, and it's under wraps that McLelas Financial is digging into your case. No one's seen us together since the hospital—and that was a legitimate concern." He reached over to squeeze her knee, the gauzy skirt crinkling against her skin. "If it becomes public knowledge we're together as any more than grant officer and applicant, it'll paint a fresh new target on us. A big neon sign on my back that says 'This Way To Emily Barton'. I'm decent enough at evading a tail, but we should discourage it anyway."

She shuddered. "They'll follow you?"

"We need to make sure that doesn't happen," he repeated. "Even if it means, for now, omitting certain details in conversation with friends."

"Omission is why you're having to run financial traces now," she reminded him.

"Trust me, if Murphy doesn't know you're mine," and she sucked in a breath at that blunt declaration, the way he said it like their relationship had staying power in daylight after all, like it wouldn't be all over once the numbers were crunched and the bad guy behind bars, "he won't have a reason to use our relationship as a hunting ground."

EMILY TRIED NOT to let the fear get under her skin, tried not to let it bother her, but she couldn't stop wondering if someone was waiting around every corner in the Partner Paws building. Or hiding in the ceiling. Under the desks. Just waiting to return her to Murphy's warehouse of horrors.

She sought refuge in the kennel room out of habit, elbows over the running pen, eyes closed. Faint threads surrounded her as if they'd always belonged and she sighed. This was her world now—a power she could barely grasp. Idly, she reached out with her mind to take a closer look. From the animals to her ran a constant stream of calm and encouragement. The same way it had when withdrawal from Shiv's drug had pulled her under, only less potent.

Emily smiled, but it didn't take long before she felt a twinge of distress. The energy reversed direction and immediately one of the office dogs limped to the edge of the pen, her nose pressing to the rail.

"It works both ways," she whispered in awe. Her fingers scratched behind the anxious pup's ears and as the emotion seeped from the thread she realized she'd come to the kennel for a reason. "It's how it's been all along, isn't it?"

It struck her that all of the times she'd thought an animal responded to her emotions so strongly, they could've been receiving a burst of her ability. Every time she was anxious, she fed that to them subconsciously. She paused in her scratching, got a bump to her palm in response. Sometimes the animals responded in direct contrast to her emotions. If she was afraid, sure, sometimes they'd skitter away, but other times they offered comfort. All the frustration she'd had trying to get the bond to send as well as receive . . . and she'd been able to do it from the start.

Emily's mental exercise took her back to Jay's thread, but she wouldn't test it or Torpedo's here. She'd save the revelation for later tonight, when they had privacy.

Soon the dog before her was ready to play again and she settled in for an active cleaning session so the place would be sparkling for the students arriving that afternoon.

"Emily? Hue's all fluffed nice!" Naomi cast a look around the kennel room and cocked her head to the side, dropping her voice to a loud whisper. "You don't think he'll come after you with everyone here, do you?"

"I hope not. But when the thug went after Julia, he didn't exactly wait until she was alone." Shoving the sponge back into her water bucket, Emily rotated her shoulder. "I think everyone will be fine."

"Does 'everyone' include you?" Naomi clicked her tongue. "You didn't put any makeup on today. It's a big day."

"Will you calm down if I let you douse me in blush?" She peered around Naomi at the yellow Labrador retriever behind her friend. "Tell me you didn't put a bow in Hue's tail. He's a boy dog, Naomi."

"Oh dear." Naomi's hand flew up to cover her mouth and she knelt beside the lab with a grimace. "Sorry, Hue. I'm gonna miss you, buddy. But you and Buster will do just fine now, won't you?"

Emily watched the redhead's careful fingers pluck the neon pink ribbon off the guide dog's tail. "Okay, I give. This isn't like you, Naomi. What's wrong?"

Naomi stared up at her from the floor. "I'm not sure. I—" She pressed her palms to the linoleum and waited until she had rebalanced on her yellow spotted heels before she continued. "Julia's the one who does the graduations. Not me."

And Julia was in the hospital. Wistfulness mingling with relief, Emily embraced the other woman.

"I know she'll be okay. I just . . . I miss her."

Hue's now-ribbonless tail thumped against Emily's bare calf

in a fast wag.

"All morning I've been thinking someone forced you to call me in," Emily admitted, stepping back.

Naomi straightened, tapping manicured nails over her forearms. She chuckled, but her bright lips twisted into a rueful expression. "Sorry to disappoint you, but no one held a gun to my head and made me get you to work today. There aren't any thugs or handcuffs to be seen. Just . . . so we're clear."

Footsteps sounded near the door to the kennel room and Emily turned to see Jay, in khakis and the casual-but-still-dressy button-up shirt he'd slid over his shoulders that morning, with his knuckle to the wall in an aborted knock. She flashed him a smile, but his eyes were wide and the set of his jaw grim like he'd overheard the tail end of their conversation.

"Everything okay?" Absently, she rubbed at her arm, and an edge of her bandage peeked out from under the long-sleeved blouse she'd picked for the occasion.

Naomi's eyes narrowed. "What is that?"

Emily tugged at her sleeve, ducking away from too-interested eyes. "I, uhm."

"No, what happened?" Naomi caught her wrist and yanked at the button on the cuff, peeling the fabric away. She threw an accusing glare at Jay. "I thought you were going to keep her safe!"

"It's just some stitches." She carefully removed her arm from her coworker's grip and a bolt of pain ran from the tips of her fingers to her shoulder. Wincing, she took a step away. The soapy bucket of water behind her tipped on its side and gushed across the floor.

"Oh!" Naomi's hand flew up to her face and her heels clattered across the floor as she went for the mop.

Jay swept into the room and took the mop from the other woman's fingers. Too-sexy blue eyes flashed Emily's way, then back to her coworker. "Emily and I aren't together, Naomi."

Ice water in her skull, her fingertips, her chest.

It hurt more than she'd expected. Because it hadn't been omission. He'd outright lied.

She knew he wanted to protect not just her, but his family, his business; going after Murphy from a legitimate angle instead of on the streets had challenges of its own. The last thing she wanted to do was make them targets. But to lie? Easily, so easily she hadn't seen a single flicker of remorse in those superpowered eyes.

"This isn't his fault." Emily stepped out of his way, watching him tackle the water. Admiring the flow of his muscles for too long would be problematic if they were going to play off his declaration in public, so she stretched out an arm to still the mop. He maneuvered out of reach. "Jay, don't. Let me get that."

"But . . . " Naomi frowned and stepped into her path. "The new spiffy apartment? Come on, I'm not stupid. We saw the place you were staying at over the video conference." She stooped to whisper in her ear, "Exactly how many men in this city could afford that rent? Are you sleeping with one of his brothers?"

"No!" Emily's eyes slid around Naomi. Jay didn't look up, but his shoulders tensed. It wasn't as easy for her, but she managed to rummage up an explanation that might work. "Their firm has been quietly working on clearing my name, and he loaned me a safe space. That's all."

Naomi looked startled and then down at Jay like she'd just realized how he'd gotten the mop in the first place. "I'm sorry. I'm gonna try to find Captain Nemo." Her eyes watered and when she fled the room, her heels barely touched the floor.

"Is your arm okay?" Jay asked.

Emily stared at the picture he made, a rich man in his version of street clothes, leaning comfortably on the worn mop handle. "You didn't have to clean it up."

"I don't mind." He pushed the mop against a stack of dog crates and reached for her arm. "Let me see. It looked like you hurt yourself when you pulled back like that."

"I'm sure it's fine," Emily said, but her words lacked conviction; she was already rolling her sleeve up over the bandages.

He ran his fingers on a slow course up the inside of her elbow. "Tell me if anything hurts. If you've pulled something out, I'll haul you to the Doctor Ninja myself." The last was for her ears only and Jay smiled. The worry in his gaze made her heart want to flip, but it was still staggering from his more-than-omission.

Heated emotions swirled through her head, ignited by his touch over bandages, for heaven's sake. How had he so easily dismissed their relationship? She felt swallowed by unease, a pang of guilt. Worse, Naomi's mention of rent had gotten to her more than she'd realized, standing in the middle of a business she'd created from sweat and hope and years of long-distance bus commutes, facing a man who'd had his wealth dropped on his shoulders and who made a midnight career out of lies just like that one. For the greater good. Even reminding herself that the youngest McLelas could have any woman he wanted with his fantastic body and limitless bank account did little to temper the attraction, even less to counter the hurt.

The warm, melty feeling in her chest that came from staring into the concern in his blue-gray eyes didn't have any doubts at all. Emily sucked in a breath and pushed the wounded and distracting emotions from her mind.

"Nothing feels out of place." Not like it had the night she'd ripped out half of them trying to wake him from his nightmare about Julia's grandfather. *Julia's grandfather!* A lightning bolt of remembrance struck her, a host of symbols colliding with the threads in her mind, and she swayed on her feet.

He stepped closer. "Emily?"

She shook her head, speechless. She'd already been excited to get to Julia's side, but maybe she could ask her about the symbols, too—maybe she'd have answers for the mysteries Jay didn't yet seem willing to explain.

His eyebrows drew together but after a moment he folded her sleeve back into place. "If your arm starts to bother you, let me know. Please. I'm at your disposal today, and I'm pretty sure the volunteer work still counts if I take you to the ER." He grinned as he pushed the pearly button through the hole in her cuff.

"Thanks. I don't think that'll be necessary." She flushed, fighting the urge to itch at the crease of pink fabric over the cut on her throat. The last thing she needed was to draw public attention there, too. A tingle caressed the nape of her neck, provoking both memories and fantasies of Jay's fingers traced over her skin, skimming over her bare shoulder to her throat where he could see for himself that her injury was healing. "But we could sure use someone to set up chairs."

Three hours passed and the man never left her side. Somehow, he managed to find work to do not far from where she tackled last-minute adjustments. When she ran into trouble looping a string of bows onto the folding chairs, his was the first set of hands to reach hers and patiently untangle her fingers and wrist from the ribbon. When Marco called in for a whole thirty seconds to apologize and tell her he'd make amends, Jay was there—with a serious one-wrong-move-and-you're-done glare at her cell phone—like he could ensure Julia's fiancé wouldn't go postal and hurt her through the phone line. When she climbed into the storage room to hunt down the missing trophy box, he provided a handy box-shuffling service while the other volunteers were busy leading the animals into the main classroom. And Jay's arms were snug around her waist to stop her fall when she tipped off the ladder with the box they sought clasped in a death-grip between her fingers.

None of which lent any credence to his lie, and by the time mid-morning and lunch were gone, everything was ready and the students trickled in for graduation, she felt back on even ground.

"Welcome, everyone," she said into the microphone on their loaner podium. "I just want to say what a pleasure it's been to work with each and every one of you. You've worked incredibly hard during your training sessions, both here, and at home." Emily tipped her head to Mrs. Bluseau—released from the hospital the previous weekend—and her voice cracked around the edges. "The past few weeks have been a little trying for us."

Her speech continued on a serious note, brushing over the attack and accusations that had made her life a living hell. Sparing everyone any personal details, she went straight to Julia's status and explained that the situation was looking up. She thanked the staff and the students for their efforts to make the latest round of classes the best yet, and a more sedated Naomi took over to call individuals up with their companions for trophies and certificates of accomplishment. With the ceremony nearing its close, she read off a list of last-minute announcements.

"I know you'll miss our smiling faces—I know I'll miss yours—so we have plans to check up on you. The follow-up instructions are in the folder you get to take home, along with numbers for some of our staff in case your companion gives you any trouble. As for you humans," she paused for a chuckle to work its way through the room, "you'd better be on your best behavior. Does anyone have anything to add?" She pulled back from the mic and sent a questioning look at the staff and volunteers standing along the nearest wall.

"I have an announcement to make, if I may," Jay said from the back of the room.

Emily nodded and he strolled up to the front. The smile he gave her warmed her insides like a toasty mug of hot chocolate and coffee all rolled into one. *I have* got *to get a grip on my hormones.* One just didn't think about a sexy man, chocolate, and coffee all with the same brain cell. That was how people got hurt. How hearts got broken.

"A few weeks ago, the young woman to my right approached me with a request on this organization's behalf."

Emily's throat tightened. *The grant?* She'd expected something about the video conference McLelas Financial had provided but now she stared at him, her mouth falling open.

"Since I started making visits to your classes and got a chance to talk to a few of you, I've learned quite a bit. You should be congratulated, staff and students alike, for your kindness, patience, and openness, even to a stranger like myself. It's sure made my job, and the committee's decision, a heck of a lot easier." Jay paused and turned to face Emily.

We got the grant! Her lungs stuttered like necessary air was trying to squeeze past her heart-blocked throat, maybe to keep her from dying of suffocation.

"Emily Barton, on behalf of McLelas Financial, I am pleased to present Partner Paws with our Rhodes grant for this fiscal year." There in his outstretched hand he held the piece of paper which would keep their non-profit running for another year. Real grant money.

Not the kind of cash a crime boss could rip out from under their feet.

A collective cheer thundered in her ears and she stepped up to take the envelope from his fingers. Brushing against his skin sent a sizzle of attraction through her so bright she wouldn't have been surprised if the whole room had seen the spark. She fought for every ounce of willpower she could wrap her mind around to restrain herself from wrapping her arms around his neck and kissing him in front of the world. Over and over her mind repeated the fact that for now, they had to lie.

"It's legitimate, every penny," he said, close enough to her ear to be intimate, and when he pulled back he winked. "I've been too busy to sway the committee."

"Thank you, Jay," she managed to say, her voice coming out far more breathy than professional.

He grinned as he stepped down from the podium and she retook the space with what she knew had to be a bright, nothing-can-go-wrong-now grin splashed across her face.

She couldn't wait to tell Julia.

CHAPTER TWENTY-FOUR

OUT OF THE ICU, Julia's room was in a less private area of the hospital, and the waiting room would fill up quickly with Partner Paws visitors. For once, Emily hadn't been thinking about alternate transportation as she rode in Jay's car. It meant she got first dibs.

"Emily!" Julia's arms lifted from the bed and Emily wrapped her in a gentle hug.

"How are you feeling?"

"Oh, much better, Em. I get to eat real food and they'll have me out again in a couple more days." She braced her palms against Emily's shoulders, a morose expression on her face. "I know it wasn't your fault. I asked them about the records that morning so they ran headlong down the wrong road, and of course I was holed up with all the blasted beeping. Think it's harder to get a phone call from the ICU than it is in prison."

"Speaking up for me from your deathbed," Emily said with a small smile. "Definitely the sign of a true friend."

"That creep who gave us the money in the first place was

behind it all. And I am so, so sorry for everything."

"You're sorry? Julia, you're the one in the hospital bed. I'm the one who should be apologizing." Emily pulled away and sank into the chair at her friend's side. In the trash can by her IV stand, a fistful of red tulips had been tossed in a heap. She flicked a glance at Julia's ring-less fingers.

Julia's dark eyes followed her gaze and narrowed. "I'm sorry about him, too. Confronting you like that? Trying to get you arrested?"

"Marco has a temper. We all know that." She sighed and fisted her hands on top of her thighs. "He's in love with you Julia. He wanted to put away the person responsible for hurting you. He thought that person was me. It's okay, really."

The primitive rage in Ninja's eyes when he'd seen Shiv's knife bear down on her throat slid into Emily's memories. He'd shot Shiv. It wasn't quite the same thing—she hadn't been actively wailing on Julia with a baseball bat—but Marco's actions were clearer to Emily than she'd ever admit to the woman she regarded like a sister.

"He hit a guard at McLelas Financial a couple days ago, trying to get in to see you."

Emily jolted upright. "What?" Why hadn't Jay or his brothers said anything?

"I don't care how much he loves me or what he thought you'd done. He can't go around punching people." She sighed. "We were working on his fits. Seeing a counselor, before I wound up in here. I thought I had it handled."

"You did. Whenever he's around you, he tries so hard, Julia. I noticed it in my office, after the break-in." Emily rubbed the flats of both fists over her skirt.

"It can't be like that. Marco can't calm down just for me. I can't build a relationship worrying about who he's going to flip out on next." Julia smoothed a hand over Emily's knuckles. "He had the gall to come by this morning to apologize for that stunt. Days without a word. He should have come to me first. Trusted me to—" Full lips curved down and she closed her eyes as if to hide the wash of disappointment from her only witness. Emily hurt for Julia, the strain in her friend's face, the fresh ache of an apology gone south. "I dumped his flowers in the trash. He wasn't angry. He wasn't tense or turning red, any of those looks he gets before he explodes on someone. He just looked sad. And then he took the ring back and walked away."

Emily squeezed her friend's hand, wishing she could soothe Julia like she was able to comfort the animals at Partner Paws. Why was the only human link among the mass of orange threads Jay's?

"But you know, I told you Young was up to something," Julia said, forcing a smile once more. "I'm so glad they've got him. Now the whole city can stop being mad at you."

"I should have listened." Emily let the subject change pass. They could talk about Marco some other time. Julia's off-handed comment rolled around in her head again and she froze, her mouth suddenly too dry to swallow. "What do you mean, 'they've got him'?"

Wouldn't Jay have said something if Murphy were behind bars?

Julia pointed at the wall behind her. There, on the TV that hung from the ceiling, streamed a headline across the bottom of the local news channel.

"McLelas accounting clears non-profit's head," Emily read aloud. Her mouth dropped open. A reporter appeared on the screen and she grabbed for the remote, cranking the volume.

"Police have named Miles Young, alias Murphy Jones, as a person of interest in this case. Thanks to McLelas Financial's forensic team, Relek City PD has issued an arrest warrant and is moving in to take him down. Guess that's one wad of cash that won't pay, eh, Mickey? Back to you."

Emily slammed on the mute button. "Why didn't Jay tell me they were already after him?"

Julia twisted to look up at her. "Jay McLelas?"

"Just this morning he said they were doing this behind the scenes. They weren't supposed to publicize this. Not before Murphy's in custody." Emily rocketed to her feet. "If Murphy sees it, he could have them killed!"

"Killed?" Julia's eyes flashed in alarm.

Emily stared at her for a second then dashed down the hallway and into the waiting area. Scanning the room, she blanched. He wasn't sitting among the other visitors. He wasn't here. Breathless, she ripped her cell phone out of her pocket and mashed buttons in a frenzy to find Jay's number.

JAY GROWLED AS he held up the cell phone to his ear, feigning a call in a mostly empty corner while Ryan apologized into his earpiece.

"I haven't even said anything yet, bro. But yeah, you're not gonna like it. Best get the growling out of the way first."

"Hurry up," he said. Guilt for snapping at his brother prompted him to add, "She's alone. Well, with Julia—"

"You gonna let me talk?"

His mouth shut with a loud click.

"We got full workups back on that drug Shiv dosed you with." Ryan paused. "It's a hallucinogen, definitely the stuff they're planning to ship in. Psychoactive stimulant of some kind. Zach says it's got mescaline in it, and he says it's mostly some kind of derivative of peyote. Stuff's designed to give a nice buzz."

"That explains a lot."

"It explains why your vision hit capacity. A little buzz to a normal person can send your eyesight into overload like that."

A clicking noise sounded on the other end of the line. "But the deal's like a ghost, Jay. We'll put more feelers out on the components to see if someone can trace shipments to any labs in Relek City. If there aren't any hits local, we'll take it wider."

He tugged on the end of his ponytail. It was more than they knew before, but it was still half-useless. "What about the plan?" Their big plan to finish Murphy—and his brothers' extra plan to take things to the next level.

"Zach and I have been going through these files this morning and I don't like the setup. My gut sense is hitting about as bad as his precog and I'm starting to think you're right. There's more to this than just moving drugs. Something big."

Jay sighed. "Not a lot of time to make different choices with the account pulls you made yesterday." Ryan had cleaned out Murphy's backup accounts but held the computer records secured so the crime boss would think he was in the clear to skip town with millions in stash. They'd be good for a couple more days before the hold recycled and the bank showed his true balance.

"Zach's meeting with some people to go over that information tonight and the theft records are in the hands of the police now."

"Hate to cut in, guys." Zach's voice popped onto the line, his tone grave. "I want you both indoors for the evening. I know you'll be good to go, Ryan, you've got that international business deal, but Jay, watch your back. And Emily's. Something ugly's about to go down."

His fingers tightened on his cell phone. "Your stomach tell you that?"

"Murphy's son was just found dead and my computer's throwing up data flags like a Fourth of July parade."

Jay beat a frantic pace across the linoleum, pacing. "What happened?" he hissed. "He should've been out of harm's way!"

Zach coughed and cleared his throat. "Word is he'd gone missing. Someone snatched him."

"That's why Murphy was so busy putting bodies in the ground this weekend," Ryan said. "He wasn't cleaning house. Someone took his son and he was trying to get him back."

"No, no. He's flipped. Out of his mind. We won't have any trouble pulling the crazy card with this crap. You should see all the records coming up on this thing." Zach's end of the line went quiet mid-cough. "Jay, they found Stefan's body in the woods, looking like he'd been chewed up by a wild animal. Maybe a feral dog."

"Wait. Zach, a feral dog?" Jay stopped pacing. Stefan had had a dog. The dog Emily was supposed to use to cure him. Fear crept back into the corners of his vision, a palpable shadow.

Zach didn't answer.

"Zach?"

"Shit, shit, shit . . . " Zach's faint voice returned, his mouth clearly turned away from the mic of the phone. "That is not the flag I wanted to see."

Much like the sound of Zach plowing a frustrated fist into something solid and most likely electrical wasn't what Jay wanted to hear.

"Murphy thinks she did it." Cold surety ground the words through Jay's teeth. He shoved the phone back in its holster and sped through the waiting room.

"Get her out before this hit goes through." Now an edge of anxiety splintered through Zach's usually mild tone. "You don't want to know how much it's worth to him to kill her."

"Emily!"

Her head jerked up as she pressed Call. The phone on Jay's belt crooned a Beatles tune, cutting off on a tuneful "Yeah, yeah, yeah" when she pressed the button a second time. His arms pulled her into a tight embrace. She gripped the back of his shirt, afraid to breathe, then looked up, her gaze latching onto his furrowed brow.

"Thank God you're okay," they said in unison. His blue-gray irises swirled, a tiny glimmer of silver flecks, alive with a host of emotions. Then he stepped back, holding her at arm's length.

"The news freaked me out a bit," Emily said first, when her vocal cords decided to work again. "Don't you think it's too soon for them to have said who they're after? And why did they mention your company?"

"What are you talking about?" Jay's expression was unusually still and he dropped his arms to his sides.

Time seemed to slow down around her. He hadn't seen the report. He hadn't seen it but was here anyway. "What . . . what were you talking about?"

He turned her, walking her back toward Julia's hospital room. "Did you get a chance to see Julia yet?"

She nodded. "We weren't done."

"Why don't you go finish up. I'll be right out here." His cell phone chirped at him and his hand flew to the device. "Do not leave this hospital without me, Emily."

She nodded, biting her lower lip. He swung around, holding up his phone without punching a button. Automatically answering—or he was actually talking to his brothers. Like some secret agent.

Emily touched the door to Julia's room and glanced back over her shoulder. The sheer relief she'd felt on seeing him, and that hug? She wanted more of that with Jay. It had felt right. Comfortable. But it was also public. As public as that newscast. Jay's fingers tugged at his ponytail and his muscles were tight with anxiety. The day had started so well . . .

"Everything okay?"

"I don't think so, Julia." Emily threw herself into the chair, propping her elbows up on the side of Julia's bed. Her fingers rubbed along the tops of her ears. Murphy had probably just added all of the McLelas brothers to his list and it was her fault. "I'm sorry I ran out of here like that."

Julia shrugged, a lopsided smile on her lips. "Anything I can do to help? I know I can't do much from the hospital bed. But make me feel useful so I can stop feeling so horrid about this forced bedrest. Anything."

Julia's grandfather. The thought sidled alongside Emily's fear and she lifted her head. "Okay, there is one thing."

She brightened, shifting to half-sit up in the bed. "Whatcha got?"

"I want to talk to you about your grandfather."

Her head tilted to the side. "What on Earth for?"

Emily ran a hand through her hair once before dropping her palms to her knees. *Here goes nothing.* "I met a guy."

"Ooh, a guy." Julia nodded at the door with a grin. "Someone I know?"

Her chest tightened at the thought of Jay standing outside on the phone. "Maybe I should start somewhere else." Spotting a pen and a notepad on the stand beside the bed, she snatched up the paper and scribbled down the loudest symbol in her head. "Have you seen this before?" The smile leeched from Julia's face and Emily's heart spun like a drill bit into the pit of her stomach. "Is that bad?"

"My grandfather was an Ohanzee shaman." Julia pinned her with a curious expression. "This symbol is for Spirit-mate."

A ripple of excitement jolted into her fingers and she closed her hands into fists. "But what does it mean?"

"Why do you want to know?" With a flip of her braid over her shoulder, she gave a weary sigh. "Does it have something to do with this guy? Is he doing research on tribes or something?"

"I saw it in a dream."

Her friend's eyes widened. "Tell me."

Emily recounted everything, from the lake, to the fire, to the tent and "the guy's" discussion with Julia's grandfather. Julia was silent except for a few clarifying questions. Afterward, she grilled her about the other symbols but Emily couldn't draw the designs right, so it was a useless tangent.

Julia popped the notepad across her knee. "You know this guy well?"

A frown tugged at Emily's lips. "Well?"

"Do you care about him?"

Emily nodded. "Yeah." Her gaze jumped, unbidden, to the blinds across the door. The back of Jay's head pressed against the glass. Beyond him, a shock of red hair bobbed in the hallway. "You know, Julia, maybe we should pick this up tomorrow. There are other important people here to see you and Jay's not letting them in." A small thrill went up her spine. Fear . . . and something else. Was he actually guarding the doorway?

"They can wait a little longer." Julia grabbed at her arm. "I'll make it quick."

She bit her lip against the pain. Her friend didn't know about the stitches, and Emily wasn't about to tell her.

"There is an Ohanzee legend, Em." Julia said. Her eyes unfocused, like she was remembering something from years past. "I'm trying to remember how he'd tell it, but I'm too tired to do it right, so bear with me. You get the layman's version." She released her hold on Emily's arm and sank back into her pillows. "In the legend, there is a great evil, and there are two wandering spirits. The spirits have a guide, who brings them together, who helps them form a bond to defeat the great evil. The belief is that when the two right spirits join together, they make a complete spirit, and they can unleash some kind of . . . power, I guess you'd call it. The two sides of the complete spirit are the Spirit-mates, and they say—"

Power. Emily stared at her, mouth agape.

The door swung open and Jay poked his head in. "I hate to interrupt, ladies, but I'm getting the third degree from a crazy woman with weapons for shoes and I think she wants to talk to you, Julia."

Julia giggled. "Okay. You were right. I better let the other visitors have some time. Wouldn't want to see Mr. McLelas get pummeled with ladies footwear."

Emily joined in her laughter, a grin spreading down to her toes. Jay abandoned the doorway and she jumped up to cross the room. "Thanks, Julia. I'll visit again as soon as I can, okay?"

"Em, this guy," Julia said when she hit the threshold. Her eyes were closed when Emily looked back. "This is a destiny thing." Dark eyes snapped open and found her face. "You're meant to be a team. To be together."

As Emily escaped the hospital out the back elevators with Jay for the second time, her heart crushed against her lungs and words completely failed her.

CHAPTER TWENTY-FIVE

GLINTING HEADLIGHTS OF MINIMAL evening traffic bore through her reflection and her hair buffeted around her cheeks in the breeze from the open windows.

"How long did you know about the grant?" Emily asked.

Shrugging, Jay studied the road with practiced intensity. "Last week. Sharing a bed did not make that an easy secret to keep."

"I'm glad you did. It was a wonderful surprise." She studied his profile for a hint of what he thought about the newscast, but he seemed determined not to talk about it.

His attention clearly elsewhere, he nodded and took another right turn. Down an alley.

She straightened. "Where are we going? Your place?"

He didn't answer, clenching his jaw and staring into the rearview mirror. Something was very, very wrong.

"You are followed." Torpedo's call cut across her skin like a dagger, raising goosebumps over her flesh.

Instead of a glimpse of brown feathers when Emily pitched

her view to the side mirror, she caught sight of a brown sedan pulling into the alley behind them. Murphy's men? She glanced at Jay and his fingers tightened on the steering wheel.

He pressed a button on his door and her window rolled up, dark glass between her and the road beyond.

"You and Julia had a pretty long talk at the hospital," he said.

"Jay, who's after us?"

He cast her a sidelong look and puffed out a lungful of air. Ahead of them, the stoplight at the next intersection, a five-way junction that long ago had bustled with bumper to bumper traffic, turned yellow. Jay slowed the car though no other vehicles were in sight, pulling to a halt when the light shifted to red.

"Plainclothes officers," he finally answered, glancing again in the rearview. "Zach sent them."

"So not Murphy's men."

"Only so many fancy cars on the street. Won't take them long."

Bitterness rose to her tongue, thick and metallic, like sucking on a penny. "Will this ever be over?"

Emily chewed on her lower lip and sent a doubtful look over her shoulder at the headlights swallowed by the lip of the BMW's trunk. He'd warned her it would happen if they were together in public. But that had been about their relationship, and this was about the evidence against Murphy.

Jay's fingers tucked a lock of hair over her ear, lingering on her skin for a moment before dropping back to the wheel. "Was Julia excited about the grant?"

She ducked her head. She rubbed her knuckles against the still-healing curve of her neck. "I forgot to tell her," she said, regret drawing her words low.

Jay's eyebrows arched in surprise, but he didn't turn his

head from the road. "Really?"

"I had some things on my mind."

"Like what?"

In the dark, she caught the glint of yellow from the opposing traffic signal. Jay crushed the gas pedal to the floor. As one of her hands grasped the inside of the door and the other braced against the dash, her body pressed back into the seat.

"Hang on."

A sarcastic reply stuck in her throat.

Rumbling under her feet, the tire seemed to skip over the road as he swung the car into a wide turn that didn't make a full U. Another side street. The smell of molten rubber made her gag.

Emily risked holding her stomach down with one hand while asking, "If they're supposed to be following us, why are you driving like we're lapping the Indy 500?"

Jay cut the curb the wrong way down a one-way lane. "If I can get a building between us and the car following *them*, our escort can keep going and we'll have a chance to run for it."

"Run . . . oh, no." Mind rebelling against more danger, Emily eyed the maniac in the driver's seat.

Lights from streetlamps zipped across his face, determination etched along his set jaw and high cheekbones.

It would be tough to fool an enemy when they were among the only vehicles on the road, but the wending in and out of streets might work. What little oncoming traffic Relek City had lurched around them and she could see hands slamming down on horns. Studying the tension in Jay's shoulders when he yanked the wheel to the left, her thoughts rattled with Julia's promises of fate and destinies.

Jay pressed a button on the car radio. "They off of us?"

"Won't last," Zach's voice hovered on the air, drained, weary. "Park somewhere and hoof it."

Her heart tumbled. The quest to stop Murphy had taken a toll on all of the McLelas brothers. She hated the note of exhaustion getting involved with her had created. "Is he okay?"

"I can hear you, Em," came the wry response.

Jay made a noise in the back of his throat. "I'm not going to lie to you."

"Sure you want to do this now?" Why did Zach sound so grim?

Fingers uncurled, Jay rubbed his palms on the wheel. "It's not just the mistake with the news. It's Stefan."

She blinked at him. "Murphy's son—"

"Murdered," Zach said.

The blow struck like a live wire. "No!"

Jay's knuckles were white.

"Not—" Horror pooled in her gut. "He's a child!"

Someone else's baby. A little, innocent boy with wise eyes and a bright laugh. Another meaningless death at the hands of madmen. Hot liquid pricked at the corners of her eyes.

"The killer framed his dog." A pause from the dash of the car. "The dog Murphy wanted you to train, Emily."

"Titan." The dog's name came out on a low moan.

"You understand what he's saying, angel?"

Quivering in the corner. Ducking away from Murphy's feet, his fists. That dog wouldn't have hurt a soul, not unless he were defending Stefan. *Stefan, oh . . . there would have been blood . . . so much blood . . .*

"Emily." The sharp tone snapped her out of her thoughts.

She looked up to see them turn one last corner, a building she didn't recognize looming out the front window. "But Shiv's dead," she said slowly. "I thought . . . why would someone . . . who would—"

"It doesn't matter who did it," Jay growled.

"It most certainly does!" She bit her lip against the brewing outburst. He couldn't be cold to that, couldn't be so ruthless.

Reaching, needing to know, Emily found the thread between them crackling with turmoil. Anger, fear, determination so fierce she jolted in her seat as though burned. No, Stefan's death had hardly left her man unaffected.

Innocent boy. Innocent pup. Had anyone found Titan? Had the killer—Emily choked back a sob.

"You two get home first," Zach ordered. "That's priority. Murphy wants blood. Don't let it be yours."

Jay nodded. "None of us are safe."

Funny how it seemed people were worse off the closer they got to her. She clenched her fists. No. This was Murphy, his syndicate, the criminals parading around the streets of a city she was coming to know all too well. She couldn't shoulder their actions any more than Jay or his brothers could.

Emily managed a ragged breath around the tightness in her chest. "We can't just let—"

"We won't," Zach promised. "Klepto won't."

"Zach, we're heading out." Jay unhooked his seatbelt.

"'Bout damn time. Don't go through the front." Zach's final words before Jay cut the radio off again.

Emily barely registered the warning. They were parked between two hearses. Definitely not a sign things were looking up. Worry felt like a host of hungry creatures attempted to make her midsection a home.

Jay leaned into her side of the car and stopped, his heated breath centimeters away from her temple. "I want to kiss you. Hold you. Make this better."

His hand hovered over one cheek. Tendrils of air wrapped her body in a web of sensual conflict. Emotions beat against her, so tangled she couldn't grab on. Struggling against the shock of Stefan's death, Emily's mind slipped uselessly around the thread that bound her to this man—and Jay looked as though he planned to conquer armies. It wasn't painful, wasn't pushing too hard, her control holding strong, but . . .

"Jay," she gasped. "It hasn't been this strong since before we started practicing."

"I know." The sensation vanished under urgency. Instead of a kiss, he pressed the button on her seatbelt and shifted out of the car.

"Jay?" she called softly.

"Stressful thoughts hurt you," came the reply. "And we have to run."

It was a long, brisk jog-walk-jog down another back alley or two, frequent stops to give her sandaled feet a break. Tense moments of waiting for something she couldn't see. Torpedo's hoots sounded overhead, too fast to interpret but talking Jay through the aerial view. The sidewalk here was neater than the ones by her old apartment—less cracks, less missing manholes. She might actually have been able to ride her bike in a straight line instead of weaving around the obstacles.

Eventually the condo was visible, though they didn't go toward the massive glass atrium. Jay pulled her into the foliage behind the building, a small garden area with a canopy of carefully placed trees. A cluster of bushes hid a ground floor window, and they burrowed into the greens.

"Amanda and Ryan's place," Jay said. He dug in his pockets for a flat, black square and dragged it over the seal of the glass. "Unless you'd like to scale the building."

"Pass." She could barely draw in enough air to function and he wanted to—"Oh."

His eyes crinkled in the corners. "Next time, then."

Brittle, her lips curved. The pressure on their emotions eased, and she breathed in a sigh of relief. It wasn't over, but a rush breaking and entering job would bring them to safety.

The window panes slid upward. Silent.

Safety for now.

"Emily," he urged once they climbed inside the darkened room. "Look at me."

She turned from stepping over the sill and her gaze locked on to eyes an arresting, irresistible silver. Before Emily could formulate an audible protest, Jay McLelas suddenly filled her personal space, wrapped his arms around her waist, and dipped firm, tantalizing lips to hers.

Oh, Emily craved these lips. This fantastic kiss. The reassurance that they were alive. They'd outrun whoever Murphy had sent.

They were safe.

When she came up for air his name was a wondering whisper. "Jay."

"I will not lose you." A vow, and it spread through her like wildfire. Fingers slid down her good arm and tangled with hers. "We're needed upstairs."

IN THE SAFEHOUSE'S living room, Jay pushed the routine series of buttons to get the video conference setup running. He blanched the instant the picture came on, Emily's gasp right beside him. "Zach, shit."

Translucent gray skin and wary, exhausted eyes betrayed the harsh demands of his 'gift'. His cheeks were hollow like his stomach had been rebelling for days. If Jay didn't know the man's ability caused the illness he'd swear Zach had a foot in death's soup kettle.

Jay's voice lowered to a broken whisper. "How bad is this?"

"It'll pass," Zach brushed a hand over his face. "Don't you worry, little sister."

Jay almost bristled, but Emily slipped her hand into his. He'd meant her. Probably.

Zach's eyes gleamed. Both, then, daring him to take the bait. "You said this involved Emily," Jay said instead.

"In that it's about the drug Shiv was using, that's all." He pushed himself back, a stool squeaking across the floor. "It's deeper into this mess than you are, Em; I didn't mean for this lout to drag you along. Figured the boy's death was plenty to handle for one night."

Dragging her further into their double-lives hadn't been part of the plan. At all. He wanted her nowhere near the next phase of what Klepto might have to do. Being his Spirit-mate was far enough and he had yet to get that right. His brother's taunt was designed to do one thing: see if his woman would stay or walk. Jay already knew what she'd choose.

She squeezed his fingers, too curious for her own good. "You think I'm going somewhere now?"

Brave, so brave, his Emily.

Zach nodded, and data popped onto the sides of the screen. "Robert says there's more than two versions of the drug—" He stopped, sighing at the startled look Jay sent him. "Robert Washburn? Our M.E. buddy?"

"Since when has the medical examiner been our 'buddy'? I thought you were just hacking his files and the coroner records, not making friends. Washburn doesn't do bribes."

"Since sixty-odd dead bodies wound up on his tables, a third of which are confirmed to have had the same substance found in your system. In Emily's."

"More bodies?" Jay frowned and Emily moved into his arms. "Does Ryan know you've been sharing intel with a stranger?"

"I haven't had a chance to tell him. As soon as Robert's files came through I jumped." Zach's lips pulled into a tight smile. "I've dodged Ry's lectures long enough; figure I'm due. Now—"

His eyes narrowed in pain and he grabbed a Kleenex from a

box on the desk. Coughing into the tissue, Zach's eyes slammed closed, and he tucked it away too slowly to prevent Jay's sharp eyes from catching the speckling of bright red against stark white.

Jay stilled. "Zach." First their brother tried to hide his pain from him and Ryan, now he was hiding its escalation. "Go lie down."

"I'm okay. You'll know when I'm not."

"I'm not there to keep you from seizing all over the floor."

Emily's soft cry was muted, her hand over her mouth. He threaded their fingers together again, pressed a kiss to her knuckles.

God, he wanted to protect her from this, from every dark and fetid corner of Relek's streets. "If you won't rest then tell me why our 'buddy' has been so busy."

"The weekend kills. From the warehouse attendees. They turned out to all be dosed; either mutilated post-mortem or killed in ways that would cover up the drug." Zach pressed his palms under his eyes, his look dire.

No, if this was bad enough, lying down wasn't going to stop his brother's ability from throwing him into a seizure.

"The drug's a hallucinogen," Zach continued, "and the way it stays active for so long will put it in high demand once it rolls into the city. What Robert found when he compared bodies though, was that it looks to be in different stages of development. He was able to match different versions to time of death. It's like they discovered that side effect and they were testing out possible fixes."

"If they can get it to stop killing, they'll find their market demand." Murphy and Ares couldn't get that far. There had been enough deaths already.

"Now, it's possible Murphy killed them to find his boy—"

Emily sucked in a harsh breath. Jay tightened his arms

around her, rubbing his chin on the top of her head.

"—or maybe this Ares character has succeeded. Regardless, he's staying in the shadows behind Murphy, testing it out, seeing how far he can go to improve it."

"Did Shiv use it on Stefan?" Emily asked. She stepped forward. Not far, just enough that he only felt the slight tremble that traveled through her in their clasped hands. "He seemed certain that he would die. Was he was waiting on the withdrawal?"

The look Zach gave her was far too calculating for Jay's comfort. "You know even if we could prove it was someone else, Murphy won't stop coming for you."

"I know," she said. "But if it was, if you could prove the drug was in his system . . . would he keep running the tests if he knew it killed his son?"

It was a nice notion. If the world played fair, it might have been an option. But the world wasn't fair. And Relek City sucked innocent people like Emily in, chewed them up, spit them back up without hope, onto dark streets with far too many cracks and not enough manhole covers. It stole parents, sisters, brothers, spouses, kids, burned whole histories to the ground, turned family into vigilantes and killers and thieves. He tugged her tight to his chest.

A sudden flutter of reassurance caught at the edge of his mind, pushing. Emily's ability, trying to reach him. Jay closed his eyes and let her in.

"I'm not sure he can stop what's already in motion." Zach was saying, instead of telling her they lived in hell. "Ares will strike a final blow before long, and our persona has to be there to scoop up the pieces."

No. Jay's brain rebelled against the idea and Emily's reassurance pushed in stronger, pulsing through him. A fierce hug, an anchor in the storm of acidic fear that struck his core.

How could he try to have a life with her? Her reassurances just a day before, her good guy-bad guy theory, surely didn't include dealing. He could barely live with the daily guilt already. Zach and Ryan's plan to usurp Murphy's role—this new, hideous turn—had to stop, now.

He lifted his head. "I will not let us sell drugs on the street. No, Zach."

His brother sighed. "There's nothing you can do."

"Watch me," he growled back.

Zach crumpled the tissue in his fist. "I'm also gonna keep looking into the bullets like the one that got you. Weapon like that'd be too messy for a sniper or a regular brawl on the street—creative, but messy." He let out a low whistle that aborted in a light cough. "Doesn't mean he's not prototyping something nasty."

"I wish you had time to rest."

Zach stabbed his fingers through his hair and tried to glare, but the effect was wasted with the pain in his eyes. "Leave it. Em, keep him indoors until the cops take Murphy down, okay? I have a bad feeling the pain pills won't stay down because the two of you have the same damned inability to stay out of trouble."

CHAPTER TWENTY-SIX

EMILY KEPT THE THREAD to Jay stable until he let her go, the loss of touch making the bridge between them less potent. He bustled around, turning off equipment.

"He has an ability too," she said. "They both do."

His shoulders tightened, but he turned to face her. "Yes. And yes, Zach's makes him sick, and yes, it sucks, and no, there's not a damned thing any of us can do about it."

"But your alter ego can do something about Murphy."

He shook his head.

"Or they think it can." She closed the gap between them and took his hand, drawing him to the couch so she could lean against his chest without him walking away.

So strong, so shaken. Her man let out a harsh breath but let her pull him into the cushions.

Squeezing the back of his neck tight, he settled his chin on the top of her head, as much curled around her as she was into his chest. "I can't lose them. You. Anyone else. I don't know what will happen if we continue down this road. Every direction I look . . . "

She tilted her chin up a tiny bit and pressed a kiss to his collarbone. "It's terrifying, Jay."

Lightly, she pushed on the bond. Just enough to try to share a glimpse of what she felt when she thought of him tangling with criminals on the streets. But it was a fight he and his brothers excelled at, and if they weren't there to do it, who would?

"I'm sorry," he whispered.

"I don't want you to apologize for that. I want you to see a way through." She tugged on the end of his ponytail. "Tell me why you and your brothers are it. Why Klepto is the only one who can do this thing with the drugs, with Ares."

"You see any other masked vigilantes on the street?" he asked. "There's no time left to embed someone else; nothing even Klepto can do from the outside. And no one else is going to do what it takes to stop them."

Half a laugh broke free. "Do you listen to yourself when you talk? I mean, really listen, Jay."

He tipped down a quizzical look.

"You keep insisting you're not the good guys, that you aren't any kind of hero. But here you are, all three of you, in the thick of things and trying to stop a drug that kills people, Jay. Trying to get it off the streets." She pressed her palm to his cheek even as denial surged through their link.

His hand fisted on his knee. The harsh emotion wavered, tempered before it could overwhelm, and her heart flipped over. *Oh, my Ninja.*

"By dealing drugs. That's not getting it off the streets; not all of it. That's just controlling maybe a tiny piece of the big picture."

She kissed the tight length of his jaw before she tried again. "It's a start. And . . . you just said no one else can do it."

"If we're outside, it'll run unchecked," he admitted as he untangled their limbs and stood. He offered her a hand up, then headed toward the kitchen. "But we won't be aiding the situation, either."

"How will you feel if you can't stop it? If you do nothing and that drug keeps killing? The weapon Zach was talking about? Out there?" Drawing back, standing toe to toe, Emily stared into eyes bleak as a winter morning. He wouldn't be able to live with that decision. Her vigilante-slash-businessman-in-sneakers was built to help. "Can you picture doing nothing, Jay? Can you picture your brothers doing nothing?"

"Taking over Murphy's resources isn't the answer. It can't be." He rubbed his knuckles over her cheek. "The glimmer of whatever you see that's good here? We'll lose all of it. Any chance we have—"

"You won't lose me, Jay. I love you."

"You—" His surprise flickered in her mind and she bit her lip.

"Love you," she repeated, and plunged in, the emotion charging through their bond like a freight train.

Hope filled his sweet, blue-gray eyes but the touch of insecurity still lingered. Worried. Did he truly still think she wouldn't accept him for who—and what—he was?

"You're not a man who can watch people get hurt." He walked backward toward the kitchen so she followed, still trying to convince him, still trying to get through. "As much as I like the idea of you playing it safe . . . "

"Emily . . . "

" . . . being off the streets . . . "

"Angel . . . "

" . . . next to me . . . "

He'd turned and she followed again but an instant later realized she was trapped, the marble counter at her back. His hands on her hips. His lips parted. They lowered to hers, faster than she could take a breath.

And then Emily regretted the necessity of oxygen.

Her body responded in a firestorm of want. Not like before, not reassurance, relief.

All blistering demand. All *now, now, now.*

She melted into his embrace. With his nip at her lower lip and desire went molten inside her, seeping into her pores.

Accepting him like tumblers on a lock.

Tingling with lust, her lips couldn't get enough of that one point of skin to skin contact. Her tongue swirled against his and she pulled him against her, tightening their embrace and oh . . .

. . . oh, at this rate he was going to kiss her blind.

Inside the blue, dark gray stars circled the pupils of his eyes. She lost herself there, his all-consuming gaze, a sound of want escaping into their embrace. The musky call of aroused male greeted her nostrils and she smiled against his lips.

Her palms smoothed the sides of his soft shirt. Traced his chest and back. Plundered underneath, seeking bare skin.

Please, please, please.

He pulled back, only to drop kisses along her cheekbone. Working upward, nibbling lightly at her ear.

Emily couldn't stop her shiver. His hands were just as mobile as her own, sliding up under her blouse, almost-tickles along her sides, stroking her arousal higher without even touching her breasts, her thighs, the heat at their junction.

More, more, more.

Encouraging, her fingernails raked along his spine. He arched his back, pressing his hard length to her thigh.

"Angel, how can I keep you?" Jay murmured against the skin on her neck. He pulled her top up and over her head before she could answer. His lips danced along her collarbone and he proceeded to explore, driving her mad with teasing kisses.

"You already have me." She kissed his temple, tugged at the band keeping his long hair in a neat ponytail so she could bunch her fingers in the thick strands. "Just have to look—mmm."

His hot mouth found her nipple through the thin camisole and bra she still wore. The fabric felt too close to her flesh, constricting, and she longed to shed the remaining layers. Urgent, she worked at his buttons, hauling his clothes off his shoulders.

He obliged by shedding it the rest of the way and gripping her face in his hands for a long, plundering taste. Her vision grew hazy with need. Her fingertips skirted the evidence of the bullet he'd taken, potent attraction beckoning her to explore every taut muscle on display.

The camisole went over her head next and he resumed his exploration of her breasts, cupping one and brushing his thumb over her nipple. He bit down through the lace of her bra, teasing. Spikes of hunger for his touch arced through her body, leaving her helplessly wet and wanting.

Then Jay came up for another kiss that left her senses reeling and her toes curling. Smooth as could be he lifted her onto the counter and Emily leaned heavily into his embrace, kissing his shoulder, across his collarbone, his chin, his intoxicating, familiar scent stealing through every inch of her lungs.

She moaned as his fingers slid under her skirt, cruising up the inside of her leg, a fantasy-fulfilling promise. Pressing light, tender kisses to the hollow of her throat where Shiv's knife had left its trace, Jay's eyes shimmered in the dim lighting like campfires.

Campfire. Spirit-mate. Destiny. Her muscles locked and she shifted back on the counter, staring down at the man she knew and didn't know, all wrapped up in one delicious, handsome package. "Jay?" The plaintive whisper left a question in her husky voice.

He stilled, gripping her hips. His breath was hot on the valley between her breasts and there was no mistaking the effort on his part to regain control, slow puffs of air flooding over her chest as he exhaled. Dragging his head up to meet her eyes, regret etched across his beautiful features. Tremors of longing she both saw and felt, the bond between them so full in her head that it hummed. She tunneled her fingers through the now-loose curtain of his hair.

"Yes?" It came out on a gasp of air. He settled a hand on her knee and she wrapped her arms around him again, resting her forehead against his good shoulder.

Her thumb rubbed across the back of his neck before she dropped her hand and turned her head to look at him. "We need to talk about something Julia told me."

A wicked glint kindled in his eyes. "Now?"

She grinned, tugging on a handful of rich brown strands. "The word Spirit-mate." She paused when his expression shifted. She'd been right to bring it up. "Don't hide from me now, Jay. That word means something to you."

The promised pleasure in his eyes faded, replaced with a softer emotion, a measure of tenderness. "Where did you hear it? Tor?"

She shook her head. "A dream, this weekend. Julia's grandfather was in it. You were in it. Talking about your ability."

His eyes went almost comically wide.

"There was a symbol . . . that's what I wanted to talk to Julia about." She resumed threading her fingertips through his hair. "I thought maybe it might help what we'd been practicing."

"This symbol: Julia knew what it meant?"

"She said it was a destiny thing." She cocked her head to one side as his eyes darted over her face. "And you knew, already."

"It . . . " he began, shook his head, and then started over, "I did know. If there'd been a way to explain it without sounding crazy—"

"Crazy." She smiled softly, then dropped her hands to his shoulders. "We've been over this. You have super-vision, I have some kind of super-emotion-sensing, we both share visions through an owl who can talk, there's this crime boss—nope, nothing you could have said would have appeared remotely sane."

An uneasy laugh, his palms closing over her arms, stroking once, then closing again, as if he couldn't decide whether to hold her close or push her away. "When Julia said 'destiny', she was only talking about the abilities we share. Not about what just happened between us."

"I'm well aware it has nothing to do with how I feel about you. No one knows that better than me, and you should be able to feel that too, if I'm doing it right."

He grinned. "You are, angel, you are."

She gripped his shoulders and tugged, and he finally slid his arms around her back. "Explain it to me now. Please."

He nipped the lobe of her ear.

"Hey! I said please!"

His lips curved against her neck in a smile that matched her own. "I told you once my brothers and I were descendants of the Ohanzee bloodline. We all went through a walk like I did with Tor."

He pulled away and hopped up on the counter beside her. Strong arms tumbled her halfway over his lap, settling her across his thighs. She stared up from his lap, bemused as his fingertips grazed the skin along the edges of her bra.

"The fire . . . we didn't just lose our mother; we lost our heritage, too. We thought we'd lost all hope of learning about our abilities at all. We didn't know anything had survived the fire until we were going through our father's things when he passed. He'd been looking for ways to help us—but he could never break the code." He shook his head. "Now we have a linguist working on the documents left over, the symbols you saw, but it's taking too long. She cracked some of it in time to help Ryan and Amanda; she hasn't managed to find anything on mine or Zach's ability at all. Yet."

Her mouth opened.

"I think maybe it's best if they tell you themselves," he said, cutting off the question. "About their abilities."

Emily nodded. "But you're telling me Ryan went through this with his wife."

"Girlfriend at the time." He shrugged. "But no, whatever it is that we share, it's not the same. Similar—but . . . you haven't been able to use my ability at all, it's only been the visions. And my sister-in-law doesn't have an ability. Not like you."

She blinked at him. Ryan's wife could use his ability . . . whatever that was. Jay's story was incredible, and as it unfolded, she began to wonder if the practice they'd attempted had merely been a glimpse of potential. Maybe she could do the same; she just hadn't figured out how yet.

One of his hands left her skin to squeeze the back of his neck. "We wish we had answers. Through the research, or . . . well . . . Shiv was our last link to that fire, so now we don't even have a tie to its cause." He shrugged. "Our bond aside, I didn't even know enough to realize I'd go blind if I used my ability too hard until after the fire took those answers from us."

She brushed the back of her hand against his cheek and he caught it, held her fingers tight. "Julia didn't understand most of the symbols I drew for her, the ones I remembered from the dream. But maybe she can help?"

His eyes brightened, silver tracing the edges. But instead of responding to the suggestion, the arm behind her back lifted her, and his teeth nibbled across her lips.

Desire ignited behind her eyelids. Not hers, though the kindling that had kept burning from the evening's world-bending kisses easily caught with the temptation he pressed toward her mind. She squeezed her thighs together and narrowed her eyes. "Jay."

"Yes?"

"That's cheating."

A lop-sided grin as the invading emotion receded. "But you can tell the emotions apart, even that strong? Yours, mine?"

"Our practice helped," she said, nodding and wondering what the devious look on his face meant. Her body was on board with everything and anything it entailed. "Maybe Julia and your researcher can find something that will help it settle more, though. Maybe . . . maybe there is a way for me to share your ability, and they can sort it out."

He swept his tongue over her lower lip and kissed her without mercy, pulling her along in a sea of temptation and bliss. This time, all of the out-of-control emotions were her own.

"Your head doesn't hurt?" he asked, as if he hadn't worked her skirt halfway off her hips.

She raised an eyebrow at his satisfied smirk. "It's stable, and it's holding without me having to wall it off," she assured him in a voice made breathless. "Or really monitor it, unless I'm curious."

"You're always curious." Jay rubbed a thumb across her cheek. "I can't see the threads at all. You are right though, there's something there. I pushed on our bond, Spirit-mate. I needed to know."

She laughed, wiggling out of her skirt the rest of the way. "Now you know it works. But why the push?"

"Because I had to be sure, when I took you this time," and with one smooth movement, he scooped her into his arms and left the countertop, her skirt landing in a heap on the tile, "all

the pleasure in your head would be 100% Emily."
"You think that first time—ah. Would sharing be so terrible? Because it was pretty amazing before."
"Angel." A look that promised this time would be even better, even without a feedback loop of emotions. "This is me, trying not to make decisions for you."
She grinned as he stopped inside the master bathroom. His finger jabbed at a single button on the blue-tiled shower wall and then he charged up and over the lip of the tub, sending her squealing. Warm water cascaded over her, soaking through her bra until the lace clung, utterly translucent, to her skin.
"I've been waiting for this shower since the day you moved in." Jay's fingertips brushed down her spine. "Imagined you under this water like some kind of mermaid."
"I'm not really a fish kind of girl." She laughed and tried to turn, but he gripped her shoulders to keep her facing the back wall. "You forgot something," she said, wriggling a still panty-clad bottom against his erection.
"I'll change the wrap out for that arm when we're done."
She shot him a look over her shoulder and was met with pure mischief. He knew perfectly well that wasn't what she'd meant.
Jay unclipped her pink, lacey bra and slipped it forward over her shoulders. Leaning back against a warm, naked chest, she let the water sluice down her body. His left hand captured one breast, a finger flicking across the taut bud, and his lips caressed the side of her neck.
He nibbled at her earlobe and her head fell into the curve of his shoulder. She moaned, closing her eyes and grinding against his pelvis, excited by the catch in his breath.
A small strangled sound against her cheek. "You keep that up and this'll be a short shower." His erection jumped against the small of her back.

"We wouldn't have to worry about the hot water running out." She reached back for his right arm, pulled the flat of his palm around her waist.

Almost wholly skin to skin, he looped his fingers around the waistband of her underwear. The wet cotton clung to her skin when he tried for a smooth removal, and she turned in his arms, smiling.

"Trouble, Spirit-mate?" she asked.

Jay grinned. Both of his hands traveled below her waist, pushing at the offending material. His thumbs traced the vee of her thighs and she moaned.

"Definitely trouble. This is still okay?"

"More than okay and don't you dare stop J—!" And then he moved lower and she moaned, kisses across and down her breasts leaving a wake of fireworks.

He removed the last remaining shred of covering, his teeth lightly dancing along the inside of her thigh. She squirmed from the sensation, and he nipped again.

"Going somewhere?"

Not with her ankles tangled in a pair of panties she wasn't.

As if they had all the time in the world, his tongue replaced his teeth, whirling in a decadent circle.

Her hands wrapped his hair around her knuckles and her hips gave an involuntary buck. Liquid gathered between her legs even as his fingers massaged the curve of her ankles. At his gentle coaxing, Emily raised her foot off the tub floor, then traded her balance for the other, but before she could put the second one back down, he'd hooked his palm around her right ankle.

"Jay?" Uncertainty drew her gaze to his.

Hunger filled the silver look he angled upward; her mouth went dry with anticipation.

As he rose, one hand slid behind her to keep her balance

steadied, the other drew her captured leg up around his thigh. The hand at her back dipped to her butt.

Thrills of sensation shot through her bloodstream. Her arms went around his neck and he backed her into the tiled wall, crushing their bodies together.

"Mmm." Her lips found his and her eyes closed, a rush of colors exploding behind her eyelids. *More, Jay. I have to have...*

I know. The words washed into her mind as water pounded around them.

No, not words, images. Impressions.

He lifted her up and the notion vanished, pinned as she was between his chest and the wall. Her ankles locked around his hips. His lips devoured her skin, kissing the droplets of water across her shoulder, licked down to the center of her chest.

Moving them slightly to the side, he reached an arm out to a shelf outside the shower. He tore open the foil packet and soon his sheathed erection pressed against her opening. Driving into her, Jay groaned.

He pulled back, a slow, deliberate tease. Emily felt her inner muscles grasping, yearning for him, and she urged him forward again.

Water coursed in a river across her belly button, lower, lapping against their joined flesh. Their pace quickened, and she gave herself up to the sensation of his fingers massaging her back, his strong thighs bunching underneath hers with every long, lingering stroke.

Her toes tingled with the buildup of their passion, everything he was, everything she was, accepted by both.

No doubts lay between them at that moment. No secrets behind shadows or personas, no more wondering about whose emotions played through her thoughts.

The air before her shimmered, color dancing across the

strange Spirit-mate bond in her head.

Destiny.

Her heart responded, the link directly between them twining with need and desire—separate but together—sweeping her away on the tide of ecstasy. For the first time she thought she saw the world as he did:

Alive, a prism of living, dancing pigmentation.

A final moan mingled with her own as he pulsed inside her. His neck had gone taut, his palms flattened against the wall. Her arms wrapped tighter around his shoulders. Her forehead pressed to his as her body quaked.

His eyes crinkled in the corners and suddenly pleasure spiked in her head.

Under again. Bliss. Sparks along her skin, colors.

So many colors.

"Jay," she managed to whisper, once the planet seemed to settle back around her body, once the lightshow receded from the fringes of her sight.

He lowered her to the basin of the tub, blue-gray eyes shining with emotion. They embraced under the soothing cascade of water for a lifetime.

A lifetime with Jay McLelas? It was an adventure she wanted more than anything in that moment.

"Those lights," she started when she'd caught her breath, "is it always like that?"

"Only with you." He chuckled. "You could be more addictive than coffee."

She grinned. "Yes, please."

He turned the water off and spare droplets fell from the showerheads. Her hand rested on the curve of her stomach, but before she noticed, Jay did. His fingers wrapped around her hand and refused to let her budge. "Are you okay?"

"We used a condom this time," she said.

"Yes."

"But there's still that maybe."

"I will be here for you, angel, no matter what that maybe turns out to be." He nudged her chin up and kissed her forehead. "I will be here for you."

The line of his mouth dipped seriously, and her fingers moved of their own accord, claiming his lips in a decadent, mesmerizing trace. "No matter what happens, I will be by your side, here to protect you. Day or night."

Always.

He spoke of now and of times past shutting down Murphy and saving her clinic, through and beyond whatever Ares brought to their city. She turned in his arms with a small smile. He raised her hand, pressed his lips to her fingertips. For an instant, an impish grin crossed his face, then fled as his eyebrows furrowed.

She reached up to smooth his forehead. "Don't," she said. "Whatever you're worrying about, stop. Think about it later."

"When?"

"When we're not naked and soaking wet and having a beautiful moment, Jay."

He kissed the tip of her nose. "Be right back."

She watched as he turned to step from the luxurious tub, and then leaned against the water-streaked tile to watch as he bent at the waist, scooping a pair of towels from a shelf built into the bathroom wall. "It doesn't bother me, you know. If the maybe turned out to be a yes."

A slow turn. Muscles rippled and her fingers twitched with remembered strokes; she longed to savor them all over again. He held out a hand and helped her onto the bathmat, holding up the towel so she could step into it.

Before he spoke, he folded it around her, rubbing gentle circles over her back. "I want . . . If I were just Jay . . . but I'm not. It's—"

He cut himself off and Emily shook her head. Her heart ached for him, at the prospect he held himself back from offering, of something long-term she now knew he craved, while he punished himself, allowing himself so little.

"I know what you're thinking." His gaze was wary when she spoke. "How could I ever presume to bring new life into the world—an innocent—when I am such a bad, bad man." She tucked her palms around his face and forced his gaze to hers. "You listen to me, Jay McLelas. After everything you've done for me, for the clinic, for this city? You are one of the best men I know. With or without a mask. You are doing the right thing, for the right reasons. Because someone has to." She paused. "Jay. I trust you. And *I love you.*"

Arms circled her hard in the next instant, his lips crashing down to hers as if she was the single most important star in his night sky.

"You will be an incredible mother," he whispered. "A man couldn't ask—"

Keening sirens blared overhead and Jay spun, shielding her body with still-damp muscles tensed for action.

No. Not again, please, no.

"What is that?" Emily's palms plastered to her ears.

He reached for his khakis, hauling them up over his thighs and scooping up a shirt on the move. "Get dressed. I'll check it out."

She managed to grab her bra and panties as she tailed him to kitchen to locate the rest of her clothes. He narrowed a cautious look around the room, the lover gone, leaving the protector—hers—her lovely white knight in a world of gray.

The alarm ceased though the security panel on the wall remained lit up like a state fair after dark. When Jay's gaze landed on her, her breath caught in her throat. His pupils had dilated until there was barely a trace of blue and silver.

Just darkness.

Then they shifted again, contracting to a normal size. She couldn't help but stare.

"Come here," he said, snagging her left elbow and shoving her clothes and his car keys into her fingers. "Get down in that corner and stay there."

Before she crouched by the stove, he dropped a final kiss on her forehead. Fear rattled through her nervous system, a far cry from minutes before when she'd been battling an altogether different species of adrenaline.

He slid a hand into the drawer that should have held silverware and pulled out a handgun, then stepped to the side of the door, armed and dangerous.

Good grief. Our kitchen gets to be an armory too? Emily leveled a frustrated look at him from around the counters. "Maybe I can just fashion another flourbomb and take whoever's attacking us out for good."

Jay bared his teeth in an approximation of a smile. "Stay there, angel. I mean it." He twisted the doorknob and bounded out to the stairway.

Seconds ticked by too slowly as she wriggled into half-soaked clothes. Her sneakers waited by the door; she slipped them on, too. *Please be careful, Jay. Love . . .* Her heart squeezed tight in elation; the truth still ached.

The door banged open and she shoved herself into a tight ball against the cabinets, wishing she could crawl under the sink to hide. At her old place, she'd hidden the trash can under the sink. Maybe there was space here, instead of a plastic bin.

Jay gave the door a backwards tap with his foot and strode into the center of the kitchen, a huge orange tabby in his arms and his gun tucked into the waistband of his khakis.

"Stray cat." He shrugged, walking toward the alarm system.

"Little guy must've rubbed against the sensor. I'll go ping Zach."

Emily scrambled to her feet, watching the "little" cat, her brain refusing to believe her eyes but the thread clear with truth. Her throat made a little squeaking sound. "Nemo?"

He wiggled in Jay's arms, letting out a little meow when he spotted her.

"What?" Jay's eyes swirled black and silver, confused.

"That's one of my office cats. Captain Nemo." How had he gotten to the condo?

Bewilderment creased his forehead. "Captain Nemo? Now who's naming things after underwater—"

A crash sounded beyond the door. The wood slammed aside to reveal a trio of gun-toting psychos.

"Jay!" she cried.

Grunting as Nemo used him for a springboard, her lover spun.

Hissing and spitting erupted from the furball. One man lunged for Emily and the male cat launched to intercept. It wasn't enough. She heard a feline howl as she struggled in her captor's grip, crying out when he twisted her arm behind her back. Pain flooded her vision.

"You got away from me once," the man's voice growled into her ear. "You're not gonna cost me a paycheck again."

"No!" She didn't know him, didn't know any of them, but she knew there was no way they could take her or Jay anywhere.

A gruff laugh vibrated against her spine.

Angry tears filled her line of sight; she blinked them away and saw Jay struggling with a pair of assailants. Metal clattered on the floor. Her assailant's hand swept over her mouth and she bit down with all the fury she could muster.

She wrenched against her swearing captor and stared in horror as the other two men took the man she loved to the floor, one with a purpling left eye but his knee to the center of Jay's spine, the other sporting a bleeding nose . . . and a long, wicked-looking needle in his outstretched hand. The second man jabbed down with the needle and Jay stiffened on the floor.

Emily screamed.

Gusts of unexpected wind filled the air. Torpedo flapped through the doorway and dove at the man who held her, then at the man holding the empty syringe. Reeling back at her captor again made the arms around her loosen, and a gun filled her vision, taking wild aim at the swooping owl.

She winced, ready for the shock to her ears this time.

"No guns, you moron!" One of them yelled instead.

The man with the wounded eye yanked another loaded needle from his pocket. "Boss said alive!"

Alive.

"Run, Emily!" Jay said through clenched teeth.

She did, stomping on the bridge of the foot behind her, but she didn't make it out the door before Jay screamed. He wasn't touching her, yet their bond twisted with his pain.

Panic ripped through her system like a virus.

Nonono . . . Alivealivealive.

She scarcely touched the stairs on her way down, and she didn't look back, Jay's keys digging into her palm like a handful of knives.

She'd never find the car. She'd never be able to drive it once she got there.

But McLelas Financial was only two blocks away.

CHAPTER TWENTY-SEVEN

EMILY SPRINTED THROUGH THE lobby, a security guard tearing across the fancy tile after her. Jay had said Ryan was in a conference meeting for the evening and a quick glance at the directory on the wall showed a particularly large conference room on the third floor. She dodged into the stairwell, lungs burning, then zipped up the stairs. Pumping her arms, Emily tore into the hallway. The room marked with glittering gold "CONFERENCE" lettering held a surprised-looking assistant.

"Ryan McLelas?" Emily gasped, directing her gaze toward the closed doorway to the right of the reception desk.

"Your name?" the tiny woman asked, grabbing for her phone.

Emily took it for a miraculous yes and lunged for the door handles.

"Ma'am, you can't go in there! Wait!"

Emily moved faster, and she flung the heavy oak doors wide, the adrenaline flooding her system giving her some kind of superhuman rush. She stood there, skirt disheveled and a bra that was soaking through her camisole, balancing a door on each hand, panting for air at the entrance to the conference room.

No less than fifteen foreign aides, one on the massive television screen on the other end of the room, turned to stare at her, and Ryan's eyes looked like they could bulge through the lenses of his glasses.

Doubt, embarrassment, and unmitigated despair crashed against her insides. Emily took a faltering step backward.

"I'll just . . . outside." She released the doors and turned her back to the room, trying to catch her breath. It came out again with a hiccup.

The receptionist flailed across the desk for her damp, wrapped arm and Emily dodged, running back out the door and down the hall.

Plan B was already rocketing around inside her head. Zach. Head of security.

Must've seen her when she came in . . .

"Down . . . stairs . . . " she huffed aloud as her feet smacked against the floor, "office . . . "

"Stop! You there!" A voice that wasn't a McLelas.

Wasn't safe.

Wouldn't save Jay.

Alive. They'd wanted him alive.

Clinging to that desperate truth, she shoved the stairwell door open. Her arm throbbed, pain mounting in her shoulder, her neck.

"Zach," she panted. Rushing. Skipping steps. Not fast enough. "Need—Nonono! Put me down!"

Her heels beat against the wall. As her vision swam, she made out two security guards. One on either side.

They'd hauled her off her feet, held her up. Good guys? Bad guys?

"Please stop! Please!"

"Get off of her," a man growled. Hands jerked away. "Back to your posts."

Her sneakers squeaked, stumbling on the floor.

Ryan's voice. RyanRyanRyan.

Help.

Help was here.

She slid down along the wall with a great, choking sob.

"Now!" As the suited legs in front of her stiffly climbed the stairs, bulky shoulders blocked them from view. "Emily? What's happened? Where's Jay?"

"Help. Have to. Need," she said. Words cracked from her lips like broken glass; Jay's pained scream replayed in her mind.

"Emily." She saw his knees hit the floor. Worried, dark brown eyes came into focus, held her gaze steady.

"Ryan?"

"Yes." He gripped her shoulders.

"He's gone. Jay . . . is . . . " Panic ate at her, fueled the tears trailing down her face. "They took him!"

"Who's they?" The back of Ryan's hand pressed against her forehead.

"I don't know, I don't know." Emily swiped at her eyes. "They had guns and needles, and they gave him a drug, and he—and he screamed, Ryan. Please, please find him."

"Emily, did they give you anything? How did you get away?"

"No, just Jay." She stared at her hands. Shaking, everything shaking. "They had two needles, and he yelled at me to get out of there. And I listened. I ran . . . I left him, Ryan." She looked up, tears spilling over harder. "I left him and they have him and they hurt him—"

How could she have just left him there?

Oh, Jay . . .

"Emily," Ryan said, shoving her guilt back. "Tell me everything."

Her lungs stuttered around her explanations, and it wouldn't help; Ryan would need every detail she could remember. She sucked in air. One deep, shuddering breath, another. More details spilled out, Nemo scratching them, the owl, every word she remembered.

"Alive is good," Ryan squeezed her shoulders lightly. "Did they say where they were taking him?"

Emily shook her head and he helped her to feet that felt like water.

A blinding, white security jacket hung in front of her for a moment, then draped around her shoulders in Ryan's stead. Another man's arm went around her waist.

"I'll back you up from the HQ," Zach said.

"Z, she's—"

"I've got this."

His face came into view for a brief moment and he looked as pale as he had over the video conference. Emily choked on a breath. They all suffered from the dual life they lived. And now Jay—she crumbled, sagging against them, her adrenaline gone.

"Easy, easy, little sister." He swiveled her by her unbandaged arm onto a step. "Where is he, Emily?"

"I don't know," she wailed.

"Shh. He'll be okay." Zach pulled her head to his chest. "His earpiece is offline, bro."

"He never takes it off," Ryan said somewhere above her.

Zach's laugh rumbled against her ear. "He does for her."

He had, and because of her, he hadn't been able to call for help. Emily sobbed. Her fault. All of it, her fault.

"None of it. Enough of that." Zach's arms tightened and his voice moved away as he added, "Tor's locked and loaded." Then his voice was close again, gruff in her ear, "He's a McLelas. We're a tough breed. And we will find him."

A tissue came into view and she sniffled into it, then it

disappeared and a fresh one showed up. The quick change startled her, and she glanced up through beaded eyelashes.

"The last time he was hurt, you nearly broke my heart with those tears, little sister." Sympathy filled Zach's keen gaze but his mouth was set in a firm line. "Murphy will not keep him long."

A trickle of sanity crept in with his confident words, settling around her like a sunrise. She shivered.

"Let's head downstairs. Bet I can hunt down something warmer for you." His lips curved. "Dry, maybe. He'll be pissed if I let you catch pneumonia."

Oh, her clothes. Zach helped her to her feet as she considered her mangled attire. Her bandage, her skirt, her top, everything was soaked through, disheveled. One bra strap and the shoulder of her blouse had been ripped apart by Murphy's goon.

"Just get him back," she whispered. "Please."

CHAPTER TWENTY-EIGHT

"I SHOULD FIRE THOSE two guards before Jay kills them." Zach pulled the thread taut across her arm and swiped at another drop of blood with a piece of gauze.

"They were just doing their job. You know, stopping the crazy half-naked lady from running around the building." Emily jerked her eyes up to stare at the wall behind Jay's brother's head, fear and panic held in check by Zach's calm demeanor. And the fact he hadn't commented further on her wet clothes and bandage.

"Fine. A nice, midnight cat-tracking mission. They can carry your Captain Nemo back, they can keep their jobs. Fair?"

She was sure he meant for her to smile. It almost worked, would have if her lips weren't numb. Nemo wouldn't be found unless he wanted to be found, and he certainly wouldn't let strangers hold him. It'd been a wonder that Jay had been able to.

But then, Nemo could sense her emotions. He'd have known Jay was hers.

She counted, measuring her breaths, determined not to sob all over the electronics as Zach rolled out a fresh length of gauze. "The stitches came out long before you showed up."

"Only these few places where it's still in danger of tearing. You heal quickly," he said.

Mortified, she wrinkled her nose. "How many times is this?"

"Just the one. Well, Two, if you count today. I worked on your palm too, but that's looking much better now." He pulled out a piece of medical tape. So ill before, Zach looked better from the short trek down to his office. It could have been the quiet coil of determination behind his eyes. "Jay had to fix you up a couple of times because he's stubborn."

Her face fell and she plucked at the sleeve of the oversized black t-shirt he'd let her borrow. Her legs were stuffed into a pair of women's jeans she wasn't about to ask after, but the shirt was Ninja Couture.

"Ry's gone to find him. He'll be fine. And so will you." He smoothed his hand over the fastener on her bandages. "We'll hang out for a little while to wait for them to show, and if they need me before then, I'll just lock you up here in the command center so you can't pull these out again."

"Must be a McLelas thing."

"What must?" He turned away from her to jab at a button on the console.

"The urge to lock women up to keep them from hurting themselves."

"And yet, strangely, it hasn't managed to work," Zach tipped a wink in her direction, slapped his palms over his knees, and shoved to his feet. "How's the arm now?"

"A little Frankenstein's monster." A tight smile worked that time. "Can I ask you something?"

"Go for it. Not much to do unless Ryan puts a call in." He shrugged and strolled to the other side of the room toward a row of jackets on the wall.

"I want to understand what you and your brothers do. What all this," and she gestured around the small room, "is for."

"Didn't get enough of a taste this afternoon?" Zach flashed his teeth. "We're shutting down the bad guys."

"Jay doesn't see it that way." She rubbed her hand over the goosebumps that traveled over her good arm.

"Sorry. I have to keep it chilled for the hardware." Zach returned with a trench coat from the wall hanger and slipped it over her shoulders, then dropped back into his chair with a shrug. After popping what looked like more than a recommended dose of painkillers, he added, "Jay has a broader definition of bad."

She pulled the coat tight around her and gave him a grateful nod. "I'd noticed. Zach, I get what you do. I'm asking how."

Zach sighed. "Okay, here. These are sensors that we set up in warehouses, apartments, places where people gather to talk about things we might be interested in." He tapped his fingers at various instruments across the panel, carefully labeled buttons and switches. Descriptions of form and function poured out of him, animated enough to make her smile easier. The middle McLelas brother seemed to find it fascinating that he'd come up with the idea for one of the re-routing techniques while standing on a rooftop in a hailstorm.

Emily's hand pushed against her forehead and Zach stopped talking.

"Too technical?"

Her smile widened. Half of it hadn't made any sense at all. "You're fine. Please, go on." Anything to get her mind off what could be happening to Jay.

He narrowed his eyes at her briefly before resuming his explanations, but this time he steered clear of pointing out his wiring methods. "We tune in, find out when shipments—

whatever they might be—will drop, learn the plans before the police. Sometimes we get there first and make sure the shipment's already gone, or replaced with something useless, so the fallout hits their bosses, sometimes we call it in and let the bigger ones get pulled in to the police station." He paused, a grim expression on his face. "Sometimes we have to kill people."

Emily nodded. "Jay's never killed anyone before, has he?"

Zach turned away from the blinking lights, quiet for a few moments, weighing his answer before he spoke. "Would you love him any less if he had?"

"No." She didn't hesitate. "I know what he's capable of. He shot Shiv to save me."

Zach shrugged. "As far as he knows, he's never taken a life. I killed Shiv."

Emily's breath caught in her throat. *As far as he knows?* "Who did he kill, Zach?"

"Drug dealer. Jay got pinned down in an alley, bullets raining over his head, and I backed him up. When it was over, I cleaned up the mess and told him he hadn't hit anyone." He scrubbed his hands across his face.

Why would he tell her, but lie to his own brother?

Emily closed her eyes. He'd been honest with her because he wanted to see if she'd accept Jay. So she'd know exactly what she'd gotten herself into before it was too late to turn back.

It was already too late. She loved Jay McLelas. With every shadow he walked in.

"We made him train at the shooting range for two weeks before we let him run any more jobs." He shrugged.

"Target practice?"

Zach grinned, but it was gone too soon. "He's my little brother, Em. And he's too much of a bleeding heart to know half the shit I get up to on my rounds. I'd rather keep it all off his conscience, and Ryan wants to keep the both of us indoors so he can fix the whole city himself."

He cast a covert look at the display. Worry chased across his face even though he tried to play it off. It reassured her, in a way, because she knew she wasn't alone and Jay's brothers would do anything and everything they could to bring him home safe.

Emily chewed on her bottom lip and did what she could to keep him from fidgeting. "Why did the reporters release the information early?"

"They decided to flash Murphy's face around in case someone spotted him and could call in a tip. But they weren't supposed to mention us." His gaze turned dangerous. "Did you see Jay's eyes when they drugged him? Even a little glimpse?"

She shook her head. "You think it's the same drug as before?"

"If it's the drug they're bringing in, it sets off his ability. Like the withdrawal did for you." Zach got to his feet and paced the room with his hands clasped behind his back. "That drug clung around his system for two days, turned his eyes into a personal hell." He paused mid-stride and moved to stare into a darkened side room. "That was one dose. I don't want to think about two."

Her chest squeezed. The sob she was struggling to hold in must have gotten loose, because he turned.

"Zach," she said, "if they really want him alive, they wouldn't use that drug, right? They don't know he can survive it."

Mulling it over, his eventual response was not as reassuring as she'd hoped, "Depends on how far the tests have come. And how far Murphy's gone to—" He held out a hand. "Worrying about it isn't helping, Em. Come here a sec."

Hugging herself to keep her hands from shaking again, she stood to join him.

"He told us about the emotion-thing," Zach said. "How you were able to project to Torpedo. Receive projections from both of them."

Emily made a sound in the back of her throat. "Emotion-thing? Is that what he called it?"

He rolled his shoulders back, adopting a thoughtful look. "Got a better word?"

She shrugged. "Empathy? I don't know."

"Are you able to access it?"

"Yes . . . " she answered, drawing out the word.

"Good. It gives you a link to Jay that we don't have, and before the night's out, we might need your superpower."

Her heart did a slow, lethargic flip. A way she could help? She'd take it. "Jay said you and Ryan could do things too. But you must not have a lot of experience with superpowers if feeling how frustrated someone else is inside my own head is your yardstick."

A short laugh. "We all get a little pizzazz from our spirit guides. Ryan has Romeo. Our older brother can overhear a conversation from fifty feet away and through a solid concrete wall. You've met Tor. He's Jay's connection to seeing in the dark, long distances, that kind of thing." He stalked through adjoining room's doorway. "And mine . . . "

Emily stepped carefully in after him. In the darkness, air rushed past her ear. A sharp, biting chirrup of sound filled the shadows.

Zach clicked the switch on the inside wall and the other room brightened, rows and rows of what could have been crates of wine. He pointed at a rod that hung over what appeared to be a remote-controlled window. In the basement. Her eyebrow went up, and that's when she spotted the tiny brown creature clinging upside down to the bar, leathery wings coming in tight to cocoon his body.

"Drak. Fastest way to get him to roost," he explained, "Flip on the light."

"A bat? Your companion is a bat?"

"Before you go for the broom, I'd like to point out the benefits of having one of these little guys around. For one, we never have to worry about bugs."

A broom? She'd been about to pet the little thing. "You do know what I do for a living, right? I most certainly do not hit animals." Emily threw him a mock look of affront, which dissolved into a grin. "He's adorable."

His mouth dropped open. "Adorable? My spirit guide is adorable?" Zach groaned. "Thanks, Emily. You sure know how to make a guy feel all strong and manly."

"So Jay's vision, Ryan's hearing, both are enhanced because of the animals they've bonded with. Where does that leave you?" She quirked an eyebrow again, this time at a cup filled with fleece fabric that sat on top of one of the cabinets. "Oh, tell me that's his."

A grumbling sound didn't answer the question, but his eyes held a smile.

Delighted, she laughed. A teeny, tiny bed for a teeny, tiny bat.

Zach coughed. "Echolocation. He can see you before you can see him."

"You have built-in radar?"

"No. My ability doesn't work like my brothers'." As quickly as he had opened up, Zach shut down, his face shuttering against the line of questions.

The loss of his candor hurt. It took her too long to realize the stinging emotion wasn't her own, but rather a thread in her mind that had swelled and then vanished just as quickly. *Drak?* She eyed the bat, reaching with her ability, but if there'd been a thread she couldn't find one now. Nothing happened. The creature didn't so much as flick an ear.

Zach's eyes had gone flat. Because he didn't want to discuss his ability? Or because he was worried about Jay? He ushered her back toward the equipment. Ryan checked in once; he'd located where they were holding Jay. And Jay was still alive.

She clung to that as the minutes passed, clung to the fact they wanted to keep him that way. After another hour, her stomach made a pitiful sound. Zach's head came up and he tugged her from her stool, into the hallway.

"Where are we going?" Emily gave him a suspicious look.

"That wasn't a monster growling. Thought you might be hungry."

They were getting too far away to hear if Jay or Ryan reported in. She pulled to a stop. "You can't just leave the speakers unattended," she said. "What if Ryan calls?"

"You're right. Why don't you grab something from the vending machine, then? It's halfway down that side, in the little alcove." He pulled his wallet out of his back pocket and shoved it into her hands, then skipped back a step. The nausea etched in the planes of his face sat at odds with the casual tone of his voice. Zach had the look of a flu patient about to hurl on her shoes.

"Are you okay?"

"No food for me," he said with a forced smile. "Just gonna head back and listen."

Emily turned and headed for the vending machines. One all the way against the back wall had a variety of chips. She was just about to feed it money when the noise of a scuffle erupted down the hallway.

"Where is my brother?" Zach's voice flew to her ears and Emily backpedaled to the alcove entrance.

In the middle of the hallway, he launched into a wrestling match with one of the men who had taken Jay. Zach clocked him in the jaw. "Who are you?"

Here? They're coming after them here? Where are his security guards?

His assailant feinted one way and Zach got off another punch. But there was another needle. It grazed his arm and he wavered. The man kicked him in the side then plunged the drug into his arm. Zach landed with a grunt.

Her hands clamped over her mouth to muffle a gasp. Movement behind her caught her eye and she ducked around the Pepsi machine, sliding along the wall. A second man passed the alcove, the gleam of a needle between his fingers. She couldn't do a thing. It was a little late to warn him. Her fingernails bit into her palms. She was so tired of doing nothing.

He knew. The thought tapped at her mind, explained why he'd been in such a rush to get her further away. It wasn't a surprise attack. Zach had landed the first blow.

A booted foot slammed into Zach's spine and she winced. Zach was down, his eyes closed. Maybe he hadn't felt it. Fury drove little holes through her fear. What could she do? Her emotion ability had no impact on people.

"Where's the other one?" The second man grabbed Zach under the arms and dragged him down the hallway.

"Beats me. I thought we'd pegged them both. Ares'll just have to wait."

"He won't like that." The stairwell door creaked open.

The other man laughed. "I don't like him."

"What do we tell Murphy about the girl?"

"Tell him she's dead. She will be soon, anyway. It'll be easier to kill her with her bodyguards out of the picture. We'll finish the job later and he won't know the difference."

The stairwell door snicked closed and Emily's fury blasted through. She peered around the vending machines. The hallway was empty. "They are not going to die. And neither am I." Conviction laced her footsteps as she returned to what Zach had called the "command center".

"At least they didn't come in here," she murmured to

herself, shutting the door. Emily's fingers splayed over the controls and her mind mulled back over Zach's meandering explanations. She picked up a desk microphone and pressed two copper buttons. "Ryan?"

A monitor switched over from a stationary camera of the private parking garage to one of the main floors. The men had stopped on one of the lower floors and Zach's security cameras traced their movements. Her fingers hovered over another pair of buttons. A red light flashed and the screen zoomed in on two other men meeting the first pair in the hallway.

"Security. Finally." Transfixed, Emily watched the silent, grainy movie play out. But no, the newcomers shook hands with the kidnappers, then one of them pulled a gun from beneath his blue dress coat.

Her breath clamped in her throat. The second pair of men didn't belong to McLelas Financial's security, but they fought with the original kidnappers and their coats reminded her of Shiv. "Who are they supposed to be?" Thick forearms wrapped around the throat of one of the first men and tightened with a jerk. His body dropped to the ground in a heap next to Zach.

Her fingertips dashed against the control panel. "Ryan!"

Static.

"Ryan, it's Emily. Can you hear me?"

Still nothing.

She stared at the motion-sensitive video. Littering the hallway with death, the two new men grabbed Zach between them and continued dragging him down a flight of stairs. The third man lay sprawled on the steps, motionless, crumpled over a cascade of blood.

"Where are they taking him?" Emily had to keep trying. She had to get through to Ryan before something happened to him, too. Tearing her gaze from the monitor, she focused on the panel under her hands and pressed down on the buttons again. Zach had explained the comm system; they were the right controls. So why weren't they working? "Ryan?"

"*Emily, what are you doing?*" Ryan's soft voice flooded her head, but it wasn't coming from the speakers. She looked down at him, hovering just out of reach, his trench coat flapping in the night air. "Emily?" He swore at his mic and yanked it out of his ear, staring at the device. "Where's Zach? Why isn't it going through?"

Her vision spun out and away, turning a slow loop around the block. Emily tugged away from the vision but it held fast, swooping first down around a grated skylight then into a patch of fog. Buoyed on air currents, she circled the grate again. Torpedo was trying to tell her something through the vision, but the owl's thoughts weren't strong enough in her mind across the distance.

Jay's spirit guide took off again, dragging her along for a ride that seemed to last forever. Finally, her gaze landed on the address of the building where Ryan stood watch. 313 Windsor. Emily knew the area; a Partner Paws' student lived nearby.

Thank you, Tor. Now, let go.

The flying persisted.

Eventually, everything paused; her owl vision coming to land near Jay's brother as an alley below flooded with headlights. Ryan crouched low. "Great. More company." His lips puckered in a low whistle. "Here's to hoping he locked her up before he decided to go in the hard way."

The barred owl let out a screech and the thudding of Emily's heart echoed the sentiment.

She was done with locks and keys.

Her eyesight returned to normal with none of the usual overwhelming sensations. "I am getting better at this." If she could handle the visions, maybe Zach was right; with the comms down and without his technical expertise, there was only one way to get eyes on where they were being held.

Torpedo.

To have the best chance for their combined abilities to get through, she had to be closer. The exact opposite of where she wanted to be in relation to Murphy . . . but he had Jay and Zach. Ryan no longer had backup.

"Here goes nothing." Groping on the desk for a pair of communicators like she'd seen Ryan wearing, Emily shoved them into the pockets of her borrowed jeans then headed for the side room.

The "window" opened to a metallic tunnel, air humid enough to be from outside. She shrugged out of the spare coat and pulled her knees up. Those super-ears Zach had mentioned meant Ryan would know she was there. She wouldn't need to be too near the action, just close enough to be heard and to project impressions, emotions.

The McLelas brothers had done more than their fair share. It was her turn.

CHAPTER TWENTY-NINE

JAY ROLLED HIS SHOULDERS against the wall and let his brain remember what it was like to think. The drug that they'd given him had run its course like a launching rocket. A weaker version of Shiv's bullet. A lot more kick on impact. His mind had taken the battering but he hadn't been able to stop Murphy's thugs from laying their hands on Emily.

At least the cat had been able to distract them. Regret slid in alongside his fear for Emily. Had the cat—Nemo, she'd called him—made it after she escaped the condo?

He groaned. She was deeply connected to her animals. If something had happened, Emily would feel it. His fault for bringing Nemo into the condo—and what if he hadn't? Jay shook his head slowly, the world rocking from side to side. There was nothing he could have done for either of them; nothing he could do now. But Emily would have gone to his brothers for help. She'd be safe. And Zach or Ryan would already have made plans to set him free.

He stared around the abandoned office space. Dark, layered

in dust, stacked with broken furniture, nothing near enough to use for escape. Possibly a chair leg or two he could use to bludgeon the guards beyond the doorway. If he could get his fingers to work.

His gaze continued toward the ceiling. Blocked by a metal grate was a skylight window, the space between the wire squares mere centimeters across. A way out. If he could stand. Jump. Work the grate out of the ceiling. And maybe climb. None of which were possible while he couldn't feel his legs.

Murphy's men still hadn't said what they wanted from him, or why he was still alive. If Murphy thought McLelas Financial had enough to send him to prison, he would have sent a kill order. If he knew Emily was still out there he would have Jay out there too, leading the way to his target. Or as bait. A pile of dust coursed forward on a harsh exhale, floating over the cracked concrete floor. His lungs barely refilled past empty.

Has he figured out who I am?

Jay blinked as swirling dust hit a solid shadow. He squinted. Pinpricks of silver speckled his vision, skirting around the dark lump on the floor. Carefully, he expanded his night vision. A headache pounded behind his eyes, but he could make out limbs. A body. A little further, and he recognized the face: Marco Ramírez. Anger rose in his throat, followed swiftly by bile. The man deserved a rotten send-off for betraying Emily, sure. But he didn't deserve to be drugged and left in a hole to die.

Excellent. Now I have to levitate two of us out of here.

A sleek shadow cut through the moonlight. He tilted back a groggy head. That'd be Tor, cutting a circuit. Not much he could do but watchful waiting. Unless the wings overhead meant his brothers were mounting a rescue.

Watcher, came the call.

Too loud, too bright in his head. Still, he struggled to send a response.

I'm here.

The spin cycle of images Tor sent next made Jay want to vomit.

In the hallway, footsteps pounded. Feigning the way his muscles sagged was easy. He'd regained some strength but not enough to put up a decent fight; everything felt like rubber. The last thing he needed was to lose the clarity he'd won back from the grip of the drugs.

The door swung open. Zach's body joined him in the makeshift cell and Jay's fists threatened to clench. He lolled his head toward the unfamiliar man who towered over them. Got a strong nudge with a booted foot in return. Mercenary. Gruesome, crocodile smile. And if this slimy reptile had hurt Zach—"Rest up, McLelas. More soon enough."

More what? More doses? More bodies? Did they have Ryan, too?

"What are you after?" Jay asked, his voice scraping the insides of his throat.

No answer. The merc just turned and left, slamming the office door. Footsteps faded from earshot and Jay tried to move. Wound up on his side like a damned pile of laundry. Helpless. Swallowing convulsively, he watched his older brother struggle for air. Zach's chest barely moved, his side riddled with fresh bruises.

Your play, Ry.

Moonbeams shifted across the floor in a grate pattern; the night's light was a foot higher in the sky by the time Zach opened his eyes.

Jay was trying to decide if he had enough energy in his newly mobile limbs to maneuver Zach into a more comfortable position when his brother drew himself up to his knees. With a wince he crawled over and nudged at Jay's shoulder.

"They run you through a trash compactor?" Zach shifted to slump against the wall next to him.

"You should talk," Jay said. He tipped a worried look at his brother's side. "They beat the hell out of you. Please tell me this isn't part of an elaborate escape plan. 'Cause it sucks."

"I'm fine." But his eyes squinted in pain when he rubbed at his bare chest. "My plan was to keep Emily out of trouble, not to rescue your sorry ass. Went a little off."

The sick feeling in Jay's gut amplified. "Emily is—"

"She's good. I provided a distraction and they hauled my ass out solo. You hear from Ryan?" Zach frowned when he shook his head. "He was with Tor. You should have heard or seen something by now."

"Tor, yeah." Jay pointed up at the window. "Bet Ry's close."

Marco moaned and Zach bolted upright, his eyes unable to penetrate the shadows. "Who's there?" he demanded.

"That's Marco. From Partner—"

"Yeah. We're pals."

As Zach slid across the floor to check on the other man, Jay lifted a heavy hand to rub at his forehead. The last of the drug still swam through his veins, but he was almost free. Strength had returned to his fingers and his body seemed to retain heat, warming to the room's temperature. Marco woke with a loud string of curses and Jay heard him scuffle with Zach, moan in pain again, and go still.

"Everything okay?" Jay asked, his eyes still shut.

"We're good. Just took Mr. Ramírez a minute to realize where he was. And who he was dealing with."

Jay nodded slowly. Zach would have gone for a pressure point to keep him quiet so none of Murphy's thugs came running. *Damn it, where is Ryan?*

When he spoke, Marco's voice had a new, subdued quality. "Will you let go if I apologize?"

VIGILANTE'S DARE

"You tried out a pair of brass knuckles on one of my guys, asshole," Zach hissed. "On what planet did you think that was gonna go your way?"

Jay throttled the urge to snort. "That happen during your interviews?"

"He wanted to see Emily, and security disagreed," Zach said as he returned to the wall with a sigh. "And he made a deal with Murphy."

Jay coughed. "Guess that went well."

"Engagement ring, was it?" Zach asked darkly, "For a woman's life?"

"The cabrón said he wouldn't hurt her! Mr. Young, he promised he'd stop pressing charges. Just had to get her there to listen." Marco's gravelly voice came closer until it seemed right in front of Jay's nose. "I saw the news. Took the damn ring back."

Zach snorted.

"Next thing I know," Marco continued, "I wake up here, the guy says his name is Murphy Jones and I'm a guinea pig. Lab rat. Said he found another way to handle Em."

Jay dropped his head back against the wall and cracked open one eye, testing his ability to focus on Emily's former coworker. The man sat close enough now for a good clock to the jaw—if enough energy could reroute to his arm to make the punch count. He cracked his other eye open and noted the bruises already decorating Marco's face. Sympathy won out over revenge. Barely. "How many times did he dose you?"

Marco frowned. "What's up with your eyes?"

"Answer the question, Mr. Ramírez."

"Twice."

Zach lowered his gaze to the floor but Jay could almost see his mental calculator crunching away. His brother's head gave an almost imperceptible shake.

"Why?" Marco shifted, winced.

"People have died from this shit, Marco. With a hell of a lot less than these bastards have already given you." Zach said.

Marco fell silent. After a long moment, he asked in a whispered rasp, "Did he get to her, too?"

"Who, the woman you tried to trade for an engagement ring?" Jay bit the words out around the pain in his head.

Zach sent him a quelling look. "As much as I like a good brawl, the two of you can barely move. It'd be like watching a couple of geriatrics go at it with canes." His lips twitched and he waved a careless hand at them both with none of the lethargy that Jay still had in his system. "No, you know what, there's a table leg over there. I'll just toss it in between you—mmkay, the freaky glowy glare says no."

Jay glared harder, something in his chest loosening as his brother laughed. "Someone's feeling better." Had he already kicked the drug out of his system?

Multiple sets of feet sounded beyond the door. Jay gestured for Zach to pretend he was still out. Marco followed suit, scooting back into the corner. It would buy them some time before Murphy's men decided to dole out another round of peyote-laced needles. Before the door wrenched open, Zach gestured wildly at Jay's eyes, and he winced, fighting down his ability. Easier than he expected, perhaps an effect of becoming used to the drug or the drug wearing off, but either way it left him near-blind.

Not blind enough to miss who joined them in the room.

"You and your brothers did quite a number on my accounts, Mr. McLelas." Two mercenaries flanked the crime boss.

Raw anger spilled through Jay's head. "Murphy Jones."

He sipped from a glass of brown liquid. "Pity none of the charges will stick."

More rum? "Oh, I think the kidnapping ones will."

"If anyone were to find your bodies."

"Murder, then." Jay leveled his gaze at Murphy's companions. "Haven't seen those two around. They dirty cops or your personal bodyguards?"

"More like babysitters," one of them muttered.

A muscle in Murphy's neck ticked. "They don't work for me."

Jay sat up a little straighter. "Then who do they work for?"

One of the mercenaries barked out a laugh. "Better try another dose."

Aw, hell. Jay's back flattened to the wall. Two syringes appeared in the second man's hand. "What is that stuff?"

"New street drug we're testing out. We call it 'pey'." Murphy smiled. "Haven't quite got the formula all worked out yet. So far the drug trials haven't gone well. The earliest subjects died after a long night of pleasure. The secondary batches caused pain, and then that irritating unconsciousness. Others, well, it's such a shame." He lifted his glass in a toast. "Don't worry. Orders were given to keep your brothers alive long enough to get a nice list of side effects. You, on the other hand, well. You're mine." The crime boss strolled out of the room, leaving his two goons behind.

No, not his goons. These goons belonged to Ares and they seemed none too happy to be following Murphy around. He flashed a look at Marco, then his eyes darted to Zach. If his brother had shaken off the drugs they could try to gang up on the mercenaries, shoot them up with their own drugs. As if sensing his thoughts, Zach's head rolled toward the floor. Negative.

Guess I'm getting inoculated. Jay kicked his leg into goon number one's shin anyway.

Possessed with an idiotic sense of 'helpful', Marco lurched out of the shadows at the nearest man, his face red with fury. In half a second he was on his back with a needle in his neck, howling. Jay kicked out in frustration, cursing the man's inability to control his temper. He'd be even more useless now. If he wasn't dead.

It took both mercs to pin Jay flat on the ground, stabbing dual needles full of pey into his own neck. Jay's eyes slammed closed. The world coasted on a green, murky lake. Then it exploded. The scream ripped from his lungs until his vocal cords gave out.

"I thought you said this batch would be better on the pain."

"I used the new one on the other guy. Leftovers of the hard pey for the McLelas's. Ares wanted it disposed of, and they can take it." Jay could hear the shrug in the man's voice. "This guy's a freak. That's what now, four? And he's not dead yet?"

A chuckle, fading as they headed for the doorway. "Want to see what happens when we tell Murphy we killed her?"

Right before the door clicked shut, Jay caught a reply that crushed his lungs and slaughtered his attempt to withstand the drug's torture.

"He'll be so disappointed. He wanted to kill the Barton woman himself."

"Jay. Come on, bro. Wake up." Zach tugged at his shoulders and hauled him upright. "Marco's out cold, but they gave him something different."

Reality didn't so much trickle back in as roar through his head like river rapids. Jay lifted an unsteady palm to his forehead. Movement. That was good. Right?

"How long was I out?" His throat blazed with each word, so it couldn't have been long.

"Fuck if I know." A snort. "It's not morning. That help?"

"Emily." Shreds of anguish, a block of solid ice in his chest.

"I'm sorry, Jay. I really thought I'd kept her out of trouble."

"She finds trouble," he said and a bitter laugh came out like a rusty pipe dragged over concrete. "Found trouble." He stared at his hands, able to see them clearly through eyesight shot with pey. "Don't think it's hit me yet."

"You gonna sit here and bawl?"

Jay rolled his head to the side. But though Zach's words held a playful overtone, the pained expression glinting in white neon on his face said his brother only sent support through the jibe. In a get-off-your-ass-and-do-something-about-it way. He couldn't force a smile through the agony, but Zach could, and he chucked his fist at Jay's shoulder.

The room spun. No, he wasn't getting off his ass anytime soon with this venom coursing through his bloodstream.

Zach stepped to the center of the room, staring at the ceiling. Moonlight criss-crossed over his face. "Did you see her die?"

Dull throbbing tugged on his heart and Jay's gaze jerked to where his spirit guide had hovered. The window in the ceiling did a neat 180. "Through Torpedo? No."

"Then maybe she's not really dead." Zach didn't meet his gaze.

Hope flooded Jay's chest then swept away ahead of a treacherous river of doubt. "What if the pey is messing up that part of my vision, too?"

"No." Zach shook his head, his eyes filling with a fierce gleam of bright silver and blue, the colors pulling forward in Jay's vision like a creepy laser show. "If anything, I think a vision of Emily while you're hopped up on this shit would be stronger, not weaker, if she were in real trouble."

Jay tilted his head back down, coughing. "You think Tor's close enough for me to get a message to her? Send her a vision, maybe, see where . . . *if* they have her?"

"He's not my spirit guide."

Jay refrained from asking about Drak. He knew his

brother's opinion on the usefulness of his own spirit guide. Zach loved the little bat, but he considered himself on his own in matters of battle and danger.

"Here's the deal," Zach said. "You do what you need to do with Tor and I'm going to try for that grate while Murphy and his boss's friends are off chatting and getting drunk. Sound good?" He pointed both of his hands at the ceiling.

"Hell, I'm not going to stop you. I can't see straight, Zach. Give me some time to try to level this out. Maybe then I'll be able to sort out that bird up there."

Zach paused, his hands on a rickety desk. He sent a worried look over his shoulder. "How bad is it?"

"Pain's gone after the first push. It's . . . better this time. Maybe getting used to it." He closed his eyes. "Just . . . a little while." Jay heard a scuffle of furniture and Zach's feet as his brother went for the wire mesh over the window. "How are you able to bounce around like that? Did they give you a pass on this stuff?"

"No. I got a couple needles myself. A crack of pain, then bam. Nothing. You heard him. Guess they screwed up and gave me one of the good batches. Even if we'd gotten the same thing, it's possible your ability makes it hit you a little worse."

Metal scraped above Jay's head.

"I feel great, actually," Zach added.

"Well, good for you." Jay angled one open eye at the ceiling. "Must be wonderful."

His brother hung from his fingers on the grate and lifted his feet up, swinging his weight from the metal rungs.

That's all I need now. To go out in a fatal familial crushing incident.

"Don't you dare fall on me, Zach." Jay tried to scoot out of the way but pain seared through his limbs. His face scrunched against the fire in his muscles.

After a few minutes he managed to find the thread of power, the hint of a connection that went beyond simply understanding his spirit guide. All he had to do—he hoped—was embrace it, and reach.

CHAPTER THIRTY

EMILY CUT OFF HER flashlight and eased around the side of the building where she'd seen Ryan. No one around. According to Torpedo, Ryan was still up on the roof. She tried whispering again. "Ryan? Can you hear me?" Not that she expected an answer. He was supposed to be the one with the super hearing. With any luck, he'd hear her and come running. "I know how to get them out."

From her frequent visions with Torpedo on the way, she had seen Zach work the grate off the skylight. He'd started battering the window. If he broke through, maybe she could get Torpedo to give Jay a message or deliver an earpiece. Talk over some kind of escape plan. And if she could track down their older brother, she'd have an ally.

She fingered the earbud communicators in her pocket. Ryan had given up on his in the last vision she had, and it now lay among cigarette butts and other debris on top of the roof. "Ry— Mmph!"

A gloved hand wrapped around her mouth. She kicked even

as her assailant dragged her backward into a recessed doorway. The hand pressed harder when the streak of a flashlight swiped across the alley. She froze. Murphy's men would have hauled her into the building, not away from it.

One of the men who'd taken Zach walked past, a handheld radio clenched in his fist.

When he was out of sight, the arms around her loosened. "Are you insane?" Ryan's voice hissed at her ear.

"Nice to see you, too." She shoved her hand in her pocket and brought out the communicators. "Here." He frowned as she pushed one into his gloved hand. "Yours broke. Maybe this one will work so I can hear you."

"How did you—Tor." He glanced up, the corners of his lips tugging even further down.

She nodded. "Now, let's get them out of there."

A thunderous look of disapproval. "I don't need your help."

"Oh, you got them out of the little room already?"

"I know where they are; it's a matter of taking down the right guard for the keys."

"You might not have to take anyone down." Emily smiled and folded his fingers over the communication device. He didn't know how far she'd come with Jay's spirit guide, how she could keep her wits on the ground while watching through an owl in flight. "There's a window up on that roof. Zach's almost got it open. You get over there and set them free; I'll stay right here and keep watch with Torpedo so I can let you know if someone's coming."

Ryan started to chuckle before she finished talking, humor sweeping the concern from his eyes for a moment. He leaned his head back against the door. "You can control the visions now?"

She bit her lower lip. Was he making fun of her? Irritation made her fingers tap on her thigh. "Is it a bad plan?"

"No."

Pride at her accomplishment gave her a boost of confidence. They could rescue both brothers now that she had an edge. No problem.

"I'm all for the plan, Emily." He smiled and shifted out into the alley. "But I'm not taking chances. You'll have to 'keep watch' from up here."

Ryan helped her up the fire escape so she wouldn't hurt her arm. They had to pause twice due to movement on the ground. A third time because Jay decided to try to use Torpedo like a message beacon at the same time a carful of men approached the compound. Ryan had shielded her eyes from sight, which he said had flared orange, and by the time they made it to the top of the building without being seen, he was cursing under his breath.

She tucked low on the roof. "It's sort of like a two-way radio. With pictures. Impressions."

"If your eyes glowed when he tried to send a message to you, his must do the same the other way." Ryan looked grim. "Don't let him try to talk to you again, and don't try to get his attention. I'll need him lucid, not sucked into some vision."

She didn't get a chance to agree. He'd already slipped back over the roof, melting into the shadows.

While he climbed into position, Emily pushed at Torpedo. Her physical body fell away from her and she sighed. *Tor, we talked about this. I'm me, not you.*

An affirmative note brushed against her mind.

But the next time she tried to direct the owl, the bond from her own ability activated too. Unexpected, the combined link struck like a whip to her soul at first, the sting of it making her flinch until all that remained was a soothing ribbon. She exhaled once, then reached for the ribbon with her mind. Stopped short.

It could help. But it might make everything worse. She had no idea what their eyes would do if she experimented with her emotional connections and Jay's visions at the same time. Mindful of Ryan's warning, she tamped down the temptation to bridge both. She and Jay would have to sort out the enhanced ability when this was all over.

When they were safe at home.

Owl-vision eased alongside her consciousness. Glass in the window's panes, shattering downward, toward the floor of Jay and Zach's prison.

"Emily?" Ryan's voice crackled at her ear.

She pushed Torpedo for another pass, a better view of the cell. "That was Zach. He's moving without you." A tour of the old building's other skylights filled her mind, a cruising pass to see if anyone had decided to investigate the noise. Nothing. "Coast is clear."

"Keep watching."

The view swooped back around, Emily merged close enough to Torpedo to feel exhilarated by the rush of city air under her wings.

They watched Ryan drop through the skylight to join his brothers. She cheered silently when he boosted Zach up through the window. Another man, limp, likely unconscious, was awkwardly lifted through the hole in the roof.

Her fingers clenched. He wasn't Jay.

Before she could take a closer look, she spotted movement. Torpedo's head swiveled and her heart threatened to buck through her chest with a single terrified beat.

"Armed men in the hall." She bit her lip. If the brothers waited any longer, all of them would be caught. "Ryan?"

"We're going."

Zach dropped flat and lowered his hand through the opening. Ryan popped up through the window, shouldered the stranger's body instead of his youngest brother's, and they dodged back into the shadows.

They left Jay behind.

Emily pulled free of the vision and held still. If she moved she'd shake apart. *They didn't have a choice. There wasn't time. Be strong. Be smart.*

Torpedo screeched from the opposing rooftop. *"The Watcher is not well."* The translation, and the images he sent, rippled smoothly into her mind like she'd been speaking owl for a lifetime.

Frustration gnawed at her bones. "There has to be something we can do."

"The Watcher cannot sprout wings and fly." The dry tone of his mental reply told her this was an argument he'd had with Jay before, and it made her smile.

It took her less than a minute to realize that had been his intent. "Sneaky."

"The Watcher is alive. We know this."

And that was what she would focus on, not the worst case scenarios to come. "Please keep an eye on him."

More minutes passed before Zach slumped to the ground beside her, his bruises thrown into sharp relief in the moonlight. "We'll get another chance." Beside him, Ryan lowered the third man's body.

Emily sucked in a harsh breath. "Marco? What happened?" He was unconscious, his expression tortured.

Zach's eyes darted to Marco. "Murphy decided to use him for drug testing. They gave him three shots of pey."

"Pey?"

"That's what they're calling it." Zach avoided her gaze, and her heart sank to her toes.

The same drug they'd given her in the warehouse, what they'd used on Jay. The drug that killed, kept killing. She recalled the blast of agony created by the drug. Jay's scream. The mournful sound that escaped her lips drew both brothers' gazes and Ryan's hand dropped to her shoulder.

"Tell us what you see," he ordered.

She sent a tentative feeler over the ribbon toward Torpedo and the bird's sudden echo of sadness shocked her. *I know they said they'd get him out of there. Stay strong with me, okay?*

But when the owl dipped toward the shattered glass, all Emily saw was an empty room.

"They've taken him," she whispered.

Ryan grimaced and his fingers tightened in silent encouragement.

Emily wrapped her arms around her knees. In her mind, the faint orange thread she knew would lead to Jay, the one that bound them together, lost some of its glow. "You didn't have a choice."

"He'll be okay." Ryan looked down at her then back up at the owl that navigated over the lip of the rooftop with a hiss in his direction.

"They're hurting Jay." Her voice cracked. The glow dimmed further and Emily felt Torpedo's concern. She closed her eyes. Walled off the dread creeping into her mind. Fear wouldn't help. She was here to save Jay. Reaching along the owl's thread with a calm she didn't feel, she fought the urge to venture down her Spirit-mate's. "I think they drugged him again."

Zach cursed. "Get Tor out of the sky, Em."

He pointed upward and Ryan ripped his jacket off, flaring his trench coat over Marco to hide his bright blue jeans. As Torpedo came to perch nearby, Emily had to flip around and peek under two pairs of overprotective arms to see for herself. A helicopter, red and white beams bouncing off the clouds.

"We need one of those," Zach murmured.

Before Emily could wrap her mind around fuel costs, Ryan hissed back, "Who's gonna fly it, you?"

"Jay's the one's been complaining about not having wings..."

Thunderous, it landed on the opposite roof, spilling lights in all directions. Murphy, along with two men in blue coats handling Jay roughly between them, boarded the sleek aircraft. It lifted up, tipped back into the sky.

"No," she murmured, echoed with a harsh whistle by Jay's spirit guide. Increasing distance drew the mental threads taut and Emily's lungs bottled her despair.

"See? Those two belong to Ares." Zach's voice barely met her ears, but she knew Ryan heard it loud and clear, even with the faded buzz of helicopter blades. "Pros, like Shiv."

"Mercenaries. And they know how the drug affects Jay. Or think they do." Ryan looped an arm around her waist as Zach dealt with Marco. "Come on, we'll follow in my car."

He tried to sound reassuring, but Emily had already caught the grim look he and Zach shared at the top of the fire escape.

CHAPTER THIRTY-ONE

THE HELICOPTER TOOK HIM back to the warehouse Murphy had first kept her, the area around it marked with unsightly new piles of trash, hollowed out cars and empty crates. Emily's back pressed hard against the warehouse wall. Cracked paneling left shavings on her jeans and t-shirt, and she stared up at the owl clinging to the roof.

"Sure you're up for this?" Zach asked, adjusting his top. He'd donned a spare black t-shirt Ryan had discovered on the backseat of his BMW while trussing a still-comatose Marco in triple-wrapped elastic cords.

The cording had been a concession. The brothers had spent the drive arguing with her about whether or not to throw him in the trunk so he couldn't wake up and see Ryan's disguise. But Marco wasn't a bad guy—merely misguided and ill-tempered—and he'd gone through enough with the pey. He'd be out for hours. With Drak on guard, Zach would know the moment he woke if he came to early, before they returned from the warehouse. Marco wasn't going anywhere tied in bungees. She counted it a victory.

"I can control it." Adrenaline building in her veins, she nodded at Zach. Torpedo was ready too, perched on the edge of her mind.

"Not the vision thing. The whole 'into the frying pan' thing."

"Okay," Ryan said. "We saw two of Ares' men go in with Jay. I can't tell how many more are in there with him, but we have to assume more."

"You don't hear anything?" Emily asked.

Ryan shook his head. "Echoes. Metal's messing with my perception. I'll have a better gauge on the inside."

Zach nodded. "Fine. We go in like there's a full squad."

"Not like Ares needs to have a full squad of those guys." Images from the McLelas Financial security camera leapt into her mind and she shuddered.

Brushing his knuckles against her shoulder, Zach tossed her a grin. "We're a little better with hand-to-hand than your average crack-selling street thug."

"You break people's necks with your bare hands?"

"When the situation allows."

Her mouth dropped open but she didn't get a chance to answer before Ryan's arm shot out across their chests.

"Shh." He cocked his head for a moment, then dropped his arm and gave her a serious look. "You okay? Scared?"

"Only a little. No, that's a lie. Yes." She met his eyes, saw the concern. "More worried than scared. But not for me."

"The ass-kicking part, we can handle. But without a comm between us and Jay, we're gonna need you and Torpedo to be our eyes, and his voice, if necessary. All we want you to do in there is stick close, tell us where to find our brother and if they've got traps set up. We'll cover you while we're inside. You'll stay closest to Zach, and Romeo will tail us." Ryan frowned again, shaking his head. "I'd rather he be in front so I can hear what's coming sooner."

Zach flicked him a cross expression. "Romeo would give us away. I'm in street clothes and we don't have time to go home for new comms. Emily's with me so both of us will be able to hear her reports; me with this one," and he tapped on the mic at his ear, "and you with your super-ears."

Irritated, Emily shifted from foot to foot. "We're wasting time."

"I want to be absolutely sure you'll be safe before we go barging in there. If we get inside and the situation isn't like we expect, plans could change. Don't need to lose you both and have Jay come back to haunt us. He'd be a sadistic little ghost." Ryan flashed his teeth. "And his eyes would probably do that glowy thing."

"Wouldn't want that." One corner of Zach's mouth lifted.

Rubbing her palms over her jeans, Emily couldn't return their smiles. She knew they forced levity for her benefit; both of his brothers shared her worry for Jay.

"If we don't move now, they're only going to hurt him worse." Her heart stuttered in pain thinking about what had already happened to the man she loved.

The two McLelas brothers exchanged a grim nod and Zach's hand snaked around her left arm. "You heard the lady, bro. Let's do this."

Ryan inched around the corner, pulling the door aside. Without hesitation, a dark, winged creature zipped into the warehouse.

Where is he? She sent the mental question to the owl swooping through the hallway in front of Jay's brothers.

Torpedo's wings didn't make a sound as he careened back and forth under the emergency lighting, searching; a giant winged shape cast across the floor. At their backs, Romeo prowled, his nose crinkling rapidly.

"*Only one way, then three,*" came the soft hooting sound over their heads.

Emily took a step after him, but Zach jerked her backward as Ryan's spirit guide let out a half-bark. Trouble. Already.

"Stick to the plan," Zach murmured.

Ushered against the wall, she huddled in shadow. The brothers split to the sides of the hallway. And vanished.

Aisle five, paper products and innocent women. Clean-up in the meat department . . . Romeo shoved against her thigh. A steady four-footed presence in the dark.

Her strangling thoughts muted, she checked on the threads in her mind. Torpedo's solid, determined. Jay's flickered like a candle flame.

Footsteps broke her focus too easily.

"Who's there?" Around the corner came a beam of light. It caught at her feet, then bounced up to her face.

Biting back a gasp, she ducked her head. The rest of the hallway was empty save for a giant man at the end with a flashlight and a gun.

Don't go toward the light. The perverse thought leapt into her mind and she rolled her eyes in exasperation. Now, *there* was a brilliant plan. Her feet skittered back to the warehouse entrance.

The flashlight beam followed, narrowing as the thug's strides picked up.

How am I supposed to stay with Zach if he up and disappears? Fear was vengeful, scores of ice along her skin. Had they gotten too far ahead of her in the dark and somehow missed the mercenary now taking broad strides across the floor? She reached her fingers down to her side but didn't find fur. Even Romeo had abandoned her? Her heart thudded wildly. It would have been nice for them to wait.

Instead of leaving her to die.

The ceiling creaked and the thug's flashlight moved up. "What the—oof!"

One of the brothers dropped from above, taking the thug in the chest. They tumbled on the floor in a flurry of punches and kicks.

"Come on," Ryan's whisper sounded at her ear. "Zach'll handle this one."

"You could have warned me you two planned to play Spiderman," she fired back under her breath. "What happened to 'Let's be sure the girl is safe so our brother doesn't kill us'?"

"I'm sure Zach was aiming for Batman, not Spiderman." His grin caught in the out-of-control flashlight beam and he shrugged. "We improvised." Ryan gestured toward the floor and Romeo slid between him and the wall, slinking into side rooms. "Where is Jay?"

Keeping pace with Ryan and safe from immediate attack, she bridged the connection effortlessly. Torpedo sent her beats of frustration.

"He doesn't see him."

"And I can't hear him, but he's here somewhere. He has to be. Murphy brought him back to this warehouse for a reason." Ryan's fingers shackled her arm. "Try again."

Emily's eyes narrowed at his forcefulness. "I'm worried too," she whispered.

His grip eased. "Sor—"

"It's the drug . . . or pain . . . making our connection to Jay unstable." She drew her link to the owl as close as she dared while still maintaining control of her body.

The orange ribbon leading to Jay resonated with life. But faint, so faint, and not from distance alone.

Torpedo continued on passing swoops through the warehouse. He was running out of spaces to look; he had to get a clear picture of Jay soon—or at least know which room he'd been hidden in.

"We'll find him, Ryan." Emily sent out a reassuring tendril along the thread to Jay as well, reaching for him without pushing on the connection.

Their link spiked.

A sharp inhale stuck in her throat and a relieved thrill thrummed into her veins. He knew she was there.

Emily glanced down at the brush of fur under her fingers. Romeo, which meant Zach had finished brawling. Just in time for them to run out of hallway.

Ryan pointed to the left. "You and Em head left; we'll take right."

Torpedo took a middle path none of them could travel, taking advantage of a gap between exposed metal ceiling beams. As Zach cleared side rooms Emily split her attention further, between the hallway, Torpedo's search, and Jay's sudden alertness.

Gunshots rang out somewhere behind them and she cringed. The distraction cost her control.

The vision sucked her under.

"No, Em, snap out of it!" Zach hissed.

She'd told them she could control it, could track Jay through the link. "No problem," she'd said.

Instead, her eyes would be glowing bright orange. Her body would be limp, her mind locked in Torpedo's body, to see and experience wholly what the owl experienced. Sights, sounds, emotion, everything. The world dipped and whirled around her even now like a 3-D adventure ride at a theme park.

Torpedo, you have to let me go. I know he's in trouble, but I can't help him like this. Do you understand me?

Zach's shake of her shoulders was miles away. "Emily. Emily, come on."

Wait. I can feel that? Hear him?

VIGILANTE'S DARE

"Zach?" she tried aloud. All that came out was the screech of an owl.

But she could still hear Jay's brother swearing. Distantly, she recognized they were in a closed room, that she was lying on the floor.

She could do this. *Torpedo. I—*

"*He is here*," the owl cut in.

Her vision zoomed to a very familiar wall and her stomach reeled.

The chains that had once held her were missing, leaving behind only the metal rings embedded in the central post. Jay's arms were lashed to the upper one with rope, suspended over his head, his ankles bound in the same way to metal rings on the floor. His head lolled on his chest.

Beat after beat, a fist closed over Emily's heart. Wringing it dry. She had to save him. She had to *do* something. Her fingertips scraped against a cold concrete floor, aching to reach out and help.

"That's it," Ryan—not Zach—said. "Fight it. Come back."

But she wasn't fighting it, not when Jay's head came up and he stared into Tor's eyes. Jay's own eyes burned with an orange tint, as if he were having a vision too—or overloaded with pey. A gag had been forced between his lips, but she still felt the twinge along their bond as if he'd spoken her name aloud.

The thread of their mental connection tightened like a steel cable.

If his eyes were already orange, there was no risk in her testing their entwined abilities. Not this time.

Using the bond, she sent careful, slow images, determined not to overwhelm him. *Jay. Help is here.*

Recognition, then relief, danced along the thread. A moment later, a symbol flashed in her mind:

Spirit-mate.

It worked! They really could—her elation quickly smothered itself.

He felt the change, concern sweeping her way. *Emily?*

I'm okay. This wasn't the time for celebration. Zach and Ryan were trying to rouse her; they needed to know where Jay was. Being able to "speak" with him wasn't an edge at all if she stayed trapped half-outside her body. *Torpedo, I see him. I know where he is. Let me go so I can—*

"You'll have to stay with her," Ryan was telling Zach when her mind jolted back like a rubber band.

"Ah!" Swimming in a rush of blinding light she rolled and tucked her knees to her chest. "That hurts."

"Emily. Okay, just breathe." Ryan gripped her shoulders and pulled her to a sitting position.

"See, I told you she'd pull it together," Zach said.

The room circled around her like a whirlpool. "That's appropriate, since everything's gone down the drain," she said.

Ryan's eyebrows creased with worry behind his mask. "Emily? Are you really here?" A shout came from the hallway. Close by. He tensed. "Don't move."

He left the room, and soon a scuffle down the hall was accompanied by Romeo's growls.

Zach's gaze flicked down to where she pushed herself off the floor. "That's moving."

Emily staggered against him and he held out his forearm to her to let her brace herself. "I can get to Jay."

Zach froze at whatever he saw in her face, but he still said, "Absolutely not. We'll stay here until we know how many—" He cut himself off with a sharp curse as a gun-toting bad guy filled the doorway.

The thug swung his gun in her direction. Zach slammed his fist into the man's wrist. The angle of the weapon shifted before it exploded, and then both of them hit the wall.

Emily threw herself forward and out the door.

"Emily! Wait!" Ryan called. A grunt came next, as if he'd taken a punch.

She couldn't wait. Tor hadn't seen any guards when he'd flown overhead. She could get to him. She could untie those ropes.

The image of Jay hanging on that wall was like fire at her heels.

Just keep running.

A bullet impacted on metal sheeting behind her and someone called her name again.

She ran faster.

She'd be useless in Zach and Ryan's fight, but she was done hiding away while the man she loved suffered. With the other brother's scrambling against the mercenaries in the hallway, untying Jay was now her sole focus.

Torpedo led the way, diving into her path and arcing toward the ceiling. Perching on a beam above Jay's head, the owl called out, *"Here!"*

They'd beaten him. Blood and bruises scattered across his face, down the exposed part of his chest, probably under his battered clothes, too. Emily couldn't hold back her cry, and his head came up as she slid into the large room. At the last moment she ducked to the side of the door. She should make sure Tor hadn't missed a guard.

But then she heard Jay's voice in her head.

Clear as crystal.

Emily, run.

She latched on to his warning and saw how he'd amplified the bond. Instead of doing as he'd said, she shoved her own thought on the matter in a tailspin down his thread. *After everything you've done for me? I am not leaving you tied to a wall.*

He clenched his fingers around the thick rope. *I told Zach and Ryan—*

They are busy. Making sure he had no guards, apparently, because there still didn't seem to be anyone around to stop her. *I'm coming for you.*

It's not safe!

She lifted her chin. *What about our relationship has ever been safe?*

CHAPTER THIRTY-TWO

TRUSTING TORPEDO TO WARN her if things changed, she ran an endless distance to Jay's side. The ropes held him fast. Too high for her fingers. She hadn't counted on that. There had to be something she could climb on.

Her lungs hauled in musk and midnight. Copper.

Blood smeared her fingers.

Jay's blood.

Emily.

"Shut up, Jay." Her voice came out watery. "I'm rescuing *you* this time."

She grasped for the gag around his mouth but he jerked back, nostrils flaring.

"Watcher!" Torpedo screeched.

"Forget to bring something sharp?" Alcohol-slurred words came from the shadows of the back room. Murphy stepped into the light, a brutal grimace on his face and a knife in his hand.

Nightmares flooded in and she went rigid at Jay's side.

Get Ryan, she told Torpedo. *Get Zach.*

An owl screech of assent. The cavalry wasn't far. Her memories shifted and her breath came easier; her muscles loosened. Fueled by a flare of anger that jetted through her veins, Emily took a step toward Murphy. "Cut him down from there."

"Aren't you adorable. So naïve. Too bad it's an act." Murphy's eyes darkened. "Come here, you murdering bitch."

"I didn't kill Stefan!" Her ears and mind barely registered Jay's muffled howl of rage.

Murphy lunged for her and she jumped back. Her spine connected with a doorframe. He was still coming so she dodged through the opening. Another door led off of the small room, and from there, a thinly carpeted hallway.

If she kept running, kept Murphy focused on her, Jay's brothers would have time to—

"Oh, nonono." The opening she'd charged through next held the horrible newspaper clippings, posters, the mattress, the stains and streaks of old blood.

Paper had been shredded off the walls and made footing treacherous.

Emily fought down a heavy smack of defeat. Not here. Not again. She turned, but the crime boss filled the door she'd come through.

Emily!

As Jay's fear bled into hers, she thinned their bond. She couldn't afford the extra emotions. A rush of air scattered papers as Murphy swiped the knife ahead of his advance.

Emily backpedaled. She slammed into the far wall, but her hand landed on a doorknob. Another way out.

Adrenaline shoved her hand into motion, yanking at the handle. She ducked again, a fist breezing past her shoulder. The door swung open wide enough for her to slide in sideways, an arm through, a shoulder—

The crime boss used his body to block the door. He shoved it inward and the pain in her shoulder burst like a firework, crashing against the tendrils of power in her head. She was pinned like a bug on a collector's display and Murphy was intent on dissection.

He smiled. Nowhere to go. It was over.

An owl screeched in the distance.

No! Jay's thread yanked tight. *Angel, no!*

"I want you to remember, once upon a time," Murphy slurred in her ear, "I asked nicely."

Suddenly, it wasn't just Jay and Tor in her mind. Support crashed in like water tossed by a storm, too many threads to count. Answering her inadvertent call. Courage, energy, hope.

Survival.

She kicked at his legs, her free hand shoving at his wrist. Desperate to keep his knife from cutting toward her face, she almost missed the fur at the edge of her vision.

I've got backup.

A liquored breath hit her nose and her stomach churned.

Backup.

She scraped at skin with her nails, wrestling for another inch of doorway.

But the fur she'd spotted wasn't Ryan's German shepherd. It was Titan. The puppy who belonged to Murphy's son. The mastiff's dark nose scrunched as his teeth bared. Letting out a bark, he launched what had to be well over 100 pounds of angry, no longer cowering dog at the crime boss's spine.

The weight on the door shifted.

Free, she fled into what appeared to be a kitchen area beyond. *Think, think, think, Emily.* No more exits here; plenty of pots and pans. *Where are the others?*

Tor heard. As owl-images of more mercenaries fired back, Emily realized Zach and Ryan wouldn't be coming after all.

Worse, she discovered there was no lock.

Tor can distract him, but you've got to get that knife away. Jay's voice forced its way over the thunder of her pulse, their bond strong, penetrating in its intimacy.

Love. He sent love along their bond and it steadied her feet, stopped the trembling that threatened before it held her immobile. The door wrenched open and Emily tugged hard, slamming it closed on the criminal's wrist. The knife clattered to the ground.

Good, kick it, Jay coached.

As the crime boss filled the doorway, she gave a flick with the toe of her shoe and the blade rocketed past him, far into the smaller room.

The impulsive kick sent her reeling backward, her arms pinwheeling. By the time she found her balance, Murphy was in. He'd shut the door in the face of the snarling mastiff.

And he wasn't smiling now. "Thought you could command that thing to kill me too?"

Despite Titan's continued thrashing against the entry, the dog couldn't help her now. She was closed off from him. Closed off from Torpedo and Jay. No amount of mental rallying could stop Murphy, not physically. Her tongue tasted of metal.

I'm still here, angel. Hold on.

A scream aborted, held back so ferociously her teeth ached. Her hands tightened into determined fists. Nerve endings burned raw with anger and her heart ached with pent-up concern for Jay even as she stood facing down a furious, drunken demon with a single goal: her death.

CHAPTER THIRTY-THREE

JAY DIVIDED HIS FOCUS, his power spiraling to Torpedo. *Okay, friend. Bring me that knife.*

The bird's talons closed around the hilt. Then it was in Jay's hand and his eyes snapped open, light scorching in from all sides.

Too much.

Rejecting the effort, his eyes shut. Murphy had forced a seventh and eighth hit of pey into his bloodstream and instead of his power finally shorting out, instead of blindness, the world had fragmented into kaleidoscoping colors. Instead of going limp, his muscles had rebounded, energy coiled inside. Nowhere to go. Stuck on overdrive. Floating. Until Emily's presence in his mind had returned him to reality. She tethered him to sanity.

And Murphy had her trapped.

Sawing at the restraints, he heaved at the frayed rope. *Damn it! Come on!*

"I will help the Watcher's Spirit-mate," Tor screeched out, winging backward in the air.

The door is closed, Jay frantically sent back in response.

Which the owl responded to with a smug-flavored image of wide open ceiling beams. *"The wall is not."*

Jay tapped the mental bond between himself and his Spirit-mate next. Terror, determination, dwindling hope. Anger. Tor showed him a glimpse, Murphy advancing, a pot thudding into his chest. She didn't have far to run in the small kitchen.

But at least she was still fighting.

Don't let him back you into a wall. Keep out of range. Instructions in the form of images drove toward her as fast as he could manage.

If she could just stay out of harm's way until he cut himself loose . . .

Jay bit down on the gag between his lips and concentrated on his bonds. His power lurched out of control, and as it did, it reached for Emily.

Pain. Eyes. Jay. Don't know how! I can't—

They'd never directly shared his ability before. Not the night-vision, and not in a place where the ambient light would fissure across it, cause pain. Blind her.

Hang on, angel. Hang on!

Ruthless, he reeled in his power. The pey-enriched energy in his body jolted, somehow growing weaker as he pulled. Siphoned off by the effort? He didn't know, but he couldn't share, couldn't allow his ability to divert itself to his Spirit-mate.

Jay!

Too much and with no way to release it, his power scalded him from the inside out.

But it wasn't Emily. He wouldn't hurt Emily.

His conscious mind splintered with the effort, part following her fight for her life, part following Torpedo. Slaps of images, jabs of emotions. Pain, so much his ears rang with it.

His woman swinging the door of a refrigerator into the

crime boss's middle.

A series of swooping attacks.

The connection with his spirit guide abruptly shattered. Darkness, smoky and thick, blistered behind his eyes. In his core, his mind, everywhere at once, Jay felt something heavy slam against a solid surface. Then nothing from Torpedo at all.

"Tor!" Emily's piercing cry was muffled through multiple partitions.

Ferocious energy redoubled his attempt to slice through the rope, a blind effort to break free. Jay jerked his wrists away from the wall with inhuman strength, shredding the last resistant strand. He ripped at the gag shoved between his lips even as he pitched forward onto his knees. Brutal agony rippled through his body and finished off his tie to his Spirit-mate.

"No, God no . . . Emily." Sensation flooded in, white light flaring through Jay's eyelids even as he felt for the second set of bonds, tied around his feet. He sliced in a frenzy, determined to reach her before the drug left him helpless. "I'm coming . . . "

He couldn't be too late. He couldn't.

Sounds of struggle filtered past the ringing in his ears. There wouldn't be a fight if Murphy had won, and he clung to those rushing and ebbing tones while life passed by in slow motion.

When the knife snapped through the rope, his body caught a rush of violent pain. Jay buckled under the onslaught to his senses, his body going prone on the concrete. Pain ratcheted into his skull, torched his spine like he was going up in a spectacular fireball.

Emily's name pounded through his veins like a mantra.

I have to get to her.

His right hand scrabbled across the floor for the gag Murphy had shoved into his mouth. Fingertips met fabric. Jay yanked the dry part of the cloth over his eyes and the brightness in the room receded.

But he could still see.

Clearly.

Through his eyelids and the thick, dark material.

"Not good," he murmured, staggering to his feet. "Emily!"

A crash of glass erupted in his ears as he made it to the doorway. There they were, facing among a lake of shattered wine bottles. The strange dog he'd heard was nowhere in sight but a mound of motionless feathers lay in a heap against the wall, one wing outstretched. Still, so still.

"He's not Klepto," Emily was protesting, her shoulders ramrod straight.

"Then both of your lovers are here," Murphy said. "I'll take them from you the way you took my son from me."

As Jay forced his burning legs to move, the crime boss's hands went for her throat.

Red, blood red, flared in a haze at the edges of Jay's vision.

His covered eyes met her watery, tormented gaze and the link between them materialized with a snap, hers reaching for his, his twining with hers. She understood what he had to do. Accepted it.

Accepted him.

In that instant Jay attacked, curving the knife through the air as he came down on the other man's back.

Murphy howled in pain, shoving Emily forward. Jay kicked at an industrial serving tray, rolling it in front of her so the side of her body hit something other than glass shards.

No more stitches, Jay sent rapid images over the gleaming link in his mind. "Run, get out!"

Murphy fought like he'd been possessed, clawing at Jay's blindfolded face and bruised torso with two wide pieces of glass, not noticing the blood he himself dripped all over the scene. Dodging another wild swipe of the man's hands, Jay barreled into the man's stomach. Murphy sprawled onto the glittering mess, snarling as glass dug its way through already torn fabric.

Jay leapt on him again, but pey made the world topple sideways. The crime boss rolled and made it to his feet first. In moments Murphy was hauling Emily back into the room with a fist wrapped into the back of her tattered shirt. Somewhere between the floor and standing, he'd located a gun, and now held it to her head.

A beautiful human shield.

Everything went still. Jay swayed, one hand extended. "Let her go." His chest shuddered with miniscule breaths. *Don't move, angel.*

"Drop the knife, Mr. McLelas." Murphy dug the barrel of the weapon into the side of her head and she closed her eyes, her eyelashes moist.

I love you.

Breathtaking images and emotions alike brushed against his heart and Jay held both hands out in surrender. The blade fell and stirred up glass.

His stunning, miraculous woman, his Spirit-mate, the woman who saw past his flaws to the man he wanted to be . . . and maybe, just maybe, the mother of his unborn child. *We will survive this. We will.* He'd accept no other outcome.

"You want this woman to live, you'll do exactly as I say. And you'll start by taking off the blindfold so I can look you in the eye."

Don't listen to him, Jay. He'll kill me anyway. He wants you dead. And Klepto. Revenge.

Jay's over-exposed eyes sought Emily's when he removed the cloth. Was the drug's grip weakening? Or was the bond they shared tempering his ability correctly this time?

She wasn't hurting. Not from anything he'd done. Her hazel gaze glimmered and a sense of her determination, her solid trust in him, warmed his chest.

If he only had that much faith in himself. Fear that the drugs would win before the battle was over beat out the confidence she'd tried to help him feel, the determination to get them through this flagging as his strength ebbed.

They didn't have time to buy time. But what other choice did his Spirit-mate have? "What is it you want?"

"That money trail to lead somewhere else. The records cleared." Murphy tightened his other arm around Emily's waist, his fingers bunching in the fabric of her t-shirt. A thin smile crossed his lips. "I don't care where or how."

"Why didn't you just go to the police? Fill a few more pockets?" He took a wavering step forward then sharply back when the gun jabbed against Emily's temple. Stainless steel cabinets streaked like silver paint smeared across a canvas.

"Because he's done with me. I'm public!" Murphy exploded. "I did everything he said. I was perfect. Business was booming. And then this slut—"

"Don't you *ever* call her that." His fists vibrated with leashed anger.

"Oh," and he dragged Emily a stumbling step, "I'm sorry, did I offend you? The records, McLelas. And then we can all go along our merry ways. Back to work, as it were."

His teeth ground together. "Ares isn't just going to let you walk away."

"Then she's useless to me."

Before she moved, Jay felt her intent, saw Murphy's finger twitch too slowly on the gun when Emily stomped on the instep of the crime boss's foot and immediately let her body go limp. She hit the floor but the bullet—a comet-trail of hot, white light—sailed toward the ceiling. Only a soft *click* came when Murphy fired a second time.

Jay rushed him without hesitation. They both hit the floor in a mad tangle. Sirens whistled and somewhere far away more bullets popped. Knuckles caught his jaw.

White-filled nothingness. *Tor! I need eyes!*

His spirit guide shrieked and confused owl-thoughts buffeted the inside of his skull. Jay couldn't make out any of the words. Too injured, he remembered; Tor so still on the floor.

"The knife!" Emily warned from a distance.

Torpedo tugged—sluggish, insistent—at his mind. That his only warning, Jay broke free from his physical body.

His vision spun out and warped to hover over his Spiritmate. Emily kicked the blade he'd dropped to bargain for her life. Through Torpedo's sight he watched his physical body palm the blade. But he felt the knife, the heft of its hilt in his hands.

And then he thrust upward. This time he drove it straight between Murphy's ribs with the force of his whole muscled frame.

The other man fell back on the floor, eyes going wide. His body spasmed once.

It was over.

Over.

Jay's eye sockets throbbed, his corneas burning. The pain won.

"Jay, no!" From somewhere high, he watched Emily collapse on the floor next to him, her arms wrapping around his neck.

"You're okay," he said, but his voice was distant.

"We have to get out of here." Her hands cradled his face and her lips—oh, her lips—would be soft where they pressed against his cheek.

Jay didn't want to go anywhere. He didn't need to. He just wanted to hold her. Forever.

"Jay. Zach and Ryan are still fighting his guys, and the police are coming. We have to go, now!" Emily tugged at his arms around her waist and pressed a palm to his cheek. He couldn't feel it, didn't know if it'd be warm or cool to the touch. "Jay?"

No. Everything was okay now. Torpedo and he were hurt but they would heal. Murphy was dead, Emily was safe, and she was right here. Right now. His vision watched their two bodies embracing on a floor of shattered glass and blood. His physical eyes flared a riot of orange. Her hands reached out and shook his shoulders.

Then she finally looked up to where he hovered.

"Tor, he's okay. We're both safe now. Help me," she said, her voice echoing in a whisper that carried. Her awareness threaded through their bond, but even the woman he loved was unable to return him to his body, unable to separate him from his spirit guide. "Send him back."

"Spirit-mate, Watcher... too far," Tor responded in broken owl-speech, and Jay couldn't tell if she understood him, from the look of frustration that crossed her face. *"I cannot."*

Emily bit her bottom lip and called into the dim warehouse. "Ryan? If you can hear me—There's something wrong with Jay, Tor's hurt, and I can't get them out of here on my own."

Jay tried to get his head to shake, his lips to respond, but the speech from his physical body slurred. His hands clamped around her waist.

"You can. Help." Torpedo landed, unsteady when he perched on a broken chair. His claws scraped over the plastic and then he stumbled, flapping haphazardly to the seat. Jay came face to face with himself as if he stared into a mirror. *"The Watcher's eyes."*

Emily started. "The blindfold." She turned in a rush, hunting on the floor for the fabric he'd discarded. It hit her fingers and his body leaned forward, allowing her tie it around his head. "Okay, Jay. Listen to me. I know you're with Torpedo. But I can't lift you and we have to get out of here."

With the blindfold on to buffer the intense light around him, it was a more manageable struggle to pull back from the owl-thoughts, but he still couldn't return to a body pumped full of drugs that warped his ability. A moment later, he felt her join him in the bond, strengthening the link, braiding directly between them and working to pull his mind free.

Angel, Emily, I love you. He managed to send her a sparse collection of images.

The bond squeezed between them, then blazed like a sudden flashbulb.

His body was his own again, and pain ruled with an iron fist. He didn't care, didn't care that he shouldn't be able to see with his eyes shut, didn't care that everything roared in his ears. Only her arms mattered, human sensations, human extremities. They'd succeeded. They'd done it. And Murphy wouldn't hunt her again.

"Emily," he whispered.

She squeezed him tight. "I'm here, Jay. I'm not going anywhere."

Ryan's taller form appeared in the doorway and Jay tipped his forehead against Emily's.

"Ares' guys are dead." Hauling him upright, Ryan settled one of Jay's arms around Emily's shoulders. "But the police . . . We'll need a cover for this."

"No problem." Jay's voice sounded slurred to his own ears. "I'll just—"

"No. I'll handle it," Emily said, her jaw set with confidence Jay had only seen when she was standing up for what she believed in. The same look she'd had, garnering help for Partner Paws. Showing up here to rescue him. Before Murphy had ensured everything would go wrong. In both cases.

But this time? Murphy lay dead at their feet.

"Get out of sight, Ryan. And take this." She shoved a shirt-wrapped knife into his gloved hands. "Jay's fingerprints."

Ryan hesitated to leave them, caught the look in her eye, then nodded. He skipped backward into the shadows. "Be careful, little sister."

"They both call me that now," she said. Her wry smile tugged at something in Jay's chest.

"Family." To keep the bulk of his weight off of Emily he had to focus more on his feet than his words. He fell back on the link between them to speak. Images weren't as convenient as words, but they worked. *What are you up to?*

"I'll talk to the cops and find you somewhere to lie down." She maneuvered him into the main room, past the wall where ropes hung severed and limp.

Talk to the cops? Emily—

"Quiet. Let me do this." She tilted her head up to his. "Just stay next to me. On the ground, not the air, okay?"

Easier said than done. He winced at the squad of flashlights that assaulted his vision, felt both Torpedo and Emily's grip on the bond between them.

"Don't move! Police!"

They were surrounded.

"Oh, rats. I know this is a bad time to have second thoughts, but are these cops clean, or dirty?" she whispered so softly he almost missed the question.

A smile crossed his lips. *You're beautiful.*

That is not an answer, Ninja.

As the brave woman under Jay's arm tensed, a detective stepped forward. "McLelas? What happened here?"

"We were rescued." Emily tilted her head up. "You'll find Murphy Jones's body in the next room. It was the masked man. The one who's been in all the papers."

Jay had to hide his own sudden tension at her announcement. *What are you doing?*

Blame Zach. Later.

"Is that so?" The detective quirked an eyebrow but motioned for the rest of his people to follow up on her words. Beside him a familiar woman with honey-streaked hair and a grim frown stayed by his side, gun out despite her lack of uniform. Roving for trouble. "There's nothing to shoot here, Lieutenant."

Amanda shook her head and continued tracking. "No disrespect Detective, but I'll judge that for myself. I don't take chances with my family's lives."

The man paled but rebounded swiftly. "What's with the blindfold?"

Only the four of them remained in the room, well, four plus two shadows over Jay's left shoulder. He could see Ryan and Zach pressed tight against the wall, grim expressions on their faces. Rather than answer the question, Emily launched into an animated harrowing tale of how she and Jay had been taken by the crazy drug-dealing Murphy.

"We cut ourselves loose, were trying to get out of that kitchen, but then there was this masked man . . . " she said.

Amanda's eyes narrowed as she slid her weapon away. "Did you see which way this masked man went?" Her hand twitched over the holster at her side.

"The way he came, but beyond that?" She shrugged. "He did say something about taking out the weak link."

Nodding in approval, Ryan crept closer in the shadows and Zach dodged down the hallway, out of Jay's peripheral.

Weak link? That ought to get Ares' attention. And them all in boiling water. Jay's fingers clamped over Emily's shoulder. Regret flowed from her and he buffered it with reassurance. *No, you're right. Zach's right. It has to be this way.*

For now, Jay, not forever. "If you don't mind," she said aloud, "we just want to go home."

"Of course." The detective looked between them once and nodded, capitulating too easily for Jay's taste. "I have questions.

But the answers can wait until morning. I want statements from you and your brothers. As I understand it, Zach McLelas was also attacked this evening but made an equally impressive getaway."

Jay's unease ramped up another notch at the mention of his brother's name. Emily helped him to the outer door and the blue and red and white beams of emergency vehicles drove like spears at his covered eyes. "Em'ly," he managed to whisper, "needa lie down."

She immediately sent him reassurance and images of cuddling under blankets over their link, turning his body away from the flashing lights. Relief was instantaneous.

Torpedo barely stirred in his mind. *"Watcher, you are whole."*

She heard it, both of them communicating across the bond. She heard his response too, a frustrated demand for more information from his cryptic spirit guide—and a cool hand pressed against his aching forehead. "Don't push it, Jay. Tor's hurting too, and we can talk when we get out of here. And get some rest." *Watcher.*

"Just a little further. You're almost to my car," Zach coaxed from in front of him. He was dressed in a suit and smiling, pushing his shoulder underneath Jay's other arm to help them forward.

"Yours? What happened to Ryan's?" Emily asked. "And when the heck did you have time to change?"

Zach swung the car door open. "Ry chased me off to get Marco to the hospital and check on backup. Amanda was already on her way so I back-filed an incident report."

"And our statements?" Jay wove the fingers of one hand into Emily's and brushed his lips across her knuckles. "Not that I'm upset about not being grilled in the back of an ambulance."

"Hey, don't look at me." Zach gave him a casual shrug of his shoulders and cracked a grin. "Could get used to having a sister-in-law on the force, though."

"Amanda will not hesitate with those handcuffs. You know that, right?" Jay sighed. His brother was far too enthusiastic about wandering down this crooked path. "Let's go home, Emily." Jay lowered a grateful kiss to her temple. Untimely sizzling coursed toward his groin, hot and demanding.

"That's interesting," Zach said, and Jay really hoped he wasn't talking about his cock. His hands caught each of their shoulders. "How long has that—Jay, can you see?"

"Through the blindfold, Zach." Though it felt as if the pey was tapering off in earnest. "Why?"

"Emily's eyes."

Jay's eyebrow shot up. He tilted her chin toward his face. His Spirit-mate's pupils were rimmed with silver coils.

"Now is not the time to play mad scientist." Emily brushed their hands away.

"It's a side-effect of the bond," Jay murmured to himself. He stared at her, transfixed, a dueling spiral of surprise and wonder fighting in his chest. "You're not just sharing visions and emotions, you're pulling at my ability, Emily. Using—No. No, you can't—Does it hurt?"

"I know what's happening. And no." She pushed him back an arm's length with a light laugh. "It did at first, but not now. It happened a couple of times tonight. My eyes are starting to sting, is all."

"Move it, then. We'll sort it out at home. Don't need two of you going nuclear. Or blind." Low whistling came from what everyone else would perceive as a darkened entryway, a lone masked shadow standing just inside the door. "And this one needs some R 'n' R."

Ryan had two dogs tailing him, the larger of whom bumped around his legs and sidled up to Emily. Jay noticed her reflexive scratch behind his ears as she watched Ryan's approach. He was so focused on watching their interaction he heard her cry out before he saw the broken jumble of feathers cradled in his brother's arms.

Shock rocked him on his feet. How had he missed how badly his spirit guide had been wounded?

Emily frowned. "He was airborne not that long ago."

Torpedo sent them a decidedly smug impression and the feathers ruffled as he settled in for a nap.

Ryan laughed. "Ah. Faker."

She shook her head. "He did take a hit, but—"

"We kept him up too long," Jay said with a slow smile. He nudged Emily with their bond to make sure she saw what he did, how exhaustion had taken its toll. When a reluctant smile touched her own lips, he added, "Enjoy it, buddy; you earned it."

Besides, he had a feeling they'd be working overtime again before long.

"He's still got a pulse!" an EMT cried from inside the building. Two other medical personnel sprinted past Emily and Jay with a stretcher between them.

They turned as one to stare at Murphy's body as uniformed personnel carried it past them, then Jay angled his head back at the lone masked shadow holding his owl. Ryan's exasperated sigh hit his ear like a brand, but his jaw didn't tic until Zach mouthed the words "shoot him again".

EPILOGUE

"Marco was on his best behavior and he's clean." Ryan plowed through the archway to Jay's living room with an unkempt pile of manila folders, Amanda and Romeo on his heels. "He won't have any dependency on the pey."

"That's good news," Jay murmured against Emily's midsection, nuzzling her with his nose. *Damn it, Ryan! When I said I was busy*... Her expression said she wanted to crawl under the coffee table. He pulled her camisole down and moved up the couch, rubbing his thumb over her stomach with a reassuring smile.

He winked at his sister-in-law. "Undercover gig all wrapped up?"

"Finally. It's good to be home," Amanda answered with a raised eyebrow. She pointed to the pants tossed out of reach on the coffee table.

Jay pantomimed knocking and she grinned, sliding into a chair to watch her husband.

Romeo disappeared into the hallway, probably hoping to

play with Titan. The two dogs were fast friends. As the young mastiff had come out of his shell, Titan had settled well into their home and become Emily's newest shadow at Partner Paws. Torpedo had been less than pleased about the shared space. Until Emily had talked to him—and neither one would tell Jay what accord had been met.

Ryan wasn't looking at any of them, his eyes scrolling down a piece of paper on top of the stack in his hands. "Julia got a real kick out of it when Zach tried to rile him up. I think the whole situation mellowed Marco out."

I thought he was supposed to have good hearing. Emily wound her arms around his neck, her embarrassment dissolving under a sparkle of humor in her eyes.

Doesn't mean he always pays attention, angel. Jay cleared his throat. "Has Brennan been in contact?"

"Yes," Ryan said with an absent nod. "And she's agreed to work with Miss Meadows."

Answers. Shiv's death might have cost them their link to the burning of Old Town—their link to the past—but if Julia and Brennan could make better progress with translations, they could finally know what the future held for their abilities. For their Spirit-mates. Zach, more than any of them now, needed that kind of advantage.

"Thanks to Emily's acting skills, we've finally got contact from this Ares guy. Gotta be honest; I expected it much sooner. But contact means now we've got leads on our drug manufacturer. Maybe if you go through these files too—" Ryan looked up and the paper crinkled in his fingers. "Whoa. Put some jeans on, bro."

Jay spared a smirk for his brother and dropped a heated gaze back to the still fully-clothed woman in his arms. At least he'd been wearing boxers . . . but now he tugged on the blanket slung over the back of the couch.

"We're shocked you didn't hear this before you walked in." He lifted Emily, tucking the cover around them both and cuddling in further. "Though you're about two minutes too early for the really loud stuff."

"I don't put my ear to the door and say to myself: 'Is that weird moaning sound coming from my little brother's living room? I better not barge in.'" An accusing look cut toward Amanda, who only laughed.

"Bet you will now." Jay smothered Emily's own light laughter with a kiss. The rest of her tension eased when their lips parted and desire flashed in her eyes.

"I'm never going to be able to sit on that couch again. You know that, right?" Ryan shook his head in disbelief and averted his gaze, a red hue creeping up from his collar.

"I'd apologize but—" Jay sucked in a breath when Emily teased his earlobe with her teeth.

"He's the one who doesn't know how to use the doorbell," Amanda said, smiling and angling for the exit. "Sorry, Jay. I'll make sure he at least knocks next time."

Ryan slid the folders onto a glass end table and threw up his hands. "I'll just leave these here."

Emily's tongue traced the length of his ear and Jay's cock jumped, an urgent demand. "Is there a timeframe on those files? I might be a while."

Ryan snorted and Emily's grin curved against his jaw. *You should tell them.*

Later. I want to celebrate with you first.

Ryan's cell phone rang, an old-school Batman theme song blaring from the holster on his belt. He mashed a button to cut it off and swung around to pace toward the archway that led back to the front door, hand to his ear.

"That's Zach," Jay whispered, catching her lower lip with his teeth.

She gasped, wiggling enticingly underneath him. "I'd never have guessed."

"Fantastic," Ryan said from the front hallway. "Yeah, I'll tell them. Okay. See you in a minute." He returned and sent a pointed stare at the round clock on the wall instead of looking at them. "Murphy's dead. Someone pulled the plug while he was sleeping."

Jay arched an eyebrow. "Someone? Who?"

Amanda's amusement died. "That's not justice."

"Zach didn't say, but I'm sure he's put resources on it." Ryan took her in his arms and rubbed a hand over her spine. "Justice or no, it does mean Emily is off the hitlist. As are we. No one will hunt without him covering the paycheck."

Amanda softened slightly. "Is Zach on his way over?"

At Ryan's nod, Jay arched an eyebrow. "You didn't warn him?"

"Why should I be the only one scarred by my little brother's pre-coital cuddling?"

Sweet, melodic laughter from his woman. Grinning, Jay dipped another kiss to her face.

Moments later, Zach burst through the door and they all turned to watch him clip a crumpled diagram to the wall. He stepped back to admire the paper and launched into a planning session without so much as a brusque hello. "So I figure Ares isn't in the city, right? We're gonna need distance from the home base . . . "

No one was listening to Zach's newest grandiose plan to revolutionize their gear. Ryan's eyes began to water with withheld glee. Jay's lips twitched and Emily shook underneath him. When he glanced down, the twinkle of mirth swirling in her eyes set off his own suppressed amusement and his shoulders quaked. He kissed her again, unable to help it when she showed him how happiness cascaded so brightly along their bond.

"So I figure I can just splice these four wires over here. Should fix the range issue. What do you guys think?" Zach finally spun around. It took him a minute. Then he blanched.

Emily giggled against Jay's lips. The short, lilting sound dragged a snort from Ryan and in the next instant the four of them exploded into outright laughter.

Zach spun back around to the wall, tilting his head toward the other couple. "You knew they were goin' at it, and you weren't going to say anything?"

Amanda swiped at her eyes, still chuckling. "Hey, you got to see them after the blanket."

Ryan nodded. "What kind of brother would let me be alone in my suffering?"

Jay's grin stayed plastered across his face as he hugged Emily tighter to his chest.

"The both of you and your women." Zach made a sound of disgust. "Kill me if I ever get that wrapped up in a girl, 'kay? No offense, ladies," he mumbled over his shoulder.

"None taken, Zach." Emily closed her eyes. "Seriously though, Jay. They're all here, and you obviously have work to do."

"There's always work. But when it can call ahead first, and doesn't, it can wait." He propped up on an elbow as her fingers threaded through his hair. The members of the growing McLelas family were all here, all alive and assembled to fix their city, their whole world, just like every other day in the office. Today though, today was different. Better. Hopeful. "Whatever plans we're making will have to be flawless, Zach. Because Emily and I are—"

"Pregnant!" He whirled with a rare, brilliant flash of teeth. "I knew it! Ha!"

Ryan tugged out his wallet and forked over a black credit card even as Amanda glared at him. "Oh, I *know* you didn't bet our honeymoon fund on the results of a pregnancy test."

"I think your family is happy for us," Emily whispered as he shifted off the couch and announced they'd be upstairs for the foreseeable future.

"Just think of it this way, angel." A balled-up pair of pants hit him in the ass as he headed for the bedroom with his Spiritmate in his arms. "When you're a McLelas, you can get a pass on crazy too."